D0725761

MIRROR SPACE

The hair on Jo-Jo's body began to prickle. His muscles bunched, ready to move quickly.

At the same instant the three mercenaries slid their face skins back into position. Jo-Jo copied them as Catchut flicked a grenade of sorts from his pouch. It should have skittered across the floor to the Extro but on first bounce it disappeared into the floor surface. The texture of the whole chamber seemed to have changed. It was no longer metallic.

'Remove all your weapons and place them at your feet,' said the Extro.

Catchut stared at the spot his small explosive had vanished.

'Do as it says,' Rast instructed.

'Capo?' Latourn's voice was tinged with uncertainty.

'Whole chamber we're in is an Extro, Lat. You wanna be goin' where your grenade just went?'

'No, Capo.' The hulky man began unbuckling his gear.

Jo-Jo felt a rising conviction. One thing he knew for sure, he wasn't going meekly into captivity again. Especially not in this place.

BY MARIANNE DE PIERRES

The Parrish Plessis Novels
Nylon Angel
Code Noir
Crash Deluxe

The Sentients of Orion
Dark Space
Chaos Space
Mirror Space

01/22

MIRROR SPACE

Book **3** of *THE SENTIENTS OF ORION*

marianne de pierres

www.orbitbooks.net

ORBIT

First published in Great Britain in 2009 by Orbit

Copyright © 2009 by Marianne de Pierres

Excerpt from *Trading in Danger* by Elizabeth Moon
Copyright © 2003 by Elizabeth Moon

The moral right of the author has been asserted.

*All characters and events in this publication, other than
those clearly in the public domain, are fictitious
and any resemblance to real persons,
living or dead, is purely coincidental.*

All rights reserved.
No part of this publication may be reproduced,
stored in a retrieval system, or transmitted, in any
form or by any means, without the prior
permission in writing of the publisher, nor be
otherwise circulated in any form of binding or
cover other than that in which it is published and
without a similar condition including this
condition being imposed on the subsequent purchaser.

A CIP catalogue record for this book
is available from the British Library.

ISBN 978-1-84149-760-0

Typeset in Caslon 540 by Palimpsest Book Production Limited,
Grangemouth, Stirlingshire

Printed and bound in Great Britain by
CPI Mackays, Chatham ME5 8TD

Papers used by Orbit are natural, renewable and recyclable
products sourced from well-managed forests and certified
in accordance with the rules of the Forest Stewardship Council.

Mixed Sources
Product group from well-managed
forests and other controlled sources
www.fsc.org Cert no. SGS-COC-004081
© 1996 Forest Stewardship Council
FSC

Orbit
An imprint of
Little, Brown Book Group
100 Victoria Embankment
London EC4Y 0DY

An Hachette UK Company
www.hachette.co.uk

www.orbitbooks.net

For Russell Hunter

ACKNOWLEDGEMENTS

Thank you to the ROR-ettes – my fellow soldiers in the trenches, especially Trent Jamieson for morale boosting. Very special thanks to Amy Parker for extra help with proofing.

And to Tara Wynne and Darren Nash, always at my side.

Sole

tyro tyro/work'm round
make'm mischief/what'm found
greedy greedy/let'm be
bring'm home/luscious

Jo-Jo Rasterovich

Falling in love was like being shot out into space wearing an EVA suit with five minutes' air supply left. At least that was the analogy Jo-Jo Rasterovich applied to it – having experienced both. The love thing was new; catastrophically, mind-screwingly new. The floating-in-space thing was old but would be forever fresh in his mind, as were the long, long moments of visceral fear he'd felt as he'd struggled for breath.

It was the visceral fear and barely breathing that Jo-Jo grappled with now. Not in the exact moment that he realised Baronessa Mira Fedor had been abducted, but right afterwards, when he knew he was prepared to give up his reason for living to find her.

If Jo-Jo had had a second for reflection he might have laughed long and hard at himself. The quintessential bachelor, fallen for his nemesis – a woman. At the very least he'd have got seriously stoned. But the biozoon that he'd travelled to Rho Junction on was, to use an obscure phrase, *about to leave the station*, chasing after Mira Fedor.

Rast Randall *should* have been watching her. Instead, the mercenary had been pursuing her own ends while Jo-Jo'd been running distraction for the idiot scholar Thales Berniere so he could act as a bio-courier for the illustrious Commander Farr. Not a situation Jo-Jo had wanted to be in, but one he'd chosen, on account of the falling-in-love thing.

Now, Jo-Jo's urge to strangle Randall was surpassed only by his desire to get back on board the biological ship . . . so that he could strangle Randall.

He clawed at the 'zoon's egress scale from where he balanced on the edge of the docking tube, with all the dignity of a drowning man grabbing for a life jacket. 'Randall! Open up! Randall you prick-bender!'

The biozoon's skin vibrated under his touch. In another moment it'd pull away from the docking tube and he'd be suctioned out in the wash of the two hundred tons of space-capable creature that was distressed and in a hurry.

'*Randall!*'

The 'zoon flexed; a ripple that ran through its huge body and sent the tube buckling.

Alarms squealed around him.

Jo-Jo hugged the barnacled outer flesh, scraping his face against it. 'Please! *Please!*'

A sob escaped.

Jo-Jo Rasterovich didn't sob! Or at least not unless he was floating in space with no air in his tank. Even then it was an angry sob. Not this pitiful, heartbroken whisper.

The emergency overrides on the docking tube kicked in and it began to retract. He stretched forward, refusing to let go of the 'zoon, until he lost his footing altogether.

He hung, like a drop of water about to fall.

Then the scale sagged inward and rough hands reached around and hauled him inside.

He fell against the mercenary, Rast Randall, who expelled a long, sour breath in his face. A panting breath like she'd been running.

'You – crazy – motherfucker,' she said. 'What – you – think – you're doing?'

Jo-Jo reefed her hands from his jacket and sent an internal message to his trembling legs to perform and hold him up. 'Changing my mind.'

Her scowl deepened to a point where he thought she might punch him, and then just as suddenly, a look of suspicion crossed her face. 'You've been blubbing.'

He didn't grace something so ridiculous with a reply.

A look of comprehension changed her expression entirely and she burst out laughing. 'Love's a bitch. Ain't she?'

She turned around and walked away.

MIRA

In those seconds of mind-sorting before true consciousness, Mira Fedor thought that she was on the Tourmaline Islands with Trinder Pellegrini. It was so tangible: the flavour of salt and sea and the faint, unpleasant scrape of wet sand on her skin; her heartbeat quick with excitement and trepidation. Unchaperoned with the young, handsome Principe. The way he watched her . . .

She rolled onto her back, luxuriating in the warm water. But the movement brought a wave of distortion and then clarity.

Insignia.

Her link with the biozoon had dwindled to the faintest of whispers. Why so distant?

Insignia, *where are you? Where am I?*

She opened her eyes and blinked painfully into a hard light. There was water – she could hear it – but the light obliterated everything else.

'Close your eyes,' instructed a voice.

Mira gladly obeyed it, shutting out the pain of the glare. Something insubstantial like gauze or silk settled on her face. It moulded to the contours of her mouth and nose and then dissolved into the warmth of her skin.

She reached to touch it but something batted her hand away.

'Do not. It is harmless but will allow you to manage the luminosity. Now open your ocular vessels.'

Ocular vessels? Mira blinked again, taking a second to wonder what kind of humanesque referred to eyes as 'ocular vessels'.

Then a cascade of recent memories and probabilities flooded over her. She'd been with Bethany at the markets on Rho Junction. Rast had left them. Siphonophores, Beth had called them. Floating globular creatures with transparent bodies and feet suckers. No – not just transparent. They'd surrounded her and—

Mira sat up quickly, wildly, clutching her abdomen. *Baby.*

'Please desist. You may injure Wanton-poda. Or yourself.'

Suddenly her surroundings came into sharp focus. She made little sense of the wider space beyond the quivering, transparent wall that encased her, save for what appeared to be sheets of undulating tissue swaying like they were caught in a breeze.

She did, however, comprehend that she was in – not a room exactly, but an amorphous space with no specific lines. A creature hovered in the air to one side of her, a curious bell-shaped thing, a little larger than her head and shoulders combined, with two sharp, earlike protrusions above large black eyes. Flaps moved constantly around the skirt of the bell, which Mira presumed kept it afloat.

She wetted her lips and let her hands fall to her side.

'This is Wanton-poda,' it said. 'Wanton is the "I" and "poda" is the cephalopod.'

Mira digested that for a moment. The creature

seemed innocuous and polite. 'You are using a cephalopod's body.'

'For the moment. Naturally there have been some modifications. Wanton-poda does not require a water environment.' It floated closer to her. 'It is normal etiquette for the other party in a conversation to identify themselves.'

'P-pardon m-my manners. My name is Mira Fedor.'

'Yes, yes, Nascent humanesque.'

'You an Extropist?'

Wanton-poda's skirt fluttered, sending it higher into the air. '"Extropist" is a term used only by Nascents. We do acknowledge the term "Post-Species", but of course that only describes a small section of our community.'

Mira swung her legs off the spongy platform she was sitting on. Her breath came too quickly, leaving her dizzy. 'I have been taken against my will, Wanton-poda. I must return to my friends and my ship. Where are they?'

The cephalopod's ear flaps flattened and it spun in circles, making little squealing noises.

Mira put her hands over her ears. 'Stop! Please! What is wrong? Have I offended you?'

But the creature took no notice, spinning faster and squealing louder.

Pressure built behind the bridge of Mira's nose. Before she realised what was happening, unwanted tears brimmed and began to fall down her cheeks.

Wanton-poda suddenly stopped and floated closer again. 'You are expressing sadness.'

Mira nodded and pressed her fingers to her eyes.

She took several slow breaths to calm herself. 'Distress. Please, tell me where I am.'

'Of course, Mira-fedor. You are in a cultivation chamber on Hue in Interim territory.'

Her panic of a few moments before turned to anger. 'In Extropy space? How far am I from Rho Junction? Who has brought me here?'

Wanton-poda began to spin.

'Why are you doing that?'

The spinning increased again and it started to wail.

Mira's head pounded. 'Stop!' she said. 'Tell me what I'm doing to upset you.'

The spinning lessened and Wanton-poda's ear flap shot up. 'Nascent Mira-fedor should not express itself to Wanton-poda in such an impolite manner.'

Mira tried to quell her rising anger. Was the creature simply obtuse or was it being cagey? She had always imagined Extropists to be highly intellectually developed. Wasn't that the point of their practices? 'My questions seem to offend you.'

'It is not the content that is offensive but the manner,' it explained. 'Interrogatives are offensive to Wanton-poda.'

Squelching noises emanated from under Wanton-poda's skirt, followed by an unpleasant odour. Mira bit her lip, not sure whether to enquire if the creature was all right. She decided to remain quiet and hold her breath until the odour dissipated.

'Better, better,' said Wanton-poda after a while, as if relieved of discomfort. 'My clarification is this. I am Highness Most Capable of Cultivation: Tissue. You – Nascent humanesque – have been brought to my chamber by Highness Most Capable of Security: Off-Hue-World. It was believed this would be a relevant location for you to take respite.'

Mira checked her desire to ask a direct question. Instead she responded with her own story. 'I was visiting the markets in the Arrivals Bell on Rho Junction in the Saiph system. It is *supposed* to be neutral territory. My . . . my escort left me for a short time and Post-Species Siphonophores surrounded me. I thought it merely an accident at first. They were transparent but then their bodies darkened. I remember being lifted up off my feet. And that is all. Now you tell me that I have been brought to Post-Species space against my will. That is abduction.'

'Wanton-poda laments your circumstance, but Highness Most Capable of Security: Off-Hue-World is most respected. It is simply my task to receive you and tend you until you are relocated, based on available information of your needs: food and liquid.'

Mira slid onto the floor and stood carefully, smoothing out her fellala. She wore the new one that *Insignia* had fabricated for her. The crispness had already gone from the folds, and stains showed along the hemline. At least she had the dignity and protection of her robe. The ambient temperature in the cultivation chamber was uncomfortably warm and moist.

As if tripped by that thought, she suddenly craved water and food. On the floor beside her she noticed a table stand holding containers of fruits and fluids.

'These should be suitable,' said the Extro, descending closer to the table stand, 'according to specifications.'

Mira sank to the floor and reached for two of the containers. The fruits weren't familiar but they smelt appealing enough. She sipped the water first, a tiny amount. It tasted so much like Araldis water that she wanted to cry again. The high calcium content had even begun to leave a white ring around the inside of the beaker. She swallowed the rest in one long, gulping draught.

'Evidence indicates the liquid is accurately reconstituted.' Wanton-poda hovered at shoulder height, its skirt frill trembling delicately. Perhaps she imagined it, but the creature seemed satisfied.

She wanted to ask how it had learned the perfect balance of mineral content but she settled for a simple compliment.

'The water is beautiful. I have so missed the taste of it.'

Wanton-poda's frill quivered and it bobbed. 'Wanton-poda is gratified. Most gratified.'

'Wanton-poda is most talented,' said Mira cautiously. If the Extro did not like direct questions, how would it react to flattery?

'Wanton-poda is happy to use its skill for an intelligent and appreciative Nascent.'

Mira felt her cheeks warm with colour. She stared at the creature suspiciously. Was it attempting to flatter her back?

Despite everything she felt a desire to smile. She converted it to humility. 'If I was an intelligent Nascent I would be able to understand why I was here and for how long. I must be too primitive.'

Wanton-poda rose and fell like a graceful jellyfish

caught in a sea swell. 'It has been decided by the Highness Most Capable: Evolution that Wanton-poda will observe and monitor the Nascent until she is cleared of contaminations, and then she and her foetus will be further examined.'

Further examined? Mira's sense of humour disappeared instantly. She struggled to think of an indirect way to find out more. 'My foetus is not due to be born for some time. I am surprised you were aware that the child existed. There is not much to see.'

'Indeed,' said Wanton-poda. 'With the technology available on your home planet that is an accurate summation, but of course you are in a vastly different place.'

'Of course,' she acknowledged.

She thought for a moment, chewing her fruit slowly. If the Extros knew her home planet then presumably they had not kidnapped her in error. Perhaps Wanton-poda would reveal more if she simply remained quiet.

'Preliminary investigation reveals that your foetus shows some interesting anomalies,' it volunteered.

Mira could barely swallow the mouthful she had chewed. She sipped the water, hoping it would lubricate her nervous, dry throat.

'It has inherited your telepathic bonding ability—' Wanton-poda stopped and spun around, hastening over to the transparent wall. It hovered in front of it, uttering soft yelping noises.

Siphonophores appeared in the outer space, weaving through the sheets of shifting tissue and bubble-incubators as they proceeded directly towards them.

They didn't halt at the transparent wall but passed straight through it. Wanton-poda shot across in between Mira and them, expelling more gusts of foul odour from underneath its frill.

An exchange of animated noises told Mira that a discussion was going on. She concentrated hard, trying to decipher something – anything – but she couldn't recognise any speech patterns or syllabic references.

She interrupted them in frustration. 'Why have you brought me here?'

But the Siphonophores didn't even seem to hear her. They turned in accord, leaving as quickly and silently as they'd arrived.

Mira attempted to follow them but the wall became solid as if she'd run into a sheet of rubber. She clawed at it in anger. The texture immediately hardened.

She took a couple of steps backward and then ran forward, trying to use momentum to break through. The wall repelled her with equal force, and she fell down.

Wanton-poda squealed. 'Please desist, Mira-fedor. You'll injure yourself and the pantomath.'

Mira climbed to her feet, clutching her hip and abdomen. She felt shaken and enraged, and fearful that she had hurt her baby. 'You can't keep me a prisoner!' she cried. 'And for Cruxsakes, what is a pantomath? Why did you call my baby that?' Suddenly she didn't care that her questions were direct and offensive.

Wanton-poda ascended to shoulder height and

excreted a light spray from under its frill. Almost instantly Mira became tired; so tired that instinct sent her stumbling over to the bed where she could lie down before—

TRIN

Trin sat on the beach under Semantic's glow, and stared out at the dark mass of water. Murmurs drifted down to him from the camp higher up along the tide line. The voices held optimism for the first time.

Many had perished in their flight from the Saqr to safety; some in the Pablo tunnels, but most had fallen to the nightwinds as they trekked to the southern islands.

Since then they had crept from island to island on stolen flat-yachts, sleeping by day and putting their lives in the hands of a young half-Mioloaquan girl.

Now Djeserit had found them an island upon which they might be able to stay, and put an end to this exhausting flight from the Saqr who'd invaded their world and devastated their towns.

Djeserit had their trust. With her unique hybrid biology she was able to fish effectively and provide them with the food they'd need for the two-day journey across the Galgos Strait. Djeserit was their hero and neither he, the new Principe of Araldis, nor Cass Mulravey, the women's advocate, had been able to give their people as much hope.

Trin wrestled with this realisation, unsure whether it pleased or displeased him.

'Trinder, darling, you've barely spoken to me.'

The voice belonged to his mother. Djeserit had rescued her from the palazzo on the Tourmaline Islands; another courageous feat that chafed at Trinder's frayed emotions.

'I have many things to contemplate, madre. They do not include entertaining you with conversation,' he said flatly.

She sat down next to him and trickled a handful of sand through her fingers, her expression unhappy. The salt had been unkind to her thin hair and ageing skin and she looked more unkempt than the rest of them despite her servant's ministrations.

'It is . . . simply . . . that I'm grateful to the Mioloaquan girl who saved me. She is . . . resourceful,' she said.

Jilda Pellegrini's artless praise of Djeserit infuriated him, in part because he agreed with her, even though he did not wish to.

'Then you should speak with her,' he said.

'I have tried, Trinder, but she dismisses me. She insists that you are the reason they have survived. She is most . . . devoted . . . to you.' She said the words carefully, as if fearful of his reaction, and yet he knew his mother. She was probing him.

'I am the Principe. Of course I have led them, as my father would have,' he said.

Jilda's face crumpled at the mention of Franco Pellegrini and she put her hand to her mouth to stifle a cry.

Trin felt irritation well in him, rather than sympathy. 'Madre!'

'Our world, Trinder. What has happened to it? We

will all perish in this harsh landscape. Caro Franco—'

'Caro Franco! He was not your caro Franco, madre. He cared as little for you as he did for me.'

'No! It was not that way.'

He grasped one thin, frail shoulder. 'It *was* that way. Only you refuse to see it.'

'Si. And will continue to.'

For the first time Trin saw a flicker of the stubbornness that matched his own. Her tragic denial filled him with guilt.

He stood and stalked away along the beach, trying to banish the anguish that she'd seeded within him.

By the next evening the rafts were assembled and the shells filled with water. The men had brought back bundles of spine bush to shade their crossing and the women had worked the tough seaweed into ropes that would tie them to the yachts if the waters became rough.

Cass Mulravey stood in the water, shepherding her women and bambini aboard their yacht while Trin watched from the beach. Her brother and the few men who had escaped from Ipo with her helped the women board. Trin couldn't remember their names, only their surliness and inclination to keep separate from the Carabinere. They talked more freely though with those from the Pablo mine.

Djes came to stand alongside him. He noticed her swaying with the effort of standing upright, her muscles more accustomed to the action of swimming now. He knew if he looked closely he would see how thick the webbing had grown between her fingers and toes.

'Stay close to my yacht,' he told her.

She inclined her head. Her hair lay slick-wet against her scalp. He had not seen it dry for days. 'I will scout and return.'

'But Djes, the xoc—'

'I will take care, my Principe, I promise.'

Her simple and endearing way released a flood of emotion in him. He reached for her and held her tight, uncaring that the Carabinere, the women and Jilda all watched them. 'We need you, Djes,' he whispered. 'I need you.'

She rested her cool cheek against his, and then pulled away gently. 'We must get them as far as we can this night. The sun will be cruel on them tomorrow.'

He let her go. 'Si.' He raised his voice. 'We go now. Keep the yachts as close together as possible. Mulravey, do you have your flags?'

The woman waved two pieces of ragged material in her hand. 'The plain colour means all is well. The bright colour means we need help. Or you need ours.'

An insult lurked in her reply as it did in all her conversations with him; it was as though she could barely contain her contempt.

He ignored it. 'You have space on your yacht. You will take some of the Pablo men.'

She shook her head. 'We travel in the group that has always been.'

Her stubborn parochialism invoked a flare of anger in him. It made no sense to adopt this line of thinking. The other two yachts were weighed down with heavier, larger men.

Djes stepped forward to intercede, but before she could speak, one of Mulravey's men took Cass's arm.

'Cass, he's right. And if anything happens out there there's only Innis and Marrat and me to help. Thom's too weak . . .' He inclined his head to indicate a man already lying on the yacht.

Trin watched Mulravey struggle between pride and necessity.

'Your man speaks well, Cass Mulravey,' said Trin.

'My name is Kristo,' the man replied. 'And I speak for the good of all of us, not to support you, Pellegrini.' His face was heavily bearded and his hair was long and ragged, but Trin thought he remembered him ministering food to Mira Fedor when she was first brought down into the Pablo mine. No supporter of the eccentric Baronessa was useful to him. Even so he tempered his reply.

'Then we should be matched in our opinions,' said Trin, 'for that is my intention as well.'

Kristo squared his shoulders as if he might react with anger, but he did nothing other than lightly squeeze Mulravey's elbow.

Mulravey stared Trin straight in the eye. 'We'll take as many as we can.' She pulled free from Kristo's grip and walked to the water.

Trin felt a small victory in her compliance. He would shatter the woman's ludicrous obstinacy yet.

He too turned to face the open sea. 'Vai!' he ordered.

Tekton

The humanesques Thales Berniere and Bethany Ionil had been much easier to persuade to leave Rho Junction than he had hoped. In fact, Tekton's free-mind told him, *they'd been easier than a Belle-Monde prostitute.*

Tekton booked a suite with an adjoining room on the cruiser *The Last Aesthetic*, and left them alone for several days while he sorted his own affairs.

First, he organised a credit line for Manruben, the metal craftsman he'd left behind on Rho. His last glimpse of the filthy old man had been as he and Thales boarded the fast-trak back to the docks. Tekton had instructed Manruben to access the credit in two days and await news of the quixite delivery. *Under no circumstances*, Tekton told him, *should you indulge in any type of sexual encounter for the duration of the contract.* The last one had killed him. Only a quickly administered HealthWatch patch had brought the randy old devil back from a permanent date with Hades.

Second, he searched for news from Araldis and looked into the authenticity of the woman that Thales had called Mira Fedor. To his dismay, the young scholar's story seemed to be true. The Vreal Studium news hub had filed reports of an attack on the backwater Latino-owned planet. Nothing had been verified by the Orion League of Sentient Species though, as communications between planet, shift station and the wider galaxy had ceased. On the subject of the Baronessa Fedor, the Lostol Patrician's Association referred him to the Latino Noble Network, which provided a simple 3D lineage tree for the exorbitant fee of 1,000 Gals. He now knew more about her family history than he did about his own.

Tekton ordered a lotion bath and luxuriated in a darkened cabin, examining the flow of Latino heritage. Despite his antipathy to feudal hierarchies, Tekton found aristocratic lineage faintly arousing; or at least the power and intrigue it promised. So much so that he indulged in a little auto-eroticism while he learned about the classes of Latino Crux.

The Fedors, it seemed, were part of the Crown Aristo class by dint of their symbiotic relationship with the biozoon species. This honour remained with the males of each generation. However, a recent addendum to the images footnoted that for the first time in history a female of the line had received the Talent.

It seemed the young Baronessa Mira Fedor, to whom Thales referred, really could pilot a biozoon.

This discovery coincided with Tekton's arrival at the point of orgasm, at which time he gave his free-mind licence to fantasise; the result being an odd vision of the head and shoulders of the young Baronessa Fedor with the body of a biozoon, conducting fellatio upon him.

Sated but a little disturbed at the oddity of the image, Tekton washed, re-robed and lay down on his sumptuous suite's bed. Next time, he decided, he would pay for pleasure.

He fell to thinking of other things. The biggest of his unanswered questions pertained to Miranda. Why on Mintaka did his colleague, the randy Dr Miranda Seeward, own a bio-lab on Rho Junction? And why had she created a virus that affected the orbitofrontal cortex? And *why* was she selling it to an illicit bio-dealer on Scolar?

Tekton set his moud about researching the orbitofrontal cortex. When it was ready he questioned it to death – or at least until it began to repeat itself.

What is its function? he asked.

As I have said, Godhead, it manages emotion and reward.

Reward?

And punishment.

Hmmm. That is why it affects decision-making.

Yes, it integrates reinforcers.

Tekton pondered further. Miranda had developed a virus that manipulated part of the brain and was selling it to a distributor on Scolar – the seat of Orion's greatest philosophers. Intriguing. He had no doubt that this was somehow intertwined with her project for the Sole Entity. Now, if he could persuade Carnage Farr to share his analysis of the virus, he could gazump Miranda, or even better, poach her ideas to gain Sole's favour.

But how did one persuade someone like Carnage to share information? The man was renowned for his brilliance – and his paranoia.

Everyone has their vulnerabilities, reminded free-mind.

Usually their family, agreed logic-mind.

And how fortuitous, Tekton thought, to be travelling with Carnage's sister.

He concluded, at that point, that Thales Berniere

might well turn out to be incidental to his needs but that the woman Bethany could be the key.

Blackmail her, proposed logic-mind.

How gauche, said free-mind. *Charm her.*

Tekton considered both options and decided on the latter for a number of reasons, not the least being that sub-light travel was so tedious.

He would need a diversion.

He began his seduction of Bethany Ionil with dinner – champagne and barbecued Mioloaquan mussels. The evening was only a moderate success, although it started well when the young scholar Thales begged off attending, saying that he felt unwell.

Bethany accepted the invitation but spent much of her time distracted and out of sorts.

'You seem pensive,' said Tekton as gently as he could manage considering he had ordered silver service and fresh flowers from the hydroponic section.

Bethany Ionil pushed her thin hair back behind her ears and sat up straighter. Her plain overalls and bare face made her look older than Tekton, though he guessed she was younger by many years.

A woman ages so gracelessly if she does not pay attention to herself, he thought, and promptly told his moud to order in some more feminine clothing.

For what or whom, Godhead?

Not for me! Tekton snapped at it in exasperation.

The moud fell silent.

'My apologies if I seem ... unhappy, Godhead Tekton. It's Thales. I'm concerned that he is unwell.' She linked her fingers together and twisted them.

Tekton poured her a second glass of champagne and put on his most affable and considerate expression.

Look sincere. Open the eyes a little wider, logic-mind told him.

Mouth too, free-mind added.

'Our journey will be relatively quick, my dear. But yours is a complex situation. I would benefit from a more detailed explanation of circumstances if I am to be of use to you.'

She shot him a straight and somewhat piercing look.

He responded to it head-on. 'I see your doubt, my dear. Why should I care, you ask? Let me reassure you that I'm a philanthropist at heart, and fortunate to be in a position to indulge my passion. Helping people is what I love to do.'

Overdoing it, logic-mind warned.

'I have also been known to make the odd wise investment when the right information falls my way.'

The doubt left her eyes. He'd offered her something she could believe.

'Godhead Tekton, if you can make money at my brother's expense, I shall tell you everything I know and shout hallelujah!'

Tekton clapped his hands together with feigned glee. 'Ah Bethany, I believe we will deal fabulously together.'

She unburdened herself then, not skimping on any details that might paint her in any better light. He heard how her passion and insecurities about her Mio husband had caused her to send her only child down to Araldis alone.

'Godhead, have you ever done something that made you wish you were dead and yet you've known that you can't take such an easy way out before you try and set things right?'

Tekton had no answer. Her heartfelt manner had taken him aback. He was not used to such ingenuousness. There was no melodrama with Bethany Ionil.

She hunched her shoulders and stabbed at the mussels on the plate before her with a tiny silver fork. 'Josef says that everyone does things that they regret, but I don't believe him. Not things they would die over.'

'Perhaps your friend's experience is more expansive than yours? You may think yours the worst of mistakes but in fact it is not.' Tekton, to his surprise, found himself speaking gently. Supportively.

Get a grip, fool. Free-mind was in a feisty mood.

'What can be worse than abandoning your own child? I'm really not sure of much any more. In fact I am sure of only one thing . . . I will do anything to rescue my child from that planet.' The direct look again. 'Can you help me?'

She loaded the last four words with so much emotion that Tekton excused himself to attend to his ablutions and digest the situation.

He vacillated between amusement and chagrin. He had thought to lure the thin woman to him and use her against her brother, but here she was attempting to use him instead.

He'd been trumped.

The notion rather dampened Tekton's appetite for seduction.

He returned to the table and told his moud to request brandy. It was no longer a champagne type of evening.

Their conversation continued into the shipboard evening. Bethany answered Tekton's questions with candour, showing not the slightest effects of the brandy that was making him drowsy.

She's drinking you under the table, said logic-mind. But the warning seemed to come from the end of a long, long tunnel.

'What brought you to Rho Junction, Godhead?' asked Bethany.

'My project. I intend to build beauty.' Tekton would have explained it more elegantly if his tongue had not been so thickened with alcohol.

'Beauty,' said Bethany mildly. 'Is beauty as subjective as our culture would have you believe, do you think?'

Tekton felt a rush of akula at the introduction of one of his favourite topics. 'Beauty is universal,' he declared with vehemence. 'I will create something that will make you weep for its perfection and writhe for its passion.'

'A noble and worthy cause, I imagine, but – pardon my ignorance of artistry – why would you feel it necessary to do such a thing?'

'For the glory, of course. I *will* be the foremost tyro,' Tekton replied without thought. 'I *will* win the Entity's favours.'

Fool! both minds cried at once.

Their emphatic rejoinder sobered Tekton somewhat. He had talked far too much.

Moud! Chilled water!

JO-JO RASTEROVICH

Jo-Jo lay on his bed, in his cabin, in a maudlin fug fuelled by some of Carnage Farr's most brutal home-grown whisky. Some of his misery he could attribute to the strains and scrapes from his last-moment attempt to get on board the biozoon. Another portion of it was due to the chronic allergy reaction that seemed to have settled into his airways and the nagging worry that Carnage Farr had given him a dose of something lethal. The major part, however, fell squarely on the shoulders of Mira Fedor.

Where in all God's hells had the Extros taken her? And why? Jo-Jo just couldn't figure it out.

Underneath the maudlin, though, was a simmering soup of other emotions; the foremost of which revolved around Rast Randall. The mercenary had left Fedor alone when she should have been watching her. Jo-Jo wanted to split Randall from orifice to orifice for her neglect, yet he couldn't. For a start, she knew Mira Fedor best. He needed her to help find the Baronessa. But also the mercenary had admitted something to him. *Love's a bitch, ain't she?* she'd said.

She hadn't levelled that just at Jo-Jo.

Randall was in love with Fedor as well.

It should be amusing. Really it should.

But Jo-Jo was too wracked with misery and rage to find anything funny.

'Rasterovich!' Rast bellowed into the ship-cast. 'Get your dismal carcass down here, we need to talk. This giant whale's freakin' out.'

Jo-Jo opened his eyes, rolled onto his side and drained the flask he held tightly. The white-haired bitch was right; the biozoon was stressed. He'd been listening for hours to the little noises that weren't normally there. And there was something about the smell of the 'zoon that had changed.

Jo-Jo got up, swaying as blood searched for brain, and tottered over to the wall. He pulled away the cabin wall drapes and swiped his fingers across the ridged flesh. It felt slimy and grainy.

Something dropped into his hair. He glanced up: thick goo had begun to seep through the ceiling covers. *Fuck.*

Jo-Jo pulled on his pants and went looking for the mercenaries.

They were in the cucina drinking beer and eating slices from a giant, stinking wheel of cheese.

'Something die in here?' Jo-Jo asked.

Randall stabbed cheese onto the end of her fork and offered him some. 'Over-matured heartbreak. The food storage enviros are screwed. One minute they're hot enough to broil pig-fat, the next they're like a damn freezer. Some of the soft stuff's complaining.'

Jo-Jo folded a chair down and sat on it. 'You think the 'zoon's sick?'

'Ailing,' said Rast.

'Gutted,' volunteered Latourn.

Jo-Jo glowered at Latourn and grabbed a knife. He

cut himself a large wedge of cheese and nibbled it. It tasted sour. 'Shit.'

'I suggest you eat up.' Rast tossed him a beer; a clean skin tube, another one of Carnage's finer brews.

Jo-Jo belched and guzzled half of it down. It tasted refreshing after the whisky. 'Why the rush?'

Still seated, Rast slid her legs off the table to the floor, lifted up a box of beer tubes and dropped it where her feet had been. Then she put her legs across the top of the carton. 'Other than the loony 'zoon . . . just a small case of us heading, uninvited, into Extro space.'

Jo-Jo paused mid-guzzle. 'You're shittin' me?' He placed the tube back on the table in front of him. He thought he did well not to tremble. 'How long we been doing that?'

The mercs broke into harmonised guffaws.

When they'd finished, Rast wiped her eyes. 'How long? Three days. Right about the time you were puking up your third bottle of No Label malt.'

Jo-Jo felt the cheese lurch around in his stomach. 'Three days. Anyone noticed us yet?'

'Hard to say. The traffic's insane out there. It's a while since I've been to the Saiph system but I don't recall seeing it like this before. Seems like everyone's going somewhere in a real hurry. Being in a 'zoon we should be OK. 'Zoons trade with everyone. Even the Extros.'

'Thought Saiph was off-limits – other than Rho Junction, I mean.'

''Tis. For OLOSS craft. Not much there though, just a bunch of dry rocks and a skinny sun. The *real* Extro worlds are somewhere else. Saiph works like an airlock for them. They let traders in from time to time if they come through Rho Junction, but the door stays shut to the real system.'

'What's the wave analysis show?'

Rast stabbed her knife into the centre of the cheese wheel and left it there. She pressed her thumb and forefinger to her forehead. 'Can't say. 'Zoon's not being very agreeable. Pings me every time I go near the buccal.'

'What about going into Autonomy to get us out of here?'

Rast dropped her hand from her face and stared at him with a deadly serious expression. 'No frickin' way am I going to try and pilot a crazy, heartbroken 'zoon.'

'I can do it,' said Jo-Jo. 'I owned one.'

She stared hard at him.

'It was a hybrid,' he admitted. 'AI-compatible.'

'No frickin' way am I trustin' *you* to do anything of the kind.' She gave the table a kick to emphasise her words.

Jo-Jo's tube rolled onto his lap. Instinctively he grabbed it and the amber fluid squirted all over him.

The mercenaries fell into their synchronised laugh again.

Jo-Jo's years of staying *out* of 'situations' flew right out of the egress scale. Maybe it was the booze. Or the fact that he was still pissed at Randall. He lunged out of his seat and flung himself at her. Surprise got him closer than he'd thought. That and the fact she had her legs up on the table.

They crashed to the floor together, Jo-Jo using his advantage to get astride her.

He got his hands to her neck and lifted her head, pounding it against the floor – a crack good enough to knock anyone out, if the floor had been concrete or wood or metal. But the floor was 'zoon, spongy and resilient. Her head almost bounced back and hit him.

He half-expected to feel the hands of Catchut and Latourn on his shoulders but they stayed put.

What he didn't expect was Randall's boot in the back of his head. The blow, as she kicked up hard and fast from behind, knocked him over her shoulder. In a single, agile move their positions reversed. Suddenly she had him pinned to the floor, her knees weighing down on his elbows. She'd punched him twice before he even began to struggle. Her next punch, though, loosened all his teeth. Jo-Jo's world disorientated, and haze spots appeared before his eyes.

He smelt the beer on Randall's breath as she leant her face close to his. 'You ever try and take me again and I'll finish it.'

Jo-Jo wet his lips. 'But then she won't have to choose between us . . . and you'll never really know,' he whispered.

A moment passed; one of those unpredictable pauses where things could have gone either way.

Jo-Jo waited, not really caring one way or the other.

Then her weight lifted abruptly from his shoulders.

Jo-Jo raised his head off the floor but before he could sit up, Rast had gone.

Catchut and Latourn lurched out of their chairs.

'What'd you say to the Capo?' demanded Latourn.

Catchut crouched down like a compacted spring.

Jo-Jo ignored them both. He picked himself up,

cupping his throbbing jaw with his hand, and fumbled in the carton for a couple of tubes of beer. Nursing them in the crook of his other arm, he left the cucina and headed to the viaduct.

No way in hell was he sailing like a sitting duck into Extro space.

He'd finished both tubes by the time he'd reached the buccal and the pain in his jaw was beginning to recede. Temporary, but he'd take it. He pushed his fist into the centre of the pucker and waited for it to retract.

Nothing.

Again. Harder this time, more like a soft punch.

Zip.

This time he ground his fist around and pushed with all his strength. A mild shock crackled up his arm to his shoulder and jolted him backwards against the opposite wall.

He recovered his footing and glared helplessly. The 'zoon had locked him out.

He stalked back along the central stratum to the cucina. Latourn and Catchut had gone, leaving their mess of tubes and the stink of overripe cheese behind them. Jo-Jo snatched up the half-empty carton and took it back to his room, where he drank it in a short space of time. They were in Extro space heading straight into the teeth of disaster and there wasn't a frickin' thing he could do about it.

Except get drunker.

MIRA

Mira opened her eyes. The taste in her mouth; the heaviness behind her eyes – the Extro had drugged her. She lay very still, trying to put pieces of recent events together but the past rose up and swamped her.

Trinder Pellegrini had raped her. *Raped*.

Adrenalin poured through her body as she remembered.

Right afterwards she'd been in shock. Anger hadn't come till later, when she escaped Araldis aboard *Insignia*. But it had stayed with her; a hidden river of it, constantly on the point of overflowing.

She sat up and stared wildly around the Extro cell, feeling the years of exercising restraint and manners breaking away.

This . . . this . . . abduction . . .

She jumped off the bed and kicked over the water container. Then she began to overturn anything unfixed. She threw herself at the wall of her prison, clawing at it and screaming. She didn't care about her madness or the self-harm.

I will not be kept like this!

Wanton-poda hastened towards her from the adjacent chamber, passing through the wall to spray her with more sedation vapour.

She tried to hit the Extro but it manoeuvred higher, out of her way.

The wooziness came as quickly as last time – more quickly.

Her legs folded.

She stayed liked that. Every time she regained consciousness Wanton-poda sprayed her again until she could not tell where the effects of one spray ended and another started. The Extro removed everything from her confinement space, including its own aquarium.

Gradually her mood calmed, making it easier to refuse food.

Siphonophores passed in and out of her cell so frequently that she barely noticed them. They were intertwined with the ghosts and the visions she began to have as a consequence of the sedation.

Time became irrelevant; it also became everything. A single moment would expand and exist for ever, and at other times Wanton-poda would tell her that days had passed.

Once, her mind cleared from the mixture of wake and sleep to the sound of Wanton-poda screaming. The Siphonophores were back, and had gathered around the little cephalopod like ghouls around a corpse.

Mira caught a glimpse of Wanton-poda spinning in an erratic, exhausted fashion as they bounced it from one to the other, each contact producing another scream.

Eventually they left. Wanton-poda bobbled over to its rest tank and sank into the rejuvenation mixture.

Mira slept again and awoke the next time feeling

clearer in the head. How long since the Extro had administered the sedation? She glanced out to the bio-lab.

Wanton-poda was still in its tank.

Noticing her movement, it emerged and floated slowly into her containment booth.

'Wanton-poda seems unwell,' she said quietly.

'Mira-fedor speaks.'

'They have hurt you.'

'Highness Most Capable: Evolution is not pleased with Mira-fedor's progress. She does not thrive.'

'That is my choice, not yours.'

'That is not relevant.'

Mira forced herself upright. 'I wish to talk to you.'

Its ear flaps lifted. 'Mira-fedor must not use aggressive behaviour.'

She nodded. 'I promise.'

'Wanton-poda does not understand that meaning.'

'I will use . . . c-calm behaviour. But t-tell me what they want.'

'Wanton-poda observes that your child is not thriving. You must ingest more nutrients or it may not survive.'

'But I don't want to survive. Not if I am to be kept here and told nothing.'

'Wanton-poda is confused. It is well acknowledged that humanesques can use resolve to change predicted outcomes but my understanding is that it is usual for that resolve to be utilised for survival, not against it.'

Mira sat straighter, holding her head against a spinning sensation. Lethargy of blood flow. She had lain still for far too long. Her fellala had gone and she wore a thin captive's robe which showed the bulge in her abdomen.

'I had thought that Post-Species like you would have retained some connection with their origins. That you would understand. Clearly that is not the case.'

'Wanton-poda senses criticism in that statement but is not sure. Mira-fedor appears to need something.'

'If I can't have my freedom then I must, at least, have knowledge. I am nothing without it. I must make sense of things.'

'Knowledge.' The creature twirled gently, a clockwise movement that Mira decided was musing. 'Wanton-poda will tell you of our worlds. Fear and anxiety emotions are known to be diminished by familiarity.'

'I need water,' said Mira.

Wanton-poda floated out through the translucent wall and returned towing a plastic tube in its small gravity field. It dropped the tube in Mira's lap and waited.

When she'd swallowed the contents, it hovered down closer to her eye level.

At this proximity she could see the cephalopod's organs beneath the bell-shaped exterior, and a small, dark tumourlike mass she assumed to be the implanted Post-Species Identity. She wondered how well it would survive outside its host. Or indeed why it had chosen such an impractical and seemingly delicate body to inhabit. If she reached quickly towards it she might be able to—

Wanton-poda shot away from her, spinning quickly counter-clockwise, as though it had read her thoughts.

'Wanton-poda acts fearful. I had thought it about to share information with me,' she said calmly.

The Extro slowed its spin and descended until it once again hovered near her face.

She peered closely again, trying to determine where the vocal projection originated. From underneath one of the head flaps, she decided. There was probably a small echo canal linked to a nano-speaker in the Identity mound. After all, cephalopods did not speak.

'While Wanton-poda is not permitted to discuss the immediate details of your presence here, it is allowed to speak of the worlds.'

'It is difficult for me to have a discussion with Wanton-poda if I cannot use the interrogative form. It is logical for my species to ask questions.'

It went into its more gentle thinking spin.

She waited.

When it settled she noticed its translucent flesh had taken on a pearl-grey colour. 'Wanton-poda will attempt to make species exception to the interrogative if Mira-fedor will be more contented.'

'Thank you,' she replied. 'I will try, if you will try. Perhaps . . . I should tell you . . . what I know of your . . . culture, then you can advise me if I am . . . misinformed.' The words came slowly despite her mind being clearer. It still seemed hard to speak fluently, as though her throat had rusted. She squeezed the last drops from the water tube and let the liquid sit in her mouth. Suddenly she longed for a steam bath and a mouth wash.

'I have heard that the first generation of your culture chose to live in virtual worlds without corporeal . . . attachment. That is, without bodies. But in the next generation there were divisions in belief. Things changed, and now your society has deviated towards the use of host bodies.' Mira found herself breathing heavily at the end of such a long speech.

Without warning Wanton-poda floated off to retrieve another water tube and a small container holding a cube of food.

She pinched off a small piece of the spicy, soft cube and put it in her mouth. As it dissolved it left an aftertaste of meat.

'It seems that Mira-fedor has a rudimentary understanding. However, Wanton-poda would not call the use of host bodies a deviation, merely a choice.'

Mira thought for a moment. The creature was not straightforward in the way it expressed itself. She needed to ask the right kind of questions. 'So others of your kind choose differently?'

The pearl-grey colour darkened to almost charcoal with her first direct question, but the cephalopod did not scream. 'Post-Species offers many choices. Mira-fedor is correct in some ways. You are correct in some ways. After the first generation, some of the Post-Species longed for some physiological reconnection. Wanton-poda's family is among them. Not all shared this desire, and preferred to remain within I context.'

'I context. Is that machine-based?'

Its flesh darkened with agitation again. 'That is a primitive analogy to how they exist and not accurate.'

'So your society is divided into corporeal and non-corporeal?'

'Again, Mira-fedor oversimplifies.'

'Forgive me, Wanton-poda, but I am trying to find my own context.'

'Let us call my family "host" then.'

'Agreed.'

'Host family has varied subsidiary families.'

'Using different species as hosts?'

'A correct summation. There is even a small branch that still favours the basic biped form.'

Mira paused. 'You mean that some Post-Species have chosen to reinhabit bipedal bodies?'

'A correct summation.'

'But that seems ridiculous.'

'Our information sharing does not require your evaluation.'

Mira closed her mouth and swallowed. She'd offended the Extro again. 'P-pardon . . . it's just that . . . I thought you pursued this line of evolution precisely to leave physical encumbrance behind?'

'We became Post-Species to increase choice. For some, that means a nostalgic connection with the past.'

'And for others that means living in a machine.'

Wanton-poda uttered an odd reverberation that Mira interpreted as frustration.

'Machine implies large metallic casings. Non-corporeal Post-Species reside in a far more sophisticated environment.'

'My experience and imagination are limited,' said Mira. 'Yet I do know a little of politics and I would surmise that there may be friction between these different streams.'

'That is not information Wanton-poda may share.'

Mira nodded. She paused again as she chewed the last of the meat-flavoured cube. 'What are the Post-Species non-corporeal like then?'

'Wanton-poda does not comprehend your interrogative.'

'What are their characteristics?'

'You may experience difficulty with Wanton-poda's

explanation. They have no comparative humanesque characteristics.'

'Is that deliberate, or a product of their interface?'

Wanton-poda hesitated before answering. 'Deliberate.'

'Are they misanthropists?'

The Extro began spinning in its thinking way, but instead of replying, it passed out through the wall into the tissue room and did not return.

Some things, Mira surmised, would be hard to find out.

TRIN

They sailed smoothly through the night, accustomed
to it as they were, and covered a third of the journey
without incident. But as Leah prepared to make its
burning journey across the sky, the winds rose. On the
far horizon from which they'd come, Trin saw the telltale pink glow of sunrise climbing the air. North and
south of them was the open sea of the Galgos and ahead
the shimmering shape of the island they sought.

'Where does this wind come from, Principe?' asked
Joe Scali. They sat close together under the weed-
strapped cover of spine bush. It felt as though the sun
beat directly on them despite the shade and their
fellalos.

'A dust storm is brewing on the mainland,' said
Trinder. Fear gnawed around the edges of his stomach
and he spoke calming words to himself. *The dust will
not affect us here.* But the winds? 'Juno!' he called to
his Carabinere scout who sat under scant cover on the
flat-yacht's bow.

'Si, Principe?'

Trin pointed east. 'A storm perhaps?'

Juno turned his attention from the island and
squinted towards the land horizon. 'I hope not,
Principe.' Dragging the brush cover with him, he
crawled along the deck to Trin and Joe Scali.

He pushed back his hood a little so that Trin could see his face. His crimson skin was almost black from sun exposure. 'The winds could break these yachts apart. I've seen it before.'

'On the islands?'

He nodded. 'I flew guard for your father one time, across the island belt. The winds forced us down on an island across the Galgos, but further south than here. We had to tie the AiV to rocks. Even so, it flipped and got carried away to sea. The wind and the water tore it apart like it was made of gauze. We waited two days for rescue.'

'I never heard that story,' said Trin thoughtfully. How many things did he not know about his father? he wondered.

'Franco did not like people to hear of his mistakes.'

'My father did not make mistakes as far as he was concerned.'

'Mistakes are the province of sons not fathers,' Juno said. 'We should alert the other yachts.'

Trin nodded. 'Everyone must be tied on.'

'But what if the yacht breaks apart, as Juno says?' asked Joe anxiously.

'Better strapped to something that floats than not.'

Juno nodded his agreement. 'I will wave the warning cloth.'

'When Djeserit comes, I will ask her to go to the other yachts and tell them.'

'That would be best, Principe.'

While Juno crawled along the crowded deck to the stern, Trin moved to the edge and let his legs trail in the water. If Djeserit was nearby she would come.

And she did, surfacing like a beautiful, elegant sea creature, her hair streaming. She rested her arms against him, blew a spray of water from her neck gills and took a land breath. Her breathing adaptation between air and water was so perfect, thought Trin. An accident of birth that turned out to be flawless. Or perhaps her parents had been truly clever and had it geneered that way. They'd taken her to a hybrid clinic, so she'd told him.

'Principe?' she rasped. When she had been under-water for a while her vocal cords took time to stretch.

'Can you see the eastern sky, Djes? We fear a wind-storm.'

She craned her head in the direction he pointed. 'The sea is disturbed. I can feel the swell building.'

'Juno thinks the winds could be strong enough to wreck our yachts. Go to the others and instruct them to tie themselves to the decks. *Everyone* must be secured.'

She frowned with concern. 'Of course.'

'You must come aboard as well.'

'I am safer below the waves, Principe. I can swim deeper.'

'But what about the xoc? They will seek the depths too.'

'We . . . I mean, *they* . . . don't feed during the storm.'

His heart lurched at her slip of inclusion. Every day she became more a part of the sea. Would he be able to win her back when they finally found a place to stop?

'Principe?' called Juno. 'No more than an hour, I estimate.'

Trin leaned down to kiss the top of Djeserit's head. 'Crux protect us all.'

She gazed up at him with the smile that never failed to soothe him; a smile of belief and love. 'Be safe, my Principe.'

She pushed off the yacht and with a flip of her legs was gone.

It took less time than Juno Genarro had supposed for the wind to whip the waves. Djeserit had not returned, but Trin could see the women preparing, shuffling about their yacht until they lay close together, clinging to each other. Then the swell began to shift the yachts in different sequence so that he only glimpsed the others when his own peaked on each wave. Juno Genarro fixed their rudder and reduced the sail width, so that they drove straight up the face of the enormous waves. Trin's fear began to abate with the regular rise and fall of the water and was replaced by exhilaration. The sea was more magnificent than anything he'd ever experienced. He listened to the shouts of the other men and wanted to join them, screaming into the face of the giant waves.

But the storm had more than elation to give them; the wind strengthened, drawing the swell into impossibly high peaks and bottomless troughs, ripping away their flimsy spine bush covers and tossing them about the raft.

Clouds scudded across the sky, giving them scant protection from the sun as they clung to each other, drenched and terrified.

We will die. Trin knew it, as surely as his fingers ached from clenching the weed rope and his muscles cramped with the effort of staying aboard. Nothing could survive such seas.

And yet, finally, the wind blew itself out and the waves gentled, and they were still afloat – desperate little barnacles clinging to their posts.

When it was possible to speak and sit upright, Trin called for a head count. They'd lost one overboard to the storm: an 'esque from the mines, a brawny fellow whose woman had died in the walk from the shaft to the Islands. Trin hadn't known his proper name. The Carabinere just called him *fratella*.

'Principe, the other yacht. It's missing,' shouted a hoarse Carabinere voice.

All the men scrambled to look to the stern.

The women. No! It was the second yacht of men. The ones who'd come from the mines. Cass Mulravey's boat seemed intact and carrying its full load.

Trin stared, dumbfounded. How could all those men have been lost, and yet the yacht with the women had survived?

'We need cover,' said Joe Scali. 'Before the cloud breaks up.'

'The spine bush is all gone. We have no other shade.'

A wild shout echoed to them from the bow, and the men turned toward Juno Genarro who stood, staring ahead, as he had done since the moment they'd begun their journey. 'There is our cover. On the island. The wind has given us wings.'

The island lay just beyond a set of gentling breakers. It loomed large and thick with brown vegetation. Tears welled in Trin's eyes, and he let them run, unchecked, down his face. *Dios and Crux. We are saved. We are saved.*

The men got to their knees, or their feet, yelling in

jubilation. Trin sat back down and let his legs trail in the water – his signal to Djes. Exhaustion and relief and sadness and elation combined into a strange and disembodied sensation. He felt as if he might float right across to the island of his own accord. Walk across water and lie beneath the lush bush.

Something splashed his face. He wiped it away. But it splashed again and again. Drawn from his daze he blinked, expecting that perhaps Djes was splashing water at him. But the taste of the drops in his mouth was different; without salt. He blinked again, trying to fathom it.

'Madre di Crux,' cried Joe Scali in disbelief. 'It is raining.'

THALES

A fever had beset Thales, leaving him shaky and sweating and with little appetite.

'But you said you didn't receive the bio-package. Perhaps it's something else?' said Bethany. 'I should call the medic.'

She sat close to him in an armchair in the luxurious cabin that Tekton the archiTect had procured for them, part of his promise to give them passage back to Akouedo system so that Thales could receive his antidote from Lasper Farr.

Tekton resided in an adjoining cabin but had kept to himself other than entertaining Bethany to dinner last evening. She'd returned restless and a little irritable and it had stayed with her.

'You're a medic.' He smiled weakly, but his comment only seemed to annoy her.

'I'm a scientist, Thales, and not at all versed in pathologies. You must get help.'

He shook his head firmly. 'Too much explanation.'

'What do you mean?'

'I think the bacterium your brother gave me has broken down the barrier earlier than it should have. He is the only one who can help me.'

'But you don't know that.'

Thales shrugged and rolled away from her. He did. He knew. Yet his HealthWatch was superior. Thales should be unable to get sick, unless he encountered something that could defeat the immune booster nanites in his system. And there was no naturally occurring disease that could do that.

Bethany clicked her tongue impatiently. 'You stubborn . . .' She didn't finish. A moment later he felt the bed move, as she sat on it and her hand stroked his arm. 'Please, Thales. I-I am worried for you.'

He sighed and rolled back to face her. 'It's only a few days until we shift.'

She offered him a glass of water.

He rose onto an elbow and sipped it gratefully. 'How was your dinner?'

'I'm not sure I trust him. He's very clever and he wants something from Lasper.'

Thales handed her back the glass. 'So do we.'

She sighed. 'I'm not sure how things will go when we get to Edo. Lasper promised to help me find Jess but with the Baronessa gone—'

'The mercenaries and your friend Rasterovich will find the Baronessa.'

She squeezed his hand. 'I believe they will. But if the Extros have taken her, will she still be alive? Or at least, will she be the same?'

'What do you mean?'

'They're Post-Species. Crux knows what they might want to change about her.'

'I suppose,' said Thales slowly, 'that it depends upon why they took her in the first place.'

Bethany nodded. 'I've thought about it over and

over. It must be something to do with her Innate Talent. What else could it be?'

'She is a most decent and refined woman. Life has brought her misfortune.'

Bethany fixed him with the piercing stare that reminded him so much of her brother. 'You admire refined women?'

'I-I am used to th-them,' stammered Thales. 'That is all. She reminds me of . . .' He trailed off, suddenly aware that he had said too much. He had not spoken to Bethany of his wife, nor would he.

'There is someone on Scolar?' she asked.

He didn't answer.

She placed the glass on the side table and stood up. 'Of course there is. How could there not be? – a young man like you . . . I suppose you intend to return to her.'

Thales's palms grew moist and the heat returned to his body. He wanted to tell Bethany how much her affection had meant to him but she became blurry before he could form the words.

'Thales. Thales, I'm so sorry . . . I didn't mean to . . .' Her voice grew thick, and distant.

And then it was gone.

It came back again – he wasn't sure how long afterwards – sounding even more desperate. 'Lasper? Is he . . .? Will he . . .?'

'He'll recover,' replied her brother.

'You said the bacterium wouldn't affect him if he brought the DNA sample back in time.'

'It shouldn't have. I checked his HealthWatch was current before we administered it but our latest blood screen analysis shows it's an inferior version to the one he should have. He's from Scolar. No one on Scolar gets substandard HealthWatch. It's in their charter. Perhaps someone wanted to harm your *friend*.'

'Substandard? But that might as well be murder.'

'Yes,' said Lasper Farr. 'It seems fate has intervened. He is fortunate that he didn't receive the DNA vaccine. His immune system would have been completely defeated. He'd be dead now.'

'Then you would have killed him.' Her voice sounded cold and angry.

'Circumstance would have killed him. Coincidence. Events. The things beyond most people's control.'

Thales listened to their conversation, struggling to make sense of his whereabouts. Wasn't he aboard *The Last Aesthetic* still? If not, then how long had he been unconscious?

He rolled his head to one side and it pounded. His skin felt raw and hot as though he'd been dipped in boiling water. He tried to think. Lasper Farr. They must be on Edo. And his HealthWatch? Was Lasper Farr saying someone had tampered with it? Someone on Scolar?

Sophos Mianos! Has my father-in-law tried to murder me?

The possibility sent a shot of adrenalin skimming through Thales's inflamed body. Mianos surely had the authority and the conniving. HealthWatch was administered at birth on Scolar and renewed at yearly intervals. Thales had attended his father-in-law's clinic since his marriage to Rene; on Mianos's recommendation. He had been quite pressing, Thales recalled, that he should do so. Perhaps good luck had kept him healthy until now. Good luck? He had had little of that.

He opened his eyes.

Bethany was leaning over him but looking at her brother, her face pinched with worry.

He shifted his gaze to the end of the bed. Lasper Farr stood there, arms crossed, the expression in his grey eyes unreadable.

'Beth?' Thales croaked.

Her glance fell to him. It was full of tenderness and something else he couldn't quite identify. 'Thank Crux,' she whispered. 'Thales, you've been terribly ill.'

He groped for her hand. 'I feel dreadful.'

She nodded. 'They had to transfuse you. You'll be weak for a few weeks. But I'll help you. Lasper says you'll make a full recovery.'

Thales licked his sore lips. They prickled as if the skin had been removed and his cheeks ached. 'Why does everything hurt so? My face?'

'The bacterium caused some necrosis.' Her saw the look in her eyes again: a nervousness. 'We've stopped it killing the tissue but there's been some scarring.'

'Where?'

'In different places.'

'On my face?'

'Yes, Thales,' she said huskily.

'It can be reconstructed though. Anything can.'

Bethany bit her lip, her eyes darting in an accusatory manner at her brother. 'The bacteria have damaged the cell structure. You'll need to have a prosthetic. Nanites won't be able to repair all of it.'

Thales let the information digest. In truth he felt so terrible it did not really mean anything.

'The more you sleep, the quicker you'll recover.'

He managed to move his head to nod. It was all he wanted to do anyway.

TEKTON

Edo entranced Tekton. Naturally he'd heard talk of the planet built solely of the larger cast-off items of billions of sentients but he had never expected for a moment that it might be beautiful. It was said the planet wasn't solid but merely an accretion of rubbish held in place by the gravitational pull of an old space station. Because of that the outer layers were less compacted and inclined to move position. A kaleidoscope of reflective surfaces.

Not only that, but he'd the good fortune to arrive on the final day of the month-long annual Trade Fest. Even *more* fortunate was the appalling physical deterioration of the young scholar Thales, which meant that Lasper Farr and his sister Bethany were immediately engaged in saving the young man's life, leaving Tekton time to explore.

One entire habitation chamber had been given over to the Fest. Tekton wandered amongst the stalls enjoying the sales talk and the inevitable boasting that went with displays of any kind. He also enjoyed the space and air in the chamber. Though *The Last Aesthetic* had been a most luxurious ship, space travel eventually became claustrophobic.

He admired the cleanliness of the entire station and stopped at an information booth to watch the advertising film. How surprising to find that rubbish could be so creatively and sanitarily recycled.

'Your first visit?' asked the Lamin behind the counter in a high, girlish voice.

Tekton gave a vague nod. He couldn't bear the creatures: vain and arrogant and fastidious. Not that Tekton didn't like things to be *just so*, but not in a Lamin armpit-picking, fingernail-clicking self-impressed way.

'Well, I suggest you hurry and take a good look. The Fest closes tonight and I can't say I won't be relieved. Two months on my feet in these heels . . . The best work is up on the dais, so they say. A couple of things causing a real stir up there: a living glass sculpture that's destined to shatter soon in a grand spectacular, and a fluid statue of a humanesque. I've heard it's made of quixite but I haven't been able to get away from here to have a look.' It sniffed.

Quixite! logic-mind and free-mind screeched at once.

Tekton scanned the chamber, locating the dais with its colossal giant glass protrusion. Without a word of acknowledgement or thanks to the talkative Lamin, Tekton made a beeline for it.

After a weapon search by a surly balol at the foot of the stairs, he was free to ascend and enjoy the sculptures.

The glass pillar inhabited by an organism was so truly spectacular that Tekton's free-mind overtook his logic-mind in a swell of creative satisfaction.

So twisted. So strained. Such glorious refraction. And the organism. *Tragic. Profound. Death in Freedom.*

It babbled for a while as Tekton drifted around the base of the column in a kind of meditative ecstasy.

Perhaps he would procure a ticket to the glass explosion. If it was timed, as the spruikers were insisting, to have twin suns shining on it, the experience would be unrepeatable.

And expensive, interjected logic-mind sternly, desperate for a way to be heard. *Without enough quixite from Araldis what will happen to our project? Without the project what will happen to our tyro placement on Belle-Monde? Without that – no fat stipend.*

Tekton jerked out of his trance and looked around. 'Where is the quixite statue?' he demanded of the closest spruiker.

'Roight behoind yuu moitey,' it carolled.

Tekton turned and pushed his way into the gathered crowd. The statue stood twice his height; a fine male figure, naked and unmistakably humanesque. The thing that so fascinated the audience though was the statue's genitals, which every few moments shifted in a carefully fluid but determined motion, from flaccid to erect.

Subtle changes then occurred in the erection, the swelling of the bulb and the enlarging of the testes.

Porn-art, concluded logic-mind.

Yes, agreed free-mind, *but the liquid play of the quixite makes it something far more intimate. A triumph of reality.*

Pah, said logic-mind. *But it does pose the question who the model was and how many times the artist needed to study his arousal.*

Who indeed? Tekton wondered. And that thought gave him quite a rush of akula. He would be eager to meet the man.

He glanced up at the face.

Upon recognition, his mouth dropped open in astonishment. *Good Sole! It's me!*

But Tekton wasn't the only one to recognise him. It began with three young female humanesques next to him who nudged and giggled and pointed; and spread through the crowd in a whisper, until more eyes were upon Tekton than the statue.

For the first time that he could ever recall, Tekton was the centre of attention that he had not specifically manufactured. And he could not even think of a way to turn it to his advantage.

He was, in fact, flabbergasted.

In an instant the spruikers roaming the dais picked up the situation and boomed it out to anyone who would listen. 'Fenr-oi-lia's model. Fenr-oi-lia's model. Come and soi-ee the man whose cock grows bigger than a soisage balloon.'

The ignominy of the situation threatened to totally shake Tekton's composure. Fenralia, the filthy little skieran, had used their acquaintance to sculpt this ridiculous likeness.

Or was it ridiculous?

A disturbingly exhibitionistic and egoistic streak ignited in Tekton. After all, his sexual prowess *was* formidable, even to the likes of the voracious Dicter Miranda Seeward. Legendary even. And perhaps there was potential for this to turn his way. He just had to figure out how best to use it.

He would, however, strangle Fenralia later. Preferably with its own rapacious and bizarrely elongated sexual organ.

But for now . . .

'Msr?'

Tekton suddenly found himself surrounded by balol soldiers wearing grey uniform. The one with the most stripes stood in front of him. 'Commander Farr requests the pleasure of your company in his lounge.'

Tekton nodded graciously and gave a little wave to his disappointed audience. 'Lead on,' he announced in a cavalier way.

The spectators began to whistle and stamp and then to Tekton's and the soldiers' astonishment, they followed them along the dais to a marquee decorated ingeniously with metal and aluminium scraps.

The soldier in charge ushered Tekton inside, then returned to keep the assembled mob in order. The crowd noise continued though, as they called for Tekton to return and deliver autographs.

'I see you're acquainted with the very talented Fenralia, Tekton of Lostol,' said a quiet voice.

Lasper 'Carnage' Farr was seated in a formal chair next to a comfortable but luxurious couch.

Tekton approached him and sat on the couch without invitation. He was quite disappointed.

He doesn't look at all terrifying, free-mind criticised. *He's so thin, and old-looking. Where are his battle scars?*

Fool, said logic-mind.

Tekton tended to side with free-mind on this. Of all the humanesques in Orion, Lasper Farr should be immense and impressive, not a lean, gaunt grey-eyed man who had clearly not taken the time to use regular rejuvenation cosmetics.

'A chance encounter of mine with the artist seems to have whetted its creative muse. I had no knowledge of the sculpture until just a few minutes ago,' said Tekton blithely.

'And yet you have already incited a near-riot.'

Tekton waved his hand. 'Amusing indeed.'

'Indeed,' agreed Farr, without the hint of a smile. 'I believe that you bought my sister passage from Rho Junction. I will arrange for your reimbursement.'

'Most appreciated, Commander Farr. And how fares the young scholar? Both he and your sister were adamant that you could best treat his condition here, even though we had access to medical help aboard *The Last Aesthetic*.'

'It is a rare bacterium, Tekton, and I have a superior laboratory. Some would say the best there is. May I offer you some champagne?'

'Delighted,' replied Tekton. Farr might not be impressive but he was refined and mannered enough for a martial type.

They sat in silence while Tekton waited for the glass to be produced and poured and brought to him by a uniformed aide.

'The young man will recover,' said Farr as an after-thought. 'He says that your appearance in the clinic on Rho Junction was providence – some might say a Godsend – if of course you are of a mind to believe in deities, which I am not.'

'An interesting conversation point, Commander, seeing as I am currently a tyro to one perceived as such.'

He's a heathen, free-mind sniffed.

He's playing you, logic-mind warned.

This time Tekton gave logic-mind free rein to

give advice. With each quiet word Lasper Farr spoke, Tekton felt less steady. The man's eyes were as cold and pitiless as Lostol's ice caps.

'In my opinion,' said Lasper, 'studium academics do not always care about their research topics. The intellectual exercise is enough for them. It also gives them a platform for dissembling and self-aggrandisement.'

'I won't take offence, Commander, but I would suggest that it is foolish to tar all academics with one brush. We might surprise you.'

Farr leaned back in his chair and folded his arms. 'Surprise me then, Tekton of Lostol.'

Truth, urged logic-mind. *Now*.

Obediently, Tekton cut to the chase. 'I know the creator of the DNA that you sent young Berniere to retrieve. Quite well, as luck would have it. I am seeking information, and so are you. A perfect set-up for . . . a negotiation.'

Farr sucked in his cheeks for a moment before he spoke, lending his face a skeletal appearance. Then suddenly he smiled. 'Or I could just torture you to find out what I want.'

The unsteadiness Tekton had been feeling began to border on dizziness, but a surge of anger came to his rescue. He would *not* be bullied as if he were some ordinary 'esque. 'What? Risk an incident that would have ramifications across Orion? And' – he waved his hands towards the entrance of the marquee – 'your own world.'

Farr gave a short laugh. 'You mean your eager audience out there? You have a high opinion of yourself.'

'I know my worth. There is an immense difference, Commander.'

'And I know what I am capable of doing, without consequence.'

Tekton's heart fluttered. He had never been overtly threatened by anyone significant before – at least, not physically – and it spawned a curious mixture of excitement and dread within him. He felt his akula swell and himself stiffen.

He longed for the Hunter device he'd been forced to relinquish before boarding *The Last Aesthetic*. Yet killing Lasper Farr outright would achieve nothing except problems. He needed, instead, to use him. 'Such aggression on your part must surely mean I offer threat, and I have little desire to do that. My request is simply a fair trade.'

'What do you want?'

'In exchange for everything I know about the creator of the virus, I wish you to undertake to support the reclaiming of the mining world Araldis.'

'Ah, Araldis. Again. Again.'

'In my conversations with the young scholar and your sibling, they informed me that you had an agreement with the unfortunate Baronessa Fedor to restore the world to its legal ownership.'

'You know the Baronessa?' asked Farr.

'I did not have the pleasure of her acquaintance, and now I believe she is in the company of the Extropists.'

Farr's expression became tense and wary. 'Not company she chose, but even so, it does call into question my agreement with her.'

'Well,' said Tekton sanguinely, 'our choices often define the choices we are left with – if you understand me.'

'Like you and I, here today.'

'Exactly.'

'So tell me why your information is worth me embarking on such an expensive and risky venture.'

'You said yourself that your laboratory is the best in Orion. Which, I would surmise, means you control most of the bio-trade. A new player of this credibility on the scene might upset things for you. You also have a personal investment on Araldis worth protecting. A niece, I believe. I would also surmise that you have some interest in why Araldis has been so aggressively overrun, and by whom. If you don't already know, that is?'

The tension left Farr's face, and a small smile played at his lips. 'You are clever enough, Tekton. I would expect nothing less of a tyro from Belle-Monde. But can you play well to the end?'

'That sounds like a challenge, Commander.'

'I'm a competitive man. It would be wise not to forget it. I'll consider your offer and we shall speak again soon. Enjoy the remainder of the Fest and your new-found fame.'

Without any obvious instruction from Lasper Farr, a soldier presented himself at Tekton's side and escorted him from the tent.

As the soldier drew back the flap, a sprinkle of spontaneous applause broke out and voices called again for autographs.

Tekton stepped graciously into their midst and gave a little bow.

The applause grew louder, as did the ribald comments.

The attention went a long way to salving the irritation and upset that Commander Farr had caused him.

MIRA

Since their conversation, Wanton-poda's behaviour had become erratic. At first Mira put it down to her ignorance of its nature, but each day she noticed a slight deterioration in its colour and physical integrity. The translucent skin had developed darker patches and its normally ever-moving fringe seemed sluggish and stiff.

The Siphonophores returned regularly, often when Mira was asleep. She knew because Wanton-poda's pitiful high-pitched wails woke her in time to see it descend into its recovery tank, away from whatever torture had been inflicted on it.

Mira waited. The next time it happened, she climbed from her bed and beat her fists against the translucent barrier. 'Stop it!' she cried. 'Leave it alone!'

The Siphonophores left without even appearing to have noticed her.

She stayed awake, leaning against the wall, thinking of *Insignia*. *Please find me. Please.*

She felt the faintest tug in response to her plea. So faint that it could have been imagined. And yet she hoped, *believed*, it was *Insignia*. What else was there for her to keep faith in? Rast Randall? Josef Rasterovich? A selfish mercenary and a vagrant wanderer; neither of them would care about her abduction.

And Thales Berniere? Would the young scholar miss her?

Now, finally, that most things had been laid bare in her life, she could admit to herself that Thales's affection for Bethany Ionil had wounded her. Was she so unappealing that he would find an older woman more attractive than her?

She sighed and returned to her bed, rolling to her side to ease the baby's weight on her backbone. How could she expect any regard from such a gracious young gentleman when she was but a pregnant refugee? Thales Berniere would be shocked if he knew what had happened to her, and repulsed.

'Mira-fedor should ingest some food.'

'Wanton-poda?' Mira's eyes flew upward.

The little cephalopod hovered above her bed looking grey and lethargic.

'It is not right that they treat you like this. I am eating and have put on weight.' She caressed the small mound of her belly. 'You told me the baby is thriving again. There is no need for them to be hurting you.'

'My circumstances are not your concern, Mira-fedor.' Then it added, 'But it is kindly of you to care for poda.'

'Is there somewhere you and I could both go?' she whispered. 'Could we leave here together? Go to a place where you won't be hurt and I will be able to have my baby without interference?'

'Mira-fedor shall not speak of these things.'

'Look at you,' declared Mira passionately. 'You are sick. I don't know much about your physiology but it appears to me that your host – poda – may die. But then I suppose you don't care much for your host.'

'Your statement lacks veracity, Mira-fedor. Poda is dear to Wanton.'

'Then save poda before it is too late.'

The creature began to spin in its thinking rhythm.

'You must know somewhere you can go, away from these . . . bullies.' Mira slid her feet to the floor, and stood so that Wanton-poda's ear flaps were at her eye level. 'I know oppression, Wanton-poda. That's where I came from. That is why I am carrying the child of a man I loathe. Oppression is wrong, whether it be amongst humanesques, aliens or Post-Species. You have a right not to be afraid.' The words tumbled so fluently from her mouth it was as if she had stored and practised them, and now was the most important time for their delivery. *Oppression had killed Faja and Estelle.* 'I have a right not to be afraid.'

Its spinning slowed down, and it moved closer so that it almost settled on Mira's shoulder. Instinctively, she reached up and brushed her fingers along its fluted edge.

It uttered a peculiar noise. 'Poda finds that soothing,' it said.

'I don't understand why they are so cruel to you.'

'Wanton-poda has had many important tasks. Before the task of Mira-fedor, Wanton-poda was charged with adapting a water species to land. Most rewarding. However, Highness Most Capable: Evolution is not satisfied.'

Something stirred in Mira's consciousness. She thought carefully about how she would elicit her next response, lapsing back into more indirect speech so as to learn what she sought. 'That must have been a complex task. I can't fathom why anyone would go to that trouble.'

'Adaptation of species receives priority amongst Host scientists. Although I do not know the specific use of this adaptation, Wanton-poda was told it would carry much prestige.'

'Not enough to stop you being hurt by the Siphonophore hosts.'

'Wanton-poda's title of Highness Most Capable of Cultivation is not as influential as some despite its expertise in genetic procedure.'

'What you describe is not unlike humanesque communities. Talent and hard work are often not rewarded. In fact, quite the opposite.'

The creature made a sound that could have been a sigh. 'Mira-fedor speaks with veracity. It is difficult to recognise the superior evolution of Post-Species some-times. Wanton-poda finds this depressing.'

The thought of a parasitical Post-Species sentient being depressed fascinated Mira. Post-Species – well, at least the Host variety – clearly retained the ghosts of emotional variations. Mira chose not to take offence that Wanton-poda considered itself a more advanced sentient than her. For the most part it was true.

'Progression is not always linear,' she proffered.

The creature lifted off her shoulder and floated in the direction of its tank. 'Wanton-poda would have had pleasure knowing how its water species has fared.'

Mira felt the stirring again. Stronger, this time, like a memory bobbing its way to the surface of her mind. 'Is it possible . . . that Wanton-poda's adaption . . . was tardigrades?'

Wanton-poda halted its forward motion and reversed, its ear flaps coming erect. 'Mira-fedor is very astute. Wanton-poda is surprised.'

Mira swallowed to ease her suddenly dry mouth. Her heart beat painfully in her chest. 'Mira-fedor has a story Wanton-poda should hear.'

The cephalopod swayed gently before her while she told it of the Saqr and their invasion of Araldis. It didn't interrupt or alter its listening pattern until she finished the telling and asked for some water.

Then it floated to its mobile canteen and returned with a fresh water tube. 'Wanton-poda has some thinking to do.' It left her and returned to its tank.

Mira drank and ate and went through the simple routine of calisthenics she'd adopted to combat the inactivity caused by her confinement. After that, she attempted the meditation exercise Thales Berniere had explained to her. At first her mind wandered, but she persisted until she gained some respite from the turmoil of questions and worries that plagued her waking moments.

Afterwards she ate again and slept, to be woken by another visit from the Siphonophores. This time they congregated around her bed, saying nothing, doing nothing that she could perceive.

Then as quickly as they appeared, they left.

Wanton-poda floated down from a high corner of her cell, descending until its fringe brushed her chest. It had never been this close to her face before.

She sensed its distress. 'What is it?'

'Mira-fedor's baby is to be removed. Wanton-poda has been directed to do it.'

Mira sat up so quickly that Wanton-poda was forced to slide down onto her lap. 'Why would they order that?'

'There is evidence that this is the optimum time to study the development of the Innate gene; optimum time to modify it.'

'Of course,' said Mira hollowly. 'Of course that's what they want.' She felt a deep welling of bitterness. 'It's what everyone wants.' She stared down at the cephalopod. 'Why are you telling me?'

'Wanton-poda suggests Mira-fedor accompany it to a safer place.'

Mira's eyes widened. 'You're saying we should escape?'

'Mira-fedor should eat and drink in readiness for a journey. Timing is crucial.'

Hope glimmered alive inside her. *Insignia*.

Her thought was rewarded with the faintest of tugs, yet something more palpable than before. She sprang from her bed and ate food cubes from the tray.

Wanton-poda hovered around her, waiting. 'In a moment, when Wanton-poda disintegrates the containment wall you must not speak again, even if directly addressed. You may not say a word until Wanton-poda uses the words "Mira-fedor, you are safe."'

Mira nodded. 'Is there anything else I should know? How should I behave?'

'It will be assumed you are a Host body that has not yet fully integrated with its Post-Species and cannot talk.'

Mira stared at Wanton-poda in shock. 'You mean hosts are sometimes humanesques?'

'Accurate,' said Wanton-poda. It spun away from her, passing through the transparent field a number of times in quick succession until the field flickered and disappeared, and she was trapped in silence, unable to get more information about the terrifying thing she had just learned.

Extropists with humanesque bodies. She had no idea. And neither, she was sure, did the rest of the Orion.

Wanton-poda had settled into a hovering position an arm's length in front of her and at shoulder height. 'Follow behind,' it said.

They left the laboratory through a spongy door similar to the walls of her confinement cell, and stepped directly out into brilliant sunshine and a warm, light breeze.

Mira took a deep, deep breath and blinked repeatedly. All her senses told her that she was standing on the shore of a small island gazing at a string of tiny atolls in a sunrise-dappled ocean. She glanced behind. There was no evidence of the door they had come through.

Turning back, she surveyed the vista again: sun, water and a myriad of islands so like the Tourmalines. But unlike the scantly inhabited waters of her home, this sea brimmed with creatures, floating around her, and across the waves, and in the waves, all moving at abnormal speeds. Hundreds of different varieties of water species.

Something scratched at her toes. She looked down as a starfish-shaped creature with twenty or more tentacles lifted its body up and crawled across her bare foot. Splashing water dragged her attention back to the ocean. A crab emerged from the waves, taller than her and with a black shiny carapace, dragging one huge heavy pincer.

A tumble of questions threatened to escape her lips so she kept them firmly closed, bottling her curiosity.

Wanton-poda moved directly forward and she followed it down the sand to the water's edge, revelling in the feel of the warm sand under her feet. But when the cephalopod floated out over the water, she baulked.

It returned and circled her several times before proceeding back out over the water.

She shook her head. Had the creature forgotten she couldn't float?

It returned again. This time it positioned itself behind her. Without warning it brushed its fringe against her neck. The sting caused her to jump forward away from it.

It stung her again.

She jumped away from it again, biting her lip to keep from exclaiming aloud. This time though, the water lapped around her feet.

Or not quite.

Tentatively she took another step.

Instead of walking from the sand and into the water, she found she was a tiny distance above it. On a cushion of air? Or perhaps the water wasn't real?

She stopped and knelt down and dipped her fingers into the rolling waves. They felt real – wet and tingling, and the scent of salt and the moisture on her skin. It had to be real.

Wanton-poda returned to her and made an irritated sound.

A large fish lifted its head from the water and turned a large silver eye on them.

Mira felt a disturbance of the air around her, as if it were vibrating.

Wanton-poda began to bob.

'Is there a problem with this Host?' the fish asked.

'Highness Most Capable of Cultivation is escorting the humanesque shell to Symbiosis Revival. There are some anomalies. It has no speech,' said Wanton-poda more calmly than she expected.

'The Host shell may need to be destroyed. Some don't revive. My own has been replaced several times in this form. But I chose carefully this time.'

Destroy the Host shell. Mira tried not to look disturbed. If she appeared too aberrant she would attract more attention.

'Most Excellent Host,' said Wanton-poda as a kind of farewell salutation.

'Most Excellent Host to you as well, cephalopod,' replied the fish.

Wanton-poda circled behind Mira and stung her until she stood and continued on.

She kept her eyes downcast after that. The fish had sounded mocking, condescending even, but she knew it could be dangerous to judge Post-Species by her own humanesque values.

They continued their walk across the water for some time – much further than she should have been able to go without tiring. She assumed this was because of the lack of friction and a sense of lighter gravity.

They traversed one large, flat island that appeared bare of vegetation, its only discerning characteristic round indentations spaced at regular intervals, in lines, in the sand.

Instinctively she avoided stepping near them, and something deep-seated urged her to move on quickly, away from them. But Wanton-poda seemed distracted by the sight of them. It fluttered down from time to time for closer observation.

As they crossed the island and passed down towards the sea again, it floated lower to observe the last line of depressions. The sand in one of the indentations began to shift and the Extro wafted back out of the way. A pearly-coloured orb the size of a humanesque's head erupted from the shallow hole. The skin of the orb bubbled and contorted for a few moments until it tore open. Thin feelers poked through, followed by larger, thicker ones with bulbous ends.

Mira's heart gave a terrified leap as one of the bulbs peeled back to reveal a moist maw.

Saqr. Smaller than the ones on Araldis but unmistakable.

She trapped the scream in her throat and ran out onto the water. Wanton-poda accelerated to put itself in front of her and they travelled for a while at a higher speed as if it comprehended her need to get away.

After they'd passed several more islands that showed no sign of the Saqr, her fear began to subside and was replaced by aching in her feet and knees. Her dry mouth told her she needed fluids.

She coughed to attract Wanton-poda's attention.

It swirled and spun a full circle around her, coming to hover in front of her face.

She swallowed and licked her lips, signalling her thirst.

Its ear flaps shot up in a way that she was coming to recognise as alertness. Though they stood on the water between islands, it changed direction heading for the closest one. When they reached it, Wanton-poda floated straight up the beach and disappeared into a thick grove of palm trees.

Mira baulked before the trees, sending a cluster of small red crabs scuttling away from her around her shuffling feet. Spines, almost as long as Mira herself, protruded from the palms' stems.

She could not see a way past them.

Wanton-poda reappeared after a time. 'We will return to functional space for refreshments,' it said in a neutral tone.

It re-entered the tree line, passing straight through the criss-cross of spines.

Mira took a deep, shaky breath. Despite the fact that she had just walked across water, her mind would not be convinced that the spines in front of her were anything other than totally real. Even in her interface with *Insignia*, she had never felt so at odds with her perception.

She took a step closer, positioning herself in the exact spot that Wanton-poda had entered. The red crabs reassembled and began crawling over her feet to enter the same space at sand level. One by one they disappeared from her view like ants vanishing inside their nest. Tentatively she reached out her hand and encountered the sharp prick of the spine.

She recoiled and sucked her finger. Perhaps the exit

to the functional space that Wanton-poda referred to was narrow or oddly shaped. She knelt down and then lay on her belly. With small, careful movements she began to crawl in under the line of the bottom spine.

'How rude!' protested a voice near her ear.

She turned her head sideways to locate it and a crab claw slapped her across the bridge of her nose.

'Wait your turn,' said the crab.

It climbed over her head, and by the time she dared to look up it had gone.

Avoiding contact with the small creatures congregating around and behind her, she crawled slowly after the crab and found herself suddenly in a tissue-walled room similar to her confinement cell, only this one appeared open-ended, leading into further cells.

Not really cells, she thought, as she dusted sand from her clothes and stood up. *More like fleshy caves. An endless, almost featureless cave system.*

She looked down expecting to see the sand she had brushed off, fallen to the floor. But it simply no longer existed.

'Mira-fedor will take refreshments now.' Wanton-poda hovered off to her right near one of the pearly walls.

Mira nodded and moved cautiously closer, the way she had approached the spine-laden palm. Wanton-poda propelled itself directly into the wall but did not bounce off as Mira had when trying to break out of her confinement. Intead, the wall enveloped the Extro, leaving only a small opaque mass where it had entered.

Mira heard a soft pop. An arm's length from the

Wanton-poda mass, the tissue wall rippled and a crab popped out onto the floor.

It raised its claw. 'You again,' it muttered in a less than impressed tone. It scuttled wide of her and off deeper into the caves.

Something bumped into her back. 'Hurry up! You're slowing everything down.'

She half-turned, and encountered the oddest-looking creature. It had the head, wet eyes and whiskers of a sea mammal but its torso tapered into humanesque-shaped legs with webbed feet.

Biting her lip, she faced the wall and stepped into it. There was no resistance this time, in fact, quite the opposite. It seemed to suck her forward.

She automatically closed her eyes and held her breath until she could no longer. Then she let it go and gulped. To her surprise, she was able to breathe normally. She felt like she was lying on a cushion of air – no sense of pressure or verticality. Only a mild, cool sensation as if someone was wiping her skin with a damp cloth.

With each wipe her aches and fatigue lessened. Even her thirst vanished. Energy filled her body as it had not done since before the invasion on Araldis.

And then . . . she was pushed back out into the cave, stumbling to catch her balance.

Wanton-poda spun agitatedly nearby, waiting.

She opened her mouth to tell the Extro how wonderful she felt and to ask what exactly had happened, but then noticed a group of Siphonophores floating near the far wall. They propelled themselves across the cave on their undulating, suckered feet until they surrounded Wanton-poda.

Mira's heart contracted in fear as they began to bully the little cephalopod as they had in the lab, converging on it with their stingers.

Wanton-poda squealed in pain.

An ungovernable rage rose in Mira, as it had before. She threw herself among them, raking at their jellylike skins with her fingernails; then slapping and punching at their swaying jelly bodies.

They returned her attack by curling their stinging tentacles around her arms.

But her anger had found a release that seemed to nullify the fear – or distance it at least.

Or was it something else that lent her strength and fury? Deep within her she felt a cold rush of adrenalin, and then a small but distinctive movement in her belly.

Child?

She grabbed some of a Siphonophore's tentacles and rent them apart. They tore easily, like worn cloth, and the creature pulsed black ink from its sac in a wide arc.

The squealing intensified: not all Wanton-poda's any more. And not just sounds of pain. Voices joined in; a cacophony of them, calling for her to be stopped.

The rest of the Siphonophores retreated, leaving her with the cephalopod and the remains of the torn Extro in her hands. Her hands and shift were stained with ink.

Other small creatures gathered around them, popping out of the walls or entering from other places, curious and shocked.

'Mira-fedor.' Wanton-poda's voice projection was barely a whisper. 'What have you done?'

'They were hurting you,' Mira said hoarsely. 'And

I . . . I . . .' She couldn't finish because she didn't know what she'd done. 'Th-the child moved.' She cupped her belly. 'And . . .'

'Mira-fedor must leave quickly,' said Wanton-poda, 'or she will be punished.' It hovered low near her shoulder. 'Mira-fedor and Wanton-poda must go into the Bare World.'

Jo-Jo Rasterovich

Jo-Jo woke flailing and shouting from the worst of over-heated, dehydrated alcohol dreams. He'd been in the mud crawling along between Rast Randall and her Capo and ahead of the balol Ilke. Rast silently signalled an enemy sighting and rolled sideways under some thick reed. Jo-Jo threw himself in the other direction, colliding with the Capo. The pair grappled with each other to be the first to reach the cover of a fallen tree.

'Get yer own,' whispered the Capo.

Jo-Jo was so close to the man that his spit made him blink. So close that he could see every minute detail of the Capo's face beneath the layer of grime. So close . . .

'Wait!' Jo-Jo sat upright. 'I know who you . . .'

'Shut the fuck up or they'll hear you,' the Capo hissed. He raised his fist to club Jo-Jo but Jo-Jo warded him off with his forearm.

'I KNOW WHO YOU ARE!' he shouted. 'I KNOW WHO YOU ARE!'

And he did.

And then the sleep dropped away and he found himself sitting upright in bed, shaking and still shouting the words.

He dragged himself straight into the wash cubicle and sat there until the tremors subsided.

It gave him time to sort his brain out – think over things.

He was on a half-crazy, pining 'zoon travelling though Extro space with a bunch of self-serving, edgy mercs.

Something new. Think harder.

Rast Randall had strong feelings for Mira Fedor. Maybe as strong as his. That meant she must be feeling guilty as hell about losing Fedor. And worried. Jo-Jo could use that, and to a degree, he could trust it.

Slightly cheered, he went to the medi-lab and connected himself up to an IV of electrolytes. When the drip ran out he moved on to the cucina and forced himself to eat some bread and dried meat.

Better.

But the effort of the walk he then took up to the buccal almost had him vomiting up the food. And the shaking was back – though not as bad.

This time when he sank his fist into the pucker it opened.

Rast was reclining in the sink they called Secondo. She didn't appear surprised to see him but her hand drifted to the weapon on her lap.

'Let's talk,' said Jo-Jo.

She sat more upright at that, eyes narrow and suspicious. 'Shoot.'

'Tell me the situation out there.' He lifted his head to indicate outside.

Rast chewed her lip before replying. 'From what I can tell we're heading to the outer reaches of Saiph. 'Zoon's sticking close to a bunch of freighters. Think it's trying to muddy up its signatures.'

'Makes sense.'

'Lots of activity around the system, especially back near Rho Junction. My Extro space nav isn't exactly sharp though.'

''Zoon's got a connection with the Baronessa – maybe it knows where she is,' said Jo-Jo.

'I'm banking on it. And on the fact that it'll let us do our thing when the time comes.'

What's your thing? Jo-Jo wanted to shout at the merc. *Desert two vulnerable women?* But he bit the words back. He needed information and commitment. He wouldn't get that from the likes of Rast Randall by being antagonistic.

His legs began to tremble, forcing him to sit down on the edge of the Autonomy nub.

'Looks like you've just trashed a kidney *and* a liver,' observed Rast.

'Gotta get my HealthWatch upgraded. Forgotten what a real hangover was like.' That was true. Jo-Jo had never felt this bad from drink before.

'Yeah. Never know what you might pick up – the places *you* frequent.'

Jo-Jo hunched, not seeing the lighter side. 'I've been thinking over some stuff. Strikes me there's a lot of things that seem connected that shouldn't be and I'm wondering why.'

Rast cocked an eyebrow and waited.

'The Lostol getting on that ship with Berniere and Bethany on Rho Junction – I know him. His name's Tekton. He's a tyro to the Entity on Belle-Monde.'

Rast's mouth fell open. '*That* was Tekton?'

'You heard of him?'

'Fedor says he's the one who's been buying up the quixite on Araldis. Carnage mentioned him too. You had some shit go down with him . . . something about a Hera contract.'

'Shit's the word for it,' said Jo-Jo grimly.

'So what's he doin' with Beth and the idiot scholar?'

'Heading back to Akouedo, I'm guessing. That can't mean anything good. Carnage and Tekton . . .' Jo-Jo shook his head, imagining the consequences of a partnership between the Commander and the tyro. He regathered himself. 'You told me before that your allegiances are your own. You stand by that?'

Rast nodded and gave him a keen look. 'Spit it out.'

'Stuff is happening . . . I keep thinking that I'm understanding it, and then something else happens.'

'Yer not making much sense, man.'

'You heard of a Dynamic System Device?'

Rast returned to chewing on her lip, taking her time to answer. 'Maybe. Thought that stuff was mostly made-up . . . DSD – wasn't that someone's idea of predicting patterns?'

Jo-Jo tapped his head. 'You've supped a bit then.'

Rast folded her arms. 'As you do . . . when you get an education,' she finished sarcastically.

'No offence,' said Jo-Jo, relieved he didn't have to explain from scratch. 'Most mercs—'

'Yeah, yeah, so what about it?'

'Carnage Farr's got one. A DSD. Saw it in virtual. He proved it by showing me some things. One of them was you wallowing in mud on some craphole during the war—'

'Longthrow?'

'Dunno – probably. You were with your Capo and a balol.'

Rast's eyes widened. 'Jancz and Ilke.'

Jancz. So that was his real name. Not Jed. 'You tripped a land mine.'

'How did you know that?'

'Saw it. Farr buys information to fuel his DSD. Combat records. Everything. And he's got eges everywhere, recording.' Jo-Jo glanced around the buccal. 'He's probably got them in here.'

'OK. So what's your point?'

'I was drinking in a bar on Dowl – followed Tekton there. Got talking to a female balol. Kinda thought I might enjoy some rough trade for a change.'

Rast sniggered. 'Ilke?'

'Yeah. She did her thing, while her friend – Jed he called himself – did his. He framed me up for importing an illegal uuli species. Problem was the judge had a grudge against me already. Anyway . . . to cut it short . . . Tekton's down there buying up quixite to help his cause on Belle-Monde. Meanwhile your Capo – Jed or Jancz or whatever he calls himself – steals my ship.'

'When was that?'

Jo-Jo gave her approximates.

Rast thought for a few moments. 'Jancz and Ilke were down on Araldis a while after that. I saw them when we were trapped in Ipo. Maybe they used your hybrid 'zoon to bring in the Saqr. They were running the show down there – no doubt about that.'

'Why didn't you let him know you were there? Sounds like he coulda got you out of that tight spot.'

Rast – almost imperceptibly – raised an eyebrow. 'You don't know mercs, do you, Rasterovich?'

'Meaning?'

'Meaning you get hired by someone then all bets are off. You might have worked with a guy on a previous job – turns out he's your enemy the next time round.'

'Yeah, yeah, Randall – I know the patter. But what's it really like? You telling me you'd kill someone who'd been your Capo?'

Randall gave him a level stare. 'In a breath. A real short one.'

A moment passed between them as the mercenary let Jo-Jo glimpse past the bravado and the jokes. He didn't like what he saw.

'So who was your *ex*-Capo hired by to bring the Saqr to Araldis?'

'Dunno,' said Rast. 'Been working my grey matter overtime on that one since I first saw them. Could be anyone . . . but . . . I'm leaning a couple of directions.'

'Tekton?'

'No. The timing's wrong. And according to Fedor, Tekton's deal had been done. He'd already paid for the mineral.'

'Who'd want large amounts of quixite bad enough to torch a planet?' asked Jo-Jo.

But before Rast could volunteer an answer, the 'zoon emitted an unnerving howl as if a ferocious wind blew along its strata.

'What the—'

An image flickered into existence above the Primo vein – a corduroy-filtered representation of the space around the 'zoon showing a cluster of ships closing on a small pulsing sphere of lights.

'Thought so,' said Rast. 'It's another shift point.' She lunged over to the Autonomy nub, elbowing Jo-Jo aside to reach the intercom. 'Lat, Catchut. Find a tubercle. We're shifting again,' she bellowed.

Then she threw herself back into her sink. 'Buckle up, we're going in rough.'

Jo-Jo saw what she meant, the 'zoon's iconic representation of space showed its trajectory towards the edge of the sphere. Imperfect Shift again. He'd done IS a few times – last time was getting out of Dowl. It was like being squeezed through a fine-meshed sieve.

Where was a bottle of Oort whisky when you needed it?

Jo-Jo slid back into the Autonomy seat and the restraints and the vibration smothers activated. This one was gonna be a total bitch.

He gave one last look at the centre of shift-space. So many ships trying to enter and exit through one point. Maybe it was as well they weren't going through Proper Shift. But why so many? Why now?

Randall grunted from Secondo. 'Funny sort of config around the shift point. Looks to me like we're in for some . . .'

Jo-Jo flicked his eyes to Rast Randall. She was hunkered down in her vein, almost indistinguishable from the sink tissue that had slithered over her, other than the outline of her boots and the mound of her breasts.

'What?' Jo-Jo rasped.

'Strife.'

The word planted itself in Jo-Jo's mind as the 'zoon went into Imperfect Shift.

Strife. Strife. Striiiffe.

It sounded over and over and over; in every possible intonation, volume, and in ways that turned it into something much more than a word.

It hammered at his temples, drilled through his ears, cascaded and crashed upon and crushed his chest, ripped strips from his skin. He cried like a baby trying to block out the sound and the sensation with his own noise but it clung to him, sticky and cutting and deeply . . .

'Rasterovich!' Rough hands shook him. 'Quit howling.'

A whiff of something strong and a stinging slap to his . . . face. *Yes.* He knew that much. Someone had hit him.

'Lemme piss on him,' offered someone else.

Jo-Jo's eyes fluttered open and his hand rose automatically to protect his face. 'Piss on me and I'll k—'

Laughter cut him off. Randall and Catchut. Clutching their sides.

'Always works, Capo.' Catchut guffawed again. Tubercle slime had stained his face an unhealthy colour. He was bent over as though there was pain beneath the laughter. Rast looked much the same, vein goo flaking off her skin.

Jo-Jo blinked a few times until the blur retreated a bit. His head was fugged and buzzing at the same time.

'You got shift hysteria,' said Randall.

Jo-Jo swallowed to see if everything was working. 'Don't handle that kinda shift well when I'm sober.'

'Yeah – or maybe it's yer bingeing that messed with you.'

Jo-Jo scowled. He wasn't interested in a lecture on sobriety from a merc. 'So where the fuck are we?'

She pointed to the space above the Primo vein where a brand new set of images floated.

'Extro space,' said Rast. 'For real this time.'

THALES

Thales stared at his reflection. The necrosis had eaten the tip of one earlobe and spread down his cheek to one side of his chin, leaving an ugly decay like slick, dark algae on a wet rock.

Bethany assured him it would dry soon but that didn't curb his despair.

'I am diseased,' he whispered. 'Abhorrent.'

But Bethany refused to let him indulge in self-pity.

'You're alive, Thales – for Cruxsakes, get over it! And what's more you're free to do what you please. We can cover the scar as soon as it dries. Now focus on the important things!'

He turned from the mirror to look at her. Farr had given them a simple but comfortable apartment to stay in: a separate bedroom from the living room and bathroom. Between them they only had some worn clothes and a handful of personal items to fill it.

Bethany sat on the couch, hugging her knees against her chest. Under the stark white Edo lighting she looked much older than she had aboard the biozoon or the cruise ship. And right now there was none of the sympathy in her voice that he sought – but neither, at least, was there the pity or disgust he felt for himself.

'You don't understand my *ahisma*. I have sworn never

to harm another sentient, but this . . . hideous . . . thing . . . I would *kill* your brother if I could for doing this to me. And for making me realise how much conviction I lack in my own belief.'

Her stern expression didn't change. 'Do you think you're the first person to change their mind? Or reassess their ethics? Thales . . .' She made an exasperated noise and held out her hands in a pleading manner. 'I am sorry for your lost ideals but life tests everything you believe. I would kill Lasper and he's my brother . . . do you understand how that makes *me* feel?'

Bethany's pragmatism foundered him. Rene would have been horrified and distraught and empathetic. But then Rene had been sheltered from most everything.

'Are you telling me that you do not mind my appearance?' he asked lamely.

A smile lit her face and lent it some youth again. 'Actually, I prefer it. You were much too pretty before.'

He stared at her, letting his thoughts and emotions well and subside within him. Beth was right. He was free now. No Gutnee Paraburd or Lasper Farr or Sophos Mianos. He could change. And the change could begin right now.

But to what?

'Where is Godhead Tekton?'

'Here still. Lasper and he are meeting.'

'What do they plan, do you think?'

She shrugged. 'Lasper will tell me when he is ready.'

'When *he* is ready, Beth? What about you?'

'I have to find Djes and I have no bargaining position.'

Thales touched his fingers to his damaged chin.

It was wet with spittle. Though the muscle weakness had gone from his body, the necrosis had left his face numb in parts. He could not feel one corner of his mouth.

Beth reached to the small side table and picked up an absorbent cloth. She offered it to him.

He pressed it to his mouth. 'And how long before I stop drooling like an animal?'

'I don't know, but it's temporary, I'm sure.' She gave him a steady look that urged him to stay buoyant.

He took a deep, calming breath. 'Have you spoken with your brother? How does he plan to send help to the planet?'

'He has not said.'

Thales held out his hand to her. He was grateful to her in so many ways. 'Then I should help convince him to do so.'

'Thales?'

Thales got to his feet. The change he so desperately wanted *would* begin now.

Tekton's apartment was close to theirs but appeared to be more lavish, with its carved wood entrance and door mould that informed him Tekton was not available. As Thales waited for Tekton to return, he sat on the cato-plasma bench outside the door and used the time to prepare himself.

Bethany had warned him not to be beguiled by the Godhead's manner and refined ways. She believed that Tekton was as calculating as Lasper beneath his civilised exterior. Though Thales thought Bethany to be some-what dramatic in her assessment, he was desperate to leave naivety behind, and therefore adopted suspicion as his keeper.

Tekton returned soon after. He did not seem surprised to see Thales and welcomed him inside like an old friend, without apparent interest in the bandage across Thales's cheek.

The Godhead's apartment was indeed more spacious and opulent than theirs, plastered white and decorated with unusual artefacts, including a large and remarkable fluid sculpture of a naked male in a state of arousal.

Thales recognised it from the display at the Trade Fest and remembered how Mira Fedor had been so discomfited by it.

Tekton stood, arms folded, as if waiting for his reaction.

Thales settled for a neutral comment. 'What manner of material is used in this sculpture?' he enquired.

'It is called quixite. Rare and beautiful. And a tolerable likeness, don't you think?'

Thales dragged his gaze from the ever-changing state of the statue's arousal, up to its face. 'Crux, Godhead. It is you!'

'Indeed.' Tekton lifted his chin and tilted his head. Clearly he was gratified. 'Fenralia, the sculptor, and I had a brief acquaintance.'

'How . . .' – Thales struggled for a word – 'flattering.'

Tekton sank gracefully into an armchair and crossed his legs. Lostolians weren't the most attractive of humanesques, with their tight, colourless skin, but Tekton managed to convey confidence and elegance despite that. His soft pastel robe seemed to ripple around his body in the same way the quixite sculpture rippled through its crude body functions.

Bethany's warning resurged in Thales's mind. *Don't be fooled by his glamour.*

'I was hoping you would be disposed to have a discussion with me.'

Tekton's eyes narrowed a fraction, though his expression remained pleasant. 'We've been through much in our short acquaintance, young Thales. I would be happy to learn more about you. Please sit.'

'And I about you, sir.'

'I shall order some wine and some food and then we shall begin.'

Thales! It was as if Bethany was next to him. 'No wine, thank you, Godhead, and I have recently eaten.'

Tekton was quiet for a moment while he accessed his moud. When he finished, he slapped his thighs. 'Now, share your concerns with me.'

'I would ask you to tell me about the substance I brought back from Rho Junction in the canister. In the laboratory, the creature spoke of it as an orbitofrontal cortex modifier. I am learned, as you know, Godhead, but not truly informed on the sciences.'

'You're best served to ask Commander Farr, young man. His laboratory has been conducting the analysis.'

'You indicated that you knew the creator of it.'

'Delicate information, Thales. Especially without knowing the intent with which it was designed.' Tekton was mild but definite.

He reminded Thales in some ways of Sophos Mianos,

but coated with another layer of manners and sophistication. 'Perhaps I should take my enquiries elsewhere then?'

'You are troubled by something, Thales?'

'As you so aptly put it, Godhead, it's a delicate matter.'

Tekton's smile faded.

Thales felt dampness splash onto his hand. He rose to his feet, dabbing at his lip. 'Please excuse me, sir; I believe I need to attend to my wound.'

'Yes.' Tekton stayed where he was. 'Shame, shame. You were such a fine-looking fellow.'

A wave of resentment surged through Thales. He left before it claimed his caution and he spoke unwisely. He would see Bethany first, and then prepare himself to seek out Lasper Farr.

But when Thales returned to his apartment the Commander was already there with his sister. They were seated, facing each other across the small faux-wood occasional table. Bethany stared down at the alpine landscape images flickering past on the tabletop while Lasper Farr's gaze fixed on her face. The animosity between the siblings poisoned the air.

Thales let his resentment turn to anger. Farr enjoyed bullying.

He leaned against the inside of the door to keep distance between them.

'You've recovered well, Thales Berniere,' said Lasper. 'Intelligent of you not to inject the DNA. Unlikely you would have survived the combination.'

As with Tekton, Thales struggled to find civil words. He felt Bethany's eyes upon him, urging composure.

'I would be pleased to know the nature of the sample I brought to you, Commander. As it was destined for my home planet, I have an interest.'

'Of course you do. It would be natural, but disclosing that information is not part of our agreement.'

'Agreement?' Thales's voice rose. 'I made no agreement. You took—'

'Thales!' Bethany warned.

Thales caught a steadying breath. 'What progress has been made on Araldis?'

Farr leaned his elbows onto his raised knees and clasped his fingers. He seemed so mild-mannered, to the point of vague at times. How deceptive. Thales remembered the strength in the man's fingers; the casual and complete callousness with which he dispensed violence.

The memory dried his mouth. How could one person's physical strength inspire such fear in another? Had humanesques evolved so little past their most primitive state? Thales wondered suddenly about the Extropists. Surely they had left such behaviours behind.

'The situation on Araldis is complicated. While the Saqr hold Dowl station they control the only means in and out of the system. I cannot even send scouts in,' said Farr.

'What of OLOSS?'

'It seems that the Baronessa has made somewhat of a name for herself; outfacing Stationmaster Landhurst has earned her kudos amongst many supporters of Consilience. Images of her and the incident have been broadcast widely. She is fast becoming a legend.' Farr seemed amused and faintly annoyed. 'It also seems her brash . . . break away from her discussion with the OLOSS envoy has stirred the League to hastily investigate the situation.'

'Investigate?'

'As we speak, OLOSS has amassed a presence at Intel and Jandowae stations. That has made it more difficult for me to move my own people around.'

Thales frowned, not really understanding the implications. 'Do you have restrictions on your movements, Commander?'

The grey eyes hardened. 'Of course not. But I am watched by both sides. I must consider all aspects and possibilities when I take action.'

'Are you saying that your only course of action is inaction?' asked Thales.

'Not inaction – caution.'

'They can amount to the same thing,' Thales challenged him mildly.

'Ah. You scholars do love to debate—'

'The answer is obvious to me, Lasper,' interjected Bethany. 'And I don't believe that you can't see it too.'

Farr raised an eyebrow at his sister, his expression so bland as to be almost obtuse. 'And what is that, Beth?'

'Find out who sent the Saqr there. Attack it from that angle.'

'Well done, little sister. I see you can still think the way I taught you, if only when pushed.'

Bethany's cheeks coloured, but she didn't respond.

Lasper went on. 'And you are correct. I do know who has sent them there. And in that lies another challenge.'

'It's the Extros, isn't it?' she whispered.

He nodded. 'And so you can see my problem. One injudicious move in either direction could spark something that cannot be stopped. Even for the life of my niece, I will not risk a war in Orion.'

'But you promised the Baronessa,' protested Thales.

'The Baronessa could well be dead,' he said matter-of-factly. 'Although I admit to a certain interest in her abduction. Perhaps the Extros have become wary of her influence.'

'She is not dead. Josef Rasterovich will find her,' said Bethany emphatically.

'The God Discoverer has some clear objectives of his own and they don't include rescuing eccentric women.'

Bethany tucked her thin hair behind her ears and lifted her chin in a gesture Thales was used to seeing. 'That is where you have always fallen down, Las. Not seeing the things driven by simple emotions.'

'While you, my dear, have always given in far too readily to simple primitive urges.'

Beth became very still, as if holding herself in check, while Lasper turned his sharp scrutiny onto Thales. The grey eyes were a weapon, needling at him. Finally, Farr looked back at his sister.

He stood to leave. 'You'll have to tell him, Beth,' he said softly. 'In the end.'

Later, Thales and Bethany lay in the bed, holding hands. A weight had descended upon them both. Thales knew his own depression to be a mingling of frustration and indecision.

'What can I do now? Lasper will not be rushed into

an intervention when the stakes are so complex,' whispered Bethany.

Thales squeezed her hand. 'While the shift station is in the hands of the Extros there is nothing you can do.'

'But I have to act in some way. You understand that, don't you?'

He nodded, although they lay in darkness. 'How can I find out about the DNA?' he asked her.

'Other than breaking into Lasper's labs?'

Thales moved his face closer to her ear. 'That's what I meant.'

She stiffened. 'Thales?'

'I know all you want to do is help your daughter, Beth. But the fact is that no one can get through to Araldis. The shift station is blocked.'

'You don't understand. I abandoned her. She's down there struggling to survive against the Saqr. I have to do more than sit and wait.'

'You can't,' said Thales flatly. 'But I can.'

'What do you mean?'

'The DNA was meant for illegal purposes on Scolar. If I can bring news of that to the Sophos, then perhaps they will listen to me on other things.'

'You want to go to Scolar?'

'I would see Gutnee Paraburd confined.'

'Is that the only reason you wish to return?'

'For the most part.' He told her then about Villon and the malaise that had overtaken his society.

She listened intently until he'd finished, then she rolled towards him, their lips almost touching. 'Do you think they killed him? The philosopher?'

'I am sure of it.' He felt her skin warming where it touched his.

'How terrible, Thales.'

'The laboratory creature on Rho Junction told Tekton and me that the DNA targeted the orbitofrontal cortex. You know more of biology than I. Is it possible that such a thing would cause behavioural changes?'

'I could make some guesses if I knew more about the DNA.'

'That is what I thought. Will you help me?'

She slipped her arm across his body and squeezed hard: her unspoken answer.

Thales felt her tremble. She cared for him, that was clear. But what could he give her in return? Could he give her love? He didn't know. Rene was still his wife. And Bethany . . . Bethany was comfort and a reasoned voice. Bethany was experience. Beth was . . .

He kissed her cheek and settled into her embrace.

Thales started awake some time later from a dream. He felt hot. The room was too warm, as though the climate setting had been altered.

And Beth was not there.

He lay quietly for a moment listening for sounds of her in the bathroom. She was not modest in the way Rene had been and didn't require privacy when at her ablutions. She'd scorned his natural reserve, describing what it had been like on Dowl in the confinement module.

'*Josef and Pet know my backside better than I do,*' she'd told him without joking.

Muffled sounds brought him more thoroughly awake.

The bathroom door was open but the door through to their living area was closed. It hadn't been before they went to bed. What was she doing out there that might cause disturbance? Was she unable to sleep?

Concern and curiosity pulled him from the bed. He moved quietly to the door, pausing to lean his ear to it. Distressed noises filtered back to him.

He pushed the door open.

Bethany stood over near the apartment's front door, her figure lit by the door icons. The front of her night-dress was open, her eyes closed and mouth creased in pain. Beside her was a stranger; a heavily gilled and scaled Mioloaquan with modified limbs and primitive facial features. The Mio's sharp teeth and fish mouth were clamped around her nipples and its fins were lashing at her side, whipping against her flesh.

'Beth!' he gasped in a strangled voice.

She swivelled, eyes flicking open, pleasure-glazed and confused. When she saw Thales her expression sharpened. The Mio pulled his teeth roughly from her breast. Thales did not miss the flush spreading across her chest and the quickening of her breath at the pain.

'What . . .' He went no further with his question, but turned and slammed the bedroom door on her. He sat on the edge of the bed feeling sick and faintly – dis-gustingly – aroused.

And angry.

Why had she done this? And almost before his eyes?

He knew of masochism. It was an ancient practice. But on Scolar it was understood that deviant sexual practices were a sign of sublimated frustrations and low self-worth, not a true, healthy expression of sexuality.

Neither he nor Rene would ever entertain such thoughts or practices.

Rene. He wanted to leave right then. Run to his home, and his wife, and his bed; to the comfort of the things that he knew and trusted.

But that was fallacy. Rene had betrayed him as well.

'Thales?' Beth switched on the light as she entered the room and came to stand in front of him.

He couldn't look at her; could think only of the pleasure in her glazed eyes.

'I'm sorry not to have been more discreet. But sometimes I need more than what we share.'

'Need more? Are you saying that I cannot please you?' he said hoarsely.

She didn't look guilty. Nor did she seem to want forgiveness. 'I care for you. You're pure, Thales; so naive and idealistic. But that is not enough. I have sought pain for a long time. It's part of me, and you are only temporary. A beautiful, temporary gift. You have a wife, Thales, who you yearn to see. You are . . . what I might have been.'

His head jerked up.

This time she gave a hollow laugh. 'You didn't need to tell me about her. Nothing could be more obvious. Even you could not pretend that what you feel for me is anything more than convenience.' She reached forward and stroked his hair. 'I don't judge you for it, Thales. So please don't judge me. You asked me for comfort and I gave it to you. Would you deny me the same even if my comfort sometimes takes a different form?'

She sounded calm, but he detected the brittleness in her voice.

'Your brother knows of your . . . preferences, doesn't he?'

She removed her hand from his head and sat on the bed, careful not to touch her body against his. 'Yes. He despises me for it, and for my attraction to alien species. Lasper is like you in many ways; an idealist and a purist about some things. That's why I don't shrink from it now. I won't give him the pleasure of guilt or embarrassment.' She took Thales's hand gently in her own. He felt her tremble. 'I don't proclaim my habits to the universe, but I won't deny them either.'

'Then why have you hidden them from me to suddenly throw them in my face?'

'Mio came to me unexpectedly. I had thought you would stay sleeping. You always sleep so soundly, Thales. Like a child.'

Like a child. Thales's throat constricted, and he had a sudden desire to be free of the apartment. He stood abruptly and reached past her for some clothes.

MIRA

'The B-Bare World?' stammered Mira. 'What is that?'

'Return to the nutrient wall and move forward,' instructed Wanton-poda. The Extro was at eye level and bobbing in agitation. 'Mira-fedor will meet resistance. Mira-fedor *must* overcome that. Wanton-poda will wait for you in the Bare World. Wanton-poda will appear different.'

The cephalopod floated quickly across the chamber and entered the wall with a soft pop.

Mira shook the remains of the Siphonophores from her hands and followed. Adrenalin still coursed through her body. She felt sick at what she'd done. And confused.

Her confusion was overwhelmed by anxiety as the wall subsumed her and she again found herself unable to tell horizontal from vertical or forward from backward.

Then a boost of energy surged through her body, and she felt light and wonderful.

'Mira-fedor.' She heard Wanton-poda's voice, but couldn't locate the creature. 'Mira-fedor, hurry.'

Mira forced her arms and legs to go through the motions of walking even though her senses told her she wasn't moving. She persisted with it until finally she felt the beginnings of some resistance.

As she continued to paddle her limbs, the force working against her grew stronger.

A peculiar contradiction of sensations assaulted her body. She felt energised as the wall continued to feed her, but the force she ran against began to weigh on her, crushing her body.

She became aware of sounds.

Other languages. Stern tones. Warnings. She selected a humanesque voice from the rest and concentrated on it.

'You are leaving the Protected Environment. Take appropriate precautions.'

And another.

'Humanesque Host, remain inside.'

Her arms and legs began to tire, despite the nutrient wall's energy infusion, and the crushing sensation turned to suffocation.

Her involuntary functions would not do their work. Her lungs would not . . .

'Mira-fedor. Follow.' Wanton-poda's voice.

She heard a loud noise, like tearing fabric.

But her legs had stopped moving and her hands only paddled weakly, as if she was waving. If she could just breathe, if . . .

And then she felt the movement again. Deep inside her belly, an agitated violent turning as though the baby would take control of her.

Volition returned. She was able to breathe and lift her knees. Her walking strides became running strides, her arms pumping in a rigid, disciplined way. A way she had never used them before. Never known she could.

And suddenly she was inside the tearing noise, and the wall peeled away from around her and she felt the wet, hot brush of wind. Something solid and real smacked against the soles of her feet and she fell forward to her knees gasping in dry air and crying and coughing.

Dashing the tears from her eyes, she gulped in some steadying breaths and looked for Wanton-poda.

But the place she had come to – the Bare World – was in darkness.

She sat on her heels and took stock.

Then cautiously, she began to feel out the area around her. Sand and rock, she thought. Little rocks, like the edge of a desert. She breathed more deeply, taking time to assess the air. It tasted and smelt dry but clear and palatable. The heat would be worse in the daylight. *If the daylight comes.*

The child within her still moved frantically. She soothed it with a rub to her belly. There was plenty of room for it yet, but in time those kicks would be like daggers to her ribs and sides.

'Mira-fedor,' said a faint voice.

She peered into the near-dark for Wanton-poda. 'Where are you?'

'I am close by. There will be daylight soon and I would warn you, I will seem different.' The cephalopod sounded so quiet and distressed.

She kept her voice as soft. 'Where are we? And how are you different?'

'The Bare World exists outside our reality. Post-Species Hosts do not come here at all. It is merely a structure, if you please; a platform for the worlds that Hosts have chosen to live in.'

'If the islands and the seawater are only virtual, then why did they feel so utterly real? Why didn't I need some device to perceive them?'

'Post-Species Host worlds are not virtual, at least, not in the primitive sense that Mira-fedor means. What Mira-fedor experienced actually existed – with some modifications. Wanton-poda, however, is different because it no longer has its Host body. Poda did not survive the transition into the Bare World.'

'Oh,' Mira whispered, shocked. 'I am sorry.' Tears spurted from her eyes and she pressed her fists to them. 'Are you in pain from losing it?'

Wanton-poda didn't baulk at her direct question. 'Yes. In *many* ways. Wanton would ask for silence now while it adjusts. Wanton will look different. Don't be frightened by the change.'

'Are we in any danger while we wait?' It had been so long now that she had feared one thing or another that it seemed a logical concern.

'Wanton does not believe that we will be followed here by its kind. However, Wanton has not been in the Bare World before, though prediction would say the dark is safe enough.'

'I have one last question, Wanton-poda.'

'Hasten, please, Mira-fedor.'

'The creature being birthed on the island, the Saqr, what do you know of it?'

'Wanton-poda sensed Mira-fedor's extreme fear of it.'

'Si. Is it a Post-Species Host like you?'

'It is a Host body being prepared for use. Wanton had much to do with its regenesis.'

'For use by one of your kind?' Mira tried to keep the impatience from her voice.

'Not necessarily,' said Wanton-poda. 'Some Host bodies are used for other things – in the way humanesques have used lesser species. Post-Species do not use barbaric behaviour modification, however. Redirection at the DNA level is much more efficient. Now, Wanton requires Mira-fedor's silence.'

Mira uncramped her legs and sank into a more comfortable position. Her questions would have to wait. She turned her attention back to her surroundings. The temperature was reminiscent of Araldis and her skin seemed to welcome it. She glanced behind her. The darkness seemed thicker there as if it harboured an object. Yet she didn't trust her senses while her body was in so much turmoil.

She continued to stroke her belly, talking to the baby in her mind for the first time in the way she did with *Insignia*. *I'm not sure how you helped me but I know that you did. What manner of person are you to exert such force of will from the womb?*

Unlike *Insignia*, the baby did not respond. And yet she felt the beginnings of attachment. Somehow the child had helped her. Perhaps it would not be like its father.

So the baby seemed to settle within her, and for some precious long moments she relaxed onto the sand.

And then the dawn came.

It crept upon her as she dozed, a subtle change of colour: inky to something less dense and then a true, colour-filled lightening. It was a sound that woke her though.

For a moment she thought a child cried. But as her senses focused she knew it not to be crying but a whining; pain-infected.

Her eyes roamed the grainy landscape ahead. Arid like Araldis but rocky, close by at least. She reined her gaze in closer to locate the sound.

It came, she thought, from a tiny dark stain on the sand, not far from her feet and no bigger than the palm of her hand. She pulled her knees in to move her feet away from it.

As the day struck in a bold dash of gold and stark ochre, she alternated between examining her surrounds and observing the stain.

The Bare World, it seemed, was just that – a barren moonscape of rock and sand but imbued with colours she had never seen in earth before. Seams of blue ran through the small ridges of rock and the sand around her glinted with hints of orange and pink and green. And yet there was a deadness about it that did not come from a lack of atmosphere.

Life had been here and then removed. She sensed it.

As the daylight brightened her perception of things, the small stain near her feet resolved into something of more substance but less appeal. It looked, Mira thought, like a slice of the livers that Faja often cooked for the alien children who needed high-iron diets. There were many substitutes for fresh organs, but Faja insisted on feeding her children as well as she could. The livers would arrive once a month, cryopacked, from one of her off-world suppliers.

Mira looked around for Wanton-poda. 'W-Wanton-poda?' she called out softly.

'Mira-fedor?' The response was thin but unmistakably emanating from the small gelatinous lump.

'I-is that you near my feet?'

'Wanton is different.'

'This is your true form?'

'Wanton is not able to disclose my true form, which is within what you see – it's illegal for my kind to do so – but this is my interactive skin.'

Mira moved closer. 'S-skin. It looks too thick.'

'It is a highly evolved material that can do and withstand many things. However, transport is an issue without a Host. Wanton would ask that you pick me up so that we can proceed.'

Mira swallowed. She felt the baby jerk, as if it had awoken and was not pleased. 'How do I best hold you?'

'Wanton would normally integrate into the Host's nervous system, but as our relationship is not of that nature I would suggest placing me against your neck, just below your ear. Without a Host it is energy-consuming for Wanton to project sound.'

Mira stared at the Extro with apprehension. 'Forgive my uncertainty, but will you hurt me? Or will you affect my control of my own functions?'

'Mira-fedor can be reassured no harm will come to her,' it replied. 'And we must hasten now.'

Mira glanced around. The landscape in front of them was as barren as before, but behind her was a different matter. Behind her everything stopped. Nothing existed past a certain point. It seemed as though the nothing was just a clear, pale sky, or something as featureless.

'The nutrient wall protects our environment. What little is left over is the Bare World.'

'That sky is the wall?'

Wanton made an exasperated noise. 'If it will help us to leave this spot, Wanton will explain as we proceed. But please, Mira-fedor, *pick Wanton up*.'

Mira reached out, stopping just short of touching the Extro. To her surprise, it sprang up of its own volition and settled on the palm of her hand.

She carefully lifted it closer to her face. It felt sticky, and had the odour of something alive and slightly bloody. She took a deep breath as it squirmed in her hand.

'Please hasten, Mira-fedor. There are things we should avoid.'

She lifted her hand to the side of her throat and Wanton squirmed across to make contact with the flesh under her ear.

The sensation was not unpleasant, like having a cool compress applied to a bruise.

Wanton made a satisfied noise and wriggled a little as it burrowed into her skin. Mira felt tiny pricks as it anchored itself to her.

In Mira's belly, the baby moved again, irritated.

'Please walk in a northerly direction.'

'Which way is north?'

'Over the ridges in front of you.'

They kept to this pattern, Wanton giving directions and Mira obeying them. The unsettling feeling of being a slave or an automaton was countered by her anxiety to find some shelter, and her fascination with the composition of the Bare World.

It was hard to digest such a place; barren tracts of land ran like tributaries around sections of the Hue much like a maze or a river delta spread across land. Geology had only figured in Mira's studium learning insomuch as it had pertained to the evolution and existence of particular alien genera. This was something totally outside that reference.

'Why does the wall – is that what you call it? – meander in such an erratic fashion?'

'I will assume that you refer to the existence of the Bare World through and around the Hue. The explanation is simple. The nutrient wall – that is a less than satisfactory term – is a fluid and ever-changing filter and protective sac not unlike the humanesque amnion. However, the wall absorbs the raw materials from the Bare World, not a parent creature. It then recomposes the proteins and acids to provide the Hue with necessary living requirements.'

'You mean food and fluids?'

'Not only. It can manipulate matter to create any manner of desired material or object.'

'That is why your world seemed virtual and yet solid.' Mira reached the top of the first ridge and stopped to stare. Ahead lay a wide corridor of flat, caked clay cracked into symmetrical patterns. On either side, though, the wall rose in such a way that she could not be sure what was sky and what was not. The peculiar visual trick made her nauseous. 'So you cannibalise the real planet in order to exist?'

'Mira-fedor's tone and choice of words imply a negative appreciation of the situation.'

'Well, what happens when you run out of raw material?'

'That is not an issue.' Wanton-poda, she thought, sounded smug. 'We have seeded the Bare World with a regeneration accelerant.'

Mira picked her way slowly down the rocky ridge. Her feet felt bruised and tender. Perhaps her soft detention stockings would fare better on the clay. 'It does not appear to be working.'

'That is why we must hurry, Mira-fedor. Wanton's references suggest that the Bare World is close to its regeneration point. To be caught in that . . .'

'What? What will happen?'

Wanton squirmed against her neck, making her flesh prickle. She wanted to scratch the area but couldn't without dislodging the Extro.

'Wanton will be unaffected, but it is unknown what the effect might be on you or your child.'

Mira's heart thumped.

'Wanton has distressed you,' said Wanton.

'Tell me where we are going.'

'Wanton is not sure, exactly. Wanton's initial thought was to escape permanent death, and now, to escape the worst of the regeneration.'

'But how can we survive until then? I need food and water.'

'That is not a difficulty. Mira-fedor can feed from the nutrient wall as long as she is subtle and sparing.'

Mira remembered the boost of energy the wall had

given her. Relief that she would not starve or dehydrate was tempered by a faint distaste at the thought of having to be in regular contact with the amnion sac around the Extro world.

'I don't understand why we have to hurry if you're unsure where we are going. We need to devise a strategy. Some way to get off this world.'

'Leave here?'

'I would wish so,' said Mira.

'But there is much prejudice against our kind. Wanton is safest here.'

'Not now that you have helped me to escape.'

Wanton issued a strange, unhappy sound, then fell to muttering something that Mira couldn't understand.

It continued its mumbling as they walked until, eventually, she could stand it no longer. The baby, it seemed, was of the same mind, delivering light jabs to the base of her abdomen.

'Wanton-poda! Where am I going? I cannot continue to walk without a destination. I am not a brainless Host.'

The Extro paused. 'Please, Mira-fedor. Address Wanton merely as "Wanton". Poda is no more. Or, perhaps, "Wanton-mira".'

Wanton-mira. The idea of it made Mira's nausea return. She halted. 'Wanton,' she said clearly and with quiet determination. 'Where are we going?'

'According to the studium notes there is a mamelon that is not affected during the regeneration.'

'Mamelon? You mean a lava flow?'

'A lava mountain.'

'Do you have a way to locate it?'

Wanton stayed silent for a moment. 'Mira-fedor's manner of speech is most shameless.'

Most shameless? She hesitated. The Extro was attempting to distract her with indignation. 'You have answered many of my direct questions now. Why would this one cause offence – unless you cannot answer it?'

'Mira-fedor sounds different.'

Mira stopped walking. The Extro was right. She was angry at so many things and the creature's tedious manner provoked her. 'I'm a long way from any friends or family, Wanton. Your species has torn me from symbiosis with my biozoon and brought me here. You may not understand humanesque feelings, so I will tell you plainly – I am angry and lonely and filled with uncertainty.'

In the silence that followed her statement Mira noticed something. The sand at her feet had changed colour, from green to a dark glinting black. With a glance, she saw the same thing happening ahead of and behind her – in swaths. Patterned swaths.

'Perhaps with me as your passenger, you will be less lonely?' said Wanton in a small voice. 'Wanton has lost poda and Mira has lost symbiote.'

She did not reply to that, her thoughts overtaken by anxiety. 'Why is the sand turning black?'

'It would seem,' Wanton said finally, 'the fertilisation process has begun. There is less time than Wanton thought.'

'Before what? The regeneration?'

'Yes.'

'But how can that be so dangerous?'

'There will be a flood, Mira-fedor. Vegetation requires water to grow.'

Mira stared at the tract of sand before them, bordered on either side by the strange, opaque sky-wall. 'Quickly. Which way do we go?' she whispered.

TEKTON

Young Thales's bandaged necrotic face was so ghastly that Tekton felt quite relieved when he left. Besides, he had things that needed some quiet reflection. Lasper Farr was stalling for time. Tekton could read the signs.

Search all 'casts for news of the planet Araldis, he told his travel moud.

While he waited for the newsfeeds, he sat back and admired Fenralia's statue. Opening his robe, he let his akula free to swell his manhood. When his thoughts became lascivious enough to engender something of suitable comparison to the statue, he observed the differences between its erection and his own.

It was indeed, he thought, a very good likeness.

Excuse me, Godhead, said the irritating moud, immediately deflating Tekton's frame of mind.

Yes, yes.

There has been some news from the planet Araldis. OLOSS has sent forward investigative fleets to a selection of connecting Resonance stations.

Are they able to shift into the Araldis system?

No, Godhead.

What in Sole are they doing then?

Waiting, Godhead. And watching.

Tekton sighed. How typically OLOSS. He went into the bedroom and lay on the wide, oval-shaped bed.

He found that space travel sapped his energy for some time after a long trip and he had his best ideas when prone.

Once comfortable, he let his minds drift into random thought and waited for patterns to emerge. Miranda Seeward and Lawmon Jise – his fellow tyros. Araldis and quixite. Lasper Farr and the Extropists. Thoughts paired together, split off and then re-formed in new pairs. What should he be seeing in these people and events that he hadn't recognised?

Step back, logic-mind suggested. *What do we know already?*

He knew that Lasper Farr couldn't move any type of force into Araldis while the shift station was compromised, and whoever had invaded the planet wanted – and was most likely helping themselves to – *his* quixite.

This left Tekton a couple of courses of immediate action. He could simply modify his designs and have Manruben create something from the small quantity of quixite already on its way to Rho Junction. Or he could divert his resources into discovering who had invaded Araldis and bargain with them. Or, perhaps, put his own project on hold and return to Belle-Monde, and unravel Miranda Seeward's intentions for the planet of Scolar with her nasty little virus.

He immediately dismissed the idea of modification; archiTects did not compromise their designs. And the Araldis questions would be answered soon enough by OLOSS, or Farr, or another group with vested interests. Which left him with Miranda Seeward.

His minds felt in accord over this. Time would

unravel the Araldis situation – in the meantime he could interfere with Miranda and Jise and their plans. And possibly keep a close eye on what his cousin Ra was up to.

Godhead?

Yes.

Commander Farr is at your door.

Tekton's heart fluttered. Had the villain come to negotiate with him, or kill him? *Does he have a weapon?*

Not that I can detect, Godhead.

That means little enough, said logic-mind. *His spit is most likely poisonous.*

Let him in, you can out-think him, free-mind bolstered his ego.

As if he could be stopped, sniffed logic-mind and sank itself into design inventory.

Tekton returned to his sitting room. *Grant him entry, moud.*

Farr entered without fanfare, closing the door gently and making his way to sit on one end of the plush lounge suite. He appraised Fenralia's statue through eyes hooded, Tekton guessed, from habitual sleeplessness. 'You purchased it?'

'Fenralia is eminently collectable. As am I.'

Farr gave a short laugh. 'You amuse me, Tekton. Such shameless vanity is rare.'

'The notion of "shame" springs from beliefs that seek to control society. I graduated from such limitations when I began to chew, Commander Farr. I would have imagined the same of you.'

'You would not begin to imagine what I am capable of, archiTect, with or without shame.'

Tekton grew hard at the man's bald statement. It was not a new thing for him to find eroticism in power – but danger? Perhaps academia had become too predictable, too familiar to stimulate him any more. 'And yet you've come to tell me that your hands are tied. OLOSS has surrounded all the stations that will allow shift to Araldis. The balance of things is delicate. And that even the enticement of details about the creator of the virus cannot persuade you to help me.'

'You have a keen mind, Tekton. But what you don't grasp is my role in this. Sentient creatures have a history of war and genocide. Balance is more important now than it has ever been and I am the only one who can maintain it. Balance is *vital*.'

Vital? 'I'm all for balance, Commander. But you intrigue me. How do you envisage keeping the peace without a superior force at your disposal? Surely you could not hope to reiterate your success as a peacemaker in the Stain Wars? Such things do not bear repeating.'

Farr lifted his hooded eyes. Something about them reminded Tekton of his cousin Ra. Self-belief. Not the kind that Tekton was imbued with, but the extreme, psychotic kind.

'My skills are outside your comprehension,' said Farr.

Tekton's erection softened a little. Psychosis was not as attractive as either power or danger, and the edge in Farr's voice strayed towards it. Did the man believe he was God?

Of course he does. It's as plain as the necrosis on the young scholar's face, volunteered free-mind.

God-deluders aren't anything new. Logic-mind shot up from underneath a weight of cost calculations.

But this man, thought Tekton, this man is no fool.

His erection came back then, harder, more convulsed, than any he could remember. If Lasper Farr thought he was as powerful as a god then maybe he had *something* to back his conviction. An edge? A source?

The notion settled firmly upon Tekton.

I must know what it is, he affirmed to himselves. *I must know what gives him such confidence. But how? How do I get deeper into such a man?*

Then inspiration struck him.

'Do you worship, Commander Farr?'

The man's grey eyes widened for a split second. 'It is a long time since anyone was brave or foolish enough to ask me about my religion.'

'In my experience, the most clever and powerful people are often the strongest believers.'

'I detect barely disguised flattery, Tekton. What are you trying to extract from me?'

'Flattery? Now who is showing their vanity?'

Farr ignored the mild barb. 'I will assume from your question that you are ambivalent about the notion that the Sole Entity is a God.'

Tekton gave a fake yawn. '"God" can be such a confusing noun, Commander.'

'Yet you've adopted the title Godhead?'

'And . . . it can be useful – if you get my meaning. Frankly, I am undecided on the nature of God, but I have a regular and personal dialogue with him. I find it clears my mind.'

'Him?'

'We are humanesque, Commander. Our pronouns are limited.'

Farr narrowed his grey eyes. 'There are many prayer venues around Edo that welcome strangers within.'

'And yours is not one of them?'

Farr got to his feet in a lithe, almost freakish, movement that belied his age. His expression lightened a little; a hint of amusement again. 'Of course, you are welcome to my chapel, Tekton. But once you have worshipped and taken reflection, I would strongly suggest you make arrangements to move on. Our pleasant acquaintanceship may, otherwise, depreciate in value.'

It took some time after Farr left for Tekton's erection to subside. To his own fascination, he appeared to be developing an erotic attraction to the idea of physical threat. Perhaps he'd spent his recent years too cocooned from the wider worlds.

That realisation did not distract him entirely from his new purpose. Foil the projects of the other tyros. He would, however, find out as much as he could about Lasper Farr before he was forced to leave.

After instructing his moud to arrange transport to the Edo shift station to connect with a res-ship bound for Mintaka, he logged a request with the porter to pack his belongings (including the statue) and take them to the loading docks.

He then bathed, ate a small meal and dressed in his most comfortable and least ostentatious robes. By the time the moud informed him that his passage was booked and that the porter would be along shortly, he felt composed and ready.

Moud. Commander Farr has extended an invitation to me to pray at his private chapel. Enquire with the mayordomo for directions.

The moud consulted with the station AI and shortly afterwards Tekton said goodbye, for ever, to his moderately luxurious suite. He found a Lamin waiting for him outside.

'The mayordomo has directed me to escort you to the Commander's chapel.' It curled its front lock with a long nail and wiggled its nostrils.

Tekton shrugged. He detested Lamins, but a guide would be useful in this instance.

Surprisingly, the Lamin took him upwards, towards the surface, not deeper into the planet-station as he'd anticipated. Leaving the central lift shaft, they found a taxi that took them across the dock bridge and through a channel in the thick wall of twisted metal. Although the taxi appeared to stay level, Tekton experienced the sensation of ascent.

His curiosity forced him to talk to the Lamin. 'I had thought the docks to be the highest level of Edo?'

The creature gave a smug smile. 'Commander Farr resides on the *surface* of Edo.'

'The surface? But there is no surface,' objected Tekton. 'The whole planet is a mound of floating rubbish.'

'The Commander's habitat is . . . fluid.'

'Fluid? What in Sole's tube does that mean?' Tekton became irritated. Lamins were obtuse at best, and altogether too arrogant for a race of tedious bureaucrats.

'You will see soon, visiting-Lostol.'

Visiting-Lostol! Tekton had an urge to smack the annoying creature across the face but thought better of it in case he tore his skin on its coarse facial hair. Lamins were known for their proclivity for diseases.

He settled for a look of crushing disdain.

Before the Lamin could further bother him, the taxi slowed to a halt outside a large hatch, big enough to have belonged to the hold of a deep spaceship. The hatch had been fitted arbitrarily into a wall of interwoven scrap, telltale trails of welding slag securing it in place.

The Lamin tapped along a section of the wall with its ridiculous nails.

The hatch popped open with a frightening sucking noise. Tekton felt a rush of wind and cold. He gasped against it and a sense of oxygen depletion.

'Fr-ree-ezing,' he chattered.

The Lamin's fur stood on end against the cold, and it gave another smug smile. 'Commander Farr likes to be reminded of the outside. The environment is within humanesque endurance limits, and the chapel itself is comfortable. Or would you prefer to return to the dock and await your departure?'

Tekton clamped his teeth together to control them. He would not let the Lamin intimidate him. He snatched the simple nose-mask it proffered and stepped through the hatch, head held high.

His next gasp was one of pure fear. The rubber collar on the other side of the hatch attached directly onto a long and fragile suspension walkway. In fact suspension, thought Tekton, was description overkill. The bridge appeared to be floating free in a void that was circled by a number of floating metal constructions.

The Lamin stepped nonchalantly onto the bridge and glanced back over its shoulder. The only sign of discomfort from the wind and cold was the shiny discharge from its tri-part nose. It licked that away.

'Are you coming, Lostol-Tekton? I cannot activate the bridge until you are on.'

Tekton forced himself to move forward, but could not stop himself from staring down. Jagged objects floated in the deep abyss below, which was periodically lit up by the flash of something silver.

'W-what is making that l-light?' he demanded in shrill, stuttering tones.

'Your moud's guest protocol will tell you,' said the Lamin, over its shoulder. It trotted on ahead, causing the bridge to undulate unnervingly.

Tekton reached for the guide rail, frozen to the spot. *Moud*, he shrieked. His akula and the erection that had been with him for hours had completely deserted him. *What is making the silver flashes?*

Transmuted-metal detrivores, Godhead. Their smaller counterparts were created to keep the metals clean and rust-free. However, the overabundance of food has allowed some mutation.

Mutated detrivores. What do they look like? Do they only eat metals?

The moud flashed a representation of one across his retina. Tekton absorbed the appearance of the creature: a roachid with a large, dull-grey dislike plate covering its head, and wide silver-veined wings. The scale showed it to be much larger than a canine.

The larger detrivores live on a primarily metal diet but there have been reported incidences of them attacking sentients whose blood contains a high level of certain minerals.

Tekton's stomach contracted into a hard lump.

A salty flavour in his mouth alerted him to the fact that he had bitten his lip sufficiently hard to make it bleed.

Turn around and go back to the taxi, free-mind urged.

If the Lamin is leading then the way must be safe, reasoned logic-mind.

Why are you even here? his free-mind demanded.

Because I want information about Farr, and this might provide it.

Might?

Tekton closed his eyes for a moment. Courage was something he'd never had to consider calling upon before. His life was largely without physical risk. Even Lasper Farr's unveiled threats hadn't been as real to him as this spindly, swaying bridge and its dreadful abyss. He desperately wanted to piss.

He cracked open his eyelids. The Lamin was already halfway across.

Across where?

His eyes opened wider. While he'd been gripping the railing, the far end of the bridge had drifted higher, and appeared to now be secured to the base of a large triangular-shaped object.

The Lamin continued onward, its thick, stumpy legs pumping hard to keep its high-heeled feet climbing.

Tekton took in a long and deliberate breath. Courage might be unfamiliar to him but pride was not. He forced his legs to move, keeping his line of sight on the Lamin's back, diverting all his thought and energy into catching the arrogant assistant. He would not be the butt of Lamin jokes about cowardice.

The creature waited for him at the end of the bridge,

where the structure coupled roughly onto a railed platform at the base of the triangle.

Tekton's sense of triumph soon faded when the Lamin gestured for him to precede it across the platform, up several flights of narrow stairs that seemed to be barely attached to the side of the triangular structure. From what he could see there was no safety net or even a harness. The railing on the abyss side of the stairs looked flimsier than those on the bridge.

'How far?' he managed to ask.

'The entrance to the chapel lies at the top.'

Tekton gritted his teeth and began the ascent. This time he kept his eyes on the steps above him. He knew that even the briefest of glances would allow the spinning sensation in his head to overtake everything else.

Within a short time, his legs trembled with effort and he couldn't catch his breath. He felt some small satisfaction to hear the Lamin breathing heavily below him.

Halfway up, he stopped to rest. With both hands gripping the rail and his backside planted firmly on the step, he allowed himself a brief glimpse down. The shape of the chasm below seemed to have shifted, like the moving outline of an enormous snake. Different structures had appeared. Or perhaps it was simply a trick of perspective.

He used his design sight to assess it. *No*. The chasm had definitely moved.

'Lostol-Tekton?' said the Lamin. 'Are you ready to continue?'

'Everything has shifted,' said Tekton aloud, ignoring him.

'The outer rim is composed of large objects less firmly caught in the gravity spin. It is an extremely fluid composition. That is why the Commander had the flexible conduit constructed.'

A clever way to confuse enemies, thought Tekton, when your home is never in the exact same place.

But dangerous.

He stood and resumed his climb, trying to ignore the possibilities of colliding structures and flying detrivores. If he lived in such a place he would certainly not use such precarious means to gain access to his private rooms. It was ridiculous to say the least.

His legs began to ache in a manner that he'd never known, and by the time he reached the top, his finely pored skin was warmed by effort.

At least, he supposed, he would not die from the chill.

His chest heaved as he finally reached the broad entry pad to the chapel. So much so that he was unable to greet Lasper Farr, who came towards him from the chapel entrance.

'Tekton.' He smiled, but did not proffer his hand in greeting. 'Enjoy your reflection time as I have mine. It is unlikely we'll meet again.'

Tekton nodded as he gasped and watched Farr walk to the other side of the platform.

What is he doing over there? It seemed simpler to ask the moud than the Lamin. And he did not have to speak to do so.

But the moud remained silent.

A moment later the sound of his impatient reiteration was drowned by the noise of an incoming air-taxi.

This time Tekton found his voice. 'You can taxi here?' he spluttered to the Lamin. 'All the way *here*!'

The Lamin's smug smile seemed to have grown a degree smugger. 'If the Commander permits.'

Farr was already inside the passenger compartment. He did not glance once at Tekton before the taxi disappeared over the lip of the pad with a groaning exhalation of air.

'That sadist!' roared Tekton. It had been a long time – if ever – since he'd lost control of his anger. Not since Ra had beaten him to the tyro position on Belle-Monde, and even then his fury had quickly turned cold and cunning.

Now all he wanted to do was slap the Lamin down.

As if sensing the possibility, the Lamin trotted away towards the chapel door.

'May I suggest we go inside, Lostol-Tekton?' it called over its shoulder.

'No!' shouted Tekton, waving his fist. 'You may not suggest anything to me. In fact you *may not* speak to me again, you simpering bag of fur and wind.'

The Lamin stopped and turned. It seemed unmoved by his anger but glanced meaningfully above Tekton's head. 'If you say so.' Then it opened the door and stepped inside, leaving it slightly ajar.

Tekton let his rage vent through a string of disgusting expletives he had not even known were in his repertoire, and would have gone on much longer if a strong and sudden draft of wind had not cooled his heated body. The very few hairs he had on his skin stiffened at the sound of a high-pitched wail; a cry of pain, amplified by echoes.

A cold, hungry sound.

Tekton glanced upward. He saw a flash of reflective silver, lent luminescence by the blinking array on the side of the chapel that had lit their ascent. The flash faded then returned in a steady rhythm as a detrivore spiralled down towards him.

Tekton learned how promptly fury could be replaced by terror, and how slowly his unconditioned body reacted when called upon, as he drove his aching, out-of-condition legs across the platform and dived for cover through the door, landing, ignominiously, at the Lamin's feet.

The Lamin leapt deftly backward, allowing Tekton to tumble inside. As it shut the door Tekton heard a heavy thud and felt a shudder.

'A large one,' observed the Lamin, nostrils flaring. 'And hungry. Does your blood, perchance, have a high iron count, Lostol-Tekton?'

TRIN

The land yachts glided onto the island shore on the gentling swell. While the men pulled the boats high above the tide line, Trin walked ahead towards the line of stunted trees, his face upturned, letting the rain drops catch in his mouth and on his skin.

Occasionally, on the Tourmalines, the lightest of rains would fall, no more than a mist, but never in his life on Araldis had Trin ever felt the full force of heavy raindrops.

He wanted to strip his robe off and let the pure liquid run over every part of his body. The salt taste on his lips could have been the seawater, or the tears that he made no attempt to stem. They'd survived and yet for those long moments during the storm he'd thought they were lost.

'Principe?'

Djes was behind him, standing on unsteady legs, her waterlogged skin wrinkled and puckered. She'd covered her nakedness by knotting together the torn signal cloths and her smile was wide and childlike as she held her webbed fingers out to catch the rain.

He embraced her for all to see. 'Thank you.'

She shook her head, dismissing her part. 'You are the one that gives us belief, Trinder.'

He hugged her tighter. Over her shoulder, he

watched the women's yacht wallow in the small waves. The stronger ones helped the weaker ones through the shallows, while his Carabinere pulled the yacht to shore. Pitifully few of his men still survived.

'The clouds will disappear soon. We should find shade,' said Djes, stroking his arm. 'I will fish now.'

While he reflected on their failures, she already looked to their survival.

'No,' he said. 'You are exhausted. The swim was too far.'

She shook her head stubbornly. 'We are safe now for a time. I can rest when we are fed. We will have time then.' She pointed into the island. 'Go past the line of trees, and to the south you'll see large rocks – boulders. There are shallow caves among them, and fresh water on the eastern side. Don't go towards the hills to the north. The bush is too dense. We will need to cut through it.'

He nodded, listening carefully. 'I will tell Joe Scali to wait for you. He will carry what you catch.'

She smiled and pressed her face lightly to his arm. Then she stepped away. Her gait was ungainly as she walked along the sand to the water. She disappeared into the waves, tossing the cloths back onto the beach. Joe Scali collected them in a bundle and waved her off.

Trin walked down to join him. The euphoria of survival and the intoxicating feel of the rain were rapidly deserting him. Fatigue replaced them.

'Wait in the bushes on the dunes for Djes until she has fished. Carry them back. She has told me the best place to take cover.'

Joe nodded, his swollen eyes roving the water for sign of her. 'But she is exhausted.'

'We are all exhausted,' Trin said sharply, to allay his guilt. 'Djes knows her limits.'

He left Joe and went further along the beach to Juno.

'Crux watched over us, Principe,' Juno rasped.

'Then let's hope Crux brings us help soon. There is shade and water just beyond the bush line.'

They reached the outcrop that Djes had described, as the last wisps of rain cloud evaporated. The Carabinere had struggled through repeat trips to carry the weakest of the women when they could barely carry their own weight. Trin felt a swell of unutterable pride for his men who had given over their fellalos at his command, and still uncomplainingly worked to his word. To the last one, they were exhausted beyond speech.

They huddled in small groups in the shallow caves that had been created by the loose arrangement of the boulders. Trin shared one with his madre, who mercifully lay in the sand and slept almost immediately. Though he had not meant to, he dozed beside her until Tina Galiotto woke him with water cupped in a pod. She had begun to serve him, as well as his madre, as if it were the natural order.

'Principe?'

He nodded thanks, and she left him.

He drank deeply and stared out across the open ground to the tree line that divided them from the beach. Leah had set, bathing the island in softer, almost bearable, warmth. Trin stood and stretched. Sleep had revived him enough to bring back the bite of hunger, and he walked from cave to cave, searching for Juno Genarro.

The Carabinere lay next to one of the women, his distant cousin Josephia Genarro, whispering. He sat up when he saw Trin. 'Principe?'

'I will go to the beach. Djes has not brought food yet.'

Juno began to climb to his feet but Trin forestalled him.

'No. Stay. There is enough light left that I will be back before dark.'

Juno slumped back gratefully. 'Walk with care. Do not get lost, Principe.'

In the fading light, the vegetation seemed altered, and Trinder broke through to the shoreline to the south of where they'd landed. He picked his way along the waterline towards the shadowy shapes of the flat-yachts. The low tide and the efforts of the men had beached them but they would need to find another way to secure them from freak waves.

He approached on feet made silent by the breakers. Where was Joe Scali? Where was Djes?

Then he heard them; the low murmur of voices coming from between the two yachts. He hastened, worried that she was hurt, or too exhausted to walk inland. He slipped past the bow of the first yacht and called out.

What had been one shadow on the sand between the yachts suddenly became two as Djes and Joe Scali pulled apart.

For a shocking moment he thought that the two of

them had been embracing in the way of lovers, but as Djes found him and threw her arms around his waist, he crushed his unworthy suspicion.

Such a thing would never happen. It would not.

JO-JO RASTEROVICH

'What is it?' Jo-Jo asked the question that was on all of their minds.

Latourn and Catchut stood on either side of Rast staring at the same image above the Primo vein that was making Jo-Jo's jaw clench. The 'zoon's buccal smelt stronger than normal; an astringent odour that reminded Jo-Jo of an aged shark he'd cleaned straight from the sea one time. Iodine. It made his eyes water. A stress smell, he decided. *The 'zoon's pining for her.*

'Looks like a frigging wheel hub,' offered Catchut.

'It's a drum,' Rast corrected. 'Or based on the design of one.'

Jo-Jo cocked his head at an angle to get another perspective. The object spinning slowly in the image captured by the 'zoon's sensors was like a giant cylinder wrapped in skin.

'What's a drum, Capo?' asked Latourn.

'They used to use instruments to make music.'

'Instruments?' Catchut had drawn a blank from the explanation.

Rast looked helplessly at Jo-Jo. 'You know what I mean?'

He nodded. 'They still get used some places where the tech's limited.' He continued to examine the image – their first look into Extropy space. 'But that wouldn't be here, I'd warrant.'

'Guess we're gonna find out first-hand anyway,' said Rast. 'Looks like we're heading straight in there with or without an invitation.'

Alongside the edge of the images, icons flickered and danced in a familiar arrival sequence. The 'zoon was letting them know of its intention to land.

'You think she's down there?' Jo-Jo's voice sounded hoarse suddenly.

'Fedor?' Rast shrugged. 'Maybe. I don't know how strong their symbiotic link is. Could be that the 'zoon's just guessing.'

'Should we arm up, Capo?' Catchut seemed anxious for something to do.

Rast kinked a corner of her lips. 'You know my motto, Cat. When in doubt, strap it on.'

Latourn and Catchut grinned and disappeared out of the buccal.

Rast stared at Jo-Jo. 'You got your head together yet?'

Jo-Jo shrugged, holding tight to his belligerence. 'Course.'

'You got any ideas why Beth and the idiot Thales jumped ship with the Lostol?'

'Why? You think it's got a bearing on this?'

'Eventually,' she said. 'Everything will.'

'Didn't pick you for a philosopher, Randall.'

'Didn't pick you for the lovesick type, Rasterovich.'

The moment of civility had passed and the tension was back.

Rast got up out of Secondo in her usual leisurely,

overconfident manner. 'Might go check out that hard-
ware myself.'

They assembled a while later inside the egress scale
as they waited for the biozoon to dock on the overrun
of the drum station. The mercs wore Latino combat
vests loaded down with bulky, antiquated weapons.
Latourn had a set of knife sheaths hanging from a utility
belt, and Catchut wore something similar with pouches
attached. Rast had two semis slung over her back, plus
a selection of grenades in her own pouches. Her vest
bulged, making her chest look twice its actual width.

She held out a vest to Jo-Jo and pulled a face. 'Best
the Pellegrinis had to offer. Vintage sweeties. Good for
getting your head blown off.'

Jo-Jo took it from her. The material felt stiff and
new, straight out of a crate.

'If the 'zoon lets the Extros on board we're better
to be here, armed and ready, than have them hunt us
down through the ship.'

Jo-Jo agreed with the merc on that score at least. He
slipped the vest on and buckled it. 'I wouldn't be
mentioning who I am to any Extros,' he said as they
took up positions around the mouth of the egress scale.

Rast nodded her agreement to Latourn and Catchut.
'Can't do any of us any good to be seen keeping
company with the *God Discoverer*. Best if he's known
as one of ours for the time being.'

Catchut scowled but said nothing.

Latourn stared at the stratum ceiling – his thoughts
were clearly elsewhere.

'Lat?'

Latourn dragged his gaze across to meet Rast's. 'Do you think the Baronessa's even here, Capo?'

Rast gave him a sharp look. 'Maybe. Why?'

Latourn reddened, his skin colour vivid enough to pass for Latino. 'If we find her, mebbe we can get off this damn 'zoon. I got a hankerin' for somethin' more military. Not complaining, Capo. Farr's paid us enough to make good for a while and I know we gotta find her to collect the rest of it, but this ain't the sort of work I'm wantin'. Babysittin' wimmen, like, and freakin' around in Extro space.'

It was the most Jo-Jo had ever heard Latourn speak but Rast never got to reply to him. The light altered, signalling that the egress scale had begun to peel back.

'Quiet!' ordered Rast. She leaned her head towards Jo-Jo, whispering. 'We got one rule in my crew, Rasterovich. My word. You ignore it, you wind up dead. Either by them, or by me. And like it or not, for the moment you're one of my crew.' She shot him a fierce glance. 'Got it?'

Jo-Jo nodded slowly. He'd already made his *big* choice, the one that saw him here on this crazy 'zoon trying not to piss himself over what was about to happen. Now it was time to swallow any arrogance on Randall's part and survive.

Rast seemed relieved. 'Right. We see trouble, you stay between me and Cat.' She fished inside her jacket and passed him a pistol. 'It's a semi. Don't fire from behind me.'

She crimped back against the wall now, pushing him along her as she squatted out of sight behind a ridge of ribbing. Latourn and Catchut did the same thing on the other side.

The egress hollow flooded with greyish light.

Nothing happened. No sound. Or smell.

Jo-Jo strained to see past Rast but she shook her head at him. Drawing a small spray pack from her utility belt, she sent the contents squirting into the air. It illuminated hundreds of minuscule beads floating in the atmosphere, glistening like diamond chips.

'Eges. Don't breathe,' said Rast. She tucked the spray away and made hand signals to Latourn and Catchut on the other side of the opening. They felt in their belts and brought out skin masks. Rast pinched her nose while she fumbled for hers.

Jo-Jo followed their cue, holding his breath while he fished in his vest to find one. He guessed the eges acted like tracers if they entered the bloodstream. He didn't let out his breath until his skin was tight across his mouth and nose.

They waited, then.

The tension increased until Jo-Jo's desire to stand up and stretch his legs became overwhelming.

Rast frowned at him, sensing his restlessness, and he was forced to admire the mercs' ability to remain absolutely still. He pressed hard against the 'zoon's ribbed wall, trying to divert his senses away from his aching, oxygen-deprived legs.

Rast hadn't sprayed the area again but Jo-Jo imagined the eges floating all around him now, measuring, calculating and relaying their data. What was the point in sitting motionless if the Extros could *see* them?

An instant later his question was answered. A spiked

ball-shaped object hurtled in through the egress scale at high speed. It dropped onto the floor, spikes digging into the 'zoon's spongy tissue, and proceeded to spin past Latourn and Catchut and on down the stratum.

'Barb sensor,' whispered Rast through her mask. 'Saw them in the war; analyses on the run. Once it's finished with the floor, it'll start on the walls. You get in its way, it'll prick holes in you. It's attracted to movement.'

A sweat broke across Jo-Jo's body. 'Will it come back?'

She nodded. 'Time to move.'

She didn't have to signal this time. As she came out of her crouch, Catchut and Latourn were already turning the corner of the rib into the egress hollow. Rast went through the open scale first, semis raised.

Jo-Jo came next, pistol quivering, then the others.

They barrelled through the short connecting junction, straight into a seamless metal chamber. Rast landed on her feet but Jo-Jo tripped and sprawled awkwardly onto his knees.

He got to his feet, nerves buzzed. 'It's sealed everywhere but the junction,' he said, glancing back to the scale. 'No way out or in.'

Rast studied the layout, then pulled out her spray pump and sent a squirt into the air. Nothing glistened.

She slipped her mask down. 'Wouldn't be too sure about that.'

Jo-Jo and the others followed suit.

'Where then?' asked Jo-Jo.

'There, Capo.' Catchut pointed to a high ceiling spot that seemed to be bubbling as though something might erupt. Did erupt; a thin tube at right angles to the surface.

'There's another,' said Lat, pointing somewhere else.

The mercs had automatically fallen into a back-to-back formation, leaving Jo-Jo standing alone.

'Get in here,' Rast ordered him.

Jo-Jo slotted his body between Rast and Catchut. Now there were half a dozen thin tubes pointing at them from different angles in the ceiling.

'Is it gas?' Jo-Jo asked.

'Could be. Extros don't use regular weapons.'

They held that formation for so long that Jo-Jo's legs began to tremble. Again he became desperate to move position.

'Randall?' he grunted.

'Hold,' she said.

He bit his lip and locked his knees.

Then, directly in front of him, a large section of the wall began to bubble. Jo-Jo lifted his pistol, working to keep his aim steady. He watched as the bubble seemed to melt into a set of metallic legs crowned by a shimmering globe where a torso should be. An Extro was in the room with them and the wall was just as suddenly back seamlessly intact.

An arm moulded from the globe and digits sprouted. A face of sorts took shape to the side of the arm: a high, angular forehead and large rolling eyes. The eyes – unnervingly – blinked.

Rast suddenly burst out laughing and dropped her weapons to her side.

To Jo-Jo's astonishment she strode over to the Extro and stopped in front of it, hands on her hips. 'EK, you bastard. Too easy.'

A square mouth-shape formed below the eyes, silver

lips and tongue protruding. 'Our eges identified, Rast Randall. EK was summoned. You brought the substance directly here?'

Randall grinned and Jo-Jo marvelled at how quickly her expression could shift from one thing to another.

'I want to change the terms of my payment. Thought mebbe it was best to discuss in . . . erm . . . person,' said Rast.

'Amusing,' said the Extro. 'Now explain better.'

'Your Host-species have abducted a woman in my protection. I want her back. That's my price for the payload.'

'Tone is demanding. Do not respond to humanesque imperatives.'

'I'm speaking this way because I'm pissed, EK. But I guess you don't know what that *feels* like.'

'Understanding of the Post-Species is limited. Advise against drawing comparisons.'

'Whatever. I have the substance and I want the woman back. Simple stuff.'

'No knowledge of her.'

'Thought you kept an eye on what the Host-species are up to.'

'Much to be observant of currently.'

Rast frowned. 'Yeah. We noticed. What's with all the traffic?'

Most of the Extro's face and its digits melted away, leaving only the protruding arm stub and lips; the globe shivered with fluidity. 'Identify the humanesque.'

'Her name is Mira Fedor, an aristocrat from the border world Araldis. We were together on Rho Junction and a bunch of flippered jellyfish abducted her.'

'Siphonophores.'

'Yeah.'

The Extro fell silent for a time. So long that Rast squatted down where she was and pulled some chewing-stim from one of her pockets.

Once more Catchut and Latourn followed her lead, though they sat behind her, their eyes roving and hands close to their weapons.

Jo-Jo noticed the dark sweat stains on Latourn's jacket and how his hair stuck to his scalp, and how his tongue worked constantly in his cheeks. Of them all, he seemed the most unnerved by the presence of the Extro. Catchut seemed more comfortable; hands steady enough and eyes darting about in cool appraisal.

Jo-Jo found himself sympathising with Latourn. He'd seen Extros before – hell, Rho Junction had been overrun with them – but not this kind. Something about the fluidity and the peculiar smell exuding from it made Jo-Jo's mouth dry.

More importantly though, how the hell did Rast Randall know it? She'd fought in the front line of the Stain Wars. That's what Lasper Farr had said, and she'd confirmed it later in their conversations aboard the 'zoon. But her manner, here, now, was too damn friendly for someone dealing with the enemy.

The merc leader turned to stare at him, as if guessing what he was thinking.

They locked glances for a long moment.

'I bought some cryoprotectant on Intel station. Landhurst runs illegal trade in it. I was supposed to deliver them to a contact. Things didn't quite work out that way. Then we end up here. Opportunity.'

'How do you know *it*?' Jo-Jo nodded towards the silent arm nub and lips of the Extro.

'You can't just know one of them. They're not like that. They just do it – appear that way – to make us more comfortable. I jus' gave EK a name so I didn't feel like I was talking to a million Extros at once.'

'So you've been trading with the Extros while you're working for both Farr and the Latinos?'

She scowled at him. 'I told you when we met. I'm nobody's bitch. I earn where I choose and so does my crew.'

Catchut nodded his agreement but Latourn looked uneasy.

Jo-Jo wanted to wrap his hands around Rast's throat and choke the life out of her. Her greediness had meant she'd left Mira and Bethany vulnerable.

And yet, if he were honest, his lifestyle resembled Rast's in so many ways: the same self-absorption but without the killing.

Until now. Now he couldn't think of anyone or anything other than Mira Fedor and the slight bulge of her newly pregnant belly. *There.* He'd allowed the thought into his consciousness. Was she really pregnant or had he just imagined it?

'The League of Sentient Species has signalled aggressive intentions towards the Post-Species,' said EK unexpectedly.

'What do you mean?' Rast stayed in her crouched position but Jo-Jo saw her muscles tense. '*Where* do you mean?'

Vibrations emanated across the chamber.

'Sounds like the whale's getting ready to blow, Capo,'

said Catchut. One hand had moved to his utility belt, where with deft fingers he eased open one pouch.

It took Jo-Jo a moment to realise he meant the 'zoon.

Rast came out of her crouch in a slow, controlled manner. 'Wouldn't do for us not to be there, Cat.'

'I'm thinkin' the same, Capo – under the circumstances.'

The hair on Jo-Jo's body began to prickle. His muscles bunched, ready to move quickly.

At the same instant the three mercenaries slid their face skins back into position. Jo-Jo copied them as Catchut flicked a grenade of sorts from his pouch. It should have skittered across the floor to the Extro but on first bounce it disappeared into the floor surface. The texture of the whole chamber seemed to have changed. It was no longer metallic.

'Remove all your weapons and place them at your feet,' said the Extro.

Catchut stared at the spot his small explosive had vanished.

'Do as it says,' Rast instructed.

'Capo?' Latourn's voice was tinged with uncertainty.

'Whole chamber we're in is an Extro, Lat. You wanna be goin' where your grenade just went?'

'No, Capo.' The hulky man began unbuckling his gear.

Jo-Jo felt a rising conviction. One thing he knew for sure, he wasn't going meekly into captivity again. Especially not in this place.

He glanced across at the junction. The egress scale was still open. Could he make it before the floor, or the wall, or the *Extro* reached out and sucked him away?

'Josef.' Rast's warning to him was clear.

'A jail's a jail, Randall. Not going back into one.'

'Who says that's where you're going?' she said reasonably. 'Might be that EK here wants to entertain us. Be the smart thing to do. Seeing as I've got all that cryo on board. Be an awful lot of disappointment if we told the 'zoon not to let them have it.'

Pretending she had control over the 'zoon was about the only thing Rast had up her sleeve. A small amount of cryo went a long way in Extro land from what Jo-Jo'd heard.

Rast's caution didn't stop Jo-Jo from taking a step backward though; or trying to, at least. But his damn boots stuck to the floor. The fear that had been gathering in his stomach sent panic messages to his limbs. He reached down and frantically scrabbled with his boot buckles.

'Don't take your feet out.' Rast gestured to stop him. 'You'll—'

A noise erupted from inside the 'zoon; a terrible groaning that drowned Rast out. An object shot through the junction as if thrown, and stopped near Catchut's feet.

Jo-Jo barely recognised the object that had spun past them earlier to sample the 'zoon's internals. Now it was coated with biozoon tissue and a thick, stinking mucus.

''Zoon's pissed,' muttered Latourn.

Jo-Jo glanced at the junction. *Insignia*'s start-up hum sent another vibration through the chamber. A fine shimmer of skin appeared across the connection junction between them and the 'zoon; a second skin growing to replace the soon-to-be-torn egress scale.

'She's blowin', Capo,' said Catchut.

Rast's expression cracked for an instant and Jo-Jo glimpsed her terror. It matched his. Then he lost all thought save the one that told him to stay with the 'zoon. Lifting his feet out of his boots, he gave one huge leap towards the junction – and fell short. The moment his feet touched the chamber surface he stuck. He fell forward and tried to crawl the last distance but his hands and elbows adhered as firmly to the floor as his feet.

Insignia's hum became something higher and stronger and a groaning tear deafened them all.

Jo-Jo craned his neck upwards to the junction. The old egress scale was still in place, a thin layer between them and the blackness, but *Insignia* had gone.

Sole

need'm that one, need'm luscious
creature find'm, bring'm
me

MIRA

Mira ran.

Wanton called out directions that took her branching down what seemed like random tributaries between the featureless plumes of Hue. The sandy terrain remained flat and firm enough for her to keep her pace for a while, but soon enough she had to stop and rest. And then sooner again. Eventually the periods of running shortened until she was back to walking.

The spreading black fertiliser kept pace with them, staining the sand in every direction. On the occasions she allowed herself a backward glance, the land had become curving dark stripes.

'The humanesque form is more limited than Wanton thought,' it commented.

'I am pregnant,' Mira snapped. Right now she could feel the drag and the ache it caused around her lower belly, and her spirits lowered with the fatigue. She did not bother to add that she was neither trained for, nor used to, extreme physical demands.

'Take the next tributary to your right side. The mamelon will be partway along. Please hurry.'

'I cannot,' said Mira. 'My body . . . cannot.'

But as she spoke the words she felt a light cooling spray of moisture on her face. She licked her lips. *Water.*

The spray grew steadily stronger.

'Mira-fedor!' Wanton's tone had changed from command to plea.

She glanced around. In an odd trick of perspective, the spray seemed to be emanating from the featureless Hue almost as though the nutrient wall had begun to leak; like rain falling from a cloudless sky – sideways. Within seconds the spray had increased into a steady side flow and then a gush. Water began to pound into the channel of sand from both sides.

Mira's exhaustion evaporated in a rush of adrenalin and she bundled her shift above her knees so she could lift them.

She ran for three lives. Hers, and her baby's, and that of the Post-Species creature that clung to her neck making concerned noises. The detention skins she wore on her feet had almost entirely disintegrated as she veered into the tributary that contained the mamelon, but she barely felt their raw tenderness.

She saw it almost straight away – a welcome mound of grey and brown boulders, rolled atop each other, towering high above the sandy floor.

Water from the sprays was beginning to puddle around her feet, turning the sand to mud and slowing her progress. Her breath rasped so hard in her chest that she could barely feel any intake of air – only the constant burning.

Several times she slid and fell.

A sound built in around her; a dull roar. She thought it to be the sound of her heart pounding to meet its body's demands until Wanton exclaimed, 'Mira-fedor. The flood! The flood!'

She looked over her shoulder. At the mouth of the

tributary she was in, the sand had assumed a bubbling, golden sheen twirled with black as sheets of water slid towards her.

She ran in complete earnestness now, fearing that the water would rise quickly and she would be swept along in it. But the air had become thick with moisture, making it even harder to breathe.

Wanton stayed silent. Inside her, the baby lay still as well. Dimly, she sensed it curling and bunching as if running with her.

She reached the lower boulders of the mamelon as the water swirled at her ankles. As she tried to climb one of the smaller boulders, she grazed her knees and forearms and fell back. Blood dripped into the circling water. Survival instinct got her clambering around to the far side of the rocks where they rested against each other in a more staggered arrangement. She managed to wedge herself between two of them and force her way off the ground.

It took intolerable effort, and too much time. The water had already caught up and was lapping at her feet again. Soon it would cover the lower boulders.

How much higher will it rise then?

She continued to climb, careless of the dreadful stinging from the layer of tiny barnacle shells that still clung stubbornly to the rock from previous floods. But her muscles struggled to sustain the demands on them and a sudden weakness assailed her limbs.

Climb, she told herself. *Climb or drown.*

She was sobbing, and couldn't stop, wasting precious energy.

Innate.

Insignia! Mira's heart thumped.

Your distress is strong.

Mira wanted to cry out for the sheer joy of hearing the biozoon in her mind again but the water surged up over her knees now, buffeting her. *Help me*, Insignia. *Find me. Please.*

I have located your whereabouts. Insignia sounded perturbed, angry even. *You have a rider.*

For a second Mira could not think what the biozoon meant.

A parasite taps your energies, Insignia explained.

You mean the baby.

No. Another.

W-Wanton. A-a Post-Species. I'm carrying it at my neck.

Remove it.

I c-cannot.

You must, or you will die before I reach you.

The link between them began to diminish. Insignia! *No!*

She reached to her neck. Wanton's outer casing was slick with moisture and prickly as it resisted her touch.

Mira withdrew her fingers from it. *Insignia* had never lied to her. At worst it had chosen not to answer her, but never, *never*, had it distorted the truth. *Insignia* did not care to protect others' sensibilities.

She grasped the Extro and wrenched it from her skin, tossing it up on top of a higher boulder.

Immediately some of the weakness left her body. With renewed energy she searched for a crevice in which to wedge her feet. Using it as leverage again, she forced her torso upward until she was able to flop backwards onto the top of the rock, alongside Wanton.

Rolling onto her side, she scooped up the Extro and knotted it into a section of her torn robe. Then she began to scramble higher, finding better hand and footholds on the dry boulders above.

The water slapped and frothed around the base rocks but she kept her eyes on her ascent, willing *Insignia* to hear her – to find her. But the climb exhausted her remaining energy, and she collapsed on a ledge just short of the summit. For a time she heard and saw nothing.

'Mira-fedor?'

Wanton's thin voice eventually drew her back.

And the baby. One sudden and intense movement that brought her, gasping, to an upright position, gripping her abdomen.

'Stop. Stop!' she pleaded, hunching over.

'What is it, Mira-fedor?'

As the wave of pain abated, Mira's breathing slowed and she raised her head to gaze at the flood. The water had risen to swirl only a body length below her, gushing around and over the larger part of the mamelon. She moved onto her knees to see better and elongate her tender abdomen. Further out, the desert tributary she had run along to reach here had transformed into a fast-moving river shaped and fed from the nutrient walls.

And yet something even stranger revealed itself from the vantage of height. While at ground level the Hue had seemed endless and seamless with the sky or the *not-sky*, but from here, looking down, Mira could see a dimpled surface – a roof – that looked like buttons pressed hard into an overfull cushion. 'What are they?'

'Please, Mira-fedor, Wanton cannot interpret data from this position.'

Mira fumbled for the knot in her wet gown. With clumsy fingers she untied it and let the Extro drop onto her palm. She raised it to eye level, holding her hand flat.

'You told me that if I carried you, you would take nothing from me, but you drained my system. I almost drowned.' There was no heat in her accusation – she didn't have the energy for it – but she made her mistrust plain. If she wanted to, she could toss the creature away into the rushing water below. It would survive, no doubt, but she would be free of it.

'Wanton took only the smallest amount for nutrition requirements. Nothing that would interfere with your own functions,' it protested.

'But when I removed you I felt my strength return.'

'Wanton is not sure why that would be.'

The Extro sounded genuine enough but how could one ever know with such a creature? 'Are you misleading me?'

'That concept is confusing.'

'Confusing!' Mira climbed to her feet. Emotion trickled into her belly. 'You pick and choose when you wish to understand me, Wanton. *That* is lying. *That* is misleading. Now tell me what those circular objects on the surface are.'

She held her arm outstretched and trembling. It would be so simple to tilt her palm and . . .

Mira.

Insignia*!*

I am closer. I have located you but it is an uncommon habitat.

It's a planet, I think. Covered by a substance they call the Hue. They live inside it and draw raw materials from the earth outside. The planet is in flood, for regeneration, and I am stranded above the waterline. Her thoughts tumbled out. *How far away are you? Are you alone?*

Some of the humanesques travelled with me to Extropy space. But circumstance has dictated that they are no longer aboard.

Circumstance? Are they alive? Thales Berniere?

I was forced to leave Rho Junction in haste to keep close to our mind-bond. The scholar and Bethany Ionil did not return in time.

Then who travelled with you?

The mercenaries.

Rast, Latourn and Catchut?

Yes.

That is all?

The God Discoverer as well.

Josef Rasterovich? Mira felt a mild disappointment that Thales was not among them.

'Mira-fedor.' Wanton unknowingly interrupted her dialogue.

'Si.'

'It is possible that you are correct. Your energy was indeed drained from you.'

'What do you mean?' Mira refocused her attention. The water level was still rising. Would it reach them even at this height?

'Wanton has discovered something.'

'What?' she cried impatiently. 'What is it?'

'There are subtleties amongst the Post-Species. Wanton's kind chose to live as individual beings, with individual hosts linked by the Hue. Non-corporeal Post-Species are different. They *are* the Hue.'

Mira felt a little surge of desperation. 'What do you mean?'

'Once Wanton left the Hue, there should have been no commonality with others of my kind.'

'But there is?'

'Wanton has run a self-analysis of its inner self. A hidden portion of its core is responsible for the drain on Mira-fedor's energy. Wanton suspects that the portion is still connected to the Hue.'

'How? No, wait . . . tell me quickly . . . what does that mean for us?'

'Wanton means that any of his kind may select information from the Hue about Wanton's location, at any time.'

'They know where we are.'

'Yes.'

'Will they come after us? You said they never leave the Hue.'

'They do leave the Hue. Mira-fedor has seen them on Rho Junction. However, ordinary Hosts do not go into the Bare World.'

'And with the flood, surely they would not risk—'

'Wanton is not sure. Mira-fedor's importance to the Hue is significant.'

'Why, Wanton?' She stopped short of closing her fist on the Extro and shaking it. 'For Cruxsakes, tell me the truth.'

'Host bodies regularly suffer degradation. Your Innate DNA is much more resilient and sustainable. It is my kind's desire to reproduce it.'

Again. Again. They sought it as the Principe Franco had. Her talent had become more burden than gift. 'But you said they were studying my child?'

'It is logical, then, that Mira-fedor's child will have a similar talent. Possibly even more refined, and stronger.'

'And does it?'

'The study was not completed.'

Mira?

Insignia. *Si?*

I sense your distraction.

The Extro in my company says its kind wish to copy my Innate compatibility. Their Hosts degrade and die. I am more resilient.

Even over distance Mira felt *Insignia*'s disapproval.

It is not for another kind to take what is unique to ours.

I agree, but it is not the first time a species has tried to steal from another.

It is more than theft. It is – to use your humanesque term – cannibalism.

'Mira-fedor. I think we are no longer safe,' said Wanton.

Mira shifted focus to Wanton again. 'Safe?' The word cracked from her throat. It had been so long since she'd been safe, she could no longer remember the associated feelings. The impulse to toss the creature into the water returned, what with its weird naivety and frustrating manner. And yet it had shown her a form of kindness; given her opportunity to escape.

She lifted her gaze to the strange, cushioned roof of the Hue and saw the reason for Wanton's concern. In the distance – hard to judge how far – several of the buttons had lifted and objects flew free from them.

'Aves,' said Wanton. '*Unvogel* most probably.'

'Extinct birds?'

'Extinction is an obsolete concept.'

Mira squinted to make out the size of the rising Aves. As large, she thought, as the Air Vehicles on Araldis. 'Are they Hosts?'

'Yes,' said Wanton. 'They are the equivalent of our soldier class. We are self-regulating within our own society but it is sometimes necessary to manage external problems.'

'Si, I have seen your self-regulation.' *Insignia?*

Yes, Mira.

Help us. Now!

THALES

Thales wandered aimlessly around the main recreation chamber. The Trade Fest was finished and only the stallholders remained, dismantling their displays and packing. Metal swarfs and leaflets and food scraps intermingled to create a carpet of litter and Au-cleaners scurried about sifting the debris into the funnels of their disposal units.

He could not put a name to his inner turmoil: disgust, frustration, anger, resentment, longing. So many conflicting emotions that one couldn't be singled out from the others.

'May I help you, Msr?' The Lamin on the information booth straightened from where it had been crouched, folding pan-films into a case.

Thales shook his head, unable to muster polite conversation.

The Lamin regarded him with a shrewd look. It trotted over to its table and snatched up a small poster streaming advertising. 'As my last visitor I would like to offer you a special diversion treatment with a new company on Edo called Ardour. Their clients are spread across many worlds. They cater to a wide variety of tastes, sir, and I'm told, are exceptionally good.'

As Thales touched the poster he felt the faint tingle

of something soaking into his skin. *Sensory Manipulative* – Sen-Man – advertising was banned on Scolar.

He nodded and moved away from the booth. Once out of the Lamin's sight he tried to throw the poster away but it stuck to his fingers. Embarrassed by the lewdness of the images streaming on it, he shoved it into his coat pocket and headed back to the taxi rank.

He had no idea where to go now. He knew no one here, other than Bethany, Lasper Farr and Tekton. Perhaps he should attempt to find a way into Farr's laboratory? Or leave? But how would he pay his fare? Where would he travel to? Was his face healed enough to travel safely?

Amid the confusion of thoughts, his mind slipped repeatedly to the memory of Bethany, and the Mio slapping her with its fins – the glazed pleasure on her face as its teeth pulled at her skin.

It repulsed him and yet the tiny trickle of desire he'd felt seemed to have seeded, and be growing stronger by the moment. Had she somehow infected him with her sexual sickness? Or had the poster saturated him with aphrodisiacs?

The taxi requested a destination.

'Here.' On impulse he pulled the poster from his pocket and ran it under the scanner.

'Certainly, sir. There will be no charge.'

Thales didn't reply. Taxis did not charge anywhere on Edo. But Commander Farr liked to remind users of the fact. Instead he settled back against the seat and closed his eyes. With slow breaths and a simple counting exercise he tried to reach a meditative state, but the calm wouldn't come to him.

He settled instead for a percolation of memories:
Rene and Villon – anything but Bethany.

'Destination arrival,' said the taxi eventually.

Thales roused himself. It had stopped outside a wall
of storage crates similar to those that Farr had first inter-
viewed them in weeks – or was it months? – before.
The higher ones were accessible by a portable elevator.

As if cued to the taxi, a door opened in one of the
crates and a cream-suited 'esque with long, smooth hair
stepped out. He tapped on the window.

Thales pulled his skin mask up across the damaged
section of his face and told the taxi to lower the window.

'Do you have your invitation?' the suited doorman
asked.

Thales waved it and it flipped out of his hand, no
longer sticky.

The doorman smiled and beckoned.

Thales had a fleeting moment of hesitation. He
needed distraction. No, more than that. He needed to
lose himself.

The first crate was an empty shell with filthy, scarred
plas walls. To his relief the doorman led him straight
through it into another.

The walls of this one – a waiting room of sorts – were
blue-tinted and covered in screens running intimate
shots of naked humanesques and aliens engaged in
explicit sex acts. The images were so enlarged that
Thales took refuge in their distortion.

'Wait here. Your entertainer will come for you.' The
doorman pointed to the row of seats.

Thales sat nervously on one, avoiding eye contact
with the other patrons. He sensed their curiosity at his

diffidence. But even the floor was a screen, and he found himself staring at his own clenched fists. His conscience pricked at him. Was this the answer to his misery?

'Good evening.'

Thales glanced up.

A beautiful, *beautiful* woman in a close-fitting dress and sharp heels stood looking down at him. Her age was impossible to decipher, but her long silken hair and sombre expression reminded him so much of Rene that he nearly cried aloud.

She saw his reaction. 'Does my appearance offend you? I can summon another.'

Thales blushed. 'N-no,' he reassured her. 'On the contrary. It is mine that offends.' He touched his face. 'My skin . . . I apologise for it. Until recently I was . . .' He trailed off. It would sound ridiculous even to his ears to proclaim his prior handsomeness.

'What is your name?' she asked.

'Thales.'

'Well, Thales-who-wears-a-mask, my name is Aleta, and you've presented with the last of our free VIP services. An exclusive offer. There were only very few available. You must be a valued member of the Commander's community.'

'I'm a visitor. That's all. The Lamin at the information desk gave it to me,' Thales said truthfully.

'How unusual.' Aleta gave the smallest of frowns. 'Our Ardour franchise is new to Edo, and the VIP offer is part of our normal entry deal to a new world. Usually it would go to a select few.' She smiled. 'But you have the ticket, Thales – so you get the experience.'

'Experience?' He began to feel a little uneasy. 'I am merely looking for distraction . . . with a woman.'

'Oh, my sweet young man, you'll get that. Now come.'

She held out her hand; so charming and so sure of herself.

He grasped her fingers without thinking, and she pulled him to his feet. His groin tightened to have her cool, firm grip upon his. He was unused to touching unfamiliar women.

She led him along a corridor that appeared to travel in an arc. Partway along she chose a door to enter – seemingly at random – and ushered him inside.

Thales stepped into another plain, clean, blue-tinted room. But something about its construction told him that it was not built from the refuse like the rest of the station. The walls were a curious malleable material and the floor was dressed with a soft, plush carpet. Two armchairs sat in one corner, and a large smooth, square, sponge-covered platform in the middle of the room. The object was twice as wide as the bed he'd been sharing with Bethany.

Aleta motioned for him to sit in one of the chairs. He did as he was told, noticing a small unopened sachet and a sealed drink tube on the side table next to him.

Instead of joining him she positioned herself close to the platform and pressed down on its surface. A small compartment unfolded and she settled herself onto its bench seat and laid her arms along the arm rests.

'Tell me, Thales, have you experienced Diversion before?'

He shook his head dumbly and wet his lips. 'Is it a . . . substance?'

She gave the same smile as before. 'In a way.' She seemed to be enjoying herself, he thought, as if his naivety amused her. 'Now we must get to know each other, so this can truly be the experience you want . . . and need. Sometimes our visitors find it difficult to talk to a stranger.' The smile again. 'On the table next to you there is small sachet. I encourage you to open it and suck out the gel. It will help us communicate.'

'What is it?' he asked nervously.

'A mild disinhibitor. The active ingredients are listed.'

She waited patiently while Thales fingered the barcode and listened to the chemical composition. The terms meant little enough to him, but he felt better for having gone through the exercise. 'I'll consider it,' he said. 'But not just now.'

Her eyes narrowed slightly. 'Very well, but feel free to enjoy a drink while I ask you some questions. It is important – for the sake of your own enjoyment – that you answer them honestly.'

He nodded and broke the seal on the drink container, supping it down. He'd never imagined that this type of service required conversation. But then he had never really considered what it might require. His physical needs had always been met by his wife, and more recently Bethany. Before Rene there had been studium girls but nothing regular or significant.

'Agreed,' he said.

'Would you be more comfortable removing your mask? I am a professional, Thales. Disfigurement is just another type of beauty to me.'

'No,' he said firmly. 'You may be accustomed to such things, Aleta, but I am still learning to . . . accept it.'

She nodded and leaned back into her compartment. 'Describe your earliest sexual experience.'

The questions flowed from there; some intimate and arousing, and others almost clinical. He managed to speak frankly for the most part and – surprisingly – found himself sharing his deep desire to change himself.

'You wish to take control of your life, Thales.'

He became impassioned at that suggestion. 'Control is supposed to be illusory and yet others seem able to manipulate and coerce me. Is it my naivety, Aleta? What is it that makes me such easy prey?'

'Perhaps it's what you secretly want, Thales. To be commanded. We could explore that idea.'

Thales wasn't sure how to reply to that. 'Just a few hours ago I found my . . . partner with . . .' He could not finish. 'Tell me Aleta, what pleasure can be gained from pain?'

She smiled so serenely that it might have been that he'd asked her to meditate with him. 'Given the right conditions, the two are as one. Perhaps I can show you?'

He shook his head. A light sweat broke over his skin. That was not what he'd meant. But why had he told this beautiful stranger so much about himself? More than he'd told Bethany even? He had refused the dis-inhibitor, and yet words sprang to his lips as if he were a gauche and ingenuous teenager.

The drink! He stared at the empty tube. *I should leave*, he thought, and stood.

'Wait!' she ordered him.

Her imperious tone overcame his volition and his legs folded underneath him. He stared across at her.

The light flickered for an instant, and the plain blue room was superseded by an authentic reproduction of his bedroom on Scolar. Aleta lay on a bed in the centre of the room, where the platform had been.

Thales sat riveted to his chair fighting a wave of emotion. 'Y-your virtual artistry is commendable.'

'It is the best there is, Thales. Come here!' She flicked her hair. It seemed longer, as long as Rene's, and her face seemed to have aged a little. It now showed the fine, beautiful lines of a well-kept older woman. Her beautiful body lay draped in the soft fabric of her attire, which accentuated her hips and caught between her thighs.

He sprang from his chair and approached her. 'How did you do that?' he demanded hoarsely. 'How did you make yourself look like my wife?'

'It is part of the service – understanding what you want most and capturing it.'

'What do you mean by "capturing"?'

'It is obvious that you miss your wife, Thales, in many ways; her love, her interest in you, but mostly you miss her firm hand. She's not just your guide, Thales, she is your Commander. Your Goddess.'

'No. That's . . . ridiculous. We are equals . . . *were* equals, at least.'

Aleta pulled the fabric down from her shoulders, revealing smooth breasts that lay heavily on her chest; larger breasts than Rene's.

Thales had longed at times for Rene's breasts to grow with the fullness of pregnancy, but she had never shown interest in such an idea.

He wetted his lips, unable to tear his eyes from her; so like his wife and yet almost . . . *more* desirable. He tried to reject the notion, but Aleta sat up straight, her expression stern.

'Remove your clothes, Thales.' The tone of her voice spoke to something deep inside him. Not his conscious or rational self, but the child who needed direction.

He stripped obediently out of his borrowed pants and shirt and stood trembling.

She looked him over. 'Sweet and youthful,' she remarked, as if to herself. 'How lovely.' She slid to the edge of the bed and placed her feet on the floor. 'Kneel.'

He dropped between her knees overwhelmed by an eagerness to please her and the need to rest his face against her thighs. The gown barely covered her womanly parts and he breathed her scent. She tugged strands of his hair, murmuring instructions to him and the order in which they would proceed.

His head swirled with anticipation and the stimulation of gentle pain.

Rene had always been directive in their lovemaking, but in a restrained and modest manner. She had never aroused him through talk of what would come.

'It is important,' said Aleta, 'that from now until our time together is over, you call me Mistress or Goddess. Do you understand, Thales?'

'Yes . . . Mistress.' He felt neither foolish nor self-aware. Aleta was as she said, and the relief of acceptance was exquisite.

'Have you been bound before, sweet boy?'

His heart thumped painfully and his throat closed. 'Not for pleasure, M-Mistress,' he managed.

'Then your training has been neglected.' She pulled his face from her lap and looked deeply into his eyes. They were so like his wife's, dark and flecked with character, and yet where he would have seen intelligence and sadness in Rene, Aleta's eyes reflected strength and confidence. She would have what she wanted from him, and he would give it willingly.

'Lie on the bed,' she said.

He did as she asked, marvelling at the softness of the covers and how long it had been since he'd felt luxury. On board *The Last Aesthetic* he'd been too ill to enjoy the fine furnishings.

She slid off the bed and walked around behind his head. Without warning she grasped both of his hands and stretched his arms out. Thales felt something snake around his wrists. He strained to see it.

'The restraints are safe and well-maintained,' she said, in matter-of-fact terms that soothed his alarm. 'You need only request it and they will be removed.'

He nodded, not daring to speak.

She glided around to the foot of the bed, where she repeated the process, spreading his legs wide and securing his ankles.

Satisfied, she lifted her negligee over her head and tossed it aside. A small triangle of material still covered her hairless pubis, and her hair flowed almost long enough to cover her breasts.

She climbed onto the bed and knelt beside him. Taking her time she looked closely at his body. Her fingers began to play lightly over his skin as she examined the contours and hollows. He had never been scrutinised in such a way, and her boldness set his body aflame.

Suddenly, she swung one leg astride his abdomen. Then, with deliberate care, she lifted one heavy breast and placed the swollen nipple close to his mouth. 'We will begin with simple obedience tasks. You will do exactly as I say, the instant I say it. With each failure, Thales, you will receive discipline. Now, open your mouth.'

He did so.

She placed her nipple inside and he instinctively closed his lips around it, sucking in its flavour and texture.

A moment later pain lit across his legs and groin, making him jerk like a puppet. Aleta sat up, letting her breast swing free, and lifted her free hand before his face, administering tiny electric shocks from the cylindrical device with the other.

'I did not tell you to do more than open your mouth. Are you not able to take simple instructions? If not, then you shall receive punishment from this.'

Despite the receding pain and his general discomfort, her tone excited him beyond belief.

'I-I didn't understand what you w-wanted,' he stuttered.

She took his nipple between her nails and pinched it hard. 'What is the correct response?'

His mind froze for a minute, confused by the conflicting sensations. 'I mean, I'm s-sorry M-Mistress.'

'Better.' She released his tender flesh and stroked his cheek. 'Now, we will begin again. Open your mouth.'

She lifted her breast again and positioned the nipple between his lips.

He kept his mouth open, lips drawn back for so long that his jaw began to ache and then quiver.

'You may suck it now,' she said finally.

Gratefully, he let his lips close. The comfort from the taste of her overwhelmed him. He wanted to thank her but dared not stop without her permission.

'Harder,' she said.

And then the muscle ache of holding his jaw open was replaced with the muscle ache of sucking.

'Stop. Release me.'

He did as he was told.

She moved her body so that her eyes came close to his. Her pupils were dilated with arousal and he felt glad that he'd pleased her.

'Better, Thales. Now, let us progress.'

After that, he lost track of time. The erotically painful sensations she inflicted upon him began to take over his mind. He sank deeper and deeper into a world of his own until nothing existed other than the stimulation that drowned his body in its own endorphins.

He flinched when Aleta first took her glass-handled whip to his thighs and arms but within a few strokes the hurting became a pleasure he could hardly bear.

She chose that moment to stop and sit astride his thighs. With confident movements she began to ride him, whipping across his legs with one hand and administering tiny electric shocks with the other.

The combination sent him towards climax but she saw, and slowed, speaking sternly to him again.

'Control yourself, young man. You will wait until you are told.'

He heard her and tried valiantly to obey her, but

the pressure in his groin had built beyond anything he had ever felt before. With shouts of ecstasy, he thrust upward into her, only dimly aware of her satisfied smile.

Afterwards, she released his bonds and lay next to him. Thales rolled on his side, curling against her. He had never felt such peace. Never been so whole. His body felt awash with happiness.

Aleta lay with him for a time in silence. Then, as if an internal timer had alerted her, she got up and slipped on her gown.

'You are permitted some extra time to wash and dress. The valet will see you out. Please feel free to recommend my services,' she said.

Thales sat up. 'Aleta,' he said hoarsely. 'Please . . . I must see you again.'

She smiled, soft and gracious. 'That would be lovely, Thales. But be warned, I am very expensive.'

'No . . . I mean . . . outside this . . .' He waved his hands, not knowing how to express himself.

The sweetness left her face, and her expression hardened. She clicked her fingers and the doorman appeared so quickly that Thales wondered if he'd been in the room somewhere.

In the moments that it took him to locate his clothes on the floor, Aleta had gone.

The doorman folded his arms. 'You have six minutes remaining. If you exceed the time limit, you will be charged.'

Embarrassed and angry, Thales quickly pulled his clothes on.

The valet showed him back along the arcing corridor

and out into the first waiting room, where a fresh load of clients waited with anticipation.

Aleta entered through another door.

He raised his hand in greeting but she walked past him without acknowledgement – without noticing him at all – and approached an older man with thick features and only a little hair.

She knelt before the man and laid her cheek against his knee in the way she had schooled Thales to do only a short time before.

Unable to contain his disgust, Thales walked out the door.

TEKTON

The Lamin did not offer to help Tekton from the floor. In fact it had already seated itself and was grooming its armpits.

Tekton got to his feet, drawing on a lifetime of aplomb to preserve his dignity. Not that anyone was watching him. In fact the Lamin and he were the only ones in the unimposing, strangely appointed prayer room.

Tekton looked around.

It was not a spiritually imbued place, in the manner of the millions of chapels spread across Orion, and neither did it have the usual other-worldly sense of quiet and eeriness. The decor suited a comfortable lounge that might be found on any moderately luxurious passenger ship. In fact, if not for the different colour schemes and unusual icons impregnating the suede walls, it could have been an exact replica of a lounge on *The Last Aesthetic*. Perhaps the whole room had been retrieved from a disbanded passenger ship?

Two long bench seats ran the length of the room divided by an equally long, low table which ended in front of a shrine. Ledges were inset into the padded walls behind the seats, and dotted with statues and objets d'art; almost as if the icons were set there to peer over the shoulders of those that sat reclining. Beautifully crafted melon-coloured matting softened the floor beneath his feet.

Tekton made his way past the Lamin to sit at the far end of one bench seat, near the shrine. The simply moulded, geometric shrine alcove housed a square black box. He bent his head and went through the pretence of prayer while he gave the box a subtle but intense scrutiny.

Despite his best efforts, he deduced absolutely nothing from it – why would Farr worship a box? – and widened his observation to include the rest of the room. For the most part, the furnishings seemed wholly at odds with Farr's personality: far too comfortable and culturally opulent.

And yet, Tekton knew that somewhere in here lay a clue to Farr's *raison d'être*. The man was deceptive. Everything about his nature, including his choice to live on the floating surface of, this constructed monstrosity called Edo, bespoke his desire to mislead.

Farr had played a spiteful mind game sending Tekton along that dangerous route here, and in mind games the player always left clues.

What secrets lurked within this odd prayer room?

Abandoning his discretion, he got up from the seat and walked a slow circuit, examining every fixed and hanging object: an eclectic mix that included a Trimium fertility goddess that looked to be sculpted from dried mucus, and a Rainbow Orbital blossoming and fading in a never-ending sequence. Tekton noted the combination of organic and astrophysical artworks.

Curious.

While he conducted his examinations, the Lamin stayed in its seat, sitting bolt upright, with knees primly crossed.

Tekton imagined it was reporting back to Farr via the mayordomo, moud or some other subvocal conduit. That notion didn't faze him. Farr wanted Tekton to play the game, or he would never have allowed him access to his private chapel.

Godhead, interrupted his moud, *you are required at the departure dock shortly.*

Hooray! crowed his free-mind. *Let's go home.*

Tekton was inclined to follow free-mind's lead. The prayer space, which he'd expected to be lofty and grand, had turned out to be oppressive – and sinister.

Sinister? queried logic-mind. *How so?*

Free-mind sought another manner of description. *It's creepy. Let's go.*

But logic-mind became stubborn. *No. Find the clue first. This is important.*

But Tekton was still siding with free-mind. Edo had become as tiresome – and if he admitted the truth, as alarming – as Commander Farr. His earlier akula rush at the ever-present sense of danger that surrounded Farr had truly begun to fade. The man was insane.

He approached the Lamin. 'I require a taxi to convey me to the departure lounge.'

The Lamin took a moment to reply while it checked in with its employer.

'Commander Farr is delighted to provide transport for you to the docks. He conveys his wishes for your speedy return to Belle-Monde. His associate there tells him the food is very good.'

His associate? 'And who would that be?' asked Tekton sharply.

'That is all the Commander wishes to say to you.'

Tekton wanted to spit with rage. Farr was taunting him with obscure hints. 'Call the taxi now. I wish to leave immediately.'

The Lamin stood up and pattered towards the exit, where it cracked the door open and peered out. 'I will inform you when it has arrived.'

Tekton nodded. He took one last sweep of the room, compartmentalising his anger so he could observe through dispassionate eyes. His gaze lingered on the shrine. What in Sole's name was significant about a black box? Was it a projector, perhaps? Or a Babushka? Or even a compression chamber of sorts?

'Lamin?' he said imperiously. 'How do you activate the shrine?'

The Lamin hesitated. 'Commander Farr says that with your intellect you should be able to work that out.'

Tekton wanted to gnash his teeth with frustration. So that's what this was, a game of superior intellect. Tekton hated to lose at anything; a family trait that his cousin Ra had taken to the worst of extremes. It seemed that Commander Farr enjoyed the same competitive attribute. His free-mind took a moment to consider Ra and Commander Farr. Their collective competitive natures gave Tekton a shiver.

Concentrate! barked logic-mind.

Tekton tried to broaden his perception of the box in relation to the figurines. It bore no comparison to the organics, but it was not unlike the Rainbow Orbital, which grew and faded over the top of its projector casing.

If the black box was also a projector of sorts, then it would likely need aural or kinaesthetic activation.

Aural, said logic-mind.

Tekton thought back over his most recent conversation with the Commander. Farr had emphasised several things. If he had more time, he could ask his moud to replay the entire conversation, but as it was . . .

'Visiting Lostol, your taxi is here.'

'Tell it to wait a moment.'

'Detrivores are very active at present. The taxi will not be able to stay grounded for too long.'

'Just a few damn minutes,' snapped Tekton. *Moud, search my last conversation with Commander Farr. Replay any verbal emphasis.*

Yes, Godhead.

Tekton listened intently then chose one word of the twenty search items. 'Shame.'

The black box remained inanimate.

'Visiting Lostol, the taxi has detected a circling detrivore. It must leave.'

'Why? There's no driver, is there?'

'Taxis have a proximity detector. Detrivores have been known to try and eat them. It is very costly.'

'Costly!' snapped Tekton. He walked quickly towards the door, listening as his moud repeated the list of Farr's emphasised words. When he peered out, the taxi was beginning to lift.

'Stop it!' he roared.

'I will try,' sniffed the Lamin. 'It is centrally programmed.'

A word from the moud's list jumped out at him, as Tekton gave one last glance into the chapel.

Balance. It seemed right, somehow. 'Balance!' he shouted.

Across the room in the shrine, an image sprang alive inside the box, in what he'd thought to be a solid interior. From where he stood it looked like a swirl of colour – nothing more.

Capture that image, he ordered his moud.

Yes, Godhead. It is captured.

Tekton turned and ran the short distance across the platform to the taxi. He flung himself inside, banging his leg against the edge of the door. It tore a gash in his thin skin. Blood streamed from the wound as the taxi lifted and pitched wildly into the abyss.

Tekton seized the handgrips and clung to them, unable to secure his seat belt while the taxi rolled and dived. The proximity alarm began to blare. Then a detrivore crashed into the taxi's underbelly. Tekton felt the shudder up through his feet; saw the dent appear like the hump from a small earthquake.

'Lift,' Tekton shouted at the automon.

But the detrivore buffeted the taxi again, this time from the side. A web of cracks appeared in the shatter-proof window. The vehicle swayed from side to side of the abyss. Tekton glimpsed struts and pylons and girders dangerously close.

'Farr!' Tekton screamed. 'Lasper Farr!'

But Lasper Farr did not appear to allay his terror.

His minds split apart under the pressure, leaving nothing to bridge the gap between them.

Free-mind was caught in the grip of bowel-evacuating fear.

But logic-mind was still making decisions. *Moud, imprint the image from the shrine on my cerebral cortex.*

May I enquire as to why you require a hard download, Godhead? the moud asked. *My function and archives are entirely transferable to your next moud.*

Do it, growled logic-mind.

A second detrivore had joined the first, ramming the small fibreplas bump under the nose of the vehicle that housed the navigation controls. The taxi began to spiral down.

Free-mind's screaming intensified.

Logic-mind held back from chiding it about a sense of dignity or courage, and settled in to observe the changes in Tekton's metabolism. Even akula had not brought such heightened responses. It also diverted some processing time to inspect the downloaded image from the shrine.

Tekton was too paralysed by free-mind to instruct the moud to identify it, so logic-mind referred to Tekton's own memory banks for a clue.

Of course, logic-mind said, after a time.

Of course fucking what? bellowed free-mind. *I'm about to die.*

It's a representation of a strange attractor. A Lorenz *strange attractor, to be exact.*

Exact? Exact? You're insane. Can't you see what's happening? free-mind shrieked back.

Why would Farr worship a strange attractor? logic-mind

pondered. *Is Farr's god an ancient theory on the behaviour of dynamical systems? And if so, in what current context is that significant?*

Tekton's moud-bolstered data recall was not sufficient for logic-mind to research anything. And frankly, free-mind was making it difficult to get sufficient blood to required areas.

The taxi was surrounded. The detrivores had stopped buffeting it and had latched on to different parts, spraying it with their metal-dissolving saliva as they prepared to feast.

Tekton, sobbing now, regained some thought control and tried to employ logic-mind to find a solution to his impending death. But it remained stubbornly resistant and preoccupied.

Chaos theory. Prediction. Prediction. Balance. Logic-mind reflected on a range of concepts. *Balance*, Farr had emphasised. *Balance* had unlocked his shrine. *Balance.*

Then it became quite excited. Farr must have some device for prediction that could help him keep the balance. It was the only explanation.

Got it! logic-mind announced.

Too frigging late, free-mind whispered.

Tekton heard a hissing noise like hot metal plunged into water and a cold shaft of wind blew straight up between his legs.

He glanced down. The slick, insectile head of a detrivore poked up through a melted gap in the floor. He screamed and kicked at it, but the detrivore's carapace snagged into the sole of his shoe and tore it from the upper. Another shaft of wind. Its wings unfolded through the crack.

Jump, ordered logic-mind.

What in—? But free-mind didn't get to finish.

Jump! logic-mind insisted.

Then the floor gave way, and he and the detrivore fell free from each other.

JO-JO RASTEROVICH

Jo-Jo was alive. Conscious. That much he knew.

That was *all* he knew. Other than that his head felt weird; full of a kind of buzzing that wasn't painful yet but might be, like the beginning of a narc hangover right before you got the headache.

He tried shifting his limbs.

He felt unconstrained, sort of . . . but he had no sense of movement. Or vision. His eyes were open, he thought, but he saw nothing.

Smell? No. Crap. What? He remembered that he'd run for the egress scale and the floor had trapped him like an insect fallen in something sticky. Then nothing . . .

A flash of fear informed him that his brain chemistry remained the same. He wondered if he was in the floor of the chamber, subsumed into the Extro the same way the grenade had been.

The idea of it made him want to puke, if only he knew where his mouth was. He tried licking his lips but sensation eluded him.

The sense-deprivation caused his mind to fracture: one thought stream devoted solely to worrying while another began reasoning furiously.

The-Extro-had-formed-out-of-the-chamber-wall-So-if-I've-been-eaten-by-the-same-chamber-then-it's-likely-that-it's-a-part-of-something-larger-Maybe-the-

whole-damn-drum-is-an-extro-the-size-of-a-space-
station-How-fucking-scary-is-that-But-does-that-mean-
a-single-consciousness?-or-many?-or-something-else—

The frantic thoughts were interrupted by the intru-
sion of a loud buzzing in his head. It sounded like an
appliance about to run out of energy, a noisy, dysfunctional sound designed to grab the consumer's attention.

You've-got-mine, he told the buzzing. *Fuck-all-else-to-
do-when-you-can't-even-feel-your-dick.*

A mournful thought, that one.

He grappled to mend the split in his conscious
thought by pooling all his concentration towards the
sound. It seemed to get louder as he gave it his full
attention. After a time – who knows how long really,
maybe no time? – the buzz turned into a wider sound.
Now it was more like the random intonations of
someone jackassing with their voice through an
amplifier.

Moooooawwwwwooooooooaaaaa

The jackassing was worse than the buzz and Jo-Jo
listened harder, hoping that it might transform again.

The next change came without warning: a sudden
plunge from amplified wail into the clamour of voices,
thousands, millions of them. He wanted to clamp his
hands to his ears – if he could find his ears.

Shut up, he mind-screamed.

Obligingly, the voices vanished but the buzz came
back, louder now, as if he'd somehow sensitised to it.
He tried to think over the top of the noise but the
sound seemed to have seeped into his mind and taken
precedence over anything else.

The buzz and his mind. *In* his mind.

He tried sleeping but his conscious state wouldn't alter. A pressure began to build around his thoughts. The buzz would send him crazy soon.

Again he tried moving his limbs. Nothing. Just the frustration of sensing – hoping – that his body was intact, but no longer his to govern.

His mind sped off again. The-Extro-thing-I'm-stuck-in-must-be-messing-with-my-brain-chemistry-So-why-hasn't-it-suppressed-my-frigging-hearing-too?-This-is-frigging-torture-what-else-could-it-be-for?-Think-Think-Think-unless-the-buzz-is-the-way-in-Shut-the-fuck-up.

But the buzz got louder.

What-do-I-mean-the-way-in?-Maybe-the-buzz-is-a-data-flow?-The-Extro-is-the-data-flow-of-sound-But-I-thought-the-Extro-was-a-drum?-I-don't-fucking-know-Fuck.

Jo-Jo gathered together the pieces of his rapidly dispersing sanity and gave it a go anyway, concentrating on the irritating noise until it broadened and became the jackass sound again.

It slipped from the jackass sound to a clamour of voices more quickly this time; though he had no measure to be sure of that, just an innate sense of time passing. He let his mind adjust to the voice-roar and listened as, occasionally, one voice rose above the rest.

After listening for a while, he caught one of the raised voices and tried to follow the sound back down into the flow. It slipped away from his auditory grasp almost immediately, but he became determined not to give up. Each time the voice peaked he grabbed for it.

Slowly, he began to feel its sense of individuality, timbre and pitch – as if he knew it.

Eventually it pulled away from him, but he floated back to the clamour and waited patiently for it to return.

When it rose from the flow, he was able to attune to it quickly, and the individual voice grew solid. This time his grasp felt sure, and it dragged him through a series of dips and peaks of sound that were speechlike, but not.

Eventually the rise-and-fall nature of it began to smooth and without warning it became a voice that he could clearly comprehend.

'For fuck's sakes, you fucking freaks!' shouted the voice. 'Somebody speak to me!'

Rast Randall, sounding thoroughly rattled. It comforted Jo-Jo to know that the woman felt fear.

'Randall?' He wasn't sure if his lips formed the words or if it was a thought. 'Randall, it's Josef.'

'Rasterovich? Where in fuck's name are you?'

'I don't know. Tell me what happened to you.'

'You made a run for the 'zoon and fell. Then I feel like I'm sinking into the floor. That's it. Next thing I know I'm awake in some kind of suspension. Can't feel any-fucking-thing. Don't even know if I need to piss.'

'I've gotta theory.'

'Shoot me with it.'

'I think we're inside the Extro. You saw it suck up the grenade. I think it did the same to us.'

'You saying we're its lunch?'

'Shit, I dunno. Y'hear the buzz?'

'Yeah it's all I could fucking hear. Till you dropped in.'

'I concentrated on the buzz real hard. For a long time. It started to change. Became more like a crowd. Just a big, big bunch of screaming voices. Nothin' I could understand.'

'And?'

'The sound was worse than the buzz but I kept listenin'. After a while I heard some voices above the rest. Kept trying to follow them. Ended up latching onto yours.'

Randall went quiet.

'Still there, Randall?'

'You telling me we're in some kinda sound machine? And somehow you found me over all those voices screaming?'

'Maybe you were bellowing louder than the rest of them. You gotta better theory?' Jo-Jo wanted to rub his forehead. In fact, he would have given away a body part just to *feel* again.

That was, if he still had body parts to give. What if his flesh didn't exist any more? What if all that was left of his consciousness was this voice and these thoughts? Maybe the Extro had 'evolved' them.

Rast must have been thinking something similar. She began to curse and didn't stop.

'Shut it, would you?' said Jo-Jo eventually.

'If I can swear, I know I'm alive,' she spat back at him.

'Yeah, well, I wouldn't be counting on that. Could be you're just a bad-mouthed bunch of neurons running around on a wave frequency.'

'That doesn't make sense.' She quietened, though. And then she laughed.

The sound made Jo-Jo feel a little better. One thing Randall could always do was laugh.

'So what's your idea? This "acoustic" connection of ours mightn't last,' she said.

He told her in more detail how he'd pursued the frequency of her voice. 'Maybe we can do that for the others. Or at least learn somethin' about this place.'

'That means you have to break contact with me?'

He thought about it. 'I guess so. I can't see how to avoid that.'

'That might be the end of it. You might not get it back.'

She sounded frightened. Rast didn't frighten easily. 'You're right,' he said. 'So maybe there are a few things that need to be said. In case . . . in case one of us finds a way out and the other doesn't.'

The silence went on so long this time that he thought he'd lost his hold on her voice.

'Deal,' she said, finally.

'Some truths, Randall. Not some cocky bullshit.'

'Practise what you preach.'

'I will. Now who do you think your ex-Capo Jancz was working for on Araldis?'

'Josef?'

He heard the softening in her tone. 'What?'

'You think just anyone can hear us?'

'Maybe. We got nothin' to lose though. I mean I don't even know it's you I'm talking to. Could be I'm just having a conflab with my imagination.'

Another short laugh. 'You do a good imitation of me then. Anyway, my thinking is that it's the Extros that wanted the quixite. They're the only ones with enough need to pull that kind of stunt. Figures that Jancz is working for them. He had as much contact with them in the war as I did. Mebbe more.'

'But why do it that way? Why send a bunch of primitive brain-suckers in to fuck the place over?'

'I been chewing that one around for a while. I'm thinking there's got to be more to it than just the quixite. Or mebbe they need the Saqr on the planet for some reason. Fedor might have an idea.'

'Why do you say that?' Jo-Jo felt raw at the mention of her.

'She says she studied alien genera at her studium. She also knows the planet better'n us.'

'You think maybe the 'zoon's found her?'

'Sure left in a hurry. Now, I got a question for you. You said Farr had a DSD. What in Crux is that?'

'You heard of Chaos Theory?'

'Sure, some old conflab to explain something that doesn't need explainin'.'

'Yeah. Whatever. Like I said, he's feeding the DSD with shitloads of info. The process lets him analyse stuff that's going to happen.'

'So what? He's trying to predict the future?'

'Nah. More than that, I think. He's trying to change it.'

'What do you mean?' Rast demanded. 'You sound as crazy as him.'

If Jo-Jo could have felt his eyelids he knew that they'd be closed in concentration. 'I don't know exactly. I've heard it talked about over the years – creating an informed system that can predict all the flow-on effects of behaviour so quickly that you can alter things before they happen. Take a diverging route.'

'Impossible.'

'Should be. Yeah. Until Sole came along. Mostly folk have fantasised about time travel to do such a thing – alter futures, I mean.

Not necessary if you have a Bifurcation Device.'

'So what's this device look like, then? A machine? An organism? Not sure that I'm getting you.'

'I don't know. I saw it work in virtual. It could be anything.'

'So how did he create it?'

'That kinda technology – if it is technology – has gotta come from the Entity.'

'How? One of the tyros?'

'That's what I'm thinking.'

'Tekton?'

'Maybe. Seems coincident he's around.'

'So what now?'

'Let's get the fuck out of here.'

'How?'

'Must be your turn to have an idea.'

Rast chuckled. 'You're all right, you know.'

'Yeah. I am. So what's your idea?'

'Not sure you'll like it.'

'Try me.'

'You know that thing we were keeping to ourselves?'

'What thing?'

'Who you are.'

'What about it?'

'You tell them – maybe they'll pay some attention to you and then you'll get an opportunity.'

'What sort of opportunity?'

'You said one idea.'

'And what are you gonna do while I go off and commit suicide?'

'Try and locate Lat and Catchut – same way as you found me.'

'And?'

'Maybe by then you'll have stirred up enough shit that we can find a crack to slip through.'

'Hummph.' This time Jo-Jo let the silence stretch.

'Josef?'

Jo-Jo was gratified that she sounded nervous again. 'Yeah, well. I can't think of anything better but I ain't rushing into that idea, either. We'll continue this later.'

'Fair enough. Hope to . . . hear you again.'

'Yeah, well, keep shouting and I'll find you.'

Jo-Jo loosened his mental hold on her voice in the way he might relax a flexed muscle, and in a moment he was back in the jackass, and then finally the buzz.

He felt tired. Not a body ache tired – he still couldn't feel a damn thing – but the kind of cloudy sensation that settles on your mind when you've thought too long or too hard. Even the buzz seemed less irritating. He slipped into a kind of numb consciousness that lasted as long as it lasted. Not sleep but something.

When it passed, his mind seemed sharper: the buzz louder.

He thought about Randall's suggestion. If he could in some way let it be known he was the God Discoverer, what would happen? Right now, he wasn't dead but he might as well be – trapped as he was like some frickin' sound bite in this weird auditory jail. What would the Post-Species do with him if they knew he'd been God-touched?

Maybe he'd try to listen in on a few things before he made that call. First thing though, he'd try to find Randall again – just so he knew he could.

He focused on the buzz, and the transition through the jackass sound into the clamour of voices was almost instantaneous this time. He floated above them and waited. The cacophony of noise had its own colour and texture. Not that he could see it, but the sounds created a mind-picture. He let that picture develop into something he could reference: an enormous spinning multicoloured wheel, like the Ferris wheels on the vacation planet Fair.

Jo-Jo's mother had taken him to Fair, once, as a child. He remembered the exotic night landscape of it; the slippery trails of the slider rides and the pounding, pulsing flash of the Sudden Drops. One thing dominated the fairground vista, the fiery little gondolas attached to the gigantic Ferris wheel. The wheel took several hours to complete one revolution, which gave the fair-goers time enough to truly appreciate the scenery. Little food traders buzzed around the gondolas, bringing water and confectionery, and the Park rangers did their own tending to the needs of passengers who'd forgotten to use the amenities before beginning the ride or had been overcome by the breadth of the spectacle.

Jo-Jo never got to ride the wheel – it turned out his mum had brought him there because the latest in her string of lovers was a ride operator. What was his name? Jo-Jo couldn't remember. But the guy had hoisted him on his shoulders and twirled him around and told him stories of how some people never came back from the Big Ride, and others grew old while they were on there, and some changed into ginkos and ate their own tails.

The more he twirled Jo-Jo on his shoulders, the more the gondola lights streamed, until the Big Ride turned into a giant blazing lollipop spinning in an endless twirl of fluorescing colour.

The clamour of voices created the same image for him now. Somewhere in the circling sound vibrations were individual gondolas – unique groups of voices – and maybe within them, single beings.

That's how he'd found Rast.

He listened for her now, concentrating on seeking the intonation and pitch that was unique to her voice.

This time he didn't have to follow it. Once he'd located it peaking out of the flow he instantaneously heard her.

She was shouting his name, over and over.

'No need to bellow,' he said.

'Josef?'

'As far as I know.'

'Thank fucking Crux,' she whispered. 'Being alone in my head with this infernal buzz is sending me nuts. I tried finding Lat and Catchut, but nothing. Just the fucking buzz.'

'I'll try.'

'Don't leave,' she said quickly. 'I mean, I don't know how long it was. I've got no way to mark time but it felt like . . . well too fucking long.'

'Yeah, the time thing is driving me crazy as well.'

'So what's happened?'

'Nothing really. I've been thinking,' said Jo-Jo slowly.

'Lemme fool around for a while; try and locate the others. I found you again real quick.'

'Why's it so easy for you?'

'Not sure, but I got a theory.'

'Tell me about it,' said Rast. 'Anything to make the buzz go away.'

'Back when I found the Entity, I died. At least, I think I did, and my HealthWatch records said the same. Sole did something to me. Split my mind in two when he reanimated me. The same thing happens to the tyros. It's the only way Sole can communicate with them. It's friggin' weird and a pain in the arse but I think it's helping me here. With this freak world.'

'I heard they did something to the tyros – didn't pick that you'd been affected too.'

'The mind split only seems to happen to me when the crap piles up. The tyros are like it all the time, though. You get the feeling you're talkin' to two people.'

'You like that now?' Rast's tone became tense. 'Are there two of you?'

'Don't be fucking stupid. I'll be back soon.'

Jo-Jo let go of Rast's voice and floated back to the clamour. He thought about how Latourn and Catchut sounded. For some reason Latourn's voice seemed easier to remember; the man had the thick, guttural tone common to Latino men. Somewhere in the kaleidoscope of sound Latourn would be suffering the same sensory deprivations as he and Randall. Catchut too. Poor bastards. He didn't like either of the mercenaries but they were humanesque. That meant a lot right now.

He concentrated on recreating Latourn's voice in his

mind and then listened for anything in the clamour that might correlate. Again without a sense of time he had no idea how long it took before he decided he couldn't find Latourn. Instead of returning to Randall though, he grasped the next peaking sound and let it pull him down.

At first the sound made little sense, at best a bunch of slurred vowels, at worst a noise similar to the mooing jackass. Instinctively, Jo-Jo stopped trying to make sense of the whole sound and narrowed his concentration to small segments.

He got a little thrill when he recognised a word. *Soon.* Another. *Hasten.* Then a whole jumble of them fell into his mind. But they weren't ordered. Not that he could tell. More like an anagram or puzzle. He played with the order of them, switching them around until they made some sense.

hasten quixite OLOSS confront

He let go, then, and floated back to the clamour, waiting to pick up another peaking sound. This one took him deep into the flow before he began to hear clearly. Like the previous voice it seemed a blur until he broke it down into smaller pieces. There was something different about this one though. A kind of hard-edged tone that clipped the ends off words.

OLOSS finis soo.

A dialect perhaps? He let go of the clipped sound and found his way back to Rast.

She was crying softly.

'Randall?'

No reply.

Jo-Jo waited while she composed herself. But the

composure didn't come and eventually she tried to talk to him between sobs. 'Can't – take – it.'

Curiously he didn't feel compassion for her, the way he might have for Bethany or Mira Fedor. The connection was there – the humanesque thing – but Rast Randall had made some hard choices in life and now she was living with the result of them.

Like I am.

'Yeah, you can,' he said. 'You have to. No choice.' He waited a bit. 'I didn't find your crew, but I tuned in to something. Not sure what, exactly. Something to do with OLOSS and quixite. Sounds like the Extros are plannin' somethin' soon.'

'Yeah?' The idea seemed to calm her down. 'You mean something's gonna change?'

'Maybe. Sounds like it. I'm gonna go dig a bit deeper, see what else I can hear.'

'Do it!' she said. The strength poured back into her voice.

MIRA

'What do you advise?' Mira asked Wanton.

The Aves had divided into small groups and flown in different directions. One group appeared to be gliding towards the mamelon in widening, shifting circles.

'As Mira-fedor climbed, Wanton observed crevices.'

'Caves?'

'Not large enough to be caves, but depressions. Wanton suggests that Mira-fedor takes cover in one of them.'

Mira peered down at the swirling water. It had steadied. 'I'll carry you in my clothes again so that I can have both hands free,' said Mira.

'It would be more sensible for Mira-fedor to reinstate Wanton's position on her neck.'

'No.' Mira spoke firmly, holding the Extro at eye level. 'Even if you do not wish me harm, it is possible they will reach me through you.'

'That is a reasonable evaluation,' Wanton agreed.

This time she slipped the Extro into the seam of her sleeve and began to climb downwards in a slow, careful spiral. Fatigue made her clumsy and slow.

There was not a lot of exposed rock left and no crevices that she could see.

She peered back out at the pillow surface of the Hue. The Aves grew larger as they closed on the mamelon; three times her size, at least, and distinct enough for her to see the tubular array along the length of their wings.

'What are those things on their wings?'

'Wanton cannot see, but would expect that they are weapons.' Wanton's projected voice was muffled.

'Guns?'

'No.'

Mira began to pick over the rock with renewed urgency, this time tugging at anything that looked loose. Over on the far side of the mamelon, a boulder shifted as she stood on it. Climbing above it, she placed her feet on the top and began to bear down. Using a rocking rhythm she attempted to dislodge it.

It came free without warning, and crashed down into the water below. Caught by the momentum, she slid after it, scraping her side as she clung to the edge of the hole it had left. But the soil came loose in her fingers and she banged into the slippery rock below as she scrabbled to stay out of the water. Her belly bumped cruelly into sharp protrusions.

This time she didn't have the strength left to pull herself higher and she hung there helpless.

Insignia, she cried.

I am close, dear one. Be stro—

But a noise above her filled her mind; a drone that sent a vibration through the rock itself. Water sucked at her clothes, weighing her down. She slipped down into it but as her head was about to dip below the frothing water, something gripped her captive's robe and pulled her back. For a moment her heart lifted.

Insignia?

Coming. I'm coming.

Then she felt the pain of a cruel grip and an Ave towed her into the sky, retracting its legs as it lifted her high above the mamelon.

She glimpsed the water racing along its course beneath her; and then the strange twisting concourses and quilted top of the Hue.

The Ave pulled her close into its belly; so close that she felt the slippery touch of its skin and the wet warmth of its body. The claws that held her were crawling with small insects that jumped onto her and ran inside her robe. She feared slipping as it swung in a sharp sloping turn back towards the place it had entered the Bare World.

Sharp squeals punctuated the flight towards the open button-top in the Hue. The other Aves gathered at its wing tips, all calling out in the same high-pitched noises, until the sound itself left her almost unconscious.

'Mira-fedor! Mira-fedor! What is happening?' Wanton's voice sounded tiny and so distant that she barely registered it.

Mira lifted her sleeve to her mouth and licked dry lips. 'The Ave is taking us back.'

'No, Mira-fedor. We must not—'

She dropped her arm away from her ear so that she couldn't hear the Extro.

'Nothing,' she mouthed at the muddy water below. 'Nothing I can do.'

Hopelessness overwhelmed her. Not even the defiant kicks from the child in her belly gave her strength. She hung, helpless, in the Ave's grasp and closed her eyes as the wind stung her, the squeals struck through her core, and she became numb with the futility of her situation and the exhaustion of a body pushed beyond its endurance.

Whatever it is, let it be quick, she thought.

Mira?

Insignia's voice was stronger in her mind, but even that failed to stir her.

I am here. Do not be frightened, dear one.

Mira didn't answer the biozoon. She was beyond fear now. Beyond feelings. She didn't hear the explosion that punctured the faux sky, or feel the Ave dive towards the roof of the Hue in terror.

She was spared the sight of the biozoon scalding the skin from the creatures that had hunted her down, just as her mind protected itself from her fall to the strange quilted surface when the Ave's claw opened involuntarily with pain; and best of all she did not see the dreadful, dreadful rage that *Insignia* loosed upon the surviving creature, ripping it apart with the spine of its hardened underbelly, and crushing the flickering life force beneath it when it set down on the Hue near its fallen Innate.

'Mira-fedor! Mira-fedor!'

Insistent, tinny shouting roused her, but she couldn't see, as if her eyes were cloaked with dark patches. She managed to roll her head but any more seemed impossible.

'A biozoon, Mira-fedor.' Wanton sounded excited, she thought distantly.

Dearest, you must come to me so I can help you.

Insignia's voice crept into her limbs but still she

couldn't move them. The baby in her stomach felt heavy and lifeless.

Mira. You must *come to me. My sensors tell me our baby is dying.*

Our baby. She found herself echoing the biozoon's words in her mind.

And with that echo, a frisson of concern grew; concern that brought with it a tiny surge of energy and will. *Insignia* would heal her baby.

She tried to awaken her other senses. She blinked repeatedly to clear the darkness. From the vague outline it seemed as though the biozoon had berthed on her right side. She would need to crawl there. But crawling required the movement of useless limbs so she began to rock from side to side until momentum took her over in one complete roll.

She waited awhile, summoning the energy to repeat the manoeuvre. Wanton called encouragement to her, though she could barely understand its speech.

The child remained inactive.

Change direction, Mira, Insignia instructed. *I am closer to your feet.*

Sluggishly, she inched her chest forward towards her belly until it would bend no more. Then she worked her legs backward away from her head.

Her breaths came slow and hard, as if her heart could barely pump the necessary blood to keep her lungs functioning.

She rested for a time before trying again.

Rock, rock, rock, became her mantra, followed by the painful exertion of tipping over: pain without energy.

After a handful of rolls she felt the hard, sharp edge

of something against her face. Her fingers moved compulsively at the contact.

Once more. Roll onto the lip, instructed *Insignia*.

But that meant a small measure of elevation that Mira couldn't manage. She drifted from consciousness but was brought back by a series of vicious stings to her hand.

Roll.

She jerked reflexively against it, enough to raise her shoulders onto the lip of biozoon skin.

It curled around her, lifting and sliding her up and then inside. Mira fell onto the spongy familiar surface of *Insignia*'s flesh and heard the muted sound of the egress scale sealing. A moment later she had the vague sense of being surrounded by softness.

I have encased you in a tubercle, Mira. I will attempt to heal you.

Nothing then.

For a long, long blissful while.

Mira avoided consciousness. Every time her thoughts tried to form into something cogent she deliberately broke them apart and sought the safety and comfort of nothing.

You must wake, Mira.

She ignored the voice. She did not need to wake. *Ever.*

The voice spoke to her sporadically, telling her things about the baby, or details of her own progress, but she did not care to hear them.

It seemed that it stopped for a time, and she welcomed the silent oblivion back. But it returned eventually with gentle persistence.

Mira, your brain activity suggests that you can hear me. Decisions need to be made.

Mira pulled the darkness over herself like a blanket. No. No more decisions. No more survival. Just the dark and the quiet.

Innate, please!

Mira stirred a little. *Insignia* had displayed anger and frustration before – but the biozoon had never begged. *What is it?*

The Post-Species are pursuing us and I am not sure of your wishes.

I wish to be left alone.

That is not acceptable within our agreement.

Then end it. End our agreement.

Equally unacceptable. You have pledged freely. Your child is part of our contract and your carelessness nearly killed it.

My carelessness! Mira opened her eyes in a rush of anger. She lay in a cabin, on a bed. Drab silk folds hung across the fleshy ceiling and she could see through to the wash cubicle and a fresh fellala laid out on the dressing rack. Her cabin. *How did I get here?*

I am able to use a form of peristalsis to move things around internally. It is tiring but useful.

Mira tried to sit up, but her muscles refused her demand. She felt a sluggish kick in her abdomen and she pressed on the spot. *My baby . . .*

Our child is alive, but weak. As you are. You should know that there have been some changes to its metabolism.

What changes?

The child's brain patterns are altered, and its endocrine and vascular systems are running at an accelerated rate.

I have compared the brain activity to those of my previous Innates, and there are no similarities.

You are saying that my child is not humanesque?

Not entirely.

Mira suddenly found it difficult to breathe and her heart contracted. *Impossible.*

That particular concept is most naive. Very little is impossible. You have brought a Post-Species entity into me. Perhaps your experiences amongst them have caused the alteration to the child.

Wanton. *I-I had forgotten. Where is it?*

The Post-Species sentient is located inside your clothing.

Mira lifted her hands from her belly and felt along her tattered sleeve. The hard, elliptical lump was still there. She fished inside and retrieved the Extro. The casing was intact and shiny, as though new.

'Wanton?'

'Mira-fedor?' Wanton's voice sounded faint and distant.

'I can barely hear you.'

'Preservation – constituents – are – degraded. Must – minimise – output.'

'What has happened to my child?'

The Extro did not reply.

Mira lifted it before her face and shook it. 'Tell me what has happened to my child or I'll tell the biozoon to expel you into the vacuum.'

'Vacuum – cannot – harm – me, Mira-fedor.'

Despite its conviction, Mira detected fear. 'It may not harm you but you will be alone for a long, long while,' she said softly. 'Maybe for eternity. You are used to symbiosis, Wanton. Loneliness must frighten even your kind,' she said.

'I will – if I . . .' The Extro's voice faded off.

Mira shook it again. 'What is it? What do you need?'

'Mycose – levels – dimin . . .' It fell silent.

Mira stared at the casing in despair. *Insignia?*

The Post-Species appears to be in difficulty? Insignia sounded suspicious.

What would it need mycose for?

I am not comprehensively informed on Post-Species. However, its request for mycose suggests that there is a difficulty with its preserving process.

Do you have mycose?

Perhaps.

Mira began to move her limbs, stretching each one cautiously to test its functionality. She then tried to sit up again.

This time she succeeded. She tucked the pillow-rest behind her back and leaned into it. Her gown, though muddy and ripped, was dry at least; cuts and scrapes from climbing the mamelon peppered her feet.

She sighed, knowing what was to come. *What do you want from me?*

There will be no more discussion about broken contracts, said *Insignia* firmly. *I comprehend that humanesques are intemperate and unreliable, but* we *are not. Integrity is vital to* us.

At another time, Mira would have argued that integrity was as subjective as art or literature, but now she did not have the energy to argue with *Insignia. I am sick . . . in my heart. Do you understand that?* Beyond *integrity.*

Dramatics. My previous Innates had considerable inner strength. Perhaps it is a difference between your reproductive roles.

Mira couldn't tell if *Insignia* was baiting her by suggesting she was not as mentally strong as her male ancestors – the biozoon didn't understand the humanesques' dual-sex evolution. *Insignia*'s species' reproductive process was more elaborate and involved the participation of several of its kind. Yet the 'zoon's comment still stung her.

Mira had travelled so far from the patriarchy of Araldis and with each world, each struggle, she'd shed the beliefs that she'd been born into. Her innate sense of equality had lain dormant on Araldis until her life had been threatened by Principe Franco. Now, her sense of entitlement grew with every passing moment.

She took a slow and deep breath to compose her thoughts. *I will not break my contract.*

As soon as she thought those words a gentle, soothing sensation burst over her. *Welcome home, dear one*, said *Insignia*. *I believe you will find mycose in the mercenary captain's cabin.*

Rast Randall?

Yes.

Where is Rast? The others? You said you left them some-where.

It is best if I show you from Primo. Do you have the strength to get there?

Did *Insignia* emphasise 'strength'? Or did Mira imagine it?

No matter. She slid her feet off the bed and placed them tenderly on the floor. She needed to wash.

TRIN

They carried Djeserit's catch back along the darkening beach, Joe Scali and Trin sharing the load of the netted fish while Djes struggled under the weight of a large octopus. Trin found his mouth watering for the food, his momentary suspicion of Djes and Joe Scali already fading before his hunger.

None of them spoke, saving energy for the exertion of the sand dunes and twisted coastal brush.

Juno Genarro was waiting for them where the brush gave way to the expanse of thinly vegetated ground, around the boulders among which the survivors rested. He immediately detailed cleaning and gutting of the catch to Tivi Scali and Vespa Malocchi, before the light faded. Semantic would be late rising tonight.

'Come and rest now,' Trin told Djes.

She was swaying against his side; partly due to the unaccustomed walking, partly exhaustion.

'Soon,' she promised. 'I would just speak to the women. Ready them to eat.'

'There is no ne—'

But she stumbled to the nearest cave before he could finish, and sat among the group of women in there.

Cass Mulravey moved in alongside her, offering her the robes that they kept in a bundle for her.

Trin watched Djes slip a robe over the scant rags

she'd worn back from the beach. Just a few weeks ago, Djes's open near-nudity would have shocked and disgusted him, and yet no one noticed her undress, so intent were they all on survival, so trusting and used were they to her ways. Djes had saved them. She would be forgiven anything.

The two women leant in close, murmuring to each other while the Carabinere moved around him, preparing the food. The sight of Djes in such intimate contact with the Mulravey woman made his empty stomach churn. How was it that she could communicate so easily with everyone? Even the difficult ones.

'Principe,' said Juno. 'The food is ready.'

'Eat!' Trin commanded in a loud, hoarse voice.

Those that could walk assembled within a few minutes, arranging themselves into a ragged circle around the small, flat rocks that Genarro had gathered to use as a table.

Djes found her way to Trin's side and sat awkwardly, as though her legs weren't sure which way to fold. He knew if he looked closely at her bare feet he would see the thick webbing that had grown between her toes.

'Where is the Principessa?' she whispered.

Trin scanned the group, suddenly made aware that his madre had not joined them. 'She was sleeping,' he said softly. 'It is best to leave her. Tina will attend her later. What does Cass Mulravey have to say that is for your ears only?'

Djes waited until Trinder had taken his share of the raw octopus flesh offered to him by Tina Galiotto before she replied.

'The weaker of her women cannot keep moving. We must wait for a time until they can regain strength.'

'No,' said Trin, as the iodine-bitter taste assaulted his senses. How he longed for cooked food. 'The cover here is shallow and an island this size may have dangers. We need better shelter from the sun, somewhere that we can defend. We are lying in cracks of shade, exposed.'

Djes nibbled at some raw fish. He wondered how she felt about eating from the ocean.

'But some of these women will die if they do not simply rest and eat for a few days. Perhaps you could send a scouting party as before.'

Trin struggled to make enough saliva to finish his mouthful while he considered what Djes had said. In truth he wanted nothing more than to stop and rest as she suggested, but something in him would not allow that. Not yet.

'I'll speak to Juno. Then I will decide,' he said.

'Yes, Principe.'

He studied her face in the faded light, and saw nothing but the usual patience and exhaustion. She didn't argue with him or try and insist. It was the reason he found her so comforting to be around. She didn't bludgeon him with her beliefs like Cass Mulravey, or whine like Jilda, or falsely fawn over him as the Latino noblewomen had done.

He thought briefly of Lancia and Chocetta Silvio and how they had shared his bed on alternate nights. Those times and that lifestyle had become dreamlike. Now he ate with his fingers and spent most of his waking hours craving food and water.

He glanced around the circle of survivors again as they struggled through their meagre meal. The divisions were still there; his Carabinere sat on either side of him and Djes, some of the surviving miners sat next to them, and then the women. Cass Mulravey sat opposite him in the circle across the flat bed of rocks. She spoke quietly to her brother. Trin wasn't sure of his name – Lennie or Innis – she seemed to call him by both names. Mira Fedor's man, Kristo, sprawled on Mulravey's other side, turning to check regularly on the alien korm that sat behind him.

Only three children had survived the walk from the mine shaft to the ocean: Fedor's adopted ragazzo, Vito, and two others. One belonged to Mulravey, but Djes had told him that she'd lost her other child, a 'bina named Chanee, to dehydration. Then there was the korm, as large as an adult but with the mentality and resilience of a child. Just a few meals of raw fish had seen it recover its strength more quickly than the humanesques.

The fact that both Mira Fedor's charges had survived was somehow a thorn to his flesh – a reminder of her. The korm's attachment to Djes aggravated him even more. It hovered near her whenever she was on land and the two spoke in the korm's language.

Would Mira Fedor come back for her children? he wondered. He'd gambled that she would, but it had been weeks already with no sign of help. Now they must create their own hope, which did not include rescue.

The group slept through the night – the first time in a while. Both Joe and Juno Genarro had agreed with Djes's suggestion to wait before they further explored the island. Reluctantly, Trin had given in. But something about the arrangement of the boulders and the smell in the air made his skin prickle. Just as the knowledge that his most trusted men had taken Djes's side against his stung his mind.

Yet as she lay next to him for the first time in days, he drew comfort from the way her muscled back curved against his stomach and her heels rested against his ankles. Her presence gave him strength and calm.

She left him well before dawn to fish again. This time Trin sent Vespa Malocchi to help her bring back the catch. The man was still grieving for his fratello, Seb, and needed distraction. They had all lost someone but Vespa had turned his grief to anger.

'Principe?' The man spoke gruffly, roused from sleep by Joe Scali.

'Wait on the beach until Djeserit returns. Gather shells for drinking.' Vespa was unhappy with the command but did not dispute it – another thing that had changed in a short time. In the Carabinere compound in Loisa, Seb and Vespa Malocchi had been the first to mock the disfavoured, inexperienced young Principe. Now he – like the others – was grateful to have Trin shoulder the responsibility.

Djes returned just before Leah blazed into the sky, draped in a brown weed that was heavy with finger-shaped pods, and dragging a weed net of pipis behind her. She slapped her bounty down on the rock table and peeled a pod off. She held it out to Trin with a wide smile on her face.

He'd waited for her, roaming the edge of the coastal brush-line, trying to decipher what was making him so uneasy about the place. Now that she was back, he felt an almost uncontrollable urge to move on.

'Weed?' he asked.

'Edible weed, from beneath the reefs. The seeds are fleshy. I've been using them for energy, Principe, but I wasn't sure if there'd be ill effects. Some weeds are poisonous. It's been days now and I've found no problems. I think it's safe for everyone.'

Trin stared at her. She looked tired and thin but not sick. Somehow she'd survived the extreme rigours of their flight better than most.

He took the seed from her and bit into it. A sweet and salty taste exploded in his mouth and he felt a surge of energy, as if he'd taken stimulants or drunk thick, strong mocha. 'Why didn't you tell me before?'

'It could've been dangerous. I had to be sure.'

Trin took another bite and experienced the same rush of energy. 'That was my decision to make. Not yours.'

Her smile vanished, and she frowned.

Trin bit back a further remonstration as Vespa staggered through the brush-line dragging something larger then himself.

'A xoc?' Trin's anger turned to incredulousness. 'You bested a xoc?'

'A gift from the ocean. It was dying in the shallows from reef cuts; bleeding to death. The storm must've brought it in too close to land.' Her voice remained steady and level, but Trin sensed her unhappiness.

She walked over to the boulders and sank down next to the korm. It chittered loudly with pleasure.

Trin did not follow her. He called Juno over. 'Make

sure everyone gets some of the xoc and the pipis. Let them have it in their caves. But do not distribute the weed yet. I will speak to you again when Leah has set.'

Juno raised his eyebrows but did not question the instruction.

Trin peeled off several of the weed pods and stalked around the boulders to the small soak of fresh water that bled out from under the rocks. He drank his fill and then carried a shell of water across to the brush-line closer to the beach. Soon the sun would preclude any movement that was not under shade, but he didn't wish to return to his own shallow cave with Jilda and Tina Galiotto. The miners and Cass Mulravey wouldn't welcome him to theirs, and his Carabinere had found women to lie with. In the daybreak light he'd seen Juno Genarro stroking the hair of the young woman Josephia as she cried silently into the sand. With even the slightest return of energies, so did emotions spill forth.

Trin stayed the rest of the day under the shade of the brush, sipping from the shell and slowly consuming the weed pods. With each pod his senses seemed to sharpen. He used the time to examine the surrounds of the boulders. At a glance, they were merely a fallen jumble of large rocks that had tumbled down from the hill to rest in a flat open space. The vegetation around them appeared to be a scant, sand-crawling creeper that flowered at night and exuded a perfume when trampled. And they had trampled it, in their trips to and from the brush-line. The creeper grew strongly near the water, but gradually thinned out as the open space stretched across to the base of the hill and sand met clay there.

The bare earth was a pale red and compacted enough that there were irregular-shaped cracks across it. Trin wondered why nothing grew on it.

He also wondered how many places on the island had fresh water leaking from the ground. He knew precious little about ecology and even less about fauna – the mining belt on Araldis was home to nothing more than checclia and lig beetles – but here, amongst real vegetation there was room for other creatures. Animals that would need to drink fresh water.

And yet they had seen no sign of their presence – no droppings or scrapings of anything other than a few small, timid checclia flicking their tongues into the fresh water. Perhaps his unease was merely a reflex. Or perhaps he sought a way to prove himself against Djeserit in the eyes of the others.

No.

Surprisingly, Jilda's voice came to mind. *Believe in your birthright, Trinder*, she'd told him when he was younger. *One day you will be Principe.*

The memory of her words shifted his thinking, and his confidence resurged. Jilda was right. Perhaps he owed his madre more than he thought.

While the others dozed amongst the shade of the boulders, Trin kept his vigil, energised by the weed pods. For the first time since leaving the Pablo mine shaft, he felt aroused both mentally and physically. It enabled him to concentrate well enough to mind-map the area right up to where the clay disappeared into the thick vines and brush at the base of the island's small mountain. Volcanic mountain or sand dune? he wondered.

It was hard to tell without getting close enough to see and feel the soil.

He felt the urge to stand and pace to order his thoughts, but he stopped himself. In this heat he would use more water than he had brought across in the shell. The weed had stimulant properties – there was no doubt. He took note of the duration of the effects and estimated how many pods it would take to get them through a night's walking.

When Leah finally dipped below the horizon, he rejoined the group around their rock table for more of the xoc. Juno Genarro had left the carcass to lie in the relative cool of the rock spring during the daylight, and it tasted waterlogged. Some of the briny taste of the sea had faded from its flesh and been replaced by a strong, earthy mineral flavour. The bite was like pepper and it disquieted Trin even more.

Yet voices sounded stronger tonight, and some of the women who had previously been unable to walk had joined them. Djeserit had been right to advise patience but he could not afford for her to be seen as more capable, more intuitive, than him. He called Tina Galiotto over.

'Where is the weed?'

'In the spring. Djeserit said it would dry out if we left it in the sun.

'Retrieve it,' said Trin.

As she moved to do his bidding, faces turned to watch. Trin stood up and stepped into the circle close to the rock table.

'We will head up into the mountain tonight,' he said.

The evening light was enough that he could see the reactions. None of them wished to leave the water. The Carabinere stayed silent, but not so Mulravey's lot and the Pablo miners.

A woman sitting next to Mulravey's brother stood up also. She was taller than most of his men. 'You been doin' most of the talking for us these past days but it can't just be that way. I think we should stay here. There's water and we're close enough to the beach for Djes to fish. When we're stronger we can help her.'

'Liesl's right,' said Cass Mulravey. 'There's no need to move. We should vote.'

Vote. Trin's stomach clenched. Djeserit's persuasion had eroded his status.

Voices joined Mulravey in agreement: the Pablo miners and her brother.

Djes and the Carabinere remained silent, still. Trin saw their discomfort. Juno Genarro and Joe Scali exchanged glances. Djes looked into her lap, hands clasped.

'What's yer reason?'

The question surprised Trin; not that it was asked, but who asked it – Mulravey's man Kristo. He sat on the other side of Mulravey's brother. His hair was so long and wild now that Trin could barely see his eyes. They were all like that, except for the women who bound their hair back with strips of thin weed.

'In truth, I have no reason, other than to say that this place does not feel safe. While we are exhausted still, these pods' – he waved at the weed that Tina Galiotto had brought dripping back from the spring – 'will give us energy to climb. In the mountains there will be bigger caves and we'll be at a better vantage to see distance.' He avoided saying 'rescue'.

'What danger?' Kristo asked. 'We've seen nothing. Only checclia.'

Trin shrugged. 'Perhaps that is it. Nothing. Surely other creatures must drink from this water. Why haven't we seen them?'

'Araldis is not a place of animals,' said Djes. 'What are you expecting, Principe?' Her tone was utterly deferential, but Trin felt the underlying sharpness of the question.

'Not the Araldis that we know. But these islands are new territory, and there seems enough flora to sustain something that could harm us. Juno?'

'The Principe is right, Djes.' The Carabinere scout glanced around the circle to make sure everyone heard him. 'I have flown over similar with Principe Franco. We saw birds and other small things.'

'Small things.' Innis guffawed. 'Mebbe the checclia might bite our toes.'

Trin contained his anger at the man's disrespect. It was not the time for tempers to be lost. 'Only fools are brash in strange places.'

Innis continued to laugh, inciting the others near him to join in, but Kristo cut across them all.

'He's right, Innis. We've got this far on his say-so. Why would we go breakin' what ain't broke yet?'

'Even if we can't see a reason?' said Mulravey. 'I say we move, if he thinks we should.'

The support was unexpected, and a moment passed around the group, brief but significant, before they stood, ready to move on his bidding.

THALES

Thales's desperation to see Aleta again settled after a few hours and left him bleak. He'd spent the hours sitting in a kafe on the main transit thoroughfare, watching Edo go about its night business. It was not a quiet world, even during the main sleep cycle.

When he finally felt he could face returning to his apartment, he left the kafe and washed in a public cubicle. As he splashed the flavoured water over his face, he felt neither remorse nor embarrassment for his evening's dalliance. Yet decency told him not to return to Bethany smelling of intimacy with another.

Shame she had not extended the same courtesy to him.

He planned to simply pack up his small stock of personal effects and find lodgings elsewhere on Edo. The thought of accepting any more of Lasper Farr's 'hospitality', or his sister's affections, made Thales sick to his stomach. It seemed he'd learned a great deal about himself in a few short hours – not all of it pleasing or uplifting.

And yet despite his bleak mood, his experience with Aleta had given him some peace back. Glimpsing into the core of his own weaknesses and vice left him feeling stronger in some way. Liberated almost.

Perhaps now was the time to shed his upbringing

and discover the person inside; the one without the ideals: the shallow, selfish, needy inner man.

He wondered if Villon had perceived that man within him, underneath the layer of naive idealism.

Strangely, the philosopher's face remained clearer in his memory than Rene's; the kindly eyes so interested in life. To the last. Villon may have had many of his own dark moments, Thales thought, and yet he'd remained buoyant and without bitterness.

I will never match Villon.

Nor was he sure that he wanted to. As he flashed his hand across the entry key to the apartment the bleakness lifted with that thought.

'Thales!' Bethany was curled on the couch naked. She looked startled, as if she'd been asleep.

'I'll just get my clothes,' he said quietly.

She sprang up. 'There is no need. I-I've been thinking a lot – and I want to talk to you. Why I did . . . that . . . and other things.'

Thales stared at her. In the darkened room she looked younger than her years and yet he knew the truth of her age, the truth of her desires.

'There is not much to be said. You were right, Bethany. I don't love you – it has been convenience, for both of us, and now that is finished. Listening to you won't change that.'

She took a step towards him, reached out her hand. 'Please, give this . . . upset a chance to heal before you make a decision.' The quaver in her voice was unmistakable, but it didn't move him.

He brushed past her into the bedroom and collected up his pitiful possessions. The total of the things he owned: a few toiletries, one set of overalls and another pair of loose travel pants and shirt all provided by Lasper Farr, and the aspect cube he'd brought from Scolar that stored his academic records and other private information. The credit clip that Rene had given him was wedged into the base of the cube. He was not completely without resources, but like Farr's handout, he had no wish to rely on Rene's guilt. On impulse he unbundled the clothes and left them on the bed.

'What are you doing?' Bethany was at the bedroom door. 'Don't be rash, Thales. It's not like I'm a—'

He stiffened. 'I know exactly what I want to do now and it doesn't involve you. In fact, it's important that it doesn't.' He swung the small bag over his shoulder.

She looked for a moment like she might try and block his path but with a sigh she stepped out of the way. He paused, and reached back to lightly touch her arm. 'You're a kind person, Beth, with a brother who is a monster. Get away from him. I hope you find your daughter.'

She didn't respond until he reached the front door.

'Thales. Wait! There's something you should know before you leave.' She switched the light on so that they could see each other properly and came over to him. 'I have some contacts here. Friends. People that support me . . . not Lasper.'

'The Mio?'

She dropped her head and then lifted it again. 'Yes. The Mio told me that Tekton was booked on a ship to leave today. He didn't make embarkation. The ship left without him.'

Thales shrugged. 'Maybe he changed his mind.'

'All his possessions were on board, including that ridiculous sculpture.'

Thales's chest constricted. He didn't like Tekton, but the man was of his own ilk and had helped them both – even if it had only been out of expediency. 'That is strange.'

Bethany came close to him. Close enough to whisper. 'My friends saw him being escorted by a Lamin to Lasper's habitat. He hasn't come back, Thales.'

'You think . . .?'

She nodded. 'It may be that he wants to keep word of the DNA you retrieved from Rho Junction from reaching the creator. I am scared for you as well. If you leave my protection then please at least use my . . . network.'

'Leaving your protection?' echoed Thales. 'You think you can protect me?'

Her anxious expression faded and she pressed her lips into a stern line that reminded Thales of her brother. 'Whether you accept it or not, while you're with me, you're safer. Lasper will consider hard before harming one of mine – and not give a second thought to your life if you are not.'

'Are you saying you can control the Commander?'

'Not control – but there are things about us that you don't know – about me.'

'More things, you mean?' He gave her a humourless smile.

'There is a group here that wants to replace Lasper with me as the leader of Consilience.'

'But you're a scientist, not a soldier. And the Stain

Wars . . . I mean, it wasn't you who averted the war. You told me that you were with the Mios.'

'Yes. Near the Mio moons at the site of the last incursion. I was with a Mio ship, dissecting dead Extropists. Recorded history leaves out all the subtleties, Thales. As a philosopher you should know that. Look what happened to your prophet Villon.' She rubbed her hand across the bridge of her nose. 'What's important is that you're safe while you're here.'

'What do you mean?'

'I mean that the truth about the war isn't recorded anywhere official. The official stories don't tell us that OLOSS was the original aggressor and that they used mercenaries to spark the fighting on Longthrow so that they could learn more about the Extros – what weapons they had and how they were evolving.'

'How they were evolving?'

'Yes, Thales. They wanted Extro fatalities so that they could find out their evolutionary secrets. Examine their Post-Species processes.'

'But why? We don't want their kind of evolution. That is the whole point of our division – our separation from them.'

'No, we don't want to follow that path. But that doesn't mean we don't want to know what they're doing. The Extros have advanced biotechnologies that we could use.'

'Then why don't we just trade for it?'

Beth touched the bridge of her nose again in a little gesture of frustration. 'It's not as simple as mere trade. There's fear and competition at stake, and a host of other things – territory and beliefs.'

He thought over what she'd just told him, and it made him even more restless. She was not the simple, sad woman he'd thought her to be.

She sensed his mood and stepped closer. 'On the outer level, the one above the docks, there's a woman called Samuelle. She manufactures the rust-eating parasite that keeps Edo clean. Ask around for her and she'll find you. I'll see to it.'

Thales pulled back from her. He didn't want her help. 'What will you do now?'

'Find a way to help my child.' She stared up at him. 'That's all there is.'

Thales nodded. He wanted to wish her luck again but it seemed pointless to say it. Luck would not rescue her Jess from Araldis. Likely nothing would.

He pressed the door open and left.

He walked most of the way back to the main recreation chamber. It gave him time to think and reconcile his feelings. Much as he no longer wished to be with Bethany, saying goodbye had been awkward, and the news of Tekton unsettling. Was Beth right? Had Farr disposed of Tekton? Or had her mistrust – her paranoia – about her brother made her leap to a ridiculous conclusion?

Today there was no sign of the Trade Fest. All the decorations had been packed away and the booths dismantled. Only the dais remained, and a Lamin with a recording dice, inspecting the walls and floors for damage. Several soldiers squatted in a corner playing a handball game.

Thales approached the Lamin. 'Pardon me. Could you direct me to a place where I might seek employment?'

The Lamin's nostrils flared and wiggled a little. It looked Thales up and down, eyes blinking.

Thales couldn't tell if it was the same one who'd given him the voucher to Aleta, or indeed the same one who'd escorted them to meet Lasper Farr the day they'd arrived. There was a likeness about their race that his less than discerning eyes couldn't recognise.

'Why would you come here to enquire?'

'There was an information booth here during the Trade Fest. I thought maybe it was a permanent fixture.'

'Nothing is permanent on Edo. Identify yourself.' The Lamin held out the dice for Thales to place his fingers on.

He hesitated for a moment, remembering Beth's warning.

'It is required that every visitor to Edo identify themselves on the request of an official employee.'

'How do I know that you're official?'

'I am Lamin,' said the creature primly. 'Official is what we are.' It twitched its head in the direction of the soldiers. 'Your reluctance is suspicious.'

Thales clicked his tongue in irritation and grasped the dice. The display flashed a set of symbols that he didn't understand.

The Lamin, however, pulled the dice from his fingers and peered at it closely. 'Proceed to the docking level. Adjacent to the inspection booth on Dock 15 is the administration office. There are many jobs currently available.'

Thales nodded. 'Thank you.'

He turned and walked out of the chamber, pleased to get away.

He caught one of the free taxis outside and rode it to the shaft. A group of workers dressed in identical overalls with a swirling logo and the name COG across the back crowded around the entrance to the pedestrian lifts. He listened in to their conversation. In the two short times he'd been on Edo, his preoccupations had kept him from acquiring any real sense of the people and their manner. If he was to survive alone, he mustn't fall into the hands of another Gutnee Paraburd. He'd find employment and learn to be an ordinary working man. Then he'd put his plans into action without the help of Bethany or any other person.

'How did the Fest treat you?' everyone seemed to be asking each other as they filed into the lift. 'Thank Edo it's over!' was the most common reply.

Thales let their chat wash over him, and relaxed into the sensation of speed without force as they ascended towards the docks. Already it seemed a very long time ago that he and Mira Fedor had caught the vehicular lift to see the Festival. She'd sought his company instead of the mercenaries', then. What had befallen her? he wondered. She was a refined and gentle woman, if not a little unconventional. He had liked her well enough, despite that, and her ability with the biozoon was remarkable.

'You see that big prick sculpture at the Fest? Was up on the dais,' said a small, stocky humanesque to his taller companion. 'Crux. And the prick who it was modelled on. He had an ego as big as his whang.'

'I saw him,' a woman chimed in. 'He's one of the Lostol tyros who've been studying that God thing they found over near Mintaka. I heard he balled Fenralia on the trip here and she liked it so much she made a sculpture of him and his better parts.'

'Fenralia's a she?' The tall one sounded surprised.

'Hard to say with ginks like that,' replied the woman. 'Fen looks like she'd stick those tentacles anywhere they'll fit.'

Most of the group laughed at that: all except the short one. He lowered his voice. 'Talking to the Jandos last night. Heard that the tyro prick's gone missing up top. He must have done somethin' to shite Farr off.'

The tall man nudged him and glanced to the back of the lift.

Thales followed his gaze. Behind the group who were crowded together, facing inward, as lifts forced passengers to do, was a solitary 'esque, standing quietly, listening. Thales hadn't noticed him before.

From what Thales could see, around the heads of the others, the man seemed unremarkable in every way, other than perhaps the intent expression on his face. He stood a little taller than Thales but was muscled and wearing different-colour overalls to the COG group. His dark uniform looked supple, the material almost elastic.

As if sensing Thales's scrutiny, the man lifted his gaze and stared at him.

Thales found the contact disconcerting, and an uncomfortable sensation settled on his chest. He glanced away.

The COG group left the lift at different levels, each one calling farewell to the rest. Others replaced them, and the pattern of exit and replace went on until they reached the level before the docks. The lift emptied entirely then, except for Thales and the man in the dark overalls.

They stood in silence while Thales watched the icon flickering upward. To his relief, the doors pinged open to the dock, and an influx of passengers separated him from the man.

He hurried straight down into the main walkway, following the large numbering sequence on the walls. Although the docks were essentially one long mooring, a mess of conveyors and passenger tubes and service modules divided one bay from the next.

Dock 15 was the farthest from the lift and took him a decent amount of walking time to reach. So much so that he was beginning to get hungry and tired.

As he passed behind a wall of containers unloaded on Dock 14, the light altered. Dock 15 was almost in darkness; only the red glow of safety lights lent an outline to the mooring mechanism and its empty berth.

Thales couldn't see an administration office or any other kind of official structure. His chest got tighter. Had the Lamin made a mistake? He turned and took hasty steps back towards the container wall.

The man from the lift jumped him before he reached it, and they both fell to the floor. Thales knew at once who it was, without seeing his face or even the colour of his overalls.

A heavy object pressed against his throat; he smelt food-sweet breath in his face. The man had just eaten, and then come to kill him.

'Reckoned you might put up more of a fight,' whispered the man.

Thales bucked against him but it was a miserable

attempt against the man's superior strength. He opened his mouth to shout, but the man forced a soft, round object between his lips that expanded as soon as it contacted his saliva. Suddenly his mouth was so full he could barely breathe. With his hands trapped underneath him, he could only writhe and twist his head from side to side.

'Might as well enjoy it then,' the man muttered to himself. He dropped the weapon and clamped his hand around Thales's neck. The suffocation came quickly, intensified by the putty filling his mouth and throat.

He attempted to knee the man in the back but his legs wouldn't work, flopping uselessly. Oblivion came quickly.

Even when the man's fingers were yanked abruptly from him, Thales barely knew consciousness. Only loud cracking sounds and a short, cut-off yelp kept him connected to the world.

The slow return of oxygen helped his brain to realise his hands were free, and he began to frantically gouge the putty from his mouth. Sitting up, he coughed and spat the material out onto the ground.

As the tears cleared from his eyes, the darkest clump of shadows on the dock became two figures: his assailant and another, his rescuer. His rescuer had the assailant trussed up by something attached to a long handle, a whip of some kind. The rescuer took what Thales thought was a spray tube from his pocket and sprayed the assailant's neck. Then he wrapped his fingers around the assailant's throat.

'You liking that?' A woman's voice. Low and soft.

A woman?

The assailant fell slack almost immediately and she kicked the man's torso over so that the whip could unravel.

'We need to hurry up before someone gets curious about the noise. Can you walk?' she asked.

Thales got onto his knees and pushed himself erect. His throat was on fire still, and his mouth felt like it was bruised and coated with dirt. 'Who – are – you?'

She curled the whip into neat loops and hooked it onto her belt. She was taller than him by more than a head, and dressed in the plain station overalls favoured by most workers. He couldn't make out the details of her face.

'Friend of a friend said you'd needed a hand,' was all she said.

Thales massaged his throat to help him speak. 'Th-thank you. B-but I don't—'

'Suit yourself,' she cut him off. 'But you'll be dead soon if you don't come with me. This one here is the softest of Lasper's men. He'll send one of the good ones after you next and that will be that. I don't plan to hang 'round here while you think about it.'

She gave a little salute and walked past him towards the container wall.

It was her pragmatism that frightened him most; the dry, flat nature of a voice that didn't bother with lies. Like the mercenary Rast Randall, but without the hint of malice in it.

'Wait,' said Thales.

She stopped, but didn't turn around.

He snatched up the small sack containing his aspect

cube and tied it to his waist. Then he hastened over to her.

'Pull your collar up and lean against me. Pretend we've been down here looking for a quiet place to shag.' She draped her arm across him and pulled him into the crook of her shoulder. Then she leaned her head down against his and led him out into the light.

Thales's heart beat as hard and quick as it had in the moments he'd been set upon. Yet they barely drew a glance from those busy loading or prepping ships.

Somewhere, around Dock 8, a balol in a lift cab called out to her. 'Hey, Fariss! Come over here and try a man your own size for a change.'

She made a rude gesture over her shoulder and steered Thales on.

When they entered the main-shaft lift she pressed the button for the level above them and pushed him up against the back wall. Then she splayed her body across his, head bent into his neck as though they were kissing or speaking intimately.

Her breath glanced hotly off his cheek. 'Relax,' she whispered. 'You're too stiff.'

He tried to do as she asked, but shock had taken over his body and he was shaking uncontrollably. Maybe it was also her proximity making him feel that way.

She grasped his arm and gave it a commanding squeeze. 'Deal with it!'

'C-cannot,' he whispered. He sagged against her, overcome by weakened muscles, unable to get his fear reaction under control; terrified that his bowels would loosen and empty where he stood. They'd left the man dead; neck broken.

She pulled Thales closer and stroked his back. Her hands were surprisingly gentle and soothing.

He opened his eyes and looked over her shoulder at those near them. Curious stares greeted him. Not just idle ones either. They knew her. Thales saw envy in some glances, and suspicion in others.

He closed his eyes again and let himself be supported by her, shivering against her body warmth until the lift announced their level.

As the doors opened, he tried valiantly to straighten but she clamped him against her side like a mother with a sickly child and manoeuvred him out of the crowded lift.

They walked in that fashion for longer than he thought the habitat could possibly stretch; through thick foil tubes and over endless adaptor couplings that joined mismatched modules. The distance and speed of their movement returned blood to his limbs and the trembling began to settle.

He began to notice that nothing they passed through seemed stable or purpose-built. On the lower public levels near the main recreation chamber, everything seemed durable enough, but here . . .

Fariss didn't speak until they veered off through the narrowest section of a tri-coupling and came to an old-style iris hatch.

She let go of him then, waiting while he steadied himself. The light in the tube, though dim, enabled him to see her face square-on for the first time. Her cheeks and forehead were broad and her nose straighter than any he'd ever seen. Beneath it, her large mouth was shaped by thick, sensual lips.

She stared back at him with equal intensity. 'What the frig happened to your face?' she said straight-up.

Thales suddenly realised his mask had been lost in the scuffle. He automatically touched his skin. It felt rough and scaly, but not wet with infection or blood. 'I . . . it . . .'

Fariss saw him struggling to find the words. 'Beth said Lasper had given you a rough time. He do that to you too?'

Beth? Thales cleared his throat. 'The Commander was responsible, indirectly.'

Her broad face coloured at the sound of his voice. 'That's a pretty sweet little accent you got. Where're you from?'

'Scolar,' said Thales automatically.

Fariss smiled. 'Well, we better get you out of harm's way until we can teach you a few survival tricks.'

'We?' he enquired politely.

She reached up to the wall and peeled off a light-weight breather mask with oxygen sacs from a large dispenser and threw it to him. 'The air's a little thin if you're not used to it. Come and meet the family.' She leaned forward then and blew into a tiny hole below the hatch's icon-pad.

The iris spiralled open.

This time she stepped through alone and waited for him to follow, as if it was somehow important that he did it without her help. She watched to see if he'd follow.

He fitted the mask, which sent a little blast of oxygen into his nose. Squaring his shoulders, he managed the step-over without tripping. The hatch shut immediately behind him, sending a rush of air against his back. The cool blast on his hot skin prickled his hair. He blinked a few times, not able to make exact sense of what he saw.

He and Fariss stood on a small platform that jutted directly into a vast hollow of space. The space wasn't empty, though. A huge building spun sluggishly inside it as though suspended from invisible cables. From the narrow tubular section of its spiralling structure to the larger, honeycombed end, it was almost an exact replica of an uncoiled seashell.

'Welcome to Ampere,' she said.

'What is it?' Thales could barely understand his own voice through the mask.

Fariss was smiling, though, and seemed to know what he asked. 'It was an island resort once built up straight from the sea onto limestone. But the owner got sick of the design and wanted somethin' new, so they plucked it off its anchorage and dumped it on land. Planetary regs said it was too large to leave there, so the owner paid to have it picked up by Savoir Hauling – Lasper Farr incorporated – and brought to Edo. I'll tell you the rest while we commute.'

She waved at the small tug that was rapidly approaching them, a flat-backed vehicle with railings around the seating like a sightseeing boat. The operator waved at Fariss and swung the tug neatly against the platform so they could step on board.

Once seated, Fariss took up her narration. She spread her large body across two seats, legs crooked up on the armrest, torso turned towards Thales. She was quite magnificent, he thought, and frightening with it.

Rast Randall, the mercenary, had been a strong, capable woman, but something about Randall's narrow, lean physique and callous laugh repelled him. The woman next to him was exuberant and commanding. His newly awakened submissive soul stirred and he had a ridiculous desire to sit at her feet.

He tried to concentrate on her narrative but his thoughts rebounded between Aleta and Bethany and her, and the man who'd just tried to kill him – how his legs had gone into spasm when Fariss strangled him. She was a murderer. The kind of person his beliefs and upbringing would have prevented him from knowing in the past.

Fariss tapped his arm. 'You listening to me? I don't do the tourist guide thing for everyone.' Then she grinned. 'Hey, I don't even know your name.'

'Thales,' he mumbled through the breather mask.

'Well, Thales, I'm called Fariss O'Dea. Now, listen and learn. Ampere isn't officially independent from the rest of Edo but we might as well be. We run our own rules here and Lasper Farr doesn't interfere.' She lifted her jaw. 'He doesn't dare. Sam provides him with all his little rust-eaters. Edo would disintegrate without them and he knows it. So you'll be safe enough while you're here with us.'

'How can you breathe without assistance?'

'Oxygen's lighter on Ampere but it's enough. I'm used to it. Better in the city than out here though. I find it hardest going down to Edo proper now. I get dizzy from the extra.'

'But how does your city do *this*?' He rotated a finger.

'You mean float out here? The outer levels of Edo

aren't as compacted as the lower levels. Gravity's doing its thing but not enough to jam us up against something. We're like a satellite kept in place by all the other stuff around us. Farr lives even further out than Ampere; right on Edo's rim where *the atmosphere's zero and the detrivores rove.*' She sang the last few words to a tune he didn't recognise.

Thales raised his eyebrows above the mask.

She laughed.

Randall used to laugh a lot, but with a hard edge that seemed like it was meant to cut you. Rene and Bethany, the women Thales'd known intimately, hadn't laughed readily. And then there was Mira Fedor. The tragedy that dogged the Baronessa had insinuated itself into her face. She seldom smiled.

Thales felt himself further drawn to Fariss as if she gave off the vigour and light that he desperately lacked.

'I'll take you to meet Samuelle and then get cleaned up. We'll sort out something for you.'

Thales wasn't sure that was what he wanted to do at all but Fariss had just saved his life and he still felt too shaken to object. He leaned back into the hard bench seat and watched as the tug hovered down onto its matching berth; a much wider platform than the one they'd left behind. This one jutted out from the large end of Ampere's honeycomb of windows. They could, Thales thought, be arriving at an exotic and luxurious hotel if not for the plethora of ugly, twisted stanchions, broken satellite towers and discarded metal structures that sufficed as Ampere's horizon on all sides.

It was unnerving to feel like you were floating free

in space and yet be hemmed in by a circumference of rubbish.

Fariss didn't speak to him again, save to tell him to remove his mask as they walked through the corridors. She did, however, shorten her stride and speed to accommodate his flagging energy, and occasionally took his elbow to guide him into a different passageway. Her every touch seemed to make his body feel better.

They received the same curious glances from other pedestrians as in the central lift, but here the faces seemed friendlier, less guarded.

Thales opened his mouth to tell her he couldn't walk any further without rest or food when she halted abruptly before a door and turned to look down at him. 'Don't lie to Sammy. It's the one thing she won't stand.'

She wanted him to make a good impression. The idea warmed Thales.

She opened the door and pushed him inside.

The room appeared to him as a once-grand suite that had been transformed into a bizarre kind of laboratory. It was brilliantly lit and dominated by a huge oval-shaped bed on a raised dais. Objects that could have been in any medi-lab, even the biozoon's, surrounded the bed. Thales recognised some of them: basic diagnostic stations, blood analysis units and a wall of freezer capacity. But a lot of the other equipment was as foreign to him as this entire man-made micro-world Fariss called Ampere.

'Sammy!' bellowed Fariss.

'Keep it down, girl,' said a voice. 'I can see you well enough.'

Fariss frowned into the bright light, swivelling her head. 'Well, I can't see you.'

'Is it him?'

'Judging from the way someone was trying to strangle him when I turned up, I'd guess so. His name is Thales.'

'Lasper's man?'

Fariss clasped her hands together like a child. 'I had to, Sammy. Didn't want him tellin' no one it was me.'

'Did you spray him?'

'Course.'

'Good girl. As long as there's no DNA residue.'

Thales heard a noise; a hiss similar to the one their hover-tug had made as it landed on the Ampere platform. A woman walked out from behind two banks of coolers and stood between them. She had the oldest face he'd ever seen.

On Scolar rejuvenation was compulsory, along with HealthWatch. While rejuve worked with variable success on individuals, it never, ever, allowed such obvious ageing. People tended to die from accidents or violent acts – but mostly they still looked young.

Samuelle's old body was encased in a grey nano-suit that quietly pumped and deflated over her skin as movement was required. She grinned, flashing a set of perfect teeth at him that looked incongruous against her lined, age-spotted skin. There were some things Samuelle chose to keep upgraded.

'Welcome to Ampere, Thales. Bethany tells me you're a learned type. Could always do with a few more of them around here. Fariss wouldn't know Villon's philosophies from a dirty ditty.'

Thales cleared his throat, forming his response in his mind. 'While I'm indebted to Fariss . . . and y-you . . . for your assistance, I have no plans to become part of your community. Bethany and I had a brief . . . relationship which has ended. It was her idea that I should come here. Not mine. Indeed if Fariss had not found me I would likely be dead and perhaps better for it. Despite my misgivings about still being alive I would like to say thank you and be on my way.'

Samuelle's sunken eyes half-closed for a moment as if she were accessing a moud. When they opened, Thales saw a hint of something grim. 'You wish to leave?' she asked.

He glanced at Fariss apologetically and nodded. 'I want to make it on my own.'

'Then let me lay it out for you, young Thales. You would most certainly be dead without our intervention, and you will be shortly, if you return. Lasper wishes any trace of you removed from Edo. It is not often that I directly oppose his wishes, but the fact that you are a danger to him is valuable to me. I also owe a great debt to Bethany. She wants you alive and so you shall stay that way.'

Anger rushed through Thales, causing him to tremble again. 'You can *not* choose whether I live or die.'

Samuelle and Fariss exchanged looks.

'You're right in that, to a point.' Samuelle nodded.

'You're better off here, Thales. I can teach you some survival skills. Make it easier for you when you're on your own again,' offered Fariss.

Thales grappled with a deep, surging instinct to obey Fariss, and shook his head stubbornly.

'Fariss,' said the old woman in a sharp voice. 'Wait outside.'

Fariss nodded and walked to the door. When she had closed herself outside, Samuelle took a step closer. Thales wasn't sure if it was the lightweight hydraulics at her knees and elbows or the nano-suit that made the hiss, but the sound unnerved him.

'I take a risk giving you this information, and you should know I will disclaim it and you should you turn out to be untrustworthy. Bethany told me what Lasper did to you, how he blackmailed you to retrieve the DNA sample from Rho Junction, and how the virus he administered nearly killed you. She said that you were desperate to find out the nature of the thing you transported here because you fear it is being used to cause problems on your homeworld. She guessed that you would try to find those answers in Lasper's laboratory and wind up stiff and vacced.'

Thales licked his lips. Black spots flickered before his eyes. He was having trouble standing now, and this was not helped by the brutal way she had cut to the chase. 'B-Bethany knows me t-too well, perhaps.'

'Sit down,' she ordered, and pointed to a bench by the blood analyser.

Thales stumbled over to it. He hadn't slept since Aleta, nor barely eaten. And then the attack . . . He sank onto the hard, cold surface with relief.

Samuelle followed and repositioned herself in front of him. 'Thales, listen to me. I want the same thing for different reasons. I don't much care what's happening to your planet but what Farr is planning affects Consilience. There're many that have devoted their lives to our belief of balance and peace. He can't be allowed to destroy that.' Her wrinkled face took on the semblance of dried carrion. 'He *won't* be allowed. We need you alive, Berniere. And you need us.'

'Why do you need me?' Thales rasped. A peculiar halo had grown around Samuelle's head, as though the hood of her nano-suit was glowing.

'We want to study your blood and your damaged skin. Find out what Lasper used to blackmail you. We need to be a step ahead of him.'

'You want my skin?' He glanced dazedly around the laboratory. *What did that mean? What did that really mean?* But the halo had made it too hard for him to think. It bleached his mind with its astringent light.

A balol materialised suddenly at his elbow and grasped his arm. He smelt it; felt the scrape of its tough exoskeleton.

'I think that you need to lie down, young man,' rasped Samuelle. 'Now.'

TEKTON

It seemed that no time at all elapsed between Tekton and the detrivore falling through the floor of the taxi, and Tekton being scooped up by the small salvage tug.

With no breathing apparatus though, he was too busy gasping for oxygen to appreciate the tug's immaculate timing. Even when rough hands forced a mask to his nose and mouth, and hauled him into the tug's small cabin, the Lostolian barely registered the gravity of his situation.

Only after moments of sucking in brackish, wonderful air did the world begin to make sense again. Tekton clung to the mask and watched the tug operator fume the circling detrivore with a hand-manipulated nozzle.

The detrivore convulsed and its muscle coordination deserted. The tug operator sent his craft scuttling beneath its erratic wing beats and deep into the shadows of a broken, but gently revolving, giant wheel. At least, that was what Tekton thought the gangling structure and attached carriages to be.

The pilot wove the tug with extraordinary skill between criss-crossed girders while the detrivore gave clumsy pursuit. Without the coordination needed for fine manoeuvring, it slammed into the metal struts and then dropped away into the chasm.

The operator cackled into his breather mask, then lifted it to spit cigar smoke out of one side of his mouth. ''Nother one down,' he crowed and snapped the mask back.

He didn't speak again until he'd threaded a path through the giant wheel, and deeper into the metal pot-pourri that surrounded the abyss. Floating along-side the wheel was a conical-shaped mass, decorated with gaudy stripes.

He tethered the tug to the base of it and popped open the cabin door. After a short crawl up an external staircase he was inside the cone. Tekton followed more slowly, his body aching from trauma and adrenalin poisoning. The steps, like the ones up to Farr's chapel, made him dizzy, and he welcomed the firm grip of his saviour, who reached down and pulled him up the last few.

Tekton almost fell into the darkened space. While he struggled to sit up, the man slammed the door shut and pressed various panels. Light flooded the cone and Tekton felt a welcome blast of oxygenated air on his skin.

The tug operator peeled off his mask and hung it on a hook near the door. He held out his hand for Tekton's.

The archiTect obediently removed it and handed it over. He inhaled the air with a sigh of relief. 'I am indebted to you . . . sir,' he managed after collecting himself. 'It would seem that Lady Luck was on my side.'

The man nodded and proffered a gloved hand. 'Jelly Hob's the name. And it ain't no luck me scooping you up. Been on the lookout since I got the word from Sam that another foreigner was about ta go missing.'

'I am no foreigner. I'm Tekton of Lostol,' replied Tekton. 'An archiTect who asked too many questions of Commander Farr, I fear. But who is Sam? And how did he know?'

'Sam is Sam,' he said, evasively. 'And . . . Lasper . . . well he don't like questions. And I should know. Was his chief pilot at one time. Saw too much.'

Tekton dabbed at his bleeding legs and tried to keep his voice even. 'Commander Farr tried to murder you as well?'

'Jus' say he had me watched. I don't much like to be watched, Tekton. 'S why I took to helpin' others who might be in trouble. But we should be fixin' your cuts and things, not gabbing. Can you get up to the top, or need I be carrying you?' He pointed upward.

Tekton looked at the central stairs that wound to the top of the cone. At every curve a platform ran across to the wall as though the stairs had wings.

'How far?'

'Three levels.' He laughed. 'But the grav's real light.'

Tekton struggled up the first two flights alone, cognisant enough to take in the odd structure and accumulated rubbish that made up Jelly Hob's home. Clothes lay draped over odd bits of furniture, food scraps littered the tops of damaged comm-desks and chipped solar arrays. Some of the equipment looked sophisticated enough to have come from the labs on Belle-Monde; other pieces appeared to be just what they were – junk. Either Hob was a genius, or he was bored and crazy, and *altogether* slovenly.

But for once, though, Tekton's sensibilities weren't offended. His life had taken a rather uncomfortable turn and he was experiencing his first taste of gratitude. Jelly Hob had saved him from certain death – Tekton could overlook a lot for that.

But by the time he passed a rather oddly obscene glass statue of a woman bent over displaying the lips of three vaginas, on the second-floor platform, he began to sway, despite the lower gravity.

'Is that a Fenralia?' he enquired woozily.

''Tis me favourite.' Hob caught him before he fell back and puffed smoke about his face. 'Can't have an archiTect falling down on my watch,' he said cheerfully.

Without any apparent difficulty, he slung Tekton over his shoulder and continued upward. The steps and the weight seemed to offer him no extra stress; he barely puffed – other than his cigar – as he stepped off the stairs onto the next level.

Hob's top level consisted of a reclining seat locked at forty-five degrees, a shelf of steel vials and a bucket full of spray-skin and other basic medi-kit products.

He dropped Tekton into the seat, and with well-practised fingers probed and prodded his wounds. He pasted probiotic paste on everything and sprayed replacement skin over the deeper cuts.

'You Lostols don't heal so quick. Need to keep the bugs out while you do. This place is a rubbish dump, y'know. Be best if I take you across to Ampere right away.'

Tekton sighed, almost enjoying Hob's competent ministrations. It was good, he thought, to be alive.

'Where is Ampere?' he asked. 'I am not keen for Lasper Farr to know that I am alive.'

Hob laughed in the rusty manner of a man who'd spent much time alone. 'Farr don't know anything about wot goes on in Ampere. Long as you don't use y'r other voice.' He tapped his head.

'You mean my moud?'

'That's the one. Don' go talking to it, and you'll be safe in there.'

'In there?'

'S'pose you ain't heard of Ampere, bein' a visitor here. Sam'll be wantin' to meet you anyways. Farr wants you dead, then like as be, she wants you alive. Not one for politickin' much – that's why I'm on me own. But Jelly Hob's smart enough to figure that out at least. And to be true, I've got a curiosity as well.'

'But who would Sam be, Mr Hob?' asked Tekton, attempting to speak in a manner that the man would comprehend.

Hob chortled. 'Mister, you call me? I be likin' that a lot, I reckon, but Jelly's good and all too.'

'Whatever you prefer,' said Tekton politely.

'Jelly's the way it been for many a while, and Jelly's the way that—'

'Who is Sam?' Tekton interrupted more curtly. His saviour, it appeared, was easily distracted and inclined to garrulousness.

'It's Samuelle, in fact, to those that don't know her. Used to work in Lasper's labs till it got so she knew more'n him. Now she sells to him. Got her own little patch not far from here.'

'Farr allows an opponent to thrive on his own planet?'

Hob chewed on his cheeks a bit before he answered. 'She's not *agin* him, as such, and she's not *for* him, neither. Hard to tell you right, how it is.' He rubbed his chin with a dirty forefinger and then his eyebrows raised as an idea formed. 'Uneasy is how it is, you see. Need each other – for now . . .'

Tekton listened intently for a while, until the details became hard to track. He found his attention drifting to the patchwork job Jelly Hob had performed on his wounds. His HealthWatch should take care of any infection, but a scan in a decent medi-lab would put his mind at rest. And Ampere sounded more comfortable, and safe, and possibly more hygienic than Jelly Hob's helter-skelter cone.

'Could we go there now?' he asked when Jelly paused to light a new cigar.

The man nodded ready agreement. 'Might as well. Got a hankering for some of Sam's rum. Best I've tasted since the war.'

As Jelly Hob helped Tekton back down the stairs to the tug and manoeuvred the squat little vehicle out of its mooring and headed it deeper into the outer rubbish rim of Edo, he kept up a monologue on the Stain Wars.

Tekton tuned in periodically, when Hob's smoking didn't muffle the words too much or when the passing scenery closed in tight as though they were flying through a narrow, jagged tunnel, and gave him claustrophobia.

It seemed that Hob had been combat-rated and damn good, if he could be believed at all.

'Saw Brigoon up close,' Hob reflected. 'And the

Mio moons. Blew the guts out of a couple of Extro Geni-carriers there at the end. No substitute for the old u-missiles in the P-class. Made such a mess it was like navigatin' through a 'roid shower afterwards. Extros got so damn close to the Mios, thought they'd mebbe wipe 'em out. That's when Lasper gave the orders to blow the fuckers. Lasper said them Geni-carriers was automated, killin' machines with no brain. Never was too sure about that. Seems Extros can put a damn brain in jus' about anythin'. I hoped after, he was right. At tha' time though I was just thinkin' 'bout the Mios. After that, Lasper told me ta change tack, sent us to intercept the OLOSS fleet. The *whole* friggin' fleet. Never been so shittin' scared in me life. Thought he'd lost his stones, y'know. Turns out he knows how to play tha' game damn good. He . . .'

It went on. And on. A recount of the last moments of the war, who'd done what and Lasper's counter-moves. At another time it might have been fascinating, but Tekton had a welter of things on his mind, not the least of which was the need to reflect on his own re-action to the first *real* danger he'd ever experienced. The encounter had left him exhausted but curiously focused. As if free-mind and logic-mind had reached a brief harmonic balance. Both of them were adamant about one thing. *Don't let Lasper Farr get away with this.*

'. . . hittin' the Geni-carrier was lucky, I reckon. Couldn't pick what they'd do next, those damn Extros. Never could see their logic. Not ever.'

'Commander Farr must have been able to.' commented Tekton gently.

Hob made a grumbling noise, as if he'd been woken

after a bad night's sleep. 'Mebbe,' he said. 'Mebbe not. Things happened. Sure. Sam's the one to talk to 'bout them Extros. She was there too.'

'In the war?'

'Yeah. Old as Lasper, she is. She don't believe in rejuve – except for organs and things. Not like me.' He puffed for a while then, lifting his breather mask to suck on the cigar and then again a moment later to blow it out. 'Third set of lungs in as many decades.'

Tekton couldn't tell if he was joking. The man looked older than most but seemed hearty and strong. He turned back to the scenery as Hob stubbed his cigar butt onto the dashboard of his display and continued his rambling story.

Edo's outer rim was a fascinating graveyard that Hob negotiated with almost casual ease. For all his verbosity, the man was undoubtedly skilled. A waste, thought Tekton, like the wasteland he'd chosen to inhabit.

For a while, the tug crept in and out and around a conglomeration of discarded fairground equipment. Gravity's processes had forced smaller objects onto larger ones, forging new, bizarre structures and making it hard to discern where one piece began and ended. Occasionally, Tekton picked out things he recognised.

As they chugged higher – or further out, he corrected his thinking – the rim became a thicker and more tortured intertwining of broken satellite towers and enormous thick cable rolls.

Hob interrupted his own monologue. 'This here's what's left of that elevator between Mintaka and her first moon. Hadda geneering fault. Broke loose from its tether. Lost about five thousand 'esques to the vac.

Took 'em weeks to scoop up the bodies floating out there.'

Tekton nodded. He remembered that fiasco and the spillover. The archiTect who'd worked on the project had been several years senior to Tekton. He'd disappeared after the accident, despite most of the culpability being shifted to the manufacturer. Tekton had always suspected the studium had spent significant money making sure the blame was transferred. The ruins of the elevator were twisted beyond redemption now and thick with a fur of lighter debris.

'Must be some magnetism in them cables. Gawd knows what crud's stickin' to 'em.'

Hob shot the tug up over one of the monumental base girders and into a rusted hole. They flew in complete darkness for far too long, save for the tug's watery forward lights. When Tekton thought he could not stand another minute of the blackness, they popped out of the other end of the girder into a yawning space.

In the centre of the space, a brilliantly lit, glorious, pearly shell-structure twirled like a tired dancer.

'Crux!' exclaimed Tekton. 'Oh my fecking gonads.'

Tekton's expletive so lacked any impact that Hob burst into his rusty laugh.

The Godhead didn't take offence; his minds were far too absorbed by the damaged beauty pirouetting before him. 'It's Murex, isn't it? The Discarded City. I never got to see it finished, although I worked on part of the design when I was a young student. My studium was devastated when they heard the owner had scrapped it. They tried to buy it but he'd already signed a deal with the Savoir company. I can't imagine how much it cost to bring here.'

'Some say they sliced it right through the middle. Top 'alf, bottom 'alf. Brought it through res shift in two goes. Sounds like a load of bull to me. Reckon it musta taken a few more than that. Anyway she's all stitched up and workin' fine now. Bit of a tilt, but good enough. If you like that type of close-up livin',' he added. 'Them people all stacked together in there makes me want ta shit a lot. When I shit—'

But Tekton was too lost in an architectural rapture to contemplate the details of Hob's claustrophobia, and in fact only remembered Hob was there when the tug smacked unceremoniously onto the landing platform not far from another vehicle.

Hob and the driver of the other vehicle exchanged waves, which made Tekton feel a little more at ease about the six or so balols that detached from their vantage points around the platform to converge on them. They weren't armed – that he could see – but their manner was wary.

Hob peeled back his mask and issued some garbled requests through the comm. The man was smart enough not to open the cabin seal.

A series of exchanged grunts later and Hob popped the cabin. 'S'right,' he said, slinging a leg over the edge. 'Sam and me go way-oh back. She's one for rules though. Usually likes a bit of notice when I come calling.'

Good-ee! Powerful women are sooo— squealed free-mind.

Dangerous, interceded logic-mind. *And mind that.*

But free-mind's anticipation was blighted before it

reached full bloom. The balols marched them inside the shell structure and down lengthy corridors. When they reached a stunning indoor atrium they shepherded Hob off in a separate direction.

'S' all right,' he called over his shoulder to Tekton. 'They're just taking you to the medi-lab. I'll be seein' you soon.'

Tekton concealed his fear at being separated from Hob and let free-mind immerse itself in the exotic and original design touches of the central reception area; the free-floating mezzanine and retractable walkway, the pond water sculptures that periodically turned to ice statues, and most importantly, the staggered skylights that flooded artificial light into the atrium in intricate, specially conceived patterns.

My skylights, thought Tekton with pride. *Mine.* His chest swelled as he watched the delicate dappling effect that moved across the floor. Imagine how it would look under true solar rays.

Tekton was possessed by a sudden mad compulsion. Ampere or Murex, or whatever it should now be called, must see sunlight again. *It must.*

The balols, however, were not mindful of Tekton's private ecstasy and hurried him across the atrium to the escalators. They descended several floors and walked another distance into an area where the lights were not as bright, and the decor less impressive.

They pushed him through a set of sliding doors into a grey room fitted with the standard range of medi-equipment. One wall of the room was lined with retractable bed-cubes.

A humanesque attendant approached him, eyeing

the wounds weeping through onto his dishevelled and tattered robe. 'You'd better get yourself over on a bed while we take a look at those legs,' said the attendant in clear Gal.

Tekton nodded with relief. Now that he was here, in something resembling proper care, he suddenly noticed how much the cuts throbbed and how nauseous he felt.

No need to suppress the pain now, logic-mind informed him in a cool tone.

He tottered over towards the bed-cubes but his eyes began to play tricks. The wall wavered, beds slipped in and out of their slots and grey patches appeared and disappeared before his eyes, heightening his sick feeling.

In desperation he fell upon the closest bed, unaware that it was already occupied.

The attendant shouted for him to stop, but he'd already lifted a knee onto the mattress and was falling forward. The momentum seemed to tip his nausea past the non-returnable point and he vomited the residue of his last meal onto the feet and legs of the occupant.

His eyes cleared after that, the grey patches abating.

An angry, surprised and horrified face confronted him. A face, surprisingly, that he knew.

'Thales Berniere,' said Tekton, spitting little bits of vomit from his mouth. 'Heavens to Crux. What are you doing here?'

JO-JO RASTEROVICH

Diving into the clamour without a particular tone or voice to focus upon was like being drowned in noise; so loud and so blurred that it caught the sides of his throat and sucked them together. Only Jo-Jo couldn't feel the sides of his throat, didn't even know if he still had one. Was the sensation imaginary? He did have a vague sense of breath – but that could well have been hindbrain memories.

As he grappled with the auditory explosion, part of his mind ventured further with that notion. He hadn't wanted to think about it properly before, but Rast's fear had sparked a deep survival instinct. He had to face all the possibilities.

His knowledge of the Extros' transformation procedures – like the rest of Orion's – was sketchy. He thought he'd heard that their trans-processes varied, dependent on what form of Post-Species sentience they wished to attain. There were the typical Extros that used a Host body, and then there were these guys; the bodiless kind.

The very first Post-Species experiments had been on humanesques, but aliens joined them quickly enough. Where their practices had taken them since then Jo-Jo could only guess. Were there second-, third-, fourth-generation Extros? Or did their population – if you could call it that – remain static?

Most importantly though, did his body still exist, and was it still alive?

Somewhere inside his mind, deep, deep below the level of the neurons that struggled to organise the crashing noise pollution into something acceptable, came an emphatic retort.

It better fucking well be, or . . .

Or what? What was he gonna do about it? Really?

Make a giant fucking nuisance of myself.

Feeling better for that conclusion, he turned his full attention back to the spinning wall of sound. There had to be a way to interpret it.

He recalled his Ferris wheel image and tried to refine it a little; not a Ferris wheel, perhaps, but a colour wheel like the ones sold to kids at fairs. In the wind they became a blur but when they were still the colours were well-defined, individual blades. He needed to slow the spinning noise right down to find the solitary voices.

It was a long time since Jo-Jo Rasterovich had practised meditation, and even then it had been part of his ploy to convince a nun at the Kanada Monastery on Kanada Keys to have sex with him. Still, he'd worked at it for a time (until, in fact, the Mother Superior had caught them at it and had him ejected from the city) and the mindset came back easily enough.

He picked out the blue sounds, listening carefully to them, much as though he was staring at the tip of his own nose, with a kind of defocused concentration. But his mind wandered all too quickly and he lost the threads.

He restarted the process, over and over, until his

concentration span increased a little. The solid blue turned into shades of blue. He picked one of them and applied the same method.

Suddenly, as with his pursuit of Rast's voice, he dropped into a clear audio space.

'**Cipher?**' asked a voice. A single word spoken but it seeded and grew into multiple responses in Jo-Jo's mind. ^what's your name?||you've never been here before||have you heard the news?||everyone's talking about it||^

'You m-mean me?' asked Jo-Jo.

'**Answer.**' Again the single word blossomed into a deluge of replies and questions. ^you first||it's not polite to crash in without introduction||are you one of the monitors?||^

Jo-Jo took one of his imaginary deep breaths. 'OK, I'm new around here. Just been transformed or whatever the frick you call it. Having a hell of a time navigating the noise.'

'**Transformed?**' ^impossible!||where from?||no transformation allowed when Medium is travelling||^

'Medium? Is that what this thing is called?' asked Jo-Jo. 'My name is Jo.'

'**Cipher.**' ^names?||what are they?||did you skip the orientation stage?||weird stuff!||JO??||^

Jo-Jo let the many responses rattle around his head for a while before he spoke again.

'I didn't get any orientation. Tell me, are you one consciousness, or many?' he ventured.

'**Question.**' ^cute question||send him back to O||weird stuff||^

'Does that mean you don't know?'

'**Alert.**' ^An aberrant!||monitor should know||enemy perhaps?||too obvious for that||cute||^

'I'm not your enemy, I'm here . . . accidentally,' said Jo-Jo. 'Can you tell me how this works? What's this monitor thing?'

'**Aberrant.**' ^Vote||Tally||30,000,132 say yes to Jo||17,128,003 say notify monitor||^

'*Thirty million say yes?* Nearly fifty million of you are listening to me? Frickin' impossible! But . . . I can only hear a few,' Jo-Jo finished limply.

'**Account.**' ^Medium is conduit to billions||Jo speaks with Minority Social||^

Even though the odd speech pattern was becoming easier to follow with each interchange, Jo-Jo wasn't sure that he was making correct, even vaguely correct, interpretations. As long as they didn't summon the monitor . . . 'So you're a Social Minority group? You mean like . . . a gossip group?'

'**Gossip?**' ^Revote||abuse||confront—^

'Whoa,' Jo-Jo interjected. 'Steady, steady. I meant . . . is your group swapping information?'

'**Travel.**' ^Medium travels||quick quick||^

'Travels where?'

'**Time.**' ^Secure the future||Leah system||tell Jo nothing||^

Leah system. Jo-Jo searched his memory. Araldis was in the Leah system. 'You mean Araldis?' If he could have, he would have spluttered, but he'd been robbed of that kind of bodily reaction.

'**Time.**' ^Araldis is prepared||ready for us||fools||^

Ready for us. That thought loosened Jo-Jo's concentration and he recoiled out of the Social Minority cache and back into the clamour. He let himself float there for a time while he assessed and organised the information he'd gleaned. To his thinking, the cache was a large – *really large* – chat group, like one you'd find on the main 'cast channels in the OLOSS worlds. Jo-Jo had always avoided those communities – other than some of the sex groups – but he knew they existed and how popular they were.

If the voices were being honest, then the Social Minority group was so huge that somehow the Medium translated or organised answers to his questions into grouped responses. Either that, or Jo-Jo was incapable of hearing and receiving all the information at once.

The latter made more sense – maybe the Post-Species brain or consciousness, or whatever the hell they were, could process many more things at once. The gist was pretty clear though. The Medium was headed for Araldis.

For the first time since coming to awareness in this weird, cerebral, auditory world Jo-Jo felt complete and utter anguish. He was heading into trouble, and he was saddled up and riding with the wrong side.

He floundered around, for a time, in an emotional fug. All his earlier bravado seemed to have deserted him; his calm, almost superior attitude in the face of Randall's disarray, gone.

He grabbed at mind-things, things from his memory that might buoy him up. But even his desire for revenge on Tekton seemed pointless now.

He wanted something to warm him, give him hope, but there was little enough. Only, perhaps, a kernel of stubbornness and a single desire.

Mira Fedor. Want to see her again.

He wasn't sure who he sent that plea out to – maybe to himself. But it was enough to rally some spirit.

He went back to Rast with the news. This time he found her cache without having to locate her voice – as though his brain was building some kind of aural map.

'You there, Randall?'

'Josef?' She sounded calmer but nonetheless relieved to hear his voice.

He told her what he'd learned and his theories on Medium and how it was organised.

'Talk about wrong place, wrong time,' she muttered. 'OLOSS will be all over Araldis by now.'

'Maybe,' said Jo-Jo. 'Remember that Dowl station was in the hands of your ex-Capo and the Saqr. Can't see them letting OLOSS in first. If this ship is shifting to Araldis then they'll be doing it under a tight window. Open the shift sphere then shut it again as soon as we're through.'

'Unless they're shifting on different coordinates,' said Rast.

'Imperfect Shift?'

'Yeah, but not the one the Savvies use. Maybe they're tuned to their own frequency. Maybe they can shift through any sphere like the 'zoons do, without using the OLOSS system.'

The very thought of it made Jo-Jo want to change the subject. 'You said you thought the Extros were after something else on Araldis.'

'They'll be after the quixite all right, but maybe more as well. You've got geo training. What do you think?'

'I think it's got to be something that needs them to be there. Physically there. Otherwise, why send this wheel rim full of billions of sentient sound waves shooting into a potential war zone?'

'Yep,' Randall agreed, but had no more answers than he did.

'You think Farr's got something to do with it?' Jo-Jo asked.

'For sure. But whether it's stoppin' them, or provokin' them, would be hard to say.'

'You think he's a hero?'

'Not much. But he's smarter than most, and more convinced.'

''Bout what?'

'Whatever it is he believes in. Attackin' those Geni-carriers with his own ship near the Mio moons was one ballsy act. But we were at war. He got lucky with the u-missiles, found some weakness in their shielding. He had a great pilot too – Captain Jeremy Hob. Don't get much better than old Jelly Hob. Lasper's got a knack for finding the good ones. Thing that got me, though, was what happened next. When he nulled the Geni-carriers, the Extros were vulnerable. OLOSS wanted to go in and void what they could: Rho Junction, Saiph, the lot. Lasper wasn't going to let that happen. Faced them down right then and there. Told them he'd take the OLOSS C-ship out.'

'How did he know which one it was?' Like everyone else, Jo-Jo had seen virtual re-enactments. OLOSS had a hidden command ship.

'He was on their side. At least, that's what they thought up until then. They must have given him the intel. The threat to the C-ship was enough to delay a decision on the Extros. By then the humanesquitarians were involved. The Extros looked like they'd showed the yellow flag and OLOSS got pressured into letting them go home. Lasper got to be hero and peacemaker in one sweet move.'

'He musta made some enemies that day.'

'You'd think. But OLOSS came off looking good in the end. Benevolent. That soothed things some. Don't imagine that there's much trust there, though.'

'So Consilience is just a farce?'

'No!' Rast was sharp. 'There's plenty among them that were . . . are . . . committed to peace. I just ain't so sure that Lasper's one of them. Nor, I'd reckon, are they.'

'They feed his fighting force though, with their members.'

'And will do until the time's right to change things.'

They were both silent for a bit.

'So you think this place is a bunch of voices or consciousnesses that can communicate at light speed, but they're socially organised as well – just like any sentient group?'

'Well, I wouldn't go thinking they're just like humanesques.'

Rast made a sound that could have been a sigh. 'You're right there.'

Another silence.

'Do you think our conversation's on some broadcast channel round this joint?' she asked.

'You and I?' Jo-Jo thought about it. 'Hard to say. It's like each voice has a private space and from there you have to consciously reach out to communicate. I found you this time even though I couldn't hear you.'

'How'd you do that?'

'Not sure. There's a marker in my brain now. You're up top left on the Ferris wheel.'

'What?'

An explanation would have sounded straight-up crazy. 'Forget it. Just an image I've got of things in my brain. I noticed something else – not sure what it means.'

'I'm listenin'.'

'The voices I heard in the chat cache were real flat – lacking normal expression. Dunno, maybe I just couldn't pick it out with all the input.'

'Or . . . it could be a downside of the transforming process,' she said.

They were both silent for a bit.

'That's the first good news you've given me,' she added.

Jo-Jo pictured Rast's lean face, her blue eyes narrow in contemplation. He suddenly craved real sight. 'How so?'

'Think about it. If they have different social cues, it might mean we can talk . . . privately.'

He so wanted to nod. She was right. 'Worth a try.'

'You first then.'

Jo-Jo thought for a moment before he spoke. 'It'd be sad to see the Extros have problems with OLOSS.' He ladled sarcasm into his voice.

'A shame,' agreed Rast, with equal mockery. 'We should do our best to support a peaceful outcome.'

'Maybe I'll go see if I can rally up a peace movement.'

'You do that, Josef. I'd like to join it – can you help me out of here so I can participate?'

'Do my best to make that happen,' said Josef. 'Back when I can.'

He let his focus drift back out to the clamour.

Suddenly, he was feeling a whole lot better.

THALES

Thales surfaced from a semi-sleep state, gasping for breath, his arms thrown wide in a startled manner. He snatched his arms back, embarrassed, and rolled instinctively onto his side towards a wall.

Where was he?

Fariss had brought him here. Saved his life and brought him here. To . . . whatever the place was called. Shell place. Sam – Samuelle – old face, young body. She wanted his DNA. He must have fainted. And now?

He heard doors open; a concerned voice speaking in Gal. Something about getting on a bed.

Thales began to roll over to see what was happening but his movements were slow. Before he could sit up a figure loomed close to him; a face and the smell of something sour. Paper-thin lips parted and vomit splashed onto his feet. Worse than sour. Acid-smelling and vile. He grabbed his bedcover and threw it off, swallowing back his own desire to be sick.

'Thales Berniere,' said an all-too-familiar voice. 'Heavens to Crux. What are you doing here?'

'Godhead.' Thales kicked out at Tekton. 'Get off me.'

Then the infirmary attendants swooped on them, easing Tekton to a bed of his own and wheeling Thales off to wash.

Though Thales returned clean, it was as though the hot, wet spew was still on him. The ignominy of being vomited on was difficult to shake, though it was tempered by curiosity and surprise.

Tekton was sitting up in his adjacent bed while the attendant pored over deep, ragged cuts on his legs.

'You appear to be in the wars, sir,' Thales commented, finally.

'And you,' said Tekton, indicating the curative skin pasted around Thales's neck and across his cheek. 'Looks like you tried to cut off your own head. And my apologies, good fellow, for earlier. I have been through some trying circumstances.'

Thales accepted Tekton's regret stiffly. When the two had last met, Tekton hadn't wished to disclose anything that might help Thales further. Bethany didn't trust the Godhead. Something had happened on *The Last Aesthetic* that she wouldn't talk about.

Thales wasn't sure if Tekton was friend or antagonist. The man was clearly brilliant but with an inflated sense of his own importance. *Don't be fooled by glamour*, Bethany had said.

And here they were, thrown together once more.

Tekton remained silent while the medi-lab attendant finished dressing his wounds.

'I wish to leave,' Thales said as she finished up.

'Sammy says you're to stay until the sample analysis comes back. We might need to run the test again.'

'And what if I don't wish to wait?' Thales heard his own petulance and didn't care.

The attendant glanced towards the guard at the door. 'Sammy said wait. So I would, if I were you.' She retired to her small, partitioned office, shut the door and turned her back on them, not prepared to get any more involved than that.

Tekton lay comfortably propped up on his pillows, his face relaxed by the pain relief flowing from the capsule stuck to the crook of one elbow. Their beds faced each other across a small array of blinking equipment.

'Where to start, young fellow? You first,' said the Godhead.

Thales set his jaw, refusing to be so easily compliant. 'I recall you had little to share with me at our last meeting, sir. Perhaps it is you who should begin.'

To his surprise, Tekton made an unhappy sound. 'You were right to be seeking information from Lasper Farr, Thales, and I was foolish withholding what I knew. Little enough as it is. I had thought to use the situation to my advantage, but Farr is a man without moral bounds.'

The Godhead then told Thales the extraordinary recount of his visit to Farr's prayer room and his ensuing near-fatal escapade.

'But why did you go there, Godhead?'

'Lasper Farr has a secret.' Tekton lowered his voice. 'I think he's found a way to predict the future. In fact I'm sure of it. He let me try and find his system.'

Thales frowned. 'Even if such a thing were possible, why would he do that?'

'It was a game, a test of intellect. See if I could work it out. Of course, on the off chance that I did, he needed to dispose of me in case I found a way to use the knowledge against him. Fortunately, someone was on hand to prevent murder. Jelly Hob,' finished Tekton, 'may be uncouth and eccentric by most standards, but he saved my life – and more so, Thales, the man can fly like a genius.'

A silence fell for a time between them as Tekton rested, eyes closed from the effort of his retelling, while Thales cogitated what he'd heard.

'It seems,' said Thales finally, 'that we are both beholden to strangers for our lives. Commander Farr also sought to rid himself of me. Why? I'm not exactly sure. I expect he wished to prevent me speaking of the details of the DNA retrieval. If that is the case then the Baronessa and the mercenaries should also be marked. For they all knew about my task.'

'But they do not know about the outcome,' commented Tekton.

'I suppose that is true. It could be that he saved my life to divert blame for my later disappearance.' His head ached with the effort of second-guessing Lasper Farr. 'Whatever the reason, I was saved by a . . . woman . . .' He stumbled on that concept. Fariss was a woman but that alone seemed an insufficient way to describe her. '. . . and brought here.'

'And now?'

But Thales was still not prepared to give away information without reciprocation. 'Yes, sir?'

Tekton gave a small and humourless smile. 'You are wise not to be as trusting these days, Thales. A lesson hard-learned. Poor fellow, I am pleased to see your face less raw.'

Thales inclined his head and waited.

'In truth I'm not sure what now. Hob tells me this

place stands independent of Farr and that I shall be safe here. I assume the same would stand for you. My instinct is to leave quickly and return to Belle-Monde, but that may not be so simple. OLOSS have gathered a force at all the res-stations that access Araldis. The Extropists have control of the planet. I think trouble is imminent. Travel may be difficult.'

Tekton shifted his injured legs with care and rearranged the bedcovers.

Beautiful linen, Thales noticed. The kind you would expect in the best of hotels. In fact, little signs of Ampere's wealth were everywhere. The infirmary, though small, was ergonomically elegant and fitted with the most sophisticated equipment. The guards he'd seen wore a ceremonial livery, not nano-suits. He snapped his attention back. Tekton was speaking again.

'Would you mind, Thales, telling me why they are taking samples of your DNA? I could offer you advice on the situation.'

Thales vacillated. The Godhead seemed different somehow, less arrogant (other than the vomiting – which given his physical state was forgivable) and more genuine. Experience could be a swift educator, Thales knew. 'They wish to prove that Lasper Farr infected me with bacteria. I expect they are accumulating evidence. And staying cognisant with the tricks he is using.'

'Ah,' said Tekton. 'But perhaps I could save them some time.'

Thales's eyes widened. 'You would tell them what you know about the creator of the DNA I collected?'

'For the right outcomes, yes.'

'And they would be?'

'Lasper Farr is a man who conducts himself beyond what is appropriate. He is also a man who is extra-ordinarily well informed. Did Bethany, by chance, ever mention how he accrues his knowledge?'

'No,' said Thales truthfully. 'But she was never comfortable with his ambitions and she was fearful of his uncanny prescience. Why do you ask?'

'Prescience, you say. Hmmmm . . . I saw something in his prayer room that would indicate that his prescience is the benefit of some advanced technology.'

'Weapons?'

'It could be thought of that way.' Tekton sat up straighter and sipped fluid from the straw-pouch dangling in front of him. 'Have you met this Samuelle?'

Thales nodded and rolled his eyes.

'What would you consider her position on affairs?'

'She is involved with Consilience, and not altogether enamoured with Commander Farr's self-serving ways.'

'She would oppose him?' asked Tekton, softly.

'I believe so. But I should not give too much weight to my opinion after one brief meeting with the woman.'

Tekton considered that for a moment. 'I have a feeling that things around us may change quickly, Thales. I would like to consider you an ally when this happens. I will do my best to help you find answers, if I can count on you in return.'

Thales stared across at Tekton. Even across the distance of two beds, he thought the tyro seemed vulnerable, even a little desperate. Thales's reserve thawed. Tekton valued him – more than that, needed him.

'I think it would be most sensible of us to help each other out of this, sir.'

'Splendid.' Tekton's pasty grey skin infused with a little colour, lending it a mottled appearance. 'Now listen carefully. The woman behind the creation of the DNA is a tyro on Belle-Monde called Dicter Miranda Seeward. Brilliant and totally untrustworthy. A woman of appetites.'

Thales blinked away the notion that the Godhead had licked his lips.

Tekton continued. 'From what my moud has been able to divine, Miranda has created something that will affect the competitive instinct in humanesques – thus the reason for targeting the orbitofrontal cortex. Scolar is obviously her blind trial – is that the term they use? Now this is where you come in, Thales. Why would she choose Scolar?'

It was a question Thales had spent hours puzzling over, even without knowing what the DNA was intended to achieve. But Tekton's précis was an illumination. Suddenly, he had an idea. 'How do you regard Scolar, Godhead? Its function, I mean.'

Tekton gave a small frown. 'Publicly, it is regarded as a source of progressive ideas and beliefs.'

'Would you agree that it has influenced OLOSS decisions over the years?'

'Indeed,' Tekton allowed. 'Think of the Beluga charter, and Villon's philosophies. Even at Tandao Ando, we were required to understand the importance of Scolar's role in the evolution of our social and political systems.'

Thales took a deep, deep breath. 'I think that Dicter

Seeward's virus is meant to nullify the genius of Scolar.'

'What?' Tekton looked momentarily confused.

Thales told him about his time with Villon and the great philosopher's fears. He followed that with a recount of his conversation with the Pragmatists in the Kafe Klatsch and the Sophos's intention to raze Villon's statue. 'There is a malaise and enervation sweeping the city – and it is real, Godhead. I had not thought that it could be caused by something as sinister as a virus deliberately spread.'

'What you've told me is preposterous, Thales. Unbelievable. And yet to think that you have spent time with the great Villon. You are a surprise package.'

'Villon was a gentleman in every possible sense of the word,' said Thales sadly. 'And I was too ineffectual to protect him.' To his chagrin, he felt tears welling.

But Tekton did not appear to notice. His eyes closed in contemplation but then opened again, abruptly. 'Miranda must be doing this for the Entity,' he muttered aloud.

'Doing what for the Entity, tyro?' said a commanding voice from the doorway.

Samuelle entered the room flanked by Fariss and a male humanesque dressed in battered leather pants and a filthy yellow skivvy. The man's face was old, like Samuelle's. They could have been siblings, if the man's body had been through the same processes and encased in a suit. As it was, his brawny shoulders slumped above a large and continuous belly that ballooned from below his rib cage and hung well below his hips.

'Mr Hob,' said Tekton as the old man came close to him.

Thales was astonished to hear the warmth in Tekton's voice.

'Tekton, meet Sammy. Or Sam-u-elle if you like,' said Jelly Hob. 'And the beeoootiful Fariss.'

Fariss gave a wide, encompassing smile that sent Thales's heart thumping madly, but Samuelle's face was a study in scrutiny. 'Don't meet many archiTects. 'Specially those that work for God.'

'Mr Hob speaks highly of you,' said Tekton politely enough, though Thales heard his tone cool somewhat.

'Looks like we've all got something in common,' said Samuelle. 'And we don't have much time to learn about it. Lasper's gone and called the decommed captains to Edo for a meeting. Seems as though we're goin' somewhere soon.'

'But he told me he wished to avoid involvement at this stage,' said Tekton. '"Balance" is what he said.'

'Balance doesn't mean peace, tyro. Balance means Lasper Farr getting what he wants.'

'Are you implying that the hero of the Stain Wars is an opportunist? I'm astonished,' said Tekton, with thick sarcasm.

Samuelle laughed. 'I might get to like you, Tekton. But right now, I need you. Farr's got some type of device he's using as a soothsayer. I want to know about it.'

'Why would I be able to help you?'

'Because the technology came from another tyro. A strange fellow with insect eyes. I met him once, a while back.'

Tekton's face turned so pale that Thales thought he might faint.

'Cousin Ra,' the Godhead gasped. 'What have you been up to?'

MIRA

Mira lifted her hand from where it rested on the wall of the stratum. A thick, gravy-coloured fluid seeped from slits in *Insignia*'s interior skin all the way along the floor of the strata to Rast's cabin. The cuts occurred at regular intervals.

What is it? What has done this to you?

It is unimportant. The mycose is contained within an object where the mercenary rested.

Mira made her way there slowly, painfully.

As the pucker retracted allowing her to enter Rast's cabin, a sense of loss welled up in her. She'd thought it impossible to feel more sadness, but the sight of Rast's scant possessions brought tears to her eyes and a sharp pain to her chest.

I'm alive. But I'm alone. Even the white-haired mercenary's face would cheer her at this moment.

The satchel she'd seen Rast carrying on Rho Junction lay behind a row of standing rifles – like a warning to anyone who might touch it.

She sat on the floor and shifted several of the rifles, laying them down next to her. The satchel's fastener was coded but inactive and opened out easily. Inside was a stack of six rectangular trays nearly the length of her arm dotted with thousands of tiny blisters.

What do I do?

The configuration of the packaging suggests that only a minute amount is required.

Mira fumbled in her sleeve and retrieved Wanton. Its casing was now so slick it reminded Mira of the large molluscs found on the jetties of the Galgos Islands.

'Wanton?'

No answer. Not even a sound.

She examined the casing as closely as her sore, exhausted eyes would permit. Despite being slippery, it was perfectly intact and she could see no place to administer the mycose.

She placed Wanton in her lap and prised the top tray from the rest. It was heavier than she expected. She dropped it next to her knee and ran her fingers along the bubbled surface. Each tiny blister rolled freely where it was embedded, like minute, smooth, malleable bearings.

They are loose.

The altered mycose is toxic. Do not let it contact your skin.

Perhaps you could have mentioned that earlier.

Insignia ignored her rebuke but fell silent in punishment.

Mira bit her lip. This was not the time for them to be at odds. *I-I'm sorry. Please help me.*

Insignia remained stubbornly silent.

With trembling fingers, Mira grasped her gown and used the material to press down lightly on one of the blisters. It popped out and rolled onto her protected palm.

She picked up Wanton with her other hand and tilted the bead so that it rolled to contact the Extro.

As soon as the bead touched Wanton it gained its

own momentum and rolled upward to the peak of the casing. A sliver of a vent opened in what had seemed a seamless surface and the bead entered.

The vent closed immediately, and despite peering closer, Mira couldn't see any trace of its existence.

'You will not see anything, Mira-fedor.'

Mira almost dropped the Extro in surprise. Its voice sounded strong again. 'Wanton?'

'Thank you. Wanton had become dysfunctional.'

'You were fortunate. One of my passengers was smuggling mycose. Otherwise I wouldn't have been able to help you.'

'Then Wanton is grateful to your smuggler friend as well.'

Mira set the Extro down on the floor next to the satchel. She was thirsty but the cucina seemed too far away to contemplate. 'Now you must show your gratitude. Tell me what has happened to my baby.' Her voice hoarsened with emotion. The baby had been so still since she'd regained consciousness that she wondered if it had really survived, even though *Insignia* insisted it lived.

'Wanton took samples of the amniotic fluid and other non-intrusive analyses. If Mira-fedor's baby has altered then the transition through the Hue into the Bare World must be responsible.'

'How?' she cried.

'The Hue is organic and intelligent and able to manipulate cells. That is how Hosts live from it.'

'It's a creature in its own right?'

'If Mira-fedor must think of it in such terms. But it is "us" as well as itself.'

Mira pressed her fingers to her temples. She craved cool fluid on her throat. *I must drink . . .*

Yes. Then you must come to Primo, Insignia insisted.

She got to her knees and then her feet.

'Take Wanton,' said Wanton.

Mira nodded to both of them. She picked up the Extro and forced her legs to walk her along the strata, denying their desire to rest. Collecting two tubes of berry pulp from the pantry, she continued on to the buccal.

With a sense of relief, she stepped through the pucker into the safest place she knew – the vaguely meaty smell, the thick, moist walls, the odd visual disparity between the biozoon's animal inner cheek and the humanesque fixtures. Home.

She placed Wanton on the floor inside the pucker and sank into Primo. As the vein engulfed her body and mind, she carried a question with her. *Insignia*'s inner skin was untouched in the buccal, unlike the still-healing cuts along the strata corridors. *What happened? What caused those wounds?*

The Post-Species use aggressive probes. It entered when I joined with Medium.

I don't understand.

Insignia projected image after image into her mind. Mira watched a spinning object enter *Insignia*, slicing and sampling everything it touched. She saw Josef and Rast and the others in a space – not a room but an area surrounded by swirling sounds. She listened to their conversation and their efforts to leave the space.

I still don't understand. What is it? Where?

This group of Post-Species refers to it as Medium. It is,

*in simple terms, a large resonator. Their consciousness is based
in sound – vibration; an ingenious evolution of the principles
behind res-shift.*

*That was not the case on the planet. They were parasitic.
Yes. They were different.*

Why did you go there?

*I needed to locate you. I took samples from their internal
'casts. Then I left.*

Y-you left the others behind?

I preferred to be without them.

Mira gasped. Though she had no enduring loyalty
to Rast or any of them, her humanesque sensibilities
contracted with fear for her own kind. *But you abandoned
them.*

*You are overly dramatic, Innate. They were not mine to
abandon.*

Can we get them back?

Insignia didn't answer immediately, and Mira was
unable to fight off the desire to sleep as Primo's recep-
tors primped and probed and replenished her.

She awoke, startled, a short time later. The baby had
kicked. She felt both relief and apprehension. Wanton
had not been in the least enlightening about the changes
to her child.

*It may be possible to negotiate with Medium for their
return,* said *Insignia,* as if there had been no time lapse
in their conversation.

Then I would wish to do that, Mira thought quickly.

If, Insignia emphasised in the annoyed fashion of
someone who'd been interrupted, *Medium was still in
local space.*

Where is it?

It has shifted to the Leah system.
To Araldis?
Yes.
But that's not possible. The Saqr have control of Dowl.
*Impossible is a ridiculous humanesque concept. Medium
would be able to shift to Dowl if it were welcome.*

Mira's muscles tightened involuntarily against the
vein's gentle massage. *Of course.* So many things made
sense now: the Saqr on the Hosts' planet, the invasion.
The Post-Species wanted Araldis. But why? For the
quixite? Or was there something else?

She fell deep into thoughts of Vito and the korm
and Cass Mulravey. Had Cass given up hope of her
return? Were they even alive still? What had transpired
in the time that she'd been gone? What was about to?

*What do you wish to do, Mira? It is not safe for us here
now that I have intruded on the Post-Species worlds. Already
I am being monitored with suspicion. If they were not in the
process of mobilisation, I would be pursued. Only the situation protects us.*

Mobilisation?

Insignia flooded her mind with more images, these
ones filtered by the biozoon's peculiar corduroy view
of space. She saw the familiar brilliant markers of shift-
space; a huge spinning drum-shaped object queuing to
enter the final layer of the sphere, flashing as brightly
as a supernova and then disappearing. Then *Insignia*'s
perspective altered, cutting across to observe the outer-
most ring of shift-space. The dazzling turquoise of the
largest ring was circled by a thick, opaque band.

What is it?
Look closely.

Perspective tightened. The band remained thick but what had looked at first to be gas and then asteroid debris defined into grey spheres as large as medium-sized asteroids. A stream of them began peeling off from the rest and entering the shift queue in an orderly fashion. Mira strained to understand; to see properly.

And then it made sense. In a horrifying way. She remembered them on the studium archivolos of the Stain Wars, but not in numbers. There must be millions. Millions upon millions. Geni-carriers OLOSS had called them, although the Post-Species had their own name: Intuitive Incendiary transporters. Some said they were actually sentient, like suicide bombers. In the final stages of the war, Lasper Farr's assailant ship had destroyed several Geni-carriers near the Mio moons. Then he'd turned on the OLOSS command ship in a bold display of assertion.

They are following Medium. Insignia's voice sounded so solemn that Mira wanted to cry.

The biozoon continued. *The explosive reaction caused by a single Geni-carrier could destroy half of Araldis. Reduce it to bare, broken rock. I have attempted to communicate the news to my pod, but farcast is restricted while we are here. I don't have access.*

We have to warn OLOSS! Mira's lips moved in agitation. *There are so many of them. In the war there were only a few, and the Commander destroyed them.*

Most believe the Post-Species withdrew because their armaments were inferior. However, it's possible that the Stain Wars were simply a trial run, to see the effectiveness of their weapons against humanesques and aliens.

Then you don't think Commander Farr was the orchestrator of peace?

From the information you have shared with me about Commander Farr, I don't believe he serves anyone other than himself. Whether his ambition is peace or not is difficult to predict.

Mira stirred in Primo, now restless in the comfort she had yearned to feel again. The vein adjusted around her, balancing her surge of adrenalin by stimulating other, pacifying chemical messengers. *Can you get us through shift without trouble?*

There are others of my kind in this system, hybrids, who have been trading. I believe that I can use them as distraction.

Then return to OLOSS space. We must try again to speak with them. And we cannot stay here.

Mira felt *Insignia*'s implicit agreement with that last thought. They were of one mind in this at least.

It will be dangerous to seek out OLOSS officials. OLOSS regards you as a criminal.

We must find a way despite that.

As the biozoon's biologics altered rhythm in preparation to join the shift queue, Mira relinquished her concentration on everything.

She would sleep again now, because later . . .

TEKTON

Samuelle received the message in the infirmary, delivered by an anxious-looking humanesque. While they stepped outside to confer, Tekton watched the rather magnificent woman – Fariss – hover over Berniere. If pheromones were visible, the infirmary would be alight with them. Tekton felt a sliver of jealousy, even in his weakened state; the look of the bold woman sent his akula rushing.

Fortunately Samuelle returned before it swelled him in a way that couldn't be ignored.

'Consilience and OLOSS are meeting on Intel station. We leave in a few hours to attend,' Samuelle announced to the room. 'Now we have to find a way to get you both on board unnoticed. Fariss?'

'I could take Thales on as my booty,' Fariss said.

Samuelle nodded and glanced at Thales. 'Dangerous, but believable.' She beckoned to the attendant, who hastened into the room.

'Cover his scars,' Samuelle ordered. 'Thales, Fariss will find you some suitable clothes.'

She turned her attention to Tekton. '*You* are more problematic, tyro. Your face is well known, and you are unmistakably Lostolian. I will have to think on it.' She tapped her finger to her cheek. Her nano-suit emitted a faint scraping sound as she turned abruptly to face Jelly Hob. 'Lasper wants you to fly his flagship.'

To Tekton's astonishment the hobo's eyes filled with tears, which proceeded to trickle down his gnarled cheeks to the skin folds of his neck.

'Truth, Sammy?' said Hob.

Samuelle nodded. 'He figured I'd know where to find you.' She displayed surprising patience, waiting for him to compose himself. 'What will you do?' she said as he palmed the tears away.

Hob shook his head and shrugged.

'We could do with you in there, Jeremy, in case things don't work out,' said Samuelle.

Jeremy? The old outcast had a real name? Tekton wanted to use his moud to verify it but stopped himself, mindful of Hob's warning.

'You know what that might mean though, don't you?' Samuelle pursed her dry lips.

A burbling noise emanated from somewhere deep in Hob's throat: indigestion of the emotional kind. He burped and cleared it. Finally, he got the words out. 'Got nothin' better to do I suppose, Sammy. Might get things right this time, eh?'

She nodded again, her face softening in understanding. 'We all might get it right this time.'

Get what right? Tekton was intrigued but knew better than to enquire at this point. 'Why do you want us to accompany you?' he asked instead.

'*You*, Tekton, are going to find Lasper's information device and steal it.'

'How did you know—'

But Sammy didn't let him finish. 'He'll have it with

him and you're the only one who's seen it other than that damn ferrety Lamin. The young one, Thales here, is our proof to the rest of Consilience that Farr's been playing his own agenda.'

'Why would you think that?' interjected Thales.

'Because we've been listening in on you two, dearie,' Samuelle cackled.

Tekton exchanged looks with Thales. How foolish of them to think they could speak freely here.

Tekton experienced a pang of regret. Perhaps he should never have left Belle-Monde. And yet the things he had learnt . . . Miranda's debilitating virus, and Ra's Dynamic System Device. Alongside those two, his offering to Sole of beauty seemed so . . . toothless. How naive he had been. He must reconsider his own design approach as soon as he could disentangle himself from these 'esques and their politics. The most important thing now was his safety. He must ensure it somehow. He must survive if he was still to beat his cousin Ra.

'What if I don't wish to go?' Tekton asked.

'You'll have trouble getting away from here even without Lasper around. Intel, though, will be full of your kind. You get hold of that device and I guarantee I'll cut you loose on Intel – Thales too, if he wants it.'

Tekton glanced at Thales again, but the young man had eyes only for Fariss.

'How will you keep Farr from discovering my presence aboard his ship?' Tekton asked her.

'You leave that to me, tyro. One thing no man will do, including Lasper Farr, is invade an old woman's privacy. There has to be some compensation for carrying around this face,' said Samuelle with a grin.

For some inexplicable reason, the words seemed to resonate deep within him, as if someone, somewhere before had uttered the exact same thing. He shrugged the foolish and worthless notion away.

THALES

His disguise appeared adequate in the milling excitement of disembarkation: artificial skin hiding his facial scars, nondescript garb and his long hair braided tightly to make him appear almost feminine.

The closer docks teemed with 'esques and aliens loading, or being loaded, into Lasper Farr's flagship. Further along later-model P-class assailants were being restocked by automon conveyors and cranes.

Thales had never seen fully functional weapon ships before. They left a cold feeling in his stomach, as did the hard-eyed mercenaries who lounged nearby on the docks in small groups.

Fariss strode along in front of him, responding when she chose to to those who called out to her. Thales heard the interest and the respect in their voices. Samuelle's main bodyguard was someone they noticed. And so, he hoped, they would not be inclined to stop and question the nervous 'esque carrying her personal weapon case.

'Got yerself some booty, Fariss,' yelled a loader operator.

'Never go nowhere without my foot-warmer,' she shouted back.

A round of guffaws from Farr's soldiers followed them along.

Not so, the mercenaries. They stared and nodded. That was all.

'Got him marked here as a body all right,' said the soldier checking entry detail. 'But I ain't got no name for him.' He looked up at Fariss, frowning. 'You gotta problem with your crew listings, Fariss?'

She shrugged. 'No problem. I ain't thought of a name for him yet.'

The soldier's eyes narrowed. 'I can't refuse you if you're on the manifest but I'm tellin' ya, there's some of the crew won't be likin' you having booty when they can't. Commander's revoked privileges for us, in case we don't come back for a while.'

'That's why I work for Samuelle. We don't come back, seems like all the more reason to have some relief, in my mind.'

The soldier made a sour face. 'Yeah, well, watch your booty's back. Might be a few that want a piece.'

Fariss's lips pursed and all her muscles tensed, making her appear even larger. 'You sayin' you want some?'

The soldier lifted his own shoulders in a defensive response. He mollified his tone. 'Watch his back is all I'm sayin', Fariss.'

'I can look after my own,' she replied and stalked on board.

Thales followed after her, his eyes downcast, not sure if he was appalled or thrilled by the charade. The idea of being at the whim of this woman enthralled him, yet their situation and the knowledge that he could be caught and killed nullified the pleasure.

He put one foot in front of the other in her wake,

locked in his own emotional battle, not really absorbing the ship surrounds. It wasn't until they reached their allotted cabin that he was forced from his introspection.

Fariss thumped her fist on the bunk, testing for comfort. 'Put the case under the lower bunk,' she told him. 'We've got the cabin to ourselves for the moment, but likely it won't be for long.'

Cabin? It was barely that, a partitioned space with narrow double bunks and a small work-entertainment station. The wardrobe was two drawers set into the cabin wall just below the comm screen.

Thales eyed the two beds. 'Floor for me?' he asked.

She gave him a good-humoured leer then lowered her voice. 'You'll be expected to sleep with me, otherwise it'll be suspicious.'

Thales felt his skin heating at the thought. 'Whatever is prudent,' he said carefully.

She continued to stare at him. 'Prudent, eh? Maybe there're some things you oughta know about booty. Booty only goes out of their cabin to eat and crap. San is down the corridor on the left. Check there is no one about before you go there. You eat in the mess with me, but at a separate table. Don't talk to anyone, and don't wander about for no good reason. Booty's fair game if they get caught out alone.' Her expression well and truly sobered. 'Farr's soldiers aren't like OLOSS military, Thales. Most of them are scum that couldn't pass the plain decency test. They'll kill you. Or whatever pleases them most.'

Thales's stomach tightened. He was completely dependent on her for his safety – his life. 'What happens when we reach Intel?'

Fariss folded her large frame into the bottom bunk. She patted the small remaining space. 'Come here and stop looking so damn scared.'

Thales obeyed her without thinking.

'You probably can guess better'n I can,' she said. 'I was a Savvy operator till Sammy offered me work. Had some kicking and punching skills. But she got me some real good lessons on fightin'. Turns out I learned quick. Been her bodyguard ever since. Not that she needs one. Her armour can do more damage than I can. She likes the extra set of eyes and ears around though. Says hers are getting old.' Fariss's hands moved in decisive gestures while she spoke.

Thales pictured them strangling his assassin on the docks. His confusion deepened. Every time he almost reached an understanding of himself or his situation, things changed; he changed. And now all he wanted was for Fariss to use her hands on him in some way.

Even so, he jumped when she leaned across and touched his face.

She was frowning. 'Your skin graft's lifting. I'll have to repair it.' She rolled off the bed and rummaged in her kit, returning a moment later with a slim cylinder of material. She settled cross-legged back on the bunk, unrolled the cylinder and fitted a tiny nozzle to a tube.

Her breath blew warm and strong on his face as she administered fresh adhesive to the artificial skin. 'Does the scar hurt?'

Thales couldn't stop trembling. She was so close now.

Bethany had never made him feel this way, and Aleta had been intoxicating but professionally aloof.

And Rene . . . he had trouble picturing his wife's face with Fariss's mouth so close to his.

On impulse he lifted his lips and pressed them to hers. The brief taste of her was breathtaking.

Then she hit him. Not a gentle slap, but a full-fisted punch to the jaw that laid him on the floor, stunned. He cupped his hands to his face in silent agony.

'See this is gonna be a fun trip,' said a strange voice.

Thales dashed the tears of pain and shock away and stared up. The 'esque who had joined them in the cabin was thick-shouldered, with a face which bore more scars than not. His eyes lay sunken under heavy lids, and he brought in with him the smell of unwashed flesh.

Fariss sprawled lengthways on the bed, hands behind her head. 'Sure it'll be,' she said casually, 'long as no one messes with what's mine. Fariss O'Dea. Can't say I've seen you before.'

'Macken. Fought with Lasper in the War. Commander asked special for me on this trip. Just got in from Mintaka to catch this ship back to Intel.'

'Long way around,' said Fariss thoughtfully. 'Why couldn't you just meet us there?'

Macken's chest swelled a bit. 'Commander wanted me on board. Keep an eye on things.' He gave Fariss a hard, pointed look. 'Guess he knows he can trust me.'

'Everyone *needs* someone they can trust, Macken. But if you're bunkin' down with me you *need* to wash.'

Thales flinched, expecting the man to react angrily to the insult, but just like the mercenary Rast Randall would have done, he laughed. 'You jus' keep your ruttin' quiet, Fariss O'Dea. I need my beauty sleep.'

He glanced down at Thales. 'Pretty one you got there. You wanna watch his tail.'

Fariss stuck out her jaw in a way that made her wide, generous face ugly. She swung her feet onto the floor and stood up, towering over Macken.

The war vet stood his ground, but like the check-in guard he mollified his tone. 'Jus' makin' an observation. No need ta get shirty.'

Fariss's lips eased into a smile. She held out her hand to shake Macken's. 'Welcome aboard.'

TEKTON

Tekton struggled with claustrophobia. Even his logic-mind had difficulty convincing him that he was perfectly safe crushed inside Samuelle's spare nano-suit. Since Lasper Farr's devious attempt to see him dead, and his subsequent rescue by Jelly Hob, Tekton's amygdala seemed to have overpowered his ability to think coherently. Sole had not factored the effect of sheer, animal terror into his mind division.

The problem was his head. It was squeezed uncomfortably into the neck section, which had then sealed itself shut. Though the suit's porous design allowed him to breathe perfectly normally, he could not shake the notion that he was in a burial wrap.

'Whatcha got in this one, Sammy? Dead body?' growled a surly voice. 'Commander's put limits on carry-on weight.'

'Quit whining, boy,' Samuelle replied. 'A woman's gotta have her extras for a long trip. Stashed me a bit of entertainment in there.'

'What? Booty?' The voice sounded surprised now.

Samuelle cackled. 'Do you know how old I am, soldier? Haven't used booty since I was a hundred and three, even then, it was in virt. Prefer the odd substance relaxation meself. But you wouldn't be telling anyone that, would you? Lest you be wanting a little free taste of Samuelle's candy.'

The 'esque paused. 'Take it to your cabin then, shall I, Sam?'

'Good lad,' said Samuelle. 'Good lad.'

Tekton endured the rough handling, disgusting grunts and loud profanity from the soldier who lugged him through the ship's corridors. But when, finally, he was dumped on a flat surface and left alone, Tekton became teary. Every muscle felt bruised and he fretted that the wounds on his legs had reopened. His life had taken a turn that he could not seem to control, and yet it seemed the only way through the circumstances was forward.

Find that device of Lasper Farr's then leave the ship at Intel and return to Belle-Monde, said logic-mind.

Free-mind was not so optimistic. *How can you make something so complex sound so simple?*

'That sniffling I can hear, Tekton?'

Samuelle peeled open the neck and suddenly he was out in ship air and feeling better. With her help, he shed the remainder of the suit and sank onto the narrow bed.

Samuelle wrinkled her nose as she lifted the suit away from him and onto a hook. 'You sure stank that up for an 'esque who don't sweat much.'

'My skin is sensitive to variations in the environment.' He tried to be arrogant and failed miserably. It seemed, since Jelly Hob had rescued him from certain death, that he did not have the heart for his usual conceits.

Samuelle moved quickly around the cabin, dropping things from her valise into the drawers and altering the environmental and comm specifications at the desk. 'I have to report to the Commander. Get some rest. I'll fix the lock from the outside. For Cruxsakes, don't use the comm while I'm out.'

Tekton stared at her, suddenly registering that he had to spend the duration of the trip to Intel in the close proximity of a strange, bossy and altogether physically unappealing old woman.

A clever and resourceful old woman, corrected logic-mind.

Free-mind would not be convinced. *But so ugly.*

As the cabin door shut and clicked to lock, Tekton fell onto the bed and curled into a ball. Sleep was always a good way to bypass unpleasant thoughts.

Tekton spent the short, sub-light leg to the Edo res-station wavering between boredom and fear. Samuelle set strict rules, which his logic-mind endorsed as sensible, and Tekton carefully obeyed, although he longed to be out of the cramped cabin and to be free to go wherever he chose.

Instead, he spent the time pondering recent events and talking to Samuelle about Lasper Farr. Though she remained guarded on the topic of Consilience, she seemed prepared to discuss the Stain Wars until Tekton hoped never to hear of them again. War stories, it seemed, were not simply the province of males.

'After the war I decided to stop rejuve,' she mused aloud. They'd quickly fallen to the habit of conversation with Tekton reclining on the bed and Samuelle at the comm-desk interfacing with the 'cast feeds. 'I found it damn useful looking like an old woman – in ways that I had never dreamt – as long, of course, as I kept my agility. Looking old's one thing, creakin' round like a bag-o'-bones is another. So I modified my suit from the combat models we used to wear on specials and kept a credit for organ renewal.'

'So you were . . . *are* a soldier.'

'Once upon a time, I was a forward scout for OLOSS. Saw the light after the war and paid out my draft. Consilience don't have those kind of structures. You get assigned to a task dependent on what you can do; organised disorder, some say. I say it's creative and effective.'

'But why do you live on Edo and work for Lasper?'

'I was with him in the war and it seemed it worked for us, for a start. He left us alone on Ampere 'cause I was valuable to him. I could do what I wanted without OLOSS breathin' down my neck. These days though, seems to be Lasper that's doing the heavy breathin'.' She leaned back in the desk-chair and in the time it took her to shut her eyelids, drifted off to sleep. The suit automatically stiffened and the collar elongated to accommodate her slackened muscles.

Tekton had already got used to her abrupt and unpredictable sleeping pattern. He moved quickly, standing and taking the four steps to the desk to peer over her shoulder. The deskfilm glowed with a representation of the Intel station and sphere. Intelspace was cluttered with the collisions of flashing icons and graphical depictions of ships and infrastructure.

As Tekton read the key on the side of the map he stifled a sharp breath. Attached to the station like the fringe of a woman's shawl, or hovering almost as close, were delegations from all over OLOSS. Above Intel's bulb, a flotilla of biozoons floated in ever-shifting formation; crowding the main landing bays were OLOSS official flagships, and jostling for position around the Scavvy docks were smaller alien deputations: uulis, skierans and others.

Tekton fancied the whole thing to be like an exotic underwater scene where sea creatures in search of food herded around the nearest reef, sucking at plankton and ducking in and out of crevices.

'Seems like word's got around, eh, tyro?' Samuelle was awake as instantaneously as she had fallen asleep. 'Lasper's got a 'cast coming through on relay.'

'How long until we shift?'

She sat up straighter and, sensing her alert state, her suit relaxed its support. She fingered through a few screens. 'Latest says an hour.'

'I'm assuming a war craft like this has group buffers. How do you propose to conduct me to one of them unnoticed?'

'Actually, tyro, I don't.'

Tekton's insides turned watery. Surely the woman had not forced him aboard merely to murder him?

Samuelle leaned back and slapped him across the back of the legs in a friendly gesture. 'You're gonna stay right here in that.' She pointed to her spare suit.

'B-b-ut I'll . . . it'll . . . I'll . . . d-d—'

'Rubbish,' she snapped. 'It's designed to withstand shift and more. I modified it that way. I'd stay in here with you but I don't want Lasper asking questions. Look, if you need reassurance, here are the specs.'

Mira

Insignia?

We are at Intel station, dearest.

Mira wrenched upward, out of her reclining position in Primo. How long had she been asleep? *Too long*, she thought. It felt that way at least. Her mind was thick and stale. The vein let her go, its sensors like sticky fingers sliding reluctantly from her flesh.

How long have I been asleep?

I assisted your rest through shift. The baby has had quite enough trauma.

I told you not to do that again.

I am not beholden to you, Mira, Insignia chided. *Our bond is my choice.*

And mine.

Perhaps.

Mira controlled her desire to argue. *Why did you bring us back here?*

I shifted to Rho Junction. When I was able to contact my pod they told me that Emergency Council had been called on Intel. Our community had already sent envoys to meet with OLOSS and Consilience. They gave me permission to join our delegation. We are safe here among the envoys. Humanesques would not know one of us from another.

As her mind began to awaken Mira sensed *Insignia*'s

improved mood, despite the biozoon's sarcasm and provocation.

Mira relaxed a little. *Can you show me?*

Of course.

Insignia's view of near-space poured into Mira's mind. Ahead of them, Intel's irregular lattice of grey landing channels invited docking, while alongside them the dark was cluttered with familiar shapes lit by the station's external lights: biozoons of varying sizes, some several times larger than *Insignia*.

Insignia changed her perspective several times.

Are we in the centre of the pod? Mira asked

Insignia made a sound that Mira had not heard in a long time; a sound of amusement. *This is not the pod, Innate, this is an Omniline.*

Mira waited, knowing *Insignia* would only explain when she was ready. Meanwhile she let the images absorb her, curious to see biozoons en masse for the first time. They floated serenely, elegantly, near each other; shifting to fit around each others' movements like a school of fish.

Omniline is a hereditary line somewhat like your familia, though much better behaved, *Insignia* told Mira.

You mean that a single family has been sent here to negotiate?

That is the manner in which we are organised. It is most expedient. I share lineage with the Envoy Omniline, so they will allow us to be present.

Mira thought about it for a moment. It really was not greatly different from humanesque social ordering. *That is kind of them.*

We are a very reasonable species. The rebuke in *Insignia*'s tone was unmistakable.

And we are not always. Mira sighed. *Often*, she corrected. *How are we to find a way to communicate with OLOSS? Landhurst is untrustworthy.*

We can use the Omniline Envoy to disseminate information to the Council, but it may draw attention to the cluster. We could be identified under close scrutiny.

Can we share what we know with the Omniline from a greater distance?

I cannot project my memories over farcast distances. Our close-sharing process requires proximity.

This time Mira sat up properly, and after a moment, stood. Despite the vein's nurturing, lengthy periods in Primo always left her muscles weakened. *I will wash and eat.*

Sensible.

'Mira-fedor?' a voice said from near her feet.

Mira started. She had forgotten Wanton. The Extro still sat where she had placed it, on the floor near the pucker. She bent down and picked it up.

'Si, Wanton?' She examined the gelatinous casing and it seemed to have regained full lustre.

'Thank you; you have perpetuated my existence for a time.'

'Circumstance helped,' said Mira. 'It was fortunate that some mycose had been . . . left here. Has it replaced what was depleted?'

'Although you will not be able to see it, I have a minute fracture in my shell. I will need frequent resuscitation until I can find a way to relayer my protection.'

Mira frowned. 'How often is frequent, Wanton?'

'From what I could see of the package, I expect to

have used the available resources within a few of your grouped cycles.'

'Months?'

'Yes.'

'What will happen if you don't get more?'

'Wanton will become inactive for a period and eventually its core will degrade. Beyond that, Wanton is not sure.'

Mira shifted the Extro to her other hand. Perhaps she imagined it, but Wanton sounded scared. She expected that death – or non-existence – was not a concept that Post-Species contemplated in the way humanesques did. Death of their Host was the closest they came to bereavement, and from her observations on the Hue world, some did not grieve for deceased Hosts at all.

Her sympathies for Wanton grew, as did the less-than-generous notion that the Extro might finally experience real fear in the way she had lived and breathed it since her graduation on Araldis.

Mira, we have an inconvenience.

What is it?

The Omniline will not agree to relay our observations of the Geni-carriers.

Why?

A section of the Omniline is concerned that evidence of our kind's presence in Post-Species space may be considered suspicious. The mood amongst the allies is precarious and changeable. We cannot predict the outcome of sharing such information.

Mira stepped back from the pucker and ran her hand through her hair. It felt long and matted from her prolonged rest in Primo. She glanced at the hand. Though her skin remained supple enough, the veins showed through and the joints of her fingers seemed painfully large against the rest. She had no fat on her. No meat to support her baby and herself. *But they must know what we saw.* She would not back down on this.

The Omniline is divided. We do not wish to be victimised by panic reactions. Humanesques can be irrational.

Mira drew a ragged breath and crossed her arms. *I understand the Omniline's fears but we must take that risk. The Geni-carriers contained enough weaponry to destroy most of the OLOSS worlds. Or lay them barren. It is not just our species who is threatened.*

The Omniline must be heeded. Insignia remained stubborn.

'Then I will go,' Mira said aloud and without hesitation.

No. You may not risk our child further. The decision rests with the Omniline.

Mira stepped back towards the buccal pucker, carrying Wanton in one hand. She would not let *Insignia* keep her captive. She pressed her fist against the sphincter and it retracted. *Then I will wash and eat, and then I will meet with your Omniarch. Please arrange for me to go to it,* she commanded.

She went to Rast's cabin on the way to her own, and retrieved the cyrotrays.

Insignia did not respond until Mira had finished with her steam bath and was dressing.

Why are you using the royal fellala? asked the biozoon suspiciously.

Because I wish to make a good impression. And it better

hides my belly. Are the arrangements made? Mira pressed along the brocade trim to seal the robe, and knelt down to lift the cryotrays of mycose onto her bed. She popped a number of the beads and formed a cluster on her desk. She then settled Wanton in the middle of them. The Extro had been quiet, conserving its energy.

'Wanton, I am leaving *Insignia* for a short while. I have placed you close to the mycose. Are you able to draw them to you as you need them?'

'Thank you, Mira-fedor, that will work adequately.'

'Use them sparingly. I will attempt to find a solution to your problem. If you have any ideas while I am gone then tell *Insignia*. *Insignia* will relay them to me.'

'How long will you be gone?' The Extro sounded anxious. 'I should not need so much if your absence is brief.'

Mira was careful not to hesitate. 'Not long at all, but I must speak with the biozoon Omniarch. It is better that you have more mycose than less.'

She left the cabin carrying a royal headdress and proceeded to the cucina, where she forced herself to eat overripe cheese and some soft dough that she mixed from a sachet. She couldn't seem to remember the last time she'd enjoyed a meal, and the prolonged time spent in Primo had left her digestive system unused to solid food. She found herself nibbling the tiniest pieces just to be able to swallow.

When she had almost finished the cheese she felt a small surge of energy. She searched amongst the shelves for something to drink and located a store of animal milk supplied by Lasper Farr. It tasted bitter and rich but washed the cheese down enough that her mild attack of nausea settled.

Our Omniarch has agreed to your presence. Go to the lower armament store.

But that is near your tail spine.

We do not have a system for coupling using our egress scales. That is a modified entry point for other species only.

Then—

Hasten to my pelvic girdle. On the outer wall you will find three vents. Insert your body through the slit into the centre one. Do not make a mistake. The outer vents are used for fertilisation and should you enter them, you will be crushed in the clasping. The centre vent is not penetrated. We use it to transfer substances through suction extraction. The Omniarch will only attempt one exchange. The area we are occupying near the station is too congested for repeated manoeuvres.

Mira hurried downward to the area *Insignia* had specified, not daring to think what the process of suction extraction might entail.

Though she knew *Insignia*'s anatomy better than her own, she hadn't ventured to the biozoon's pelvic cavity on *Insignia*'s own warning of infection. Now she counted her way along the gill bars to the pectoral stratum, until she reached the thick cartilage wall that divided it from the pelvic section.

Wait. My pelvic girdle is inhabited by bacteria that are not deemed safe for your kind. I will flush the area with acid. That will give you a short time to transfer safely.

Will the acid residue harm me?

No more than if you emptied the contents of your own stomach onto me.

Mira found herself able to smile. *I think I have done that several times.*

Yes. You have. Please remember your manners when you are with the Omniarch.

Mira faced the barrier of gristly, grey membrane and waited. There was little ambient light at the narrow end of the biozoon's body, barely enough to see her way; and even that she sensed *Insignia* had manufactured for her comfort.

After a time, a bubble appeared in part of the membrane between the cartilage deposits. It grew larger and larger as if filling with gas, and turned a deep purplish colour. Mira stepped back automatically and a moment later it ruptured, trickling blood onto the floor and leaving a narrow, rucked slit.

Step through now. I heal very quickly in this area, Insignia ordered.

Mira forced her body through the gap, though it was barely large enough for someone half her stature. *Not for someone at all*, she realised as she pressed against the stickiness. *It's porous to allow for transference of fluids – not objects. Insignia* had deliberately torn the membrane to allow her to pass.

As she squeezed through, the hole was already closing on itself, and she was forced to drop the royal headdress. She found herself pressed into a narrow gap – nothing as wide as a chamber. The three vents *Insignia* had spoken of were higher than her head and surrounded by spongy tissue, thicker and more resilient than the membrane, and dotted with dentricles.

Tentatively she pushed her toe into *Insignia*'s flesh. It depressed enough for her to find purchase. Reaching as high as she could, she grasped a dentricle in each hand and began to climb towards the middle vent. But her pregnant belly hampered her agility and she over-balanced backward, falling hard against the cartilage and banging her ribs.

The child inside her moved, jabbing her lower belly, and making her nauseous as it spun rapidly in her womb. She tried to calm it by pressing her abdomen, but the child seemed frantic. The next strong jab hit up under her breastbone, bringing tears to her eyes.

'Be still if you want me to succeed!' she cried aloud. She struggled to her feet and tried again.

The child settled as she climbed. In the back of her mind she sensed *Insignia*'s behaviour changing as well. The biozoon seemed almost submissive. Though she could feel no movement, an image formed in her mind, of *Insignia* arching its long back and curling its tail carefully out of the way.

Fear and urgency gripped her. Clasping was immi-nent, and she had no idea how far the Omniarch's stems would penetrate the other vents, or how much dis-tortion would occur in the tissue. She had to be inside the central one to be safe.

She scrabbled over the lip and slid forward into the wetness as the biozoon's entire pelvic girdle began to shudder. She felt building waves of vibration and the vent began to contract against her as if being squeezed shut. For a moment she feared she'd be crushed, but with each contraction she was sucked deeper into the vent.

At some point she was no longer on board *Insignia*. She knew that from her mind-bond, not from any change in the vent's shape or consistency.

The vibrations had stilled and she lay in the dark, pressed uncomfortably on her stomach, without room even to roll onto her back.

Insignia?

Your mind-bond with your mate will be much weaker while you are with me.

Omniarch?

You may address me as Ley-al.

I am Mira Fedor.

Yes, Innate. I am aware of who you are. Why do you insist upon meeting with me under these circumstances?

Ley-al, if you please, I am most uncomfortable lying upon my unborn child. Is it possible for me to move?

Very well.

Mira felt a constriction around her shoulders and hips again, as the peristaltic action of the vent moved her forward. Pain shot through her abdomen and dimly Mira felt *Insignia*'s protest.

Then she was squeezed out of the vent into a small ribbed space.

Follow the passage to the central stratum. It is a direct link to my buccal.

Mira got to her feet shakily. Though her limbs trembled under the energy demand and her belly ached, stubborn determination lent her strength. She'd failed to bring help to Araldis; she would not fail to warn OLOSS of the danger, even if she must face

Stationmaster Landhurst and Sophos Mianos again. *I will be heard. And after that . . .* She shrugged to herself. After that, it didn't matter.

Ley-al's buccal was large and divided by membranous struts like supporting trunks shot down from an over-sized tree. A familiar iodine smell assailed Mira as she entered, but that was where Ley-al's similarity to *Insignia* ended. There was no Autonomy nub and the Primo vein was buried under a layer of pulsating skin. There was no concession to humanesque passengers. The biozoon's cheek cavity was purely animal.

I had an Innate once, Mira Fedor, but it was not to my liking.

Now that she was closer to its brain she felt the full force of the Omniarch's imposing presence.

How is it that you can mind-speak with me even though we are not bonded?

All the negotiators of our species can do so. Now, explain why you have requested this visit in the midst of such difficult circumstances.

Mira felt for *Insignia* but Ley-al's presence over-whelmed her senses. She hoped that meant *Insignia* would experience the same clouding. *You've seen the threat from the Post-Species. You would agree it is disturbing and dangerous for all sentients?*

Ley-al made a sound that Mira interpreted as a grunt. *It is terrifying, but I will not risk a spontaneous reaction against the pod by revealing this information.*

I understand. Mira attempted to be sympathetic. *And I have a solution. If you allow me to disembark then I will be the one to do it.*

Ley-al paused, considering Mira's offer. *Why did you need to offer this course of action personally? Tasy-al could have conveyed this to the Omniline.*

Tasy-al? Did Ley-al mean *Insignia*? Of course. *Insignia* was merely its Latino name.

Mira walked deeper into the buccal, until she stood as close as she could to the wall that separated it from Ley-al's brain cavity. It was time for the truth.

I am carrying a child to which Insignia – *Tasy-al – is very attached. Tasy-al will not permit me to risk its life in any way.*

Tasy-al is holding you captive? Ley-al's tone lifted from a thunderous rumbling to a concerned roar.

We are in disagreement about my ability to care for myself – that is all, Mira explained hurriedly, *and I don't believe there is time enough for us to reach an amicable agreement.*

Ley-al indulged in another protracted silence.

Mira glanced down at herself while she waited. Drying mucus flaked from the folds of the royal fellala and the robe was badly crumpled even by a mercenary's standards. Without looking in a mirror she knew that she appeared much less than aristo. She touched her hair: stiff with the same substance.

A wave of dizziness came over her then. She searched for somewhere to sit and saw nothing that would suffice. Instead she settled for leaning one arm against the wall. Her other hand strayed to her belly.

I have conferred with the group, and it is agreed that you should proceed. It is important that you are not seen to be associated with the Omniline. Go to the section of my pelvic girdle that you would know as the hold, and secrete yourself in a milk bladder. They are our gifts to the OLOSS delegation.

I will send a shuttle across and servitors will remove them. Once you are on the station you are responsible for your own survival.

A retort rose to her lips but she suppressed it. It was her Innate talent, her ability to communicate with these creatures, that put her constantly in danger. Couldn't these sophistic creatures see that? Instead she nodded. *Thank you, Ley-al.* She hesitated. *Does* Insignia *know?*

Tasy-al is unaware of our agreement. Tasy-al will be informed once you have debarked.

And not before. Please.

Agreed. The Omniline bids you farewell. It is most likely, in our estimation, that you will not return. Be assured we will console Tasy-al with a suitable replacement.

At one time the Omniarch's blunt comment might have upset or offended her, but she had grown accustomed to the biozoons' manner. Now, strangely enough, as she made her way along the main stratum she could only feel grateful.

THALES

Fariss's fingers tugged at Thales's waistband and her lips pressed against his ear. They lay sandwiched together on the bunk, in the dark, Fariss's large naked frame taking up most of the space. She smelt of sweat and something sweeter.

'He'll be expecting to hear us,' she whispered. 'Otherwise he'll be suspicious.'

Thales's heart fluttered with excitement and nervousness. 'You . . . do you . . . I mean . . .'

Her hand slipped below inside the loose waistband and cupped his testicles. She began to massage them with strong, practised fingers that fell just short of inflicting pain.

He hardened almost reflexively.

'I mean . . . get on top of me,' she ordered.

In a clumsy, inexpert move, Thales rolled onto her. With their heads level, his toes scraped above her ankles. She put her hands on his shoulders and pushed him down so that their groins met. Then she wrapped her legs around him and used her hand to guide him inside her.

Thales listed in a sea of conflicting emotions: arousal, embarrassment – a woman had never handled him so perfunctorily before – and fear, what if he couldn't perform? He'd never had to like this – not on demand.

Fariss must have sensed his turmoil, his softening. She put her lips to his and filled his mouth with her tongue. With unreasonably strong arms and legs, she crushed him against her.

He felt helpless in her grip and with that came a surge of desire. He hardened again and began to strain. She loosened her hold, enough for him to move. Within moments he climaxed, unable to stifle the sounds.

In the bunk above them Macken rolled over and grunted.

Thales lay on top of her panting and embarrassed, hoping that the mercenary was asleep.

Fariss shrugged Thales off her and grabbed his hand. Without a qualm she placed it between her legs. 'Don't think you get to have all the fun,' she whispered.

She guided him then, showing him how and where to stimulate her, forcing his fingers to slide swiftly against the wet nub of her clitoris.

She orgasmed easily, giving loud, unguarded cries.

When she'd finished, she crooked an arm around him and drew him against her chest. Thales felt peculiar in that position – not a man's position – although Rene had often liked him to put his head on her lap. But that had been comforting, like a parent tending her child. Nothing about Fariss was motherly. And yet, as she fell into a quick and deep sleep, he felt protected and for the briefest moment – content.

The contentment disappeared when he woke to Fariss rolling out of bed. Macken was already on the floor next to her, swearing and pulling on his pants.

'We're shifting early,' Fariss explained. 'Gotta get

into the cans.' She hooked Thales's clothes up with her foot and flicked them at him. 'I need to check in on Sammy. Wait here for me.'

'I'll take him to the cans if you want,' Macken offered.

Fariss leant over to the wall and palmed on the lights. She stared hard at the merc. 'That a straight-up offer?'

Macken shrugged. 'Sure thing. I'm goin' there, ain't I? Not planning to stay here and rattle to death.'

She nodded slowly. 'All right, but don't mess with my booty, Macken. I'll come after you.' She looked down at Thales.

'Sh-shouldn't I stay with you?' he asked.

'Sammy's up a few levels. Don't want to run out of time getting back and have to leave you here during shift.'

Thales licked dry lips. He didn't want that either.

'F-fine.' He got up and began pulling on his borrowed clothes.

Fariss dragged her weapons case out from under the bunk and removed something – a rifle, he thought. She closed the lid and keyed the lock. Then, to his surprise, she dropped a light kiss on his head as she bent to pull on her boots. 'See you soon.' With the hand Macken couldn't see she pushed something small and hard into the pocket of Thales's pants.

She was gone then, leaving him alone with the mercenary and his stale sweat smell.

Thales straightened up. He was shorter and much slimmer than the man, but he squared his shoulders.

'What's yer rush, booty?' Macken slouched over between Thales and the door. 'Siren gives us the final call. Wouldn't want to get you in there too soon 'mong all those wantin' types. Not without yer missus. Tho' can't see what's drawing her fanny to the likes of you. Bit fuckin' scrawny I woulda thought.'

Thales stayed quiet, containing his anger and chagrin. The man was as uncouth and vulgar as any he'd met – and pleased with himself, as well. Not in a harmless, boastful manner either. Macken's ego made him dangerous.

'Yer don't say much tho'. Mebbe that's why she likes you. Something to be said for booty that doesn't gab. I'm more partial to wimmen in the sack meself, but they c'n bend yer ear so fierce you wanna snap their damn necks.'

Thales backed away until he felt the opposite wall against his shoulder blades. He prayed for the siren to sound, calling them to the vibration buffer. 'What do you think will happen when we reach Intel?' he asked, seeking distraction.

Macken stiffened for an instant then his mouth split into a less than pleasant smile. 'My, my, now ain't that a pretty little accent you got going there? You come through one of those expensive whorehouses then?'

Thales nodded quickly to cover his error. 'Yes.'

Macken persisted. 'Which one?'

Thales racked his memory for the name of Aleta's group. 'Ardour.'

Immediately he knew he'd made an even bigger mistake.

'Ah, no wonder that big bitch brought you along.' Macken's face reddened, sending shivers of alarm shooting through Thales's stomach. He wanted to run out into the corridor but knew he'd never get past the mercenary.

'Planning to sell you to some to rich OLOSS type, is she? Mebbe she's smarter than she looks.' He took a step forward. 'Think I might be tasting a little bit for free first though. Whores is whores in my mind – and I don't pay for them, no matter how ejicated.'

He took another step.

Thales lurched to one side and tried to duck around. He got his hand to the door before Macken dragged him back. The brawny man threw him up against the wall.

Thales struggled, but Macken flattened against him, crushing him with his superior weight.

Thales screamed for help.

Macken smacked him across the side of the mouth and punched him in the soft part of his back.

Thales crumpled to the floor.

Macken wrenched Thales's pants down to his knees and partly lifted him to his feet. 'You don't act like any whore I've ever had. So let's have a little taste of what makes you special.' He rolled Thales over and threw him forward over the comm-desk.

Thales tried to twist away from him but Macken struck him again; an open-handed smack across the side of the jaw, connecting with the same spot Fariss had hit earlier.

The bruising accentuated the pain, and a sick feeling climbed the back of his throat. He curled further forward and felt the hardness of Fariss's weapon press into his thigh.

Kill him. The desire overwhelmed every other thought and sensation.

He slipped shaking fingers into his pocket.

As Macken attempted to penetrate him in a brutal first thrust, Thales found the trigger slot. He fumbled the pistol free of his pocket and turned the nozzle backwards, so that it pointed between his legs.

It discharged into Macken's groin, sending the mercenary flopping back onto the floor.

Thales remained frozen by what he'd done, even when the warning sirens began to blare and the door opened abruptly.

Fariss burst into the cabin, bearing her blunt, stubby rifle. She assessed the situation in a single breath. Bending down, she wrapped her hands around Macken's thick neck and jerked it sharply to make sure he was dead. Then she stepped over his still form and pulled Thales's pants up.

'We have to get to the cans,' was all she said. 'Hurry.'

Thales clung to her in the vibration shelter. He couldn't help it. The steady pressure of her arm around him as he pressed his face into her chest was the only thing that stopped him from screaming or sobbing.

The catcalls and smutty comments from the soldiers packed alongside them on the benches were blank noise. His consciousness centred on Fariss, and the slight vibration and movement of her chest as she breathed and spoke – countering them with her own remarks.

When the res-shift was over, she didn't lead him back to their cabin but took the crowded lift down to the ship's hold. They wove between rows of containers until she found a small, plax-partitioned cubicle.

Through the daze of shock, he watched her enter and speak earnestly to an 'esque dressed in standard work overalls. The 'esque nodded as Fariss handed him something.

She left the cubicle and came back to him. Her eyes showed him a kind of impatient sympathy. She grabbed his shoulders. 'We'll be docked in a few hours. You have to stay out of sight until then. Understand?'

Thales tried. The words made sense but he couldn't react to them.

She shook him gently. 'Macken was slime, but there'll be fallout. They'll come looking. I'll say I shot him because he was chasing my booty. I'll say you got scared and disappeared. So much will be goin' on now we're here; they won't have time to search for you. I've paid the operator to get you off the ship when they start unloading.' Her expression softened a fraction. 'Find somewhere safe and contact Sammy through the station comm.'

'You?' Thales managed to get the question out, but his voice sounded so distant, so foreign, he wasn't sure if he'd even spoken it.

'I shouldn't have left you with him. I shoulda known.' Her brow creased in intense frustration so that her wide face seemed full of anger. She pulled him to her in a rough hug and then pushed him away.

He watched her stride off between the rows of containers.

'Get yer arse in here, mate.' The 'esque was behind him, pointing to an open refrigerated carton used for food transport. 'I'll leave the cooler off and the vents open. The automons'll move you out in a few hours to the quarantine area. Intel likes to spray everything down before they convey 'em to the refill depot. Get out before they fumigate.'

Thales nodded dumbly. He climbed into the carton and a moment later was in complete darkness.

MIRA

You will soon be removed to the station quarantine area. It is my recommendation that you vacate before the fumigation process. The Omniline will not recognise your status should you be discovered in the quarantine area. Farewell, Innate.

The Omniarch's mental presence had already started to diminish in her mind. As a servitor jostled the mound of milk bladders out of the biozoon's pelvic cavity and into a shuttle, Mira felt it drop away altogether to be replaced by *Insignia*'s fury.

What have you done, Mira Fedor?

I have made an agreement with the Omniline.

You heedlessly risk the life of our child?

It is not heedless, neither is it our *child*, she corrected.

You made *an agreement with me.*

Mira clenched her jaw. *And I will keep that promise. But I have to warn OLOSS, otherwise I will have failed at everything. Don't you see? It's not just Araldis at risk now. The Post-Species threaten our existence.*

Several jolts shook her as she was lifted and stacked ready for transport. Then stillness followed while the shuttle covered the short distance from Ley-al to station quarantine.

Your higher ambitions don't concern me, Insignia persisted.

They are not higher ambitions. I was the only one who

could bring help to little Vito and Cass Mulravey and the korm. Do you know how it feels to have left your bambino to die?

The child you call Vito is not your baby.

Not my own flesh, but as dear to me.

That doesn't make sense.

Mira clenched her jaw in frustration. *How can you be so self-interested?*

How can you *be so irresponsible?*

She fell silent. *Insignia* did not – would not – see her viewpoint.

A second series of jolts sent Mira tipping forward onto her knees, as another automaton collected her from the shuttle and trundled down a steep incline. When it evened out, she was tipped back, jarring her spine. Cramps beset her legs and feet, and she bit her lip to stop from crying out. She massaged her legs with her fingers and prayed for the servitor to hurry.

Finally, all was still again.

She waited for a while before she allowed herself to prise open the bladder's flexible seal.

The quarantine area was a large, gloomy, flat expanse littered with cartons and containers and divided by conveyors. Automons ducked in and out of rows, unstacking and ordering and placing things on the maze of stationary tracks. A soft pulsing noise filled the air. She glanced upward, noticing the large, fat pipes protruding from the ceiling. When the time came to spray the incoming cargo, they would extend down to the middle of the warehouse. Already she could see the hydraulic hoses flexing.

Hampered by her thicker robe, she took long minutes

to wriggle out of the sour-smelling bladder. The exertion made her light-headed and she pressed her hand to her mouth to stave off sickness. It seemed that every time she placed a demand on her body it reacted with nausea or fatigue. The 'bino drained her.

She threaded her way between containers, stopping to peer around each one, fearing discovery, but the quarantine area seemed fully automated and devoid of 'esque or alien.

An automaton had already picked up her empty bladder and distributed it to a conveyor. When she reached halfway to the exit, the ceiling tubes began to descend.

Mira increased her pace, careless of discovery now. She had to get out before the spraying started. But the door was too far. She glanced around frantically. The nearest conveyor disappeared into a narrow cavity in the wall. She ran alongside it, planning to climb onto the conveyor and crawl through its tunnel. As she reached the wall and climbed up onto the track, she heard a noise. Not the hissing of the tube hydraulics or the whine of the scurrying automatons – more like an animal caught in something.

She climbed onto the track and glanced backwards. One of the containers behind her on the conveyor was making erratic, rocking movements. Had something alive been trapped in there?

Above her, the bottom of each ceiling tube had opened and projected a directional nozzle.

She crouched, preparing to crawl through the rubber-fringed entrance to the cargo tunnel, but the container noise became louder and punctuated with sounds that could have been grunts. Not animal, perhaps ... but surely not ...

She climbed around the cartons between her and the moving container and bent to inspect it. It was adorned with icons denoting it as a refrigerator, and she sighted the refrigerant bar along one side. Now she was closer, she could see the door partially opened but the latch caught on the carton next to it.

Using her knees and lower body she shifted the neighbouring carton a fraction closer to release the latch.

The door of the refrigerated container flew open and a body spilled out, almost knocking her off the conveyor. She scrambled onto the top of the carton and clung to it.

The 'esque emitted a moan or a sob, she could not tell which, and glanced wildly around. Eyes fixed on her, unfocused at first and then slowly, incredulously widening.

'Baronessa?' The male 'esque's voice was hoarse with emotion and distress.

She stared into the stranger's face. How did this man know her?

She inhaled sharply and then stopped. The taint of something sickly sweet filled her lungs. She let out her breath. 'Quickly,' she said. 'The spray.'

He followed her back along the conveyor, crawling into the wall cavity behind her. The conveyor veered off at a right angle, disappearing through a slot under a closed shutter. There wasn't enough space for them to follow it.

'We're trapped,' said Mira shrilly.

The 'esque seemed even more frantic than she,

flailing at the first shutter with his fists in a way that seemed familiar.

'It's unbreakable,' she said automatically. Something about his panic had the reverse effect on her. She felt calmer; more able to think. 'There must be a failsafe option. Automated facilities are required to have them.' She knew that from the flight manuals she'd studied. 'Look for a flywheel or an embedded disc.'

The 'esque obediently began searching one side of the small tunnel section while she looked over the other. The sweetly poisoned scent was creeping in.

'Here,' he cried, pointing overhead.

'Spin it,' she instructed. 'Quickly.'

He worked the embedded wheel with frantic fingers but it was stiff and unresponsive. 'It won't move,' he gasped.

'Harder!' she urged him. She put her sleeve to her mouth. The scent was stronger in only a few breaths.

He grunted with effort, the way he had when still trapped in the container, biting his lip, screwing up his face. As he did a flap of skin moved along his cheek as though it might slough off altogether.

He wiped the sweat from his face against his sleeve as he pressed on the wheel. The skin peeled off and fell onto the belt. Beneath it was an ugly, blackened scar.

'It's moving!' His voice raised, and slowly, as he wound, so did the screen.

When it was just high enough for them to crawl under she bade him leave the winding. He followed her again and she could hear him coughing and grabbing his throat.

Mira wanted to do the same. The fumes were caught in her chest and mouth, coating them. As soon as she was through, she was up on her feet searching for the next failsafe.

'S-same p-place,' she gulped.

The 'esque reached up to the wheel but couldn't hold his body steady. He collapsed forward, hands on the floor, mouth open wide.

'Close it.' She didn't urge him this time, she demanded. 'Wind it closed, *now!*'

He reached up again and began the reverse process. This wheel worked more easily. In a few movements he had closed the screen behind them.

They both fell to the floor either side of the conveyor, shielding their noses and mouths with their clothes.

Mira's eyes streamed and the 'esque began to cough violently.

Neither spoke until the fumes lessened and their symptoms began to abate. 'Climb onto the belt,' she managed finally. 'As soon as the pipes retract it will move.'

Her instruction brought them closer together. The 'esque was shuddering, his chest heaving against the poisoned fumes still. 'Don't – you – know me?'

She looked at him, close as he now was. So much of his face seemed familiar, but the fear in his eyes and the haggardness and scarring were not. 'Who?' She was still not able to waste breath on unnecessary words.

'I am Thales,' he said. 'Thales Berniere.'

THALES

Thales watched the Baronessa's face fill with confusion. 'Th-Thales? Thales Berniere?'

He swallowed, trying to wet his dry, irritated throat. 'I-I have had much m-misfortune since we p-parted.'

'You had had much misfortune when we met,' she whispered, with the ghost of a smile.

Thales could not return it. 'It follows me.'

Her eyes roamed his face, and he saw her try to connect what she knew of him with what she saw. 'Our circumstances must be equally dire if we meet again in such surroundings.'

'Then you first, Baronessa.' He mustered some gentlemanly manner. Not just his appearance had changed, he knew, but even the patterns of his speech.

Yet he was not alone in change. Mira Fedor was even gaunter than before, and her smooth skin showed the beginnings of lines at the corners of her eyes and mouth. More significant, though, was the change in her expression. The confusion and softness had left her. He saw only determination and below that, perhaps, a deeply embedded anger.

She nodded. 'But quickly. The conveyor will start soon and we will need to move with it.'

'I was told that the Extros had kidnapped you,' said Thales.

'That is true. As you can see, I have escaped . . . but with dire news. The Post-Species have amassed a huge scale of weaponry. I must find my way into the OLOSS assemblage and inform them.'

'But you are sought by OLOSS for questioning. They won't believe you.'

'I can make them believe, but not if I'm prevented from presenting what I know by Stationmaster Landhurst.' Mira shifted position and he suddenly noticed her swelling belly.

She saw Thales staring and waited.

'Baronessa? Are you . . .'

She placed her hands across the small mound. 'I was raped on Araldis by my Principe. He saw it as the only way to ensure the survival of his bloodline. I was the only surviving Crown Aristo.' Her eyes met his without embarrassment or upset.

'Then all the time that we travelled together, you were . . .'

'Si.' She nodded.

A muffled alarm sounded and the shutters lifted. The conveyor began to move. The rocking forced them both to grab the edges of the belt.

'I know a woman who will be at the meeting, Baronessa. But . . .' *But what?* Could he tell this poor, ragged woman that he had just killed a man to avoid his own rape, and that he now had to stay hidden? *No. Not yet.* But he could do his best to help her. 'We should find fresh clothes and a safe place for a few hours. The meeting is scheduled for station morning.' He peered ahead. 'It's hard to tell, but I think it's evening.'

Mira stared at him with a hint of suspicion. 'A contact?'

As the conveyor trundled them on he gave her an abridged account of events. 'Samuelle will be at the meeting. She'll help you.'

'Who is Samuelle? A safe place? New clothes? But I have no lucre and no credit.'

Thales felt in his pocket. His aspect cube was still there. He pulled it out and removed Rene's credit clip. 'But I do.'

The conveyor stopped in the recesses of a food depot storage area, and began its loop back to the fumigation chamber. The dim lighting and lack of 'esque or alien presence confirmed Thales's impression that it was station evening.

They crept past the automons and large refrigerated containers, and into the warren of narrow service corridors. Eventually one led them out into a busy food court.

Thales hesitated, crouching down behind a row of cleaning trolleys. He gave Mira the credit clip. 'My face . . . I'll wait here.'

She nodded and returned shortly with warm bread and berry tubes. Thales ate his ravenously but the Baronessa sipped her drink slowly, nervously glancing around.

'I'll watch now,' said Thales, brushing the crumbs from his fingers and standing.

With obvious relief she sank down behind the trolleys and began to nibble on the bread. But her whole body started to tremble, as though the food somehow made her weaker. When she tried to stand her legs collapsed underneath her.

Thales leant down to her. 'Baronessa?'

'The child . . .' she cried, clutching her stomach. 'Thales! Help me!'

TEKTON

Tekton paused at the door to Lasper Farr's cabin and reviewed the spatial image of the map he'd committed to memory. Samuelle had been showing him the route on the comm-desk when something had sent her wheezing out of the cabin with unseemly haste.

It had occurred to Tekton right then that using Samuelle's spare nano-suit might be a clever way to reach the upper levels of the ship's bow without too much fuss. The Commander's soldiers were, after all, used to seeing Samuelle in it.

And up to this point, his idea had worked. He'd proceeded unhampered through the ship, disguising his face by pinching the suit's hood so tight that only his eyes remained visible.

He'd scarcely been given a backward glance by the soldiers running to their docking duties, and now he stood on the brink of entering Farr's cabin.

According to the suit's 'cast link, the Commander had already left the ship. It was possible he'd taken the device with him but Tekton didn't think that likely. Farr wouldn't risk having it on station.

Tekton tried the door but it was locked.

Pacing a few steps either way, he checked for observers. Satisfied that no one was close enough to hear, he returned and experimented with the suit's various add-ons. To his delight it confused the locking system into opening with a simple jamming device. Samuelle had shown a certain flair when she'd had this made.

Farr's cabin was a replica of Samuelle's, though larger and furbished with an infinitely superior comm-desk. Clothes hung neatly in a cupboard, and the tightly tucked bed sheets looked unused. The black box arte-fact that Tekton had seen on Edo sat to one side of the comm.

He wheezed his way to it in Samuelle's suit and sat down. 'Balance,' he said.

The box sprang a beautiful three-dimensional representation of a Lorenz attractor.

Now what? asked free-mind.

Ssshh, I'm thinking, logic-mind replied.

It was the first time since Jelly Hob's timely rescue of him that his minds had been vocal.

Need another cue word, logic-mind decided.

Hampered by his own limited memory, Tekton was forced to take a risk. *Moud, activate and synchronise with ship's AI.*

The delay was short.

Good evening, Godhead. I am your new moud. Fully synchronised with your previous assistant.

Yes. Yes. Review of all my conversations with Lasper Farr. Rank verbally emphasised words.

Review shows the greatest verbal emphasis on the words 'shame' and 'balance', it replied almost instantly.

Ah. Yes. 'Shame.'

A light beam shot from the undulating image and hit Tekton squarely in the eyes. His surroundings darkened, and he fell into a mind-space occupied by a pond of spinning lights like a shift sphere, though infinitely denser. The lights looped and spun and knitted in an elegant and never-ending fashion.

Fascinating. Logic-mind was entranced. *Endless possibilities, dependent on changes made to the parameters of the closed dynamical system.*

How do you know that? free-mind asked with suspicion.

A Bifurcation Device. Thought only to be a fancy.

Explain, demanded Tekton. *Quickly. The ship's security will have detected my moud activation.*

It's an organic system representing sentient behaviour. With this level of information it's possible to predict outcomes. Altering the course of precursor events will change those outcomes.

God-meddling, thought Tekton.

Indeed. Logic-mind was in agreement. *Commander Farr is using a system that should not be possible.*

Unless a god created it.

For whom? Logic-mind pondered.

For its most deserving acolyte. Cousin Ra. But why would Ra supply an object of such potential to Lasper Farr?

Who better to play OLOSS against Post-Species? free-mind chimed in.

What can be gained from such meddling? Tekton peered closer at the spinning, weaving lights. *Can it be interpreted?*

Of course, said logic-mind.

Then get it to explain how I best find my way out of this hapless situation, and back to ranking most highly in Sole's favour.

The twinkling lights brightened and he found himself

awash in rapidly moving images; scenes of what had been and what would be. At odd instants, an image would freeze, allowing his mind time to create a sequence.

The deluge continued as he made a series of choices and the narrative ravelled: his rescue by Jelly Hob, meeting Samuelle, sharing her cabin aboard ship, and finally an image of a distraught and dishevelled woman, clutching her stomach in a dirty corridor.

Who in Sole's prickless body is that? asked Tekton.

Baronessa Mira Fedor, logic-mind declared.

What's she doing there – in my future? Tekton might have stamped his foot. He wasn't sure.

She is significant to it somehow.

Tekton stared at the Baronessa's round belly. *Good gonads, the woman is having a baby!*

Yes. That seems to be rather the point.

Tekton didn't like the idea of his life being tied up with the pregnant Baronessa at all. *Review previous sequences.*

New images flared: Lasper on the bridge, the Baronessa again with an equally unkempt Thales Berniere in a tiny and unrecognisable room. And then a final picture of the Baronessa, Thales and Samuelle in intense conversation.

'What does it mean?' Tekton cried aloud in frustration.

Actual events and potential outcomes, surmised logic-mind.

'But which is which?'

'Tekkie?' A familiar voice dragged him away from the hypnosis of Farr's Bifurcation Device and back to the present.

Jelly Hob was standing on one foot in the doorway

of the cabin. He looked ill at ease and edgy. 'You ain't supposed to be in here. Commander'll have your conkers.'

Tekton fixed the old pilot with his most appealing smile. 'Jeremy? I want you to fly me to Belle-Monde near Mintaka.'

Jelly Hob's expression fell into perplexed lines. 'When?' he asked. 'In what ship?'

'Quite soon,' replied Tekton. He widened his smile. 'In this one.'

TRIN

Trin wanted to shout at them. It was taking too long to allocate the carrying of the shells and the remainder of the xoc and weed, and his desire to leave this place had suddenly become acute.

They'd all ingested the first of their weed pods, which seemed to engender confusion rather than energy as the stimulant began to rage through their depleted bodies.

Djes was next to him. She'd said nothing since Kristo had spoken out in support of Trin.

'What is wrong?' she asked him now.

Trin swivelled, glancing around. Semantic was rising at least, giving them light to travel by. 'Something . . .'

'We're ready, Principe,' said Juno Genarro.

'You will go ahead, Juno, and I will lead the group. Vespa, stay at the back, make sure nobody lags behind.'

'I'll watch our backs with Malocchi,' said Kristo.

It was the first time one of Mulravey's men had offered freely to help. Trin glanced at Juno, and the Carabinere nodded.

'Si,' Trin agreed.

'But Kristo, I need you to help with Thom,' protested Cass Mulravey.

'C'n walk on my own, Cass,' snarled the subject of her concern.

Trin looked at him. They were all thin, but Mulravey's man Thomaas seemed the weakest of the men. He scratched his skin constantly as though bitten by unseen insects, and his hands had the tremor of a person either ill or addicted.

Cass Mulravey shrugged and reached for her ragazzo. The child climbed onto her shoulders and grasped her mother's knotted hair. 'Hurry, mama,' he cried in a soft voice.

The ragazzo felt it too; the thickening of air and the smell of . . . lig.

Trin began walking, tracking Juno, who'd set off at a run, and the group followed him. As they stepped off the carpet of creeper onto the cracked earth, something landed near their feet. One of the women screamed in fright, setting off reactions in the others.

'Settle,' yelled Mulravey. 'It's just a lig.'

'B-but it's h-huge,' called out Josephia. She stood near Tina Galiotto, who lent her shoulder to Jilda Pellegrini.

The lig's body was the size of Trin's forearm, its wings like stiff, transparent curtains. Tivi Scali kicked at it, and it lifted lazily to settle again not far away.

More came then, landing on the edge where the sand-creeper met the cracked, heavier clay.

'They're feeding on the flowers,' said Mulravey loudly. 'Nothing to fret about.'

It seemed that way, as if they were dipping deep into the white star blossoms that opened only at night.

Trin glanced back over to the boulders. More ligs had alighted near the base of the rocks and were crawling into the cracks that they had just vacated. *Why so many of them? Why so large?*

They moved forward again, but it was only a few steps before one of the Carabinere gave a hoarse shout. 'Principe! Madre di Crux!'

Everyone stopped again.

'Principe!'

The second shout came from Juno Genarro. He waved in the moonlight to Trin, indicating that he'd found a way up the mountain through the tangle of brush.

Trin waved back to him, then turned to the group. 'Cue?'

They had spread out – instinctively, perhaps – around a Carabinere, who was on his knees. Before him was a hole. A clod of dirt lay alongside, the hole as though a piece of earth had simply flipped open.

Trin moved closer.

It has. One of the cracked surface segments had been knocked from its place by pressure from below. Something dark and thick and moist snaked out from the hole and licked at the man's worn boot.

He scrambled backwards, out of reach.

'A tentacle,' said Joe Scali. 'Saqr!'

Trin heard the terror in his voice. Joe knew what the Saqr could do – what they'd done to his sweetheart, Rantha, and all the others in Malocchi's enclave. Herded them like pitiful animals and drained the fluid from their bodies. Thrown them atop each other in a used pile. Trin would never erase the memory of young Nathaniel clutching Rantha's body.

'It's the Saqr. The Saqr are here!' someone else screamed.

'No!' said Trin quickly, cutting off the panic. He pushed past Cass Mulravey and her Thomaas, and knelt down to observe the flicking flesh. 'See how it is thicker, closer down to the hole, and the way it is retracting. I think it is more like a . . . tongue.'

'But what creature has a tongue like that?' Joe asked the question that they all wished answered.

'Trinder!' said Djeserit. She placed a hand on his shoulder and tugged. He felt gratified at her anxious tone.

'There's another one, Principe,' said Tivi Scali. 'Over there.' He pointed towards the point where the sand-creeper met the clay.

Everyone began to shift, lifting their feet, searching in the moonlit dark for anything unusual. Little eruptions began occurring all around them; more clods of earth overturned.

'We should not wait to find out,' said Trin, suddenly.

But his decision came too late.

A creature the size of a large dog erupted from the first hole, collapsing a swath of earth around it. It shook off the dirt with heavy, rolling movements and snapped powerful jaws at the kneeling Carabinere.

The man stumbled to his feet and kicked it, but it lunged at his leg, snagging his ankle. He punched its head and it let go, momentarily stunned. Dark, multi-faceted eyes reflected dully in the moonlight. It seemed to be looking at the ligs feeding from the creeper – deciding which it preferred.

Trin saw the thick, ridged, red skin and long, sweeping reptilian tail.

Checclia. Huge checclia.

It flicked its tail, catching the Carabinere with an almost insolent whip across his forearm, and bounded towards the ligs. The insects tried to lift and scatter but seemed sluggish from ingesting the flowers.

The checclia leapt upon the back of the closest one, ripping its abdomen in half in one bite. It clawed the lig's wings, which made a sharp crackling sound as they tore.

'Vai,' shouted Trin. 'Vai! To Juno Genarro!'

The group broke into a run, energised by fear and fuelled by the weed stimulant. Even the weakest of the women found strength. But other checclia were emerging rapidly from their holes. Trin tripped over one, lurching to recover his balance.

Thomaas and Cass Mulravey and her ragazzo were next to him. One of the reptiles sprang from its hole and ran up Thomaas's back, digging claws deep into his shoulders. He stumbled and fell, shrieking in pain.

Cass Mulravey stopped to help him, dropping her ragazzo to the ground. She beat at the checclia with her bare hands.

It twisted its articulated neck and snapped at her flailing arms, hissing.

Trin ran back and pushed her aside. He kicked the checclia in the side of the head with his boot, as the Carabinere had done. It stopped snapping at Mulravey and turned its attention to Trin. The dark, lidless eyes seemed to regard him in a calculating manner. In a considered move, it bit deep into Thomaas's neck.

The man writhed with uncontrolled agony.

Panicked, Trin kicked it again and again until it released its hold. Dark blood trickled from its jaws.

It flicked its tongue to catch the drips and launched itself towards Trin.

He dived sideways, knocking Mulravey over.

But the checclia's intention was elsewhere. It connected with a descending lig and hooked its teeth into the end of its abdomen. The lig struggled for altitude and lost, pulled to earth by the checclia's weight.

Its fight was short-lived and pitiful.

A sweet and cloying scent filled the air as the lig perished.

Trin and Cass Mulravey dragged the small, thin Thomaas to his feet and forced him on towards the rest of the group, who waited in the shelter of the brush-line.

Joe Scali had hold of Djeserit, who was trying to return to them. He pushed her into his cousin Tivi's arms and came himself, but Mulravey wouldn't relinquish her hold of Thomaas.

'Can – do – it,' she gasped. 'Take – 'bino and get back.'

'Principe?'

'Back – Joe,' said Trin. 'More – coming.'

Joe snatched up the ragazzo, and ran as the ground around them turned into a mass of emerging checclia.

Thomaas had become a dragging weight against his shoulder, and Trin's own strength faded. He fought an overwhelming desire to shrug the man off and leave him. A flash of memory brought with it the same rush of emotion he'd felt in Loisa when the silos had exploded. Seb Malocchi had fallen as the fire rushed towards them. Trin hadn't wanted to stop and help him. But the moment took him out of himself, to another place.

Suddenly, Thomaas wasn't connected to the irritating

Cass Mulravey; he was simply a fragile 'esque, one of his kind, and his kind were too few.

Trin fumbled in his pocket for a weed pod and crammed the stimulant into his mouth. He repeated the action, this time forcing Thomaas to take it.

'Chew and swallow,' he ordered.

Mulravey reached for her own supply, and did the same without waiting for his bidding.

Trin felt his vigour return almost immediately, and he hoisted Thomaas higher. Mulravey responded with the same energy. They covered the last distance on a rush of adrenalin, falling into the waiting arms of Juno Genarro and Vespa Malocchi.

The Carabinere dragged them deep into the shelter of the thick undergrowth, where they lay, breathing hard.

Trin's muscles twitched compulsively, and his heart pounded. Djeserit crawled to his side as he jerked and spasmed.

'You saved Thomaas, Principe,' she said. All the wonder and devotion had returned to her voice. 'We should have kept moving, as you said. You knew . . . you knew.'

She cradled his head until his tremors settled, and the constriction eased in his chest. And when he was able, she helped him sit upright.

Cass Mulravey was near him, resting against the thick trunk of a small broad-leaved tree. Juno Genarro knelt next to her, leaning over Thomaas, pressing his hand against the wound on the man's neck.

'The bleeding has almost stopped, Principe. The effects of the pod have slowed the flow. We'll be able to travel again soon, but he'll need help.'

Trin looked over Juno's shoulder. The rest of the group were scattered through the undergrowth, within hearing distance.

'The checclia seem to like the open ground and the ligs. I think it will be safe for us to rest here a while longer,' he replied.

Juno nodded, but it was Cass Mulravey who spoke.

'Your instinct was right, Pellegrini. We should have listened to you on this.' She said it loud enough for everyone to hear. 'Next time, we will.'

Then, more quietly, she added, 'Thank you.' Her face was worn out with effort and the after-effects of the weed.

Trin knew he must look the same. But a strong emotion buoyed him. He *had* been right. And now they would *all* look to him.

MIRA

Mira? Is our baby coming?

Mira shut *Insignia*'s concern from her mind as another cramp spread across her belly and forced her to curl forward and grasp her knees.

Thales Berniere stared at her helplessly. 'What should I do, Baronessa?'

His look of fear steadied her panic. She must stay calm and think. The baby was too young to be born yet. These pains would settle if she could rest for a time. 'I must find a-a room. Somewhere I can lie down.'

Perspiration stood out on his scarred face. He licked his lips nervously. 'Can you walk if I help you?'

She nodded. 'I think so.' She stood slowly, grasping Thales's arm. The pain had faded quickly, as if it had never occurred.

He glanced out into the emporium. 'Where would we find such a thing?'

She pointed across to a brightly veneered kiosk, sandwiched between food vendors. From their vantage point behind the refuse bins, the attendant looked to be a Lamin hybrid. 'Transit units.' She paused, taking a couple of shallow breaths to ease a building discomfort under her breastbone. 'Randall spoke of them. They have sleeping couches and comm-soles.'

They walked across to the kiosk, Mira leaning on Thales's arm. The young man was stiff and trembling.

'Try to be still,' she whispered. 'We mustn't appear jittery.'

He took a deep breath and dropped his bunched shoulders but the trembling didn't stop. She sensed a still-fresh trauma in him – something more recent even than the terrible disfiguration of his face.

'What's yir pleasure?' The Lamin hybrid's face was unusually broad and sallow. Mira studied it, trying unsuccessfully to identify its mixed heritage, while it wiggled its nostrils at them and blinked its sloe eyes at her enlarged belly. 'Double, I presume?' it said in a patronising voice.

Thales hesitated, glancing at Mira for guidance.

'Twin. And we would wish to wash.'

'Yaaas,' it said, as if to imply that they needed it. 'Is extra.'

Mira nodded and handed over Thales's credit clip. She hadn't asked him how he had come by it, but she doubted it was his. Although the Scolar emblem was reassuring – suggesting it wasn't stolen.

The half-Lamin clacked its long fingernails through several booking screens and selected a pass-key from a storage sleeve. It handed the small pliable chip over and pointed to a narrow escalator on the other side of a crêpe stall. 'Turn left at the top. Numbers are on the door plates.' Then, as an afterthought, it added, 'Blood residues are extra; deducted automatically. Refer to yir contract.' It activated the screen at the front of the booth and set it to scroll through the rules and regulations.

Mira frowned at the creature. 'That won't be necessary.' She collected the chip and the clip and turned away towards the escalator. Thales hastened to position himself at her side and they rode to the next level in silence.

Fortunately, their room was near the beginning of a row that stretched back further than Mira could see. It would arc eventually, she guessed, and curl back until it met the escalator on the right side. The row was periodically inset with other escalators that allowed access to the units above.

Mira opened the door and light flooded the space, illuminating a cabinet that doubled as comm-sole and ablution station with a pop-up stool, and behind it, two beds. The room was no wider than the door, and only just long enough for the furnishings.

She ushered Thales in front of her and shut the door firmly behind them, checking it was locked. He stood awkwardly in her way, but she pushed past him and sank onto the lower bed.

'Baronessa?'

'Just let me rest a while, and then we will speak,' she said wearily. The abdominal pains had not returned, but she suddenly felt completely exhausted. She yearned for the soothing replenishment of Primo vein, but it would be a while before she was reunited with her ship – if ever. If Landhurst found her . . . *Necessary risk*, she told herself as she drifted.

Her sleep was heavy at first – a good while of it – and then became interspersed with the sounds of Thales climbing down from the top bunk to wash.

He switched on the station news and she listened

to the low, droning report of the OLOSS summit. Though she could barely hear the details, she recognised the newsreader's solemn tones.

When Thales requested a search on someone called Fariss O'Dea, however, she jerked fully awake. 'Stop!' she gasped.

His hand obediently blanked the screen, and he swivelled on the stool to stare at her.

Mira licked dry lips, and struggled to an upright position. As she moved, so did the baby, giving a sharp, reassuring dig under her ribs. 'Station communication may be monitored for anything suspicious. Searching for anyone specific may draw attention to our comm-sole. Even an idle search.'

He reddened. 'I-I am sorry, Baronessa. I didn't think. The woman – Fariss – who saved my life, I'm concerned to know her fate.'

Mira closed her eyes and rubbed them gently with her forefingers; she felt grimy from being inside the milk bladder. 'I think it is time you told me your story. We must be clear on the risks.'

He nodded.

'Change places with me, and speak while I wash,' she said.

He did as she instructed without comment or protest. He hadn't been difficult or assertive when they'd last been together, but even so, Mira sensed a change in him. His volatility seemed to have been replaced by compliance.

She closed the comm-sole and opened the basin segment, sighing with pleasure at the sight of the tube of scented liquid soap. Her life lacked even the most basic of pleasures. She squeezed some onto her dry hands and mixed it with a spray of water, revelling in the slippery, gentle feel of it. She craved to unfold the larger basin and wash her entire body, but modesty denied her. 'Tell me.'

'When you were taken from Rho Junction, we – the mercenaries, the God Discoverer, Bethany and I – all went our separate ways. Circumstance had brought about my meeting an educated Lostolian gentleman at the medi-clinic where I went to receive the DNA. The man was called Tekton. He is a tyro with the Sole Entity. A man I believe you have mentioned before – though at the time, his name meant little to me.'

'Tekton? The archiTect?' Mira stiffened. 'What brought him to Rho Junction?'

'He did not disclose the details of his visit, though he brought a metallist to the clinic for urgent medical help, so I presume his business was in that line.' Thales screwed up his forehead, remembering. 'A craftsman, I think. A filthy old man who looked more like a vagrant.'

'Did they mention which metal? Was it quixite?' Mira's thoughts flew in several directions at once. Could this be proof of Marchella's dealing with Tekton, the Lostolian? If so, what was he crafting from the alloy? How close she had been to meeting him . . .

Thales was speaking again, and she dragged her attention back to him.

'. . . but something told me not to allow myself to be injected with it, and instead the gentleman helped me take it from the attendant – with some force.'

Mira nodded, encouraging him to continue. She felt

his eyes fix on the movement of her hands as she moisturised them.

'The gentleman and I exchanged stories, and he offered Bethany and me quick passage back to Edo. I accepted. It was a rash decision, but I was panicked by the things he told me. I wanted to get back to Edo as quickly as possible. And, truthfully, I was eager to be free of Rast Randall and her confidants.'

'I understand that desire,' Mira agreed. 'They are not the finest company to keep.'

'Please understand, Baronessa, that I was sorry for your disappearance, as was Beth. But I didn't think myself able to contribute in any way to finding you. Lasper Farr had injected me with a virus that would break down the barrier substance administered by Gutnee Paraburd. Returning to Edo to receive the antidote was uppermost in my mind.' He seemed embarrassed but not acutely so. His life had been under constant threat since before he left Scolar and she couldn't blame him for his decisions. Hers might have been the same.

'I know,' she said. 'I saw you in the infirmary. *Insignia* told me the results of your blood analysis.'

He nodded. 'I wondered if the ship was aware of such things.'

Mira pursed her lips. '*Insignia* is aware of everything but chooses to only tell part of it.'

Thales gave another nod, though his thoughts were clearly moving forward. 'As it was,' he said, 'I became acutely ill on the return ship. Lasper Farr's virus eroded the barrier substance sooner than it should have because my own HealthWatch had been compromised –

tampered with – and my immunity was low. It is how I got this.' He touched the ugly, blackened scarring on his face. 'Necrosis set in. Fortunately, we arrived at Edo in time for me to receive the antidote.'

Mira damped her face with a disposable cloth. Applying a tiny amount of the soap to her cheeks, she began the same gentle pattern of rubbing. It helped her stay calm as she listened and absorbed. 'Who, do you think, tampered with your HealthWatch?'

Thales's expression became bitter. 'I believe that my father-in-law did so. Sophos Mianos. He wished me out of his daughter's life once I began to question their ways. You met him, Baronessa. Do you think him capable of murder?'

Mira leaned her face into the basin and let the spray rinse it. Then she smoothed the drops from her face with her fingers. She turned to look at him calmly. 'Si, I do. So let us hope that he was flung into space when *Insignia* tore away from her docking connection. Let us hope that his insides boiled and burst from within him.'

Thales's eyes widened and his mouth opened in surprise.

'I am beyond wishing well to cruel and greedy humanesques, Thales. Now please continue,' she said, not giving him time to dwell on the callousness of her comment.

Thales swallowed several times and picked up the thread of his story. From there he told her of his decision to leave Bethany, the subsequent attempt on his life by Farr's man, and Fariss's timely rescue.

'But why should Commander Farr attempt to harm

you later on, when he could simply have let you die from the infection?' Mira interrupted.

'Bethany spoke as if I was *under her protection* while I was still in her company. I d-didn't believe her. Nor did I believe it when she told me that some members of Consilience wish her to replace Lasper. I mean . . .' – he stumbled to find a way to express himself – 'she is n-neither charismatic n-nor dominating like her brother.' A strange emotion crossed his face as he spoke. 'She is . . .'

'A woman?'

Thales jerked his head up. 'No, Baronessa. I am not like your Latino males. But I did not see qualities of leadership in Bethany. She seemed frightened of her brother, and plagued by her own weaknesses.'

'Like all of us,' added Mira. 'Perhaps those things would make her a better leader.'

Silence fell between them and Thales gazed at the floor.

Mira supposed that his preoccupation was with the other things that had transpired between him and Bethany; delicate, private things that should stay unrevealed.

'Bethany saved your life by having others watch out for you?' she said, prodding him gently.

Thales chewed his bottom lip in embarrassment, continuing to avert his gaze. 'Fariss and Samuelle – yes.'

Mira sighed. Though intelligent and sensitive and refined, Thales had not grown any more in his understanding of human nature. And now he no longer had his beauty to compensate for his naivety. She felt jaded next to him and much, much older, although their ages must be quite similar. Something deep inside her feared for Thales's survival.

She realised, in that instant, that the quiet attraction she'd felt for him was born of a mothering instinct, and nothing more. She poured a drink into a disposable cup and took a sip, savouring the peculiar tang of the station water. Understanding her feelings came as a relief. Things became clearer. She would protect Thales as best she could, as she would Vito, or the korm, but her future was not invested in his.

Thoughts of Vito brought an instant sharp pang to her chest. She must warn OLOSS of the Post-Species threat, and they must find a way to save the survivors on Araldis. Foolish hope, perhaps, but one she would cling to.

Strangely, her thoughts moved directly on to Josef Rasterovich. She wished him here to ask his opinion. Or Rast Randall. Both of them were worldly, and smart enough to see the many sides to each situation.

She suppressed the sound that rose in her throat. How ironic that she would wish for their company, having just told Thales the contrary.

One thing she knew with certainty, though – both Randall and Rasterovich would find a way to meet with OLOSS officials and make them believe the threat to all OLOSS sentients. So must she. 'So the woman, Fariss, is another mercenary?'

'Of a type,' he admitted. 'But she's more . . . like-able . . . than Rast Randall.'

Mira twisted her lips. 'That would not be difficult. Randall could be described as an acquired taste, at best.'

'She abandoned you and Bethany, Baronessa. She was supposed to be your safeguard.'

'Truly, she did. She cannot be trusted. But then, few can.' She added softly, 'We do not have to dig very deep to find out what principles we can abandon.'

He didn't reply to that, but once more appeared to be swallowed by his own thoughts; disturbed thoughts, by the tense, unhappy curl of his lips.

'Can you tell me any more?' she pressed.

He nodded and continued with a halting explanation of Samuelle and the city of Ampere, and Farr's abrupt summoning of them here, to Intel. He hesitated as he described the ship journey, struggling to find the words to explain it.

She waited in silence, sensing something important teetered on the brink of being said.

Finally, it came out in a rush – Macken's bullying and his own desperation to avert rape, what it made him do, and then Fariss's decision to help him escape and take the blame herself. By the end of it, he was speaking in breath-robbed gulps.

Mira felt mired in her own memories. How she wished she had killed Trin Pellegrini. 'You say that Samuelle will be present at the OLOSS meeting.'

'I believe so.'

'What is her position on the Post-Species?'

He shrugged. 'I have heard some things that suggest she is not enamoured with Commander Farr, but yet is committed to the Consilience cause. She supports Bethany, I know that much.'

Mira wiped her face and hands on the absorbent film in the dispenser and dropped it into the basin. They both watched it curl up and disintegrate.

She pushed the basin back into its cabinet and

opened the cover on the comm-sole. 'Was Bethany on the ship that brought you here?'

'It's possible. I didn't leave the cabin or speak to anyone other than Fariss. Fariss didn't mention her name.'

'You didn't enquire?'

Thales bowed his head again as if expecting her judgement. 'I was brought on board as her consort – it would have caused suspicion if I'd shown an interest in such things. We only spoke about trivial matters.'

Mira felt the weight of his humiliation, and yet he didn't shirk from the truth. 'We've both been forced to do things we wouldn't choose. We are not less for it, Thales – we have survived. There is some triumph in that.'

For a moment his head lifted and his face lit with a smile that transcended his scars and apprehensive expression. Mira saw a glimpse of the beautiful, passionate young man she'd rescued from the OLOSS ship. Had she contributed to the ruin of his life by bringing him aboard *Insignia*? He'd been so ill-prepared for the wider worlds – worse, even, than she.

And now he had killed a man to save himself.

As if attuned to her thoughts, his smile faded. 'Though I am grateful for your perspective, Baronessa, I cannot allow myself to adopt it. When I left Scolar I was a Jainist. I had sworn to adhere to those non-violent tenets, and yet I've done nothing but cheat on my beliefs since I left Scolar.'

'Ideals are seldom practical, Thales.'

'That does not excuse me.'

She shrugged. 'We must each console our own consciences. Mine does not find shame in survival.'

'Nor should it,' he said. 'Your inner strength is inspiring.'

He said it in such a heartfelt manner that Mira was silenced, unsure of how to respond. She didn't consider herself to be strong-minded, and felt only irritation at her own limitations.

And yet his simple statement lifted her spirits.

'Then let us inspire each other,' she eventually replied. 'How can I get to the summit meeting?'

'If we convince Samuelle of your story then I'm sure she could arrange it.'

Mira thought for a moment. If the woman he spoke of, Fariss, had shouldered the blame for the death, then it should be safe enough for Thales to move about Intel station. 'Can you make contact with Samuelle without using station comm-sys?'

He straightened his posture, as if gaining some purpose. 'I can try, Baronessa.'

THALES

Fear and excitement lent Thales energy, but did nothing to assuage the trembling that had set in from the instant he'd discharged Fariss's pistol into Macken. Even for the last few hours when he had lain in the bunk above Mira Fedor, his body had been plagued by uncontrollable movements and periodic fits of shivers.

Now, as he crossed the early-station-morning plaza to the station Directory booth, his trembling had subsided to a low, manageable tremor that he hoped would barely be noticed. Action – movement – was a relief from sitting in the confinement of the tiny sleeper unit.

From watching the station comm-news while Mira Fedor had rested, he'd learned that the summit was scheduled to start in just a few hours, watched on farcast by most of OLOSS Orion. Traffic around and inside the station had already been restricted, but once the proceedings had begun, a full curfew had been scheduled. He had to find Samuelle before then, or Mira Fedor's hope of presenting what she had seen to the joint meeting would disappear.

On his request, the Directory kiosk displayed the complete ball-and-flute design of the station. It reminded Thales of one of Rene's precious crystal vases. It also explained the nature of each location he placed his finger upon, and the most direct route there. It was a completely different configuration from Edo – the only other station he'd spent any time upon. Here, on Intel, the circular plane of the docks fed into the narrow neck of the flute, like a skirt flaring stiffly from a woman's narrow waist. Immediately above it was the lower stem, which housed a food plaza and short-term accommodation, and beneath it, in the bulb of the station, were the reactors that kept Intel spinning.

The permanent residences and retail outlets nestled in the mid-flute section, whilst station admin spread across the entire expansive top section. Like Edo, Intel had a central lift shaft but it was complemented by smaller conduits that ran up the sides of the flute at regular intervals.

Thales studied the pictures and tried to think practically, like Mira Fedor. In normal times, he expected that station visitors and general travellers would be lodged in the short-term accommodation, but for something so important, with a self-imposed curfew, he imagined that the Stationmaster would like his visitors close by the designated conference room, to minimise movement and risk.

Yet the news had spoken of a delegation of biozoons congesting a large area of dock availability. Mira Fedor's *Insignia* was hidden out there among them. How did they partake in the summit? he wondered. Would the meeting somehow be brought to them?

No. OLOSS would never inconvenience themselves for minority aliens.

He asked the Directory to show him the traffic flow. The colours of the shifting icons told him that all lifts were busy. When he asked the Directory to confirm this, it told him that there were delays in moving around the station as Station Security performed random checks.

Thales's trembling increased. If Fariss had taken the blame for Macken's murder then he wouldn't be listed as a criminal but he had no identification other than his aspect cube. Would that be enough to pass through Station Sec? How else could he reach the conference area?

Then he remembered how Gutnee Paraburd had taken him into the unseen corridors of Scolar station. *All large transit stations have service areas*, Gutnee had said.

'Show me the service maps,' he instructed the Directory.

'Please provide your clearance details,' it intoned.

Thales stared at the screen unable to think of what to do.

'How much longer you gonna be there?' demanded an annoyed voice.

Thales glanced behind him. A queue had formed while he'd been lost in his own thoughts. The bald-headed 'esque behind him in line scowled.

'P-pardon me,' Thales stammered, and walked quickly over towards a juice bar.

As he pretended to consider which mixture of flavours he might like, he saw uniformed 'esques enter and move with quick purpose across the plaza. They converged around the Directory and began to question those in the queue. The angry, bald 'esque looked around, searching for Thales.

Thales walked quickly in the other direction. As he passed the narrow passage lined with cleaning equipment that he and the Baronessa had followed from the unloading facility, he stepped inside it, and crouched down behind a trolley.

He waited for shouts or the sound of running feet, but neither came.

'Watcha doin', luv?'

This voice belonged to a woman, squatting like him, chewing on an unlit cigarillo. Her lined face held a cagey expression. She wore a stained blue cleaner's uniform with the station logo stamped into the shoulder.

'Hiding,' he said truthfully.

She plucked the cigarillo from her mouth and grinned. 'Me too. Damn Station Sec makin' double tha work for us. Stompin' around, pokin' about in things, turnin' stuff inside out.'

'It is difficult to go anywhere,' Thales agreed, thinking of the congestion shown by the Directory.

'Stinkin' hard I'd call it. Ree-diculous. All fer some hob-nobs' meetin'.'

Thales nodded, not knowing what else to say – but the wrinkled old woman didn't need his encouragement.

'S'all right for us Dowdies though,' she continued.

'Dowdies?'

'Cleaners.' She frowned. 'Where you from that you ain't heard of Dowdies?'

'I just arrived. F-from a place called Scolar. It would seem to be a bad time to be sightseeing around Orion,' he added lamely. His lie seemed so obvious.

She stuck the cigarillo back in her mouth and chewed

a bit. Then she removed it again. 'So what you doin' back here wi' me?'

Thales scrambled for a more plausible story. 'My identification was stolen last night when I arrived. I don't wish to be detained while Station Security authenticates my story. With things the way they are, it could take altogether too long to be verified.'

The woman nodded. 'Big words yer using, but I get the idee of it. Things not so good around here wivout yer ID right now. Likely they'll slam yer in the containers orright.'

Thales gave a completely involuntary shiver. He didn't have to fake his nervousness. 'I-I have a . . . colleague. She's staying at the top end of the station. She'll vouch for me but I need to speak with her first.'

The old woman nodded sympathetically and waggled her finger in the air. 'Might be able to do somethin' there. Us Dowdies can get anywhere quick.'

The dawning of possibility quickened his heartbeat. 'Y-you would help me?'

'Could do. Could do.' She returned to chewing her cigarillo while Thales waited. The woman seemed quick-witted enough, though uneducated. But why would she help him?

'Kinda feel sorry for you,' she said, as if answering his thoughts. 'What with all the ugliness on yer face, and on account of yer bein' a bit simple and having yer ID nicked.' She gave a phlegmy chortle. ''Ere, 'elp me up.'

He put out his hand and pulled her. She was light and wiry and at full standing height she only reached his shoulders.

'Come on, then,' she said.

She led him down the same corridor that he and Mira Fedor had emerged from earlier, but instead of entering one of the adjoining passages she walked on until she came to a blind corner. She turned to face a grubby section of the wall.

He waited again, wondering if she had simply been teasing him; or was she, perhaps, demented?

But the woman positioned herself side-on, and laid a thin, knobbly finger against a seam in the titanium. The seam parted and slid open.

She entered the hidden lift and beckoned him. 'In 'ere, Mr Big Words.'

Thales hurried to join her and stood watching the level counter while she continued to prattle.

The trip to the top of the station passed in an agony of inane remarks as Thales felt the claws of claustrophobia sinking into him. The lift stank of cleaning fluids and stale cigarillos, and the proximity of the old woman made him edgy.

Small spaces. The cabin on Farr's ship, the refrigerator container, the sleeper unit and now this. He had a sudden longing for the vast, inky night skies of Scolar, unlit by any moon. He wanted to breathe unfiltered, real-world air and feel cool wind. He wanted . . .

''Ere we go, luvvy.' The door finally opened into a corridor just like the one they had left. She waved him into it without ceremony. 'Luck and all,' she said.

The door closed on her crafty old face, and he experienced an instant of panic. What did her haste mean? Nothing. *It means nothing.* He discarded his unnamed

fear as paranoia. He was closer to Samuelle, he hoped.
That was all that mattered.

Resolutely, he walked down the corridor and found
his way to the edge of a large open space filled with
'esques seated at workstations. He retreated quickly
and took another door. This one led to a long, sweeping
passage and past low-lit doorways that had the appearance of more luxurious lodgings than the plaza sleeper
units. He listened at several of the doors but heard
nothing. It was still early station morning.

Partway along the arc he stumbled upon an open
common room furnished with couches and comm-soles
and a spread of breakfast pastries and fruit that made
his mouth salivate. A Dowdie sucked up the floor dust
with a silent extraction nozzle, while a uniformed
attendant fussed over the food.

He looked up and down the corridor. Voices drifted
towards him; visitors leaving their station cabins to find
breakfast. It was possible that Samuelle would be one
of them.

Thales ran a few steps in one direction, and then
changed his mind and ran back the other way. As
quickly as his fumbling fingers would allow, he prised
open the door of a fire-hydrant housing and pulled
several extinguishers free. He juggled them over to
the doorway and put them down. Then he raced back
and forced himself into the tiny space, pulling the door
closed.

The claustrophobia that assailed him this time was
profound. His body heated and he began to sweat. He
curled his fingers tight into his fists and tucked them
under his knees to keep from flinging the door open.

He used his meditation breathing in the hope that the fierce shaking that had beset him would subside.

Voices came closer and passed.

Once. Twice. Three times. Small groups, chatting in quiet tones.

Then he heard a familiar hissing noise. He tried to peer through the crack in the door, but his efforts to control his breathing had become ragged gasps to get enough air in his lungs. Pinpricks of light exploded before his fluttering eyelids at the oxygen deprivation. Unable to control his body, he burst from the cupboard and sprawled into the corridor.

He heard an exclamation of recognition and felt himself lifted into the air. Strength-enhanced arms and augmented legs conveyed him away from the fire housing and into a cabin. The door sucked shut and he was dropped into a small armchair.

'Berniere! What in Edo's name are you doing?'

He forced his eyes open to confront Samuelle's ferocity. Everything that he needed to say rushed to his tongue at once and he found himself unable to be coherent.

She made a frustrated noise and thrust a water tube into his mouth. 'Drink, then breathe.'

He obeyed her simple instruction. The cool water somehow made it easier to catch his breath. And then speak. 'S-small spaces,' he managed after drinking half the tube. 'I-I dislike s-small s-spaces. 'Pologise.'

Her sharp eyes blinked at him. 'Fariss has been arrested for Macken's murder. What do you know about that?'

Thales's stomach cramped with anxiety. 'Have you seen her?'

'She's in station containment, for Cruxsakes. But where have you been, Berniere? How did you get off the damn ship unnoticed?'

'Fariss helped me. She said it was better for me to leave through the hold. She arranged it.'

Samuelle pressed her forehead. 'Well, as things turned out, mebbe she was right. Macken's death brought a lot of attention her way.' A glint of tears showed in her eyes. 'Can't figure out what she was doing though . . . murdering one of Lasper's treasured.'

'Perhaps it wasn't murder,' whispered Thales. 'Perhaps it was self-defence.'

'You know that?' she said.

Thales shook his head dumbly.

Samuelle shrugged. 'If only the damn girl'd talk to me about it, but she won't say a shitting word.' She sank deep into her own thoughts for a moment, then pulled herself back to the present. 'And why are you falling out of cupboards at my feet?'

Thales told her, as quickly as his scrambled thoughts would allow, about Mira Fedor and everything that she'd seen in Post-Species space. As he spoke, Samuelle's expression altered. Disbelief replaced irritation.

'You say both Landhurst and OLOSS want this woman for different crimes.'

'Neither are real crimes,' said Thales. 'Self-defence.'

'Like Fariss, eh?' Samuelle gave a humourless laugh. 'You have a mastery of understatement, Thales. This Fedor woman nearly tore the side off an OLOSS ship and somehow convinced a bunch of decommed warships to turn their weapons on a station.' She paced back and forth across the room as she spoke. 'It's too risky to align myself with someone of her reputation, though truth be known, I'm curious to meet her.' She shook her head. 'Can't help you. You wait here now, in case I need your testimony.'

'No!' cried Thales, forcing himself to stand. 'You must hear her out at least.'

'There is *nothing* I must do.'

Thales took a ragged breath. 'Fariss is incarcerated?'

The sharp eyes bored into him. 'And?'

'What will happen to her?'

Samuelle considered. 'At home on Edo she'd have been executed if I hadn't been able to get her off-planet. Here, with things the way they are, I don't know. Lasper will have to use station court. She'll wind up in containment, but at least she'll be alive.'

Containment. The very thought of being locked away was too much to bear – but not as great as the guilt and remorse he harboured over Fariss's sacrifice. He took a deep breath so that he could say the words in one attempt. 'I will admit to Macken's murder on the condition that you help Mira Fedor.'

Samuelle stiffened, though her suit kept working, strengthening and massaging her muscles with little movements that looked like a ripple across her body. 'What's that?'

'I killed Macken,' he said clearly. 'He tried to rape me. Fariss left me with a pistol when she went to see you, just before we shifted. It happened then. She came back and found me. After shift, she took me straight down to the hold. I hid in a refrigerated carton.'

Samuelle sank into one of the two armchairs as if winded. 'You? *You* did it?'

Thales stared at the floor. The matting was clean, but worn with use by countless, nameless occupants. Had any of them talked of murder before? he wondered. The tremor came back. He'd killed a man.

When he looked up again, Samuelle was staring at him.

'Seems,' she said, 'that you've got an introduction to make.'

MIRA

The uniformed men who came to the door of the
sleeper unit bore the same air as Randall, Catchut and
Latourn. They were not mercenaries, but soldiers with
strong bodies and watchful eyes. For an instant she
thought they were Station Security, until the tallest
one spoke.

'Samuelle wants ta speak with ye. Brought you something to wear to get ye past Sec.' He looked her up
and down and grunted. 'She didn't say nuthin' about
ye bein' preggers.'

He pulled a pack free from his back and fished out
a hooded uniform and boots. 'Put this on. Stuff somethin' down the top. Make ye chest look big ta hide ye
belly. Come out when ye ready. But hurry – we ain't
got much time.' There was no leer in his voice, no
curiosity, just a businesslike urgency.

With shaking fingers Mira donned the garb, tucking
the pants into the too-large boots. She wrapped the
bed sheet around her chest until it equalled the girth
of her stomach and then she donned the shirt, pressing
the seams tightly together. The mirror showed her as
a stocky, short figure, not a pregnant one. She pulled
the hood up and tucked her hair under it.

Then she stepped outside, acutely aware of the pants
rubbing between her legs. She had never worn such

clothing before, and it felt strange and uncomfortable and . . . obvious.

'Stay between us, and don't walk like a lady. Don't speak either,' said Samuelle's soldier. 'We'll handle the rest.'

Station Sec stopped them several times. In the plaza, leaving the lift well up-station, and then again entering the top level of station space.

Each time Mira kept her shoulders square and willed herself to appear as one of them. She tried to remember Randall's swagger, the way she stood with her legs apart and her chin high.

When they finally arrived at their destination, Mira's own legs were trembling with the strain of keeping up her disguise and the effort of walking at the soldiers' pace.

The person who opened the door they stopped at wore a black, quilted suit made of material that Mira had never seen before. The face and body encased by the suit was old and female – humanesque. The suit made a faint sighing noise as she lifted her arm and waved them all inside. Thales stood behind her, his hands clasped together.

'Any trouble?' said the woman after she closed the door.

The soldier shook his head. 'Luck more'n anythin', Sam. So many people comin' and goin', Station Sec can barely cope. They're lettin' the likes of us through quicker. Didn't look too close. A good thing, at that.'

The old woman nodded. 'That's what I figured. Now catch some downtime.' Then she added, 'Go by Fariss first, see if they'll let her have visitors. Tell her I said that this is only short-term.'

The soldier raised an eyebrow but didn't comment. He nodded to the others and they left.

When they'd gone, Thales stepped into the space between Mira and the woman. His eyes were bloodshot but he seemed calmer than when he'd left her. 'Baronessa, this is Samuelle.'

Mira pushed back the hood and shook her hair free.

Samuelle stared baldly at her lumpen body. 'What in the Crux're you carrying in there, girl?'

'If you would excuse, I will remove the extra padding I wore to disguise my pregnancy.'

Samuelle's mouth dropped open. 'Pregnancy?' She glared at Thales. 'You didn't say nothin' about pregnancy.'

'I-it seemed i-inconsequential to the i-important matters,' stammered Thales.

Samuelle made a snorting noise and pointed Mira towards the small adjoining bathroom. 'I have a meeting to git to, Baronessa. Move it.'

Mira didn't miss the sarcastic way Samuelle used her title. She hastened to the bathroom and removed the sheeting from around her chest, feeling her breath come easier as she resealed the shirt.

When she returned to the main room Thales was seated in one of the chairs watching Samuelle pace. Her body moved with remarkable agility.

'Sit yourself down, girl, before yer pass out.' She poured Mira some water from a dispenser in a cupboard and passed it to her. 'Git to it.'

Mira nodded. She'd been rehearsing this while she waited for Thales, and the words came freely. 'I was kidnapped on Rho Junction by a group of Post-Species. They took me to their world in Extropy—'

'What did they want?' interrupted Samuelle.

'I have the Innate gene, which allows me to fly a biozoon. They wished to analyse it. They have trouble with keeping their host bodies alive.'

'Women don't get that gene.'

'I know,' said Mira. 'But I have.'

The woman gave a low whistle. 'Go on.'

'The story is detailed but I managed to escape with the help of one of them. *Insignia*, my ship, came for me. As we left Extropy space we observed something utterly dreadful.'

'What could be so bad?'

'Intuitive Incendiary transporters.'

'Geni-carriers? How many? Five? Ten?'

Mira closed her eyes, remembering the sight of them – like an asteroid belt colliding with a shift sphere. 'Millions. *Insignia* can quantify it more exactly.'

'Millions? Bullshit.'

Mira stared without blinking. 'It's the truth. They were shifting.'

'To where?'

'Araldis, I assume. But I could not be sure.'

Samuelle's suit propelled her to the narrow bed and she sat down. Her face had lost its colour. 'How could they have so many? When did they . . . Baronessa Fedor.' Her head jerked up quickly. 'Yer not insane are yer?'

Mira felt her lips almost stretch into a smile. 'Indeed, I am. But not in relation to this. I wish that I was.'

'The biozoon will confirm yer story? The biozoon is here?'

'Si.' Mira said it confidently, though she was not

sure – *Insignia* was angry enough with her to be spiteful. 'It is among the Envoy pod.'

'Then we have ta find a way to git you to this meeting.'

'That could be . . . difficult. You know of my problems with OLOSS and the Stationmaster?'

Samuelle nodded. She stood again, a tinge of colour returning to her face. Her eyes darted about with thought, and then fell upon Thales Berniere. 'Time for yer confession, young one. I need me best soldier back.'

JO-JO RASTEROVICH

Jo-Jo was getting the hang of things. Navigating the Extros' aural landscape wasn't much different from a holo map. He found himself increasingly able to glide between layers and pick up conversations at whim. His adaptability had to be related to Sole's interference with his brain function. He could think of no other reason.

Rast Randall, on the other hand, was struggling to fight her way out of listening isolation. Jo-Jo heard the relief in her voice every time he returned to speak to her.

'What's the news?' she asked with strained lightness. 'Found Catchut or Lat yet?'

He hesitated. He'd located Catchut, but the merc was gibbering. No amount of talking on Jo-Jo's part had been able to penetrate the man's broken mind. 'Catchut's not making much sense. Think the process might've cracked him.'

'The process.' Randall's voice rose. 'What frigging process? We're stuck in some frigging sound chamber with a bunch of faceless echoes. Where's the frigging process in that?'

'*Randall!*'

The merc fell silent for a time. No tears, but Jo-Jo sensed something else. Rast couldn't hold on much longer. Soon she'd be like Catchut. Jo-Jo didn't have much affection for Randall but he didn't want to be left alone here.

'Hold on. I can see daylight,' he said, using the shorthand way they'd developed to speak to each other.

'Truth?' she asked in a subdued tone.

'Truer than.'

'I need to see light soon then. Or I won't.' She knew she was losing it.

'Back in a flash.'

Jo-Jo left her and slipped back into the wider stream. He floated on the noise, thinking. His ability, and Rast's, to have an emotional response suggested that their bodies were still intact somewhere. He wasn't sure why, but that made sense to him.

If he was right about that, then there had to be a way back to them.

The Medium was an object run by a system, which meant it had to have a back end, a functional space where maintenance occurred. Something had to look after the physical demands of the ship, or drum, or whatever it was.

With that in mind he opened his senses to the clamour. The most common thread among the conversations he sampled as he skimmed was devoted to travel and destination. They'd reached Araldis, he heard. Preparation was being made for some type of transformation. Quixite was the word on every cache's metaphorical lips.

To be precise . . . transformation||quixite||

He dipped deep past these exchanges and sought out the low-end frequencies. But the roar of voices had intensified. If there was a subtle set of sounds that denoted the physical workings of the Medium, he would never hear it unless he could get them to all be quiet.

He found Rast and told her, 'I'm going to try something.'

'Make it good,' she whispered. Her voice sounded hoarse with defeat, or maybe he just imagined it.

He flipped away and began to skim and dip again, the way he'd been practising. But instead of sampling conversations, seeking information, he began to spread a very simple rumour, phrased as closely as he could to an Extro manner.

silence||transformation needs||silence

At first there was nothing. No change to the din. No response. But he continued to dive in and out of the voice-gondolas on the giant Ferris wheel that he imagined, repeating his rumour until the words became a meaningless kaleidoscope of sound in his own mind.

Then suddenly he found he'd stopped, whether from a bodiless kind of exhaustion or in response to something else; not silence, but a hush.

Yes. The clamour had lessened.

And underneath the listening quiet of the trillion Extro consciousnesses he heard the thrub of something different.

With all the concentration he'd ever had, and ever would have, Jo-Jo dived down to catch that slow thrub. He clutched at it. The long, slow sound wave dragged him along like a swimmer caught in the undertow of the surf. Unlike drowning though, this gave him a sense of solidity. He was near the bottom, or the top, or the end – a base line.

He smiled with satisfaction. *Smiled?* Yes, a smile. He was sure. He felt the tug of flesh and the stretch of lips. Sensation returning? He tried breathing. Sound of breath. Something rising and falling. A vague sense of physicality.

In his excitement, his concentration on the thrub wavered, and the physical sensations receded. Panicking, he refocused on the sound until he felt the wave pulling him along again.

When the sense of feeling began to return, he tried to isolate his fingers and hands. Wiggle them.

He touched something. Warm and moist. Skin. His heart pounded. Jubilation streaked though him. Bodily sensation was like a gift, an ecstasy. But also strange and disorientating.

He moved the fingers. Crept them along a skin carpet. Little increments, recognising surfaces, guessing: stomach, ribs – count them all – shoulder curve, throat, hair-coated jaw, teeth, eyelash.

Something was wrong. He retraced his fingers, pushing them over the ridge of his nose. No skin to touch, there, and a much duller sensation. He experimented a little, finding the border where the sensation sharpened again. At that point he pinched and prised until something soft and pliable peeled off.

He ripped it with force, flicking it away.

Full body consciousness came at him with the speed of air rushing into a vacuum. Suddenly his eyes were open and staring at unrecognisable surrounds, and his muscles were telling him he'd been inactive for too long. He blinked at the blurriness, but it refused to clear properly. He was prone, surrounded by a substance with no sense of pressure or buoyancy. He put his hand in front of his face. Intact, but blurred as if underwater.

Then he began to choke, his mouth and airways filling with whatever it was surrounding him.

He flailed and kicked, trying to swim through it – until his head broke a surface. His whole body popped out of the substance, like a child propelled from a slippery, contracting birth canal, and settled on top, bouncing slightly.

He gasped and spat and tried to order his perception. He was in a bland space, similar to the one they had entered originally; perhaps even the same one.

Yes. The same one, he decided. He could see a mark, like a scar, where the biozoon had been connected. The floor was the pliable, jellylike substance under him. He stabbed his fingers downward and they sank deeply into it yet his body stayed on top. *Some kind of surface tension*, he mused. *Need to move slowly.*

As he withdrew his fingers and widened his field of view, the blur cleared. The ambient light was low and the place smelt of . . . unwashed flesh. Probably his own.

He sat up carefully. A distortion in the jellylike floor caught his attention. Slowly, palms flat, he eased along on his butt to get a closer look. With every sliding movement his feet broke the surface and he had to pull them back out.

The distortion was variegated in colour, the closest part to him being dark. He screwed up his eyes, trying to make out the shape. It seemed large and square.

He plunged his hand below, and contacted a wet clump of hair. Then gristly flesh. An ear. He worked his way across the face and felt for contours he might recognise. The bridge of the nose was broad. Latourn maybe?

He reached further down and tried to tug the body towards him but only succeeded in dragging himself back under. Arching his back, he closed his fingers and paddled up until he was above the surface again.

He slid sideways on his stomach, about to try another angle, when he noticed something white next to Latourn.

Randall.

He reached his hand through the jelly-floor and touched matted hair. Then, he plunged his other hand down and hooked his hands under the mercenary's shoulders. He began to pull, but his face sank below the surface and his mouth filled. Panicking, he rolled onto his back and lay there, panting and spitting, until the floor stopped moving.

The surface tension was fragile, and he needed to move more carefully if he wanted to stay on top. This time, when he rolled back onto his stomach, he only thrust one hand down. Feeling his way past Rast's forehead to her nose, he touched a waxy seal like the one that had been over his. He scrabbled at it until it began to peel. When he'd ripped it off, he rolled carefully away and waited.

Why didn't Latourn have one? he wondered.

Too many long moments later, Rast erupted from the floor in much the same way he had. He grabbed one of her flailing arms and croaked out, 'Stop struggling, or you'll go under again. I'm right next to you.'

Immediately she stilled. After a while the floor ceased to move.

'Josef?' she coughed.

'Right here,' he said.

'We're alive.'

'For the moment. Open your eyes.'

'I won't ever forget that you got me out of there.' Her voice was strangled and dead serious.

'We're not out yet.'

Rast tried to sit up, but her sudden movement sent her partially slipping back beneath the floor.

Jo-Jo reached across and grasped her arm. When the floor stopped moving again, he gave her some instructions: 'Move real slow, palms flat. Make your body surface as wide as possible.'

'Gotcha. Now what?' Her voice sounded stronger with every word she spoke.

'Look over your left shoulder. See that mark on the wall? I reckon that's where the 'zoon was connected. Somehow we gotta get that open.'

'And what? Get sucked out into the vacuum?' Her confident tone diminished a bit.

'I listened to a bunch of conversations when I was spreading my rumour. I can't be sure, but I think we've landed on Araldis.'

'You can't be sure? Are you nuts? What if you're wrong?'

'Well, we could stay here. Sink back underneath and become Extros for good.'

He felt the floor vibrate as she craned her neck around.

'How about we try sliding in different directions? See what we come up against?' she suggested.

'I prefer to try the door idea first.'

'First? There won't be a second, if you're wrong.'

'I'm not wrong.'

'How do you know?'

'Something's different. There's no vibration. And the Extros were all talking about quixite and transformation. They're expecting something to happen soon.'

'Not convinced,' said Rast stubbornly.

Jo-Jo felt a rising annoyance. They didn't have time for a difference of opinion. The Extros would already know they were no longer submerged. 'We hang around here exploring and we'll end up like your crew.'

Rast rolled slowly onto her side so she could see Jo-Jo's face. Her blue eyes were bloodshot to hell and her face and hair were glazed with floor goo. 'Where – are – they?'

'On the other side of me. I've felt down there. I think it's Latourn. Long hair.'

She began to turn over. 'Lemme past you.'

'Wait,' he ordered. 'I'll move first. Both of us at once will cause waves.'

Surprisingly, she listened.

With painfully slow movements, he slid his body around behind hers in a semicircle until their heads almost touched. 'Now you go.'

She rolled more slowly this time, until she was positioned above the spot where Lat's body was encased.

Jo-Jo closed his eyes, not wanting to see her reaction. He felt the surface tremor as she plunged her hand below.

'I can't get him to move,' she gulped, struggling to keep her own face from being pulled beneath.

'I know,' said Jo-Jo, still studying the inside of his eyelids. 'I checked him.'

'What's that mean?'

'Means his lungs are full of goo.'

'And?'

'Unless they're set up like the tubercles in a biozoon, I'm thinking he's dead.'

'But the floor was solid before. I don't get it.'

'I bet Medium's capable of changing lots of things internally.'

'Medium?'

'That's what it's called. Maybe it transforms into something more liquid when it's in travelling mode. Maybe sound travels better through the goo.'

'Well that shoots down your theory about it being planetside already.' Rast's calm reaction told Jo-Jo that she didn't believe him.

'Maybe,' he conceded. 'Whatever. But if I'm right, best to be on top than underneath it, I reckon.'

She made a disgruntled noise. 'How did you get me out?'

'I pulled a plug off your mouth and nose seal. You started to drown and reacted by swimming to the top.'

'Why didn't Lat do the same?'

'His mouth and nose seal was already gone when I found him. He had no breathing reflex.'

'What about Catchut?' Her voice sounded grim now.

Jo-Jo opened his eyes and turned his head to try and look at her, his eyes widening. 'Dunno. But he was making noise down there, so maybe he's . . .?'

Her blue eyes blinked and fixed him with a fierce look. 'Find him,' she said.

They began to move away from each other, taking turns to roll; Jo-Jo towards the scar, Rast in the opposite direction.

Jo-Jo found the movement getting easier, as if the surface tension had increased. Just short of the scar, he saw something opaque below the surface. 'Over here.'

With a single, careful movement he delved downward. The resistance was definitely greater, but he touched something solid. 'Randall! Hurry over.'

'I know, I can feel it.' She was sliding back toward him quickly.

Jo-Jo felt the seal over Catchut's nose. It was intact but moving his fingers had become an effort, and he felt pressure building up around his arms.

Rast was able to balance on her knees by the time she reached him. The jelly-floor was solidifying. 'Get him out,' she cried.

Jo-Jo ripped the seal off and forced his other arm under. It was like reaching into a vat of cold honey.

Rast was doing the same.

Even though the surface gave them more purchase, the pulling was harder. Catchut started moving of his own accord but not with the vigour that Jo-Jo or Randall had been able to. He was asphyxiating in the hardening gel.

'More,' gasped Randall.

Jo-Jo strained his muscle-weakened shoulders until he thought his arms would dislocate.

Between them, they dragged Catchut's head and shoulders out. The layers of drying Extro fluid cracked into shards as soon as his skin reached air. He clawed at his nose and mouth to clear them.

'Again!' Rast hauled with strength she shouldn't have had. The rest of Catchut's body cracked free, his clothes tearing from it, boots left behind underneath.

They let go of him and he fell onto the surface, shivering and mostly naked.

Rast's eyes were wild now, pumped with survival adrenalin.

Jo-Jo figured his looked about the same.

'Josef.' She pointed to the mark left by the biozoon's abrupt departure.

'You game?' he said.

She nodded and gave a mad, almost unhinged grin. 'You're a persuasive man. Now, how do we get the fuckin' thing open?'

MIRA

Mira's heart contracted. She glanced back and forth between Thales and Samuelle. 'Thales,' she said. 'What confession?'

The young man flushed with emotion. 'I-I—'

But his answer was cut short by a noise at the door. Before any of them could react, it was thrust open and the room filled with armed Station Sec.

One of the guards opened his combat hood. 'Here,' he commanded.

A figure crept up to stand next to him; a small woman, older than Samuelle and gaunt with it. Her face crinkled with pleasure. 'Thet's him orright. Damn terrorist. Wanted to git up here without bein' seen.'

Thales's mouth opened helplessly. He shut it again. Mira saw the hopeless defeat in his eyes from being betrayed again.

'What's yer beef, sergeant?' demanded Samuelle. She seemed composed, but her eyes were narrow with concentration.

'That's the Stationmaster's concern, ma'am.'

Landhurst. Mira felt the blood rushing away from her head.

'But I'm due at the summit meeting,' argued Samuelle.

The Sec sergeant didn't blink as he raised his weapon.

*   *   *

Mira walked next to Thales and behind Samuelle. Guards both led and flanked them. Curious glances followed them as they were taken down-station.

'What did you tell Samuelle?' whispered Mira.

'She refused to see you. Said it was too dangerous. I told her I would confess and set Fariss free, if she changed her mind,' he replied in a low voice.

'Do you know what that means?'

He nodded. 'I would have done it anyway. I couldn't let Fariss . . . I just needed time to think it through. I panicked on the ship, but now I know what to do.' He was silent for a moment. 'At least this way something was gained from it . . . or would have been if the old woman hadn't betrayed me.'

Mira did something she'd never done before. She reached across and squeezed his hand. She didn't let go. 'We'll be in detention together.'

'That will,' he said, with a shaking intake of breath, 'make it infinitely more bearable.'

Mira kept looking ahead, her heart heavier than it had ever been.

The guards took them through a contortion of corridors that seemed to get narrower. The last one they entered was wider, and long, and the lining was worn, the floor scuffed. Most detainment modules were adjoined to the larger station, not part of it, in case the Stationmaster chose to disconnect it – in times of emergency.

The thought made Mira sick. Landhurst could vac them if he wanted to. She tried to stay in the present, concentrating on the light whispering noise of Samuelle's suit and the sticky moisture of Thales's palm.

The Station-Sec guards stopped at the detention module junction, waiting for it to cycle open. Then they instructed Mira, Samuelle and Thales to move through.

Mira stepped over the junction lip after Samuelle, and felt the blast of cooler air.

The detention processing chamber was bulb-shaped, and crowded with different kinds of soldiers. These ones were clothed in matt black uniforms that bore the OLOSS insignia. They stood, alert, as Station Sec filed in behind Thales.

'What's this?' said the Sec sergeant, pushing his way to the middle of the room.

An OLOSS captain matched his position. 'OLOSS sanctions the release of the prisoner Fariss O'Dea and the three you're about to process: Mira Fedor, Thales Berniere and Samuelle Sansarin.'

'What do you mean, OLOSS?'

The captain handed him an audio-plant.

The Sec sergeant fitted it in his ear, authenticated the voice and listened. His face tightened into disapproval, but he ordered his guards to stand away.

Mira's heart quickened. What had happened? Where were they to be taken now?

The two groups of guards waited in a tense silence as the detention administrator arranged for Fariss's release.

Samuelle filled the quiet with accusations and demands. 'What in Crux's name is goin' on, Captain? Landhurst's got some nerve bringing me down here. Wait till Commander Farr hears about this.'

'Commander Farr already knows, Ms Sansarin. That

is why you're returning to the station with us, not being detained.'

'Sammy?' The tallest woman Mira had ever seen was stooped in the low doorway into the containment area. Samuelle nodded reassurance, and the tall woman's eyes flew to Thales. 'What's goin' on?' Her stare shifted to Station Sec, the OLOSS guards and then Mira.

'Not sure,' Samuelle frowned. 'But I say we find out. Captain?'

The Sec sergeant accompanied the OLOSS contingent back the way they'd come and up a short escalator. After passing a series of checkpoints they entered the ante-room of a large chamber.

'Commander Farr has permitted these witnesses access to the summit meeting,' the captain informed the door guards, and produced another audio-plant.

Witnesses? Mira glanced at Thales, but his eyes were riveted to Fariss.

They were all scanned and physically searched, before the door guards disarmed the door. Samuelle entered first, followed by Fariss, then Mira and Thales. Only the captain and the Sec sergeant followed them in.

And for good reason. The room was already filled with 'esques and aliens, mostly seated, in a semicircle around a liquid translator hub.

They fell silent as Samuelle walked directly around the outside to stand near Landhurst.

The Stationmaster had changed little since Mira had seen him last, his hooked nose still like a badly drawn line down the middle of his face, his bow legs and wiry torso encased in blue station overalls. Only the matt comm-patch above one ear distinguished him from any other station worker; that and his arrogant air.

In fact, the entire room was thick with confidence.

Lasper Farr sat to the right of Landhurst, but not next to him. Mira recognised other faces around the semi-circle from newscasts. Lutinous the skieran ambassador, the Lostolian President Gan, the uuli Convenor, Balol Butnik, and numerous other dignitaries. Between Landhurst and Farr was JiHaigh, the OLOSS All-Prime. JiHaigh was said to be the most powerful individual in OLOSS Orion. Her physical presence in this chamber was a testament to the gravity of the summit. Like Samuelle, JiHaigh wore a protective skin suit, though hers was a subtle skin tone and lay underneath her clothes. It gave her face an unusual shininess. Mira imagined that most of the others wore some kind of physical safeguard, too – protection that she couldn't see.

Landhurst's eyes flicked from Samuelle and Fariss straight to Thales, then settled on Mira. It took only a moment before she saw recognition light in them.

'Baronessa Fedor?' his and another voice said simultaneously.

Landhurst leapt up from his chair and a second figure lifted on a float-form that supported his partially paralysed body.

'Sophos Mianos,' hissed Thales through his teeth.

Mira took in the livid expression of the Scolar Pre-Eminence who had tried to imprison her and *Insignia*. Was his injury her fault? Had the paralysis occurred because of *Insignia*'s abrupt detachment from the OLOSS ship?

Mira straightened her back, bracing herself against a wave of anguish. What would Landhurst do? Would Mianos blame her?

'Who allowed this?' Landhurst spluttered.

Lasper Farr rose. 'I did,' he said in a mild voice. 'I believe that these witnesses are in possession of crucial information that should be heard.'

'Witnesses? This is not a court of law, this is a security summit,' said Landhurst.

'This is,' said Commander Farr more pertinently, more dangerously, 'a dialogue about the continued survival of our species. Now, Samuelle, before we begin, explain to me what you're doing in the company of Baronessa Fedor and Thales Berniere.'

'I see you do know her, Lasper. Proves that part of her story, at least,' Samuelle said with relief.

Landhurst interjected. 'Baronessa Fedor will be placed under arrest and taken immediately to confinement. Sergeant, do as—'

'Wait!' ordered Farr.

The Sec sergeant hesitated, not sure whom to obey.

'Commander?' Landhurst's face reddened with fury.

The tension between the two charged the room. Mira saw glances and subvocalisations fly between the other participants. Eges danced close to the ceiling, recording and relaying to the common-casts. This was Landhurst's station, but Farr was a hero. Billions of people would be watching.

Landhurst swallowed down a lump of pride and said in more emollient tones, 'What is it that you'd like to hear, Commander Farr, *before I detain this woman*?'

'First, what's her supposed crime?'

'The woman incited decommed assailant ships to act in an aggressive manner towards my station, *inside* shift-space.'

'Which decommed warships?'

'Captain Dren from *Audacity*.' Mira found her own lips and tongue forming and speaking the words. 'I did not incite him – he chose to protect me when Stationmaster Landhurst tried to appropriate my bonded biozoon.'

Farr's head whipped in her direction. 'Dren you say? Can't imagine veteran Dren getting involved in something for no good cause.' He glanced around the rest of the room. 'Dren was one of my forward scouts in the war.'

'It's the war that brings me here, Command—' began Mira.

'She's not a reliable source,' interrupted Landhurst. He had not sat down and now he leaned across his comm-sole with undisguised threat.

'Landhurst.' Farr again. Not loudly, but with clear intent. 'Let the woman speak.'

'*This* is the woman who evaded my investigation and nearly cost me my life,' Mianos hissed. 'She is from Araldis. Or so she says. I believe that she killed the royal family and stole their biozoon.'

The soft murmuring around the room increased to a loud discussion. All the participants, it seemed, had heard at least one of the stories.

Mira caught snatches of their comments, some enraged, and others curious. Lutinous's dialect was incomprehensible, but the Balol Butnik was openly admiring. 'The woman is a warrior,' he bellowed above all of them. 'Let her speak.'

His declaration quieted the room long enough for Thales to find his voice. He'd stood behind Mira as they'd entered the room. Now he stepped in front of her. The summit participants seemed to hold their breaths. This young man looked so worn and damaged, yet he bore himself with quiet dignity.

'I am Thales Berniere, from Scolar. Sophos Mianos tried to imprison the Baronessa unlawfully, as he did me back on Scolar. I was married to his daughter, a fact that he could not accept. When I questioned his staid and reactionary philosophies he incarcerated me with the prophet Villon.'

Villon. It was as though Mira could hear the billions of sentients watching the proceedings repeat the great philosopher's name in one accord.

But Thales had not finished. 'Sophos Mianos had Villon killed and used his death to silence me. I believe that he also interfered with my HealthWatch, compromising my immune system. This' – he gestured dramatically to his scarred face – 'was the result. I also have evidence that my planet has been infected with a virus that affects the orbitofrontal cortex of the humanesque brain. The virus impairs decision-making and enervates cognitive function. Sophos Mianos is no longer capable of making informed, useful decisions for the good of OLOSS. I would not trust *him*.'

'Preposterous,' spluttered Mianos. 'The fellow is a lunatic, in the company of a felon. Both should be in containment. Landhurst, I insist—'

Landhurst waved to the Sec sergeant, but as he moved closer to Mira and Thales the OLOSS captain stepped between them. From one side of the room,

Mira heard a ripple of objection. The skieran and uuli ambassadors were signalling their disagreement. One of the uulis, a large semi-opaque alien, began to flare crimson, and its voice blared out through the translator.

'These accusations are most serious. We wish the humanesque woman to speak,' it said.

An altogether different voice cut in immediately afterward and an image of the biozoon ambassador Ley-al appeared on the screen above the translator hub. 'Baronessa Fedor should be heard. It is our opinion.'

The captain placed his hand on Mira's shoulder. She wanted to shrug it off but forced herself to stay still. Any reaction on her part could be misinterpreted, and tip the balance of favour.

'We shall vote on her right to be heard,' intervened Commander Farr. He gave Mira a penetrating look that sent a clear warning. She must be careful how she portrayed him or he would affect the outcome. Somehow he had known she had been arrested by Landhurst and he wanted her here to . . .?

Thales stood close to her while the vote occurred silently.

Hordes of thoughts swarmed through Mira's mind. She wanted to thank Thales for speaking up for her, and berate him for confiding the truth of the murder to Samuelle. Why had Ley-al spoken in her favour? And the skierans? What was Lasper Farr planning? If he was as sinister as Thales believed him to be then his motives could be anything.

'The vote is cast,' droned the translator. 'Baronessa Fedor will be heard.'

The captain released his grip on her shoulder and stepped away.

'Baronessa?' said Lasper Farr.

Mira drew a deep breath. *Insignia?*

Yes, Mira.

I am at the summit meeting.

I can see you on the 'cast. As can the rest of Orion.

What shall I tell them?

You do not appear to need or value my counsel.

Lasper Farr is dangerous. And the information I have will send panic throughout OLOSS.

They are all dangerous. You have taken this action of your own accord. Now you must see through the consequences of it.

You are angry, still.

'Mira Fedor!' Lasper's voice was sharp. Urgent.

'Sophos Mianos is correct. I did flee from him and the OLOSS ship. He wanted to impound my ship and keep me in containment. You must understand' – she turned a pleading face to the summit – 'I was desperate.' She told them the unadorned truth of the Saqr invasion and her escape from Araldis.

'What took you to Rho Junction, Baronessa?' asked the uuli Convenor.

She was careful not to look at Farr. 'I was promised help for my world, in return for a favour. That required that I travel to the Saiph system. Upon our arrival, there appeared to be much Post-Species activity around the station.'

'Our reports have also said so,' agreed the Convenor.

'I was abducted from the docks by host Siphonophores.' As she spoke an image of them appeared on the central screen. Her mouth dried at the vivid reminder. She licked her lips, plunging on with a recount of her time on the Hue world.

'All very fascinating, Baronessa,' said President Gan. 'And it would seem that the Post-Species are responsible for the Saqr adaptation. But what is the significance?'

'I have sought to build a picture, President Gan, so that you understand the gravity of what I am about to tell you next. As *Insignia* approached the shift sphere leaving Post-Species space, we came across a terrifying sight. Millions of Geni-carriers. Shifting.'

The room buzzed with reaction.

'Millions, Baronessa?' Even Lasper Farr had paled. 'An exaggeration surely. There were only three in the Stain War. Manufacturing on such a large scale in the time since then is impossible.'

'My biozoon can verify this.'

'Then instruct it to do so,' said JiHaigh.

'I do not instruct my biozoon,' said Mira quietly. 'But I will request.'

Mira heard Thales exhale next to her as the OLOSS All-Prime frowned.

Insignia? Will you show them? Please.

Silence.

Insignia, *so much is at risk. Don't let your anger at me prevent us from warning our species.*

You have warned mine. Perhaps we would be better off without humanesques. They are untrustworthy.

Do you think the Post-Species would spare you in a mass invasion?

Your Innate speaks the truth, Tasy-al.

Ley-al? The Omniarch's voice was almost as strong as *Insignia*'s.

Yes, Mira Fedor. Tasy-al, the Omniline wishes that you support your Innate and reveal the images you have stored.

But you don't wish to be associated—

We have reconsidered.

'It appears that the Baronessa has no evidence to substantiate her wild claims.' Landhurst was standing again. 'Sergeant, arrest her.'

The sergeant strode past the OLOSS captain and seized Mira's hands, forcing them into a restraint.

'No!' cried Thales. He grabbed the sergeant's arm but the guard discharged a stun into his side. He fell to the floor, quivering.

Mira heard shouts of condemnation. Saw the big woman, Fariss, run to Thales's side.

The sergeant dragged Mira towards the door, wrenching her arms with unnecessary force. Cramps tore at her abdomen, and she felt a gush of wetness between her legs.

Insignia! Mira cried.

Tasy-al! said the Omniarch.

'Wait!' Lasper Farr's voice drowned out the ones in Mira's mind.

The sergeant stopped and allowed Mira to straighten. The wetness had spread down the legs of her borrowed pants, but no one noticed the embarrassing stain of body fluid. All eyes were back upon the hub-screen as a series of images began to project.

The Geni-carriers, as seen through the corduroy filter of *Insignia*'s vision; from the seeming, asteroid collection on the edge of the Post-Species shift sphere, to the more intimate vision of the ammunition carriers. Millions of them.

Lasper Farr leaned, white-knuckled, onto his commsole while JiHaigh fell back in her chair as if stabbed in the chest. Each of the summit participants was as aghast as the next.

All except one.

Landhurst's expression was grim, but not surprised.

A terrifying thought entered Mira's mind. Wanton had told her that there were Post-Species who still chose the humanesque form. And what was it that *Insignia* had said? Landhurst had offered his station as a venue for the summit; a noble gesture for an ignoble man.

Had he deliberately drawn all the OLOSS leaders to one place at one time?

Was Landhurst an Extro?

The summit meeting erupted into shouts and arguments, and guards poured through the door, recalled by their various leaders. Suddenly the crowded room was too congested to move in. The Sec sergeant let go of her and plunged into the mêlée.

Mira, there is a rumour that the Dowl station is operational again. The Omniline believes we may be under immediate threat. The anger and resentment had gone from *Insignia*'s tone. Mira heard only undisguised concern. *You should return to me quickly.*

How?

Ley-al has rerouted the transportation shuttle to me. The same one that brought you to the station. The Omniarch wishes that you hasten. As do I.

Which dock?

Sub-25. A level below the quarantine deck.

I'm coming. And there will be others.

Mira pressed through the throng of bodies to Thales. Fariss had lifted him to his feet and was holding him with one strong arm. With the other, she fended off the buffeting crowd.

There was drool on the young scholar's face and his body trembled and jerked with the after-effects of the stun.

Mira grabbed his chin and stared into his eyes. 'Come with me now,' she said fiercely. Then, to Fariss, 'Both of you.'

'I can't leave Sammy.' Fariss's response was clipped and automatic. Her eyes roved the chaotic milling. 'There.'

Samuelle's nano-suit stood out amongst the formal robes and uniforms. She was closer to the door than them.

'Stay with me,' said Fariss. Still holding onto Thales, she forced a path over to Sammy using her strong, wide body to push others aside.

Mira followed closely in her wake and found herself face to face with the old woman again.

Samuelle grimaced at her. 'You made your point, Baronessa.'

Over Samuelle's shoulder Mira saw the Station Sec sergeant trying to reach her.

'There's room on my ship,' said Mira. 'I'm leaving now.'

Samuelle shook her head. 'I've got my own battles to fight. We all have now.'

'Sammy, can I take Thales there?' said Fariss.

Samuelle gave the big woman a keen stare then

nodded. 'It's best. Macken was Lasper's favourite. He won't forget.'

'Security's coming,' Mira said. 'We have to—'

'Go!' said Samuelle. She turned her back on them and planted her body in a direct line to block the sergeant.

Fariss pushed on, but the guards in the doorway had their weapons out.

'Stop. No one leaves,' ordered one of them.

Fariss shoved her huge hand into his face and sent him sprawling with a violent push. It set off a chain reaction of falling bodies and shouting. She lifted Thales clear of the confusion and lent a free hand to pull Mira along until they were outside the ante-chamber.

The corridor was eerily deserted. So were the escalators. The three of them moved unhindered to one of the subsidiary lifts. The only people Mira glimpsed were gathered around a public screen, riveted to the events unfolding in the summit room.

'Where're we going?' asked Fariss, as the lift door closed. Thales straightened and tried to take his own weight. Colour had returned to his face and he wiped the saliva from his chin.

'Sub-25, below quarantine. A shuttle will be waiting,' said Mira. Insignia?

Fariss nodded and pressed the button. She stared at the moist patch on Mira's pants.

'You piss yourself?'

'M-my waters. I think . . .' Insignia? *Is the shuttle here?*

Fariss's eyebrows shot up. 'You having a fuckin' baby? Now?'

'I don't know.'

'Shit.'

Mira dropped her hands self-consciously in front of her. *Insignia?* she pleaded.

It is waiting.

Thank Crux.

When Ley-al's shuttle attached seamlessly to the egress scale, Mira stepped on board first. As she hurried along *Insignia*'s ribbed stratum to the buccal, cramps bit into her lower belly. Fluid soaked steadily down her legs onto the pants of her borrowed soldier garb.

The baby couldn't be coming now? It couldn't be. It was only a few months old in her womb; too young to be born. Too young for a humanesque bambino. Too—

The biozoon's buccal pucker was already dilated, waiting for her. She heard Fariss close behind, swearing under her breath, while Thales moaned with effort.

'Put him in the second vein,' Mira gasped, as she fell into Primo. The biozoon's symbiosis function folded around her in a loving embrace. Nano-sensors slipped in through the pores in her skin, reading electrolyte levels, gauging dehydration and trauma. She felt the flush of replenishment.

Fariss staggered across to the Secondo vein and laid Thales in it.

Mira?

See to the scholar.

I will see to you both. Our baby is distressed.

My amniotic fluid has ruptured. Can you repair it?

I can slow the fluid loss but I cannot prevent the birth. This is what I feared.

No! Anguish tore right through Mira and turned her mind inside out.

She'd warned OLOSS about the Extropists' amassed weaponry. She'd risked everything to bring them news of the great threat. Wasn't there some grace in that? Some balance that should swing in her favour? Some universal justice?

Insignia, *please. Please. My baby must not die.*

Sole

bring'm home/pretty pretty
bring'm baby/know'm all
bring'm baby/burn'm others

extras

www.orbitbooks.net

about the author

Marianne de Pierres was born in Western Australia and now lives in Queensland with her husband, three sons and two cockatoos. She has a BA in Film and Television and a Postgraduate Certificate of Arts in Writing, Editing and Publishing. Her passions are books, basketball and avocados. She has been actively involved in promoting Speculative Fiction in Australia and is the co-founder of the Vision Writers Group, and ROR – wRiters On the Rise, a critiquing group for professional writers. She was also involved in the early planning stage of Clarion South. Marianne has published a variety of short fiction and is collaborating on a film project for Sydney-based Enchanter Productions. You can find out more about her at www.mariannedepierres.com

Find out more about Marianne de Pierres and other Orbit authors by registering for the free monthly newsletter at www.orbitbooks.net

if you enjoyed
MIRROR SPACE
look out for
TRADING IN DANGER
book one of Vatta's War

by

Elizabeth Moon

Kylara Vatta came to attention in front of the Commandant's desk. One sheet of flatcopy lay in front of him, the print too small for her to read upside down. She had a bad feeling about this. On previous trips to the Commandant's office, she had been summoned by an icon popping up on her deskcomp. Those had all been benign visits, the result of exams passed in the top 5 per cent, or prizes won, and the Commandant had greeted her with the most thawed of his several frosty expressions.

Today it had been 'Cadet Vatta to the Commandant's office, on the double,' blaring out over the speaker right in the middle of her first class period, Veshpasir's lecture on the history of the first century PD. Veshpasir, no friend to shipping dynasties, had given her a nasty smirk before saying, 'Dismissed, Cadet Vatta.'

She had no idea what this was about. Or rather, she hoped she didn't. Surely she had been careful enough . . .

'Cadet Vatta,' the Commandant said. No thawing at all, and his left eyelid drooped ominously.

'Sir,' she said.

'I won't even ask what you thought you were doing,' he said. 'I don't want to know. I don't care.'

'Sir?' She hated the squeak in her voice.

'Don't play the innocent with me, Cadet.' Rumor had it that if his left eyelid actually closed, cadets died. She wasn't sure she believed that, but she hoped she wasn't about to find out. 'You are a disgrace to the Service.'

Ky almost shook her head in confusion. What could he be talking about?

'Going outside the chain of command like this' – he thumped the sheet of paper – 'embarrassing the Service.'

'Sir—' She gulped, caught between the etiquette that required silence until she was given leave to speak, and a desperate need to find out what had the Commandant's eyelid hovering ever nearer to its mate.

'You have something to say, Cadet?' the Commandant asked. His voice, like his face, might have been carved out of a glacier. 'Do go ahead . . .' It was not a generous offer.

'Sir, with the greatest respect, this cadet does not know to what the Commandant is referring . . .'

His lips disappeared altogether. 'Oh, you can play

the innocent all you want, Cadet, and maintain that formal folderol, but you don't fool me.' He paused. Ky searched her memory, and came up empty. 'Well, since you insist, let's try this: do you recall the name *Mandy Rocher*?'

'Yes, sir,' Ky said promptly. 'Second year, third squad.'

'And you can think of no reason why I might connect that name and yours?'

'Sir, I helped Cadet Rocher locate a Miznarii chaplain last weekend, when Chaplain Oser was away . . .' A dim glimmer of what might be the problem came to her but she couldn't believe there would be that much fuss about a simple little . . .

'And just how did you locate a Miznarii chaplain, Cadet?'

'I . . . er . . . called my mother, sir.'

'You called your mother.' He made it sound obscene, as if only the lowest criminal would call a mother. 'And told your mother to do what, Cadet?'

'I asked her if her friend Jucha could refer me to a Miznarii chaplain near the Academy.'

'For what reason?'

'I told her that one of the underclassmen was overdue for confession and the Academy chaplain was out of town.'

'You didn't tell her what he wanted to confess?'

Ky felt her own eyebrows going up. 'Sir, I don't know what he had to confess. I only know that he was in distress, and needed a chaplain, and I thought . . . I thought it would save trouble if I just got him one.'

'You're not Miznarii yourself . . .?'

'No, sir. We're Modulans.' Actually, they were

Saphiric Cyclans, but that was such a small sect that nobody recognized it, and Modulans were respectable and undemanding. You could be a Modulan without doing anything much at all, a source of some humor to more energetic sects. Ky found Modulan chapel restful and had gone often enough to acquire a reputation for moderate piety – the level most approved by Modulans.

'Hmmph.' The Commandant's eyelid twitched upward a millimeter; Ky hoped this was a good sign. 'You had no idea that what he wanted to confess concerned the honor of the Service?'

Her jaw dropped; she forced it back up. 'No, sir!'

'That he made a formal complaint to this Miznarii, in addition to his confession, which the chaplain took immediately to the Bureau of War, where it fell into the hands of a particularly noxious bureaucrat whose *sister* just happens to be on the staff of *Wide Exposure*, so that I found myself on the horn very early this morning with Grand-Admiral Tasliki, who is not amused at all . . .?' It was not really a question; it was rant and explanation and condemnation all in one. 'The bureaucrat spoke on *Wide Exposure*'s "Night Affairs" program at 0115 – clever timing, that – and this morning all the media channels had something on it. That's only the beginning.'

Ky felt hot, then cold, then hot again. 'S-sir . . . ,' she managed.

'So even if you did not know, Cadet Vatta, what Cadet Rocher wanted to confess, you may be able to grasp that by going outside the chain of command you have created a very *very* large public relations problem, embarrassing the entire general staff, the Bureau of War, and – last but not least – me personally.'

'Yes, sir.' She could understand that. She could not, she thought, have anticipated it, and now she was consumed by curiosity: what, exactly, *had* Mandy Rocher said? They weren't allowed access to things like *Wide Exposure* except on weekends.

'You are an embarrassment, Cadet Vatta,' the Commandant said. 'Many, many people want your hide tacked on the wall and your head on a pike. The *only* reason I don't—' His eyelid was up another millimeter. 'The *only* reason I don't, is that I have observed your progress through the Academy and you have so far been, within the limits of your ability, an exemplary cadet. When I thought you'd done it on purpose I was going to throw you to the wolves. Now – since I suspect that you simply fell for a sob story and your entire barracks knows you have a soft spot for underdogs and lost lambs – I'm simply going to take the hide off your back in strips and see your resignation on my desk by 1500 hours this afternoon.'

'S-sir?' Resignation . . . did that mean what it sounded like? Was he kicking her out? Just because she'd tried to help Mandy?

Now the eyelid came all the way back up. 'Cadet Vatta, you have – unwittingly, perhaps – created a major mess with implications that could damage the Service for years. Your ass is grass, one way or the other. You could be charged, for instance, with that string of articles beginning with 312.5 – I see by your expression that you have, belatedly, remembered them . . .'

She did indeed. Article 312.5 of the Military Legal

Code: failure to inform superior officer in a timely manner of potentially harmful personnel situations. Article 312.6: failure to inform superior officer in a timely manner of breaches of security involving sensitive personnel. Article 312.7: failure to inform superior officer in a timely manner of . . . rats, rats, and flying rats. She was majorly doomed.

'I . . . wasn't thinking, sir.' That was not an attempt at apology, merely a statement of fact.

'Fairly obvious. What did you think might happen?'

'I thought . . . Mandy – Cadet Rocher – was so upset that day – I thought if he could see a chaplain and confess or whatever, he'd settle down until the regular chaplain got back. He had those exams coming up, and they were group-graded; if he didn't do well, his squad would suffer for it . . .'

'What you don't know, Cadet, is that Rocher had been avoiding the regular chaplain's cycle; his so-called emergency was of his own making. He wanted to talk to someone outside the Academy, and you made that possible.'

'Yes, sir.'

'And you didn't tell anyone at all about this, did you?'

'No, sir.'

'Easier to get forgiveness than permission, is that what you were thinking?'

'No, sir . . . not really.' One of the places where Modulans and Saphiric Cyclans disagreed was about the giving of aid. Modulans felt that moderate assistance should be moderately public – one did not make a huge display of charity, but one allowed others to know charity was going on, to set a good example. Saphiric Cyclans, on the other hand, believed that all help should be given as anonymously as possible. Now was probably not the time to talk about that difference.

'I am so reassured.' The Commandant's eyelid quivered. 'Cadet Vatta, it is unfortunate that you have to suffer for a generous impulse, but we need naval officers with brains as well as kind hearts. You will not return to class. You will, as I said, present a letter of resignation which does not mention any of this, and cites personal reasons as the cause, by 1500 hours. Sooner, Cadet, is better than later, but first you will go to Signals, and make contact with your family, so that you will be able to leave quietly and quickly when that resignation is approved.' The look he gave her now was warmer by a few degrees, but still not cordial. 'Staff will pack up your things; they will be at the gate when you depart.'

'I . . . yes, sir.'

'And yes, you infer correctly that you are not to speak to any of your former associates. Your departure will be explained as seems most expedient for the Service.'

'Sir.' Not speak to anyone. Not to Mira or Lisette . . . not to Hal. *Only another few months, and we can* – but not now, not ever. Please, please, let no one figure out . . .

'You are dismissed.'

'Sir.' Ky saluted, rotated correctly on her right heel, and left his office, her mind a blur. Signals. She knew where Signals was. She passed without really seeing an enlisted man in the passage, and another at the head of the stairs down to the classroom level. Halfway to

Signals, her mind clicked on long enough to panic . . . She had to call her family, tell her father and, oh heavens, her *mother* that she was disgraced, dismissed . . . Her brothers would all . . . her cousins . . . Uncle Tomas . . . Aunt Grace, worse than Uncle Tomas, who would say again all she had said when Ky first went to the Academy, laced with *I told you so* . . .

She felt the tremor in her hands, and fought to still it. Now, for this short period of time, she was still a cadet, and now, for this short period of time, she would act like one. Even as the dream went down in smoke and ashes, even then . . . her stomach looped wildly once and settled.

At the door of Signals, a uniformed guard stared past her.

'Cadet Vatta, on order of the Commandant,' she said.

He stepped aside, and she heard him murmur into his com-unit 'Cadet Vatta at Signals, sir.'

Commander Terry had the watch in Signals; his expression suggested that her family were loathsome toads, and she was toad spawn. 'Vatta,' he said, minus the honorific.

'Sir.'

'Which contact number?' As if having more than one number were also a crime.

'Vatta Enterprises,' Ky said. 'They have a relay—' Wherever her father was, they could reach him, or give her a link to the senior Vatta onplanet.

'We would prefer that you make a direct call.'

She knew her father's mobile number, of course, but he'd often said he hated the damned thing, and would leave it on the bedside table as often as not. That meant her mother might pick it up, the last person she wanted to talk to. Vatta Enterprises would ring his skullphone, which he couldn't take off. She didn't have that number; no one did but the communications computer at VE.

She rattled off the string for the mobile, and mentally visualized the arc of blue, best fortune, of the Saphiran Cyclan wheel, as Commander Terry nodded to the rating who entered the string.

'Name?' Terry asked abruptly. Ky startled. 'The name of the person you are calling,' he said.

'Sir, my father, sir. Gerard Avondettin Vatta. But if my mother—'

'You are permitted one call, to one recipient, Cadet Vatta.' Commander Terry picked up the headset and held the receiver to his ear. Ky waited, the blue arc fading in her mental eye. Then his hand twitched. 'This is Commander Terry at the Naval Academy; I need to speak to Gerard Avondettin Vatta.' A pause, then: 'Kylara Vatta will speak with you.' He held the headset out to Ky.

She was not even allowed to speak from a privacy booth. She had known the call would be recorded, but at least a semblance of normal courtesy would have helped. She could feel tears swelling now, stuffing her nose. She fought for calmness as she took the headset and put it on. Enough of this; she turned her back on Commander Terry without permission.

'Dad, listen—'

'Ky, what's wrong? Are you hurt?'

'Dad, no, I'm fine, please listen. I have to leave, I have to leave today. Can you send somebody to the gates?'

'Ky, what is it?'

'Dad, please. I have to resign. I have to leave. I don't have any money for transport; I need a way to get home—'

'What—!' She could hear the explosion building up, the familiar prelude to the famous roar. Then it ended, surprising her into silence. His voice gentled to a soft growl. 'Ky, listen, whatever it is, we can help. Let me call the Commandant—'

'No, Dad. Don't do that. I'll explain when I get there, only help me get there, please?'

'When do you need transport?'

She looked at the chronometer. Only 0935. Surely she could write a resignation that would satisfy the Commandant by noon.

'By noon, if that's possible.'

'For you, Kylara-mish, five minutes would be possible. Only tell me, has someone hurt you?'

Later, she would consider whether Mandy Rocher had hurt her; now she wanted only to get away. And even if Mandy had, she had made it possible; it was her own fault. 'It's not that, Dad.'

'Good. Because if any one of those fisheaters had laid a finger on you—'

'Dad, please. Noon?'

'At the gates. On Vatta honor.'

'Vatta honor.' The signal died, and she handed the headset back to Commander Terry. He took it without comment, and gave a curt nod.

'Get on your way, Vatta.'

'Yes, sir.' She needed a place to write the resignation; if she was forbidden to return to her quarters, where could she go? Outside, she found the answer, of sorts: the wiry gray-haired senior NCO who had been her year's nemesis in the first four quarters, and an increasingly valuable resource ever since. She had not, she remembered, taken MacRobert's advice on the matter of Mandy Rocher.

'Commandant's library is empty, Cadet Vatta,' he said now. 'Fully equipped.'

'Right,' she said. She would not cry. She would certainly not cry in front of this man. He turned to lead the way and she followed.

'Right mess you made of things,' he said, when they were around a corner from Signals.

'Yes,' Ky said.

'I won't say I told you so,' he said. He just had, of course, but she didn't answer. 'I daresay you feel bad enough already.'

A shadow of a question in that. Anger stirred suddenly, beneath the anguish. 'Yes, I do,' she said, hearing the sharp edge to her own voice.

'Thought so,' he said. 'Here you are.' He opened the door for her. She had never been in the Commandant's private library before; the long narrow room held not only racks of ordinary books and journals, but shelves of ancient books like those in her family's oldest house. A long table ran down the middle of the room, and at one end someone had set out a stack of white paper and a selection of pens. 'It's appropriate that a resignation of this type be handwritten,' MacRobert told her. 'You can use the voice recorder or the keyboard to rough it out, but it's better to stick to the simplest format . . .' Someone had also laid out a copy of *Naval Etiquette: Essentials for Officers*, and the hand reader.

'Thank you,' Ky said. It was still not 1000 hours. Her world had ended less than an hour ago. She had another couple of hours . . .

'What time did you arrange transport for?' MacRobert asked.

'Noon,' Ky said.

'I'll see that your gear is at the gate by 1130,' MacRobert said.

'Thank you,' Ky said again. She felt unreal, still, as if this were a dream, as if she were floating a few centimeters off the floor.

'I'll leave you alone,' MacRobert said. 'When you're finished, you can leave the resignation here—'

'The Commandant said on his desk,' Ky said.

'That's right. And so it will be; just tell me when you're finished.' He nodded and went out, shutting the door silently behind him.

She put *Naval Etiquette: Essentials for Officers* into the reader and found that someone had already book-marked the section on resignations. Voluntary and involuntary, sections of the legal code relating to, forms of appropriate and inappropriate . . . She paused there and looked at the appropriate wording for resigning one's commission while in command of a ship, while in command of a flotilla, while between commands, while on leave, while suffering an incurable mental or physical condition precluding further duty . . . That's me, Ky thought. Suffering from an incurable tendency to trust people in trouble and help lame dogs.

She turned to the keyboard – she didn't trust her voice to use the speech-activated system – and copied in the phrasing. 'I, [name], hereby resign my [cadet-ship/commission] for reasons of [reason.]' 'I, Kylara Evangeline Dominique Vatta, hereby resign my cadet-ship for reasons of overwhelming stupidity and weak sentimentality.' No, that wouldn't do. 'For reasons of totally unfair blame for something I didn't do.' That wouldn't do either. 'For reasons of a mental illness called gullibility?' 'Soft-heartedness?' No.

Tears blurred her vision suddenly; she blinked them back. Memory stirred, bringing her Mandy Rocher's image as he sat, shoulders hunched, hands trembling a little, telling her that he had to find a chaplain, he really did. Had his hands trembled with secret laughter that she was so easy to fool? Had he looked down to hide the scorn in his eyes? He was such a little . . . little . . . she searched her vocabulary for a sufficiently descriptive phrase. Insignificant. Forgettable. Boring. Pitiful. Nonentity. And to lose her cadetship because of *him*!

She would get him someday. Vengeance, said her grandmother, was an unworthy goal, but this was a special case. Surely this was a special case.

'I, Kylara Evangeline Dominique Vatta, hereby resign from the Academy for reasons that reflect on my ability to carry out the duties of a naval officer.'

Close. Not quite yet.

She looked around the room, squinting to bring the titles of the old books into focus. Herren and Herren's *Chronicles of the Dispersion*, all ten volumes. Her family owned III through X, but I and II were very rare indeed in paper form. Cantabria's *Principles of Space Warfare*, evidently a first edition. She longed to pull it down and check, but was afraid to. A row bound identically in blue-gray cloth . . . logbooks, the old-fashioned kind. Those would be centuries and centuries old; she got up and looked at the names on the spines. *Darius II, Paleologus, Sargon, Ataturk* . . . she felt the gooseflesh come up on her arms, and looked quickly at the last, least-faded volume. *Centaurus*. Not in fact centuries old, not even one century: these were logs that the Commandant had kept, his personal logs from every ship on which he'd served. She'd once memorized the sequence on a dare. Her fingers twitched. What had he thought, felt, done as a young man on his first ship?

She would never know. She had no right to know. The adventures she had hoped to write into such logs herself would never come her way now. She made herself step away from that shelf and look at another. History here, biography there, reference works on all the neighboring states, on the biota of First Colony, on the ecology of water gardens . . . Water gardens? The Commandant studied water gardens?

A sound outside in the passage startled her and sent her back to the table, but the footsteps passed by. She stared at the screen again. 'For reasons of . . .' Back to the hand reader. Alternate phrasing: 'due to.' Clumsy.

Never say more than you need, her father had said; her mother had muttered that Kylara always said more than she needed.

She'd stop that right now.

'I, Kylara Evangeline Dominique Vatta, hereby

resign from the Academy for personal reasons.' Short and . . . not sweet. Nothing about this was sweet.

She stared at the screen a long time, glaring at the tiny blue words on the gray screen. Then she moved the paper over and copied the words very carefully, in her best script, the handwriting of a properly brought-up child and good student.

Panic gripped her when she had signed it. She did not want to do this. She could not do this. She must do this. She looked at the time, 10:22:38. Had destroying her life really taken so little time?

A tap on the door, then it opened. MacRobert again, this time with a large silver tray. A teapot, incongruously splotched with big pink roses. A pair of matching cups, gold-rimmed, on saucers. A small plate of lemon cookies, and another of tiny, precisely cut sandwiches.

'The Commandant will be joining you,' MacRobert said. He set the tray on the end of the library table, picked up her resignation, and walked out with it. Ky sat immobile, staring at the steam rising from the teapot's spout, trying not to smell the fragrance of cookies obviously fresh from the oven, trying not to think or feel anything at all.

The Commandant's entrance brought her upright, to attention; he waved her back down. 'You've resigned, sit down.' He sighed. His left eyelid was back up where it should be, but his whole face sagged. 'Pour out, will you?'

Ky carried out the familiar ritual, something she didn't have to think about, and handed him his cup of tea. He waited, and nodded at her. She poured one for herself. It was good tea; it would be, she thought.

He took a sandwich and gave her a look; she took one, too.

He ate his sandwich in one bite, and sipped his tea. 'It's a shame, really,' he said. 'Here I had a perfectly good excuse to remove your internal organs and hang them from the towers, make an example of you . . . It's my job, and I'm supposed to relish it, or why did I ask for it? But you were a good cadet, Mistress Vatta, and I know you intended to be a good officer.'

Then why did you make me resign? That was a question she must never ask; she knew that much.

'In consideration of your past performance, and on my own responsibility, I've chosen to let you keep your insignia and wear it as you depart; I trust your sense of honor not to wear it again.'

'No, sir,' she said. The bite of sandwich she had taken stuck in her throat. She had not even considered that he might demand their removal. The class ring on her finger – Hal's ring, as he wore hers – suddenly weighed twice as much.

'It's hard for you to believe now, I'm sure, but you will survive this. You have many talents, and you will find a use for them . . .' He took a long swallow of his tea, and actually smiled at her. 'Thank you for not making this harder than it had to be. Your resignation was . . . masterful.'

The sandwich bite went down, a miserable lump. She wasn't hungry; she couldn't be hungry. She ate the rest of the sandwich out of pure social duty.

'I understand you've arranged transport for noon?' he asked.

'Yes, sir.'

'You don't have to say *sir*, Ca – Mistress Vatta.'

'I can't help it,' Ky said. Tears stung her eyes; she looked away.

'Well, then. I would advise that you go out at 1130, while classes are in session. MacRobert will remain with you until your transport arrives, to deal with any . . . mmm . . . problems that may come up. Since the story broke on the early news, the media have been camped at our gates; it'll be days before that dies down.'

For a moment she had been furious – had he thought she'd do something wrong? – but the mention of media steadied her. Of course they would be trying to get in, trying to interview cadets. Of course the daughter of the Vatta family would interest them, even if Mandy hadn't mentioned her, and someone would be bound to have a face-recognition subroutine that would pop out her name.

'And there's another thing.' She had to look at him again, had to see the expression of mingled annoyance and pity that was worse than anything he might have said directly. 'The Bureau demands – I realize this isn't necessary – a statement that you will consider all this confidential and not communicate with the media.'

As if she would. As if – but she took the paper he handed her and scrawled her name on it in a rough parody of her usual careful handwriting.

'You have almost an hour,' the Commandant said. 'MacRobert will fetch you when it's time.' He drained his cup and picked up one of the lemon cookies. 'And – if you'll take advice – drink the rest of that tea, and eat those sandwiches. Shock uses up energy.' He rose, nodded to her, and went out, shutting the door softly behind him.

To her shame, Ky burst into tears. She snatched the tea towel off the tray and buried her face in it. She could always claim she'd spilled the tea; she wasn't a cadet; she didn't have to tell the strict truth. Five hard sobs, and it was over, for now. She wiped her face, spread the tea towel out again, and set everything back on the tray in perfect order. No – her cup was almost full. She drank the tea. She ate another sandwich. Disgusting body, to want tea and food at such a time.

The silent room eased her, made calm possible. She got up and paced the circuit, looking at the titles again. Then she took down the logbook labeled *Darius II* on the back. Just this once – and what could they do to her if they disapproved?

When MacRobert came for her at 1127, she was deep into the logbook, and calm again.

Outside, the weather had changed, as if her fortune changed it, from early morning's sunshine and puffy clouds to a dank, miserable cold rain with a gusty wind. Her luggage made a pile in the relative safety of the gateway arch; she stood in the shelter of the sentry's alcove, where she could just see the street beyond, and the gaggle of reporters on the far side. She was still in cadet blue; the sentry ignored her, and MacRobert checked off her bags on a list before turning to her.

'They'll be near on time?' he asked.

'I expect so,' Ky said. The lump in her throat was growing now; she had to swallow before she could speak.

'Good. We'll have to frustrate the mob over there . . .' He cocked his head. 'You're not half-bad, Vatta. Sorry you stepped in it. Don't forget us.' His voice seemed to carry some message she couldn't quite understand.

'I won't,' she said. How could he even suggest she might forget this? Her skin felt scorched with shame.

'Don't be angrier than you have to be.'

'I'm not.' She might be later, but now . . . anger was only beginning to seep toward the surface, through shock and pain.

'Good. You still have friends here, though at the moment there's a necessary distance—' He looked at the clock. 1154. 'Excuse me for a few moments. I'll be back at 1200 sharp.'

Ky wondered what he was up to, but not for long. The chill dank air, the gusts of wind, all brought back to her the enormity of her fall from grace. She was going to have to go out there, in the cold rain, and pick up those bags and put them in the vehicle in front of everyone in the universe, obviously disgraced and sent away, and be driven home to her parents like any stupid brat who's messed up. Like, for instance, her cousin Stella, who had fallen in love with a musha dealer and given him the family codes. She remembered overhearing some of that, when she was thirteen, and telling herself *she* would never be so stupid, *she* would never disgrace the family the way Stella had.

And now it was on all the news, whatever had actually been said, and it was all her fault.

A huge black car whizzed past the entrance, flags flapping from its front and rear staffs, and she saw the reporters across the way turn, and then rush after it. 'The back entrance!' she heard one of them yell. Their support vans squealed into motion, turned quickly across the street, and sped after the black car. She glanced at the clock. 1159. She stepped out of the alcove into the archway and saw a decent middle-aged dark blue car swerving over to stop at the archway. Twelve hundred on the dot. Two men – the driver and escort – got out of the car.

'I'll help with these.' MacRobert was back, and already had two of her bags in hand. 'Vatta, you get in the car. Jim, get her trunk,' he said to the sentry. In moments, Ky was in the backseat, her luggage stowed in the trunk or beside her, and the two men were back in the car.

'Take care, Vatta,' MacRobert said. 'And remember what I said; you have friends here . . .'

At the last moment, she stripped off the class ring and handed it to him. 'You'll know where this should go,' she said. She couldn't keep it; she could only hope that MacRobert would get it back to him discreetly, that Hal would understand.